**Praise for the novels of Nina Bruhns,
three-time overall winner of the Daphne du Maurier Award
for Excellence in Mystery/Suspense**

"Sexy, suspenseful and so gritty you'll taste the desert sand. A thrill ride from start to finish!"
—*USA Today* bestselling author Rebecca York

"A provocative, sexy thriller that will get your adrenaline pumping on all levels. A riveting breakout novel that will shoot Ms. Bruhns straight to bestsellerdom. Move over, boys, and see how it's really done!"
—Award-winning author Tamar Myers

"Intense pacing . . . powerful characters . . . searing emotions and explosive sexual tension! Once I started reading *Shoot to Thrill*, I couldn't stop! This is high-action suspense at its very best!" —Bestselling author Debra Webb

"The stuff legends are made out of."—*Midwest Book Review*

"Shocking discoveries, revenge, humor, and passion fill the pages . . . An interesting and exciting story with twists and turns." —*Joyfully Reviewed*

"[A] delightfully whimsical tale that enchants the reader from beginning to end. Yo ho ho and a bottle of fun!"
—Deborah MacGillivray

"This is one you will definitely not want to miss!"
—*In the Library Reviews*

continued . . .

if looks could

CHILL

NINA BRUHNS

BERKLEY SENSATION, NEW YORK

THE BERKLEY PUBLISHING GROUP
Published by the Penguin Group
Penguin Group (USA) Inc.
375 Hudson Street, New York, New York 10014, USA
Penguin Group (Canada), 90 Eglinton Avenue East, Suite 700, Toronto, Ontario M4P 2Y3, Canada
(a division of Pearson Penguin Canada Inc.)
Penguin Books Ltd., 80 Strand, London WC2R 0RL, England
Penguin Group Ireland, 25 St. Stephen's Green, Dublin 2, Ireland (a division of Penguin Books Ltd.)
Penguin Group (Australia), 250 Camberwell Road, Camberwell, Victoria 3124, Australia
(a division of Pearson Australia Group Pty. Ltd.)
Penguin Books India Pvt. Ltd., 11 Community Centre, Panchsheel Park, New Delhi—110 017, India
Penguin Group (NZ), 67 Apollo Drive, Rosedale, North Shore 0632, New Zealand
(a division of Pearson New Zealand Ltd.)
Penguin Books (South Africa) (Pty.) Ltd., 24 Sturdee Avenue, Rosebank, Johannesburg 2196,
South Africa

Penguin Books Ltd., Registered Offices: 80 Strand, London WC2R 0RL, England

This is a work of fiction. Names, characters, places, and incidents either are the product of the author's imagination or are used fictitiously, and any resemblance to actual persons, living or dead, business establishments, events, or locales is entirely coincidental. The publisher does not have any control over and does not assume any responsibility for author or third-party websites or their content.

IF LOOKS COULD CHILL

A Berkley Sensation Book / published by arrangement with the author

PRINTING HISTORY
Berkley Sensation mass-market edition / December 2009

Copyright © 2009 by Nina Bruhns.
Excerpt from *A Kiss to Kill* by Nina Bruhns copyright © by Nina Bruhns.
Cover illustration by Craig White.
Cover design by Rita Frangie.
Interior text design by Kristin del Rosario.

ISBN: 978-0-425-23152-4

BERKLEY® SENSATION
Berkley Sensation Books are published by The Berkley Publishing Group,
a division of Penguin Group (USA) Inc.,
375 Hudson Street, New York, New York 10014.
BERKLEY® SENSATION and the "B" design are trademarks of Penguin Group (USA) Inc.

PRINTED IN THE UNITED STATES OF AMERICA

10 9 8 7 6 5 4 3 2 1

*This book is dedicated to all my friends
in the Kiss of Death Chapter of RWA.
A more amazing group of women
is simply not to be found.
Thanks for a dozen great years
of murder and mayhem!*

Acknowledgments

I would like to acknowledge the invaluable help of CJ Lyons on the medical elements of this story—any and all errors and/or truth-stretching are strictly my own—and Dorothy McFalls for being the best first reader and critiquer in the universe. Thanks, ladies!

And once again a bow to my fabulous editor, Kate Seaver, and incomparable agent, Natasha Kern. You're both a true joy to work with!

ONE

"SHE seems young."

Marc Boudreaux Lafayette flicked a glance over at fellow STORM operator Bobby Lee Quinn, who was lounging against a pillar in an elegantly tailored tuxedo, sipping a martini, appearing for all the world like he attended embassy parties every day of his life.

Marc knew better. Quinn was a Bama redneck with gun grease under his fingernails from all the ground ops he'd led in the past six or seven years working for STORM Corps. Still, for some obscure reason women loved him.

"Too young for you, *boug*," Marc warned. For all the good that would do. If it wore skirts, Quinn was all over it. He returned his gaze to the newest CIA officer to hit Istanbul this summer. Darcy Zimmerman. Fresh as a summer rain, and pretty as a bayou orchid in a strapless blue gown that had their Arab hosts either frowning or drooling. Her cover was assistant to the cultural attaché at the U.S. embassy. But already she was attracting too much attention for a spook.

He gave the blond ingénue a week in this cauldron of politics, jealousy, and backstabbing. Tops.

"Wonder if she's even legal," Quinn mused.

Dieu. Less than a week, if Quinn got his hands on her.

"Why? You plannin' some kind of mischief, *mon ami*?"

"You got a problem with that, friend?"

Yeah. He did. The girl looked right out of college, and no way was she ready to handle whatever Quinn had in mind to dish her way. But . . .

Not his business. Besides, they'd assigned her to Istanbul, so she must be able to look after herself. As long as she didn't compromise his mission or need her ass rescued, Marc didn't care what she looked like. They weren't here at the Dumani Embassy decked out in penguin suits to pick up women. They had a job to do. And Quinn was a pro. He wouldn't get distracted. *Alors*, if he did, *he* could do the *foutu—fucking—*rescuing.

CIA had brought in STORM to help on this dash-and-grab because of the deniability factor. Strategic Technical Operations and Rescue Missions Corporation—STORM Corps—was a nongovernmental spec-ops outfit that hired out to private companies and individuals, mainly to recover and defend hostages and other assets. But they were often used to carry out sensitive or controversial covert ops in locations and situations where official government agencies couldn't or wouldn't go.

Such as this one.

Upstairs on the third floor of the Dumani Embassy was a safe containing an antiterrorist's wet dream. First, new identity papers for Jallil Abu Bakr and Abbas Tawhid, the two men suspected of being the driving force behind al Sayika, one of the worst terrorist organizations to burst onto the international scene since al Qaeda. This year alone, al Sayika cells had blown up the Dutch stock exchange, poisoned a Saudi princess actively advocating for equal rights for women within Islam, and murdered a female French National Police commander for clamping down on the race riots in the Paris *banlieues*.

Just as fanatical as bin Laden, and far more sophisticated in their long-term planning, Jallil Abu Bakr and Abbas Tawhid were way up there on everyone's Most Wanted lists, right under their fuckbuddy. Unfortunately, Abu Bakr was an enigma; no Western agent had ever seen his face. Abbas Tawhid was a cruel, ruthless, misogynistic sociopath who had risen through the ranks on sheer brutality. His face was well-known but the aliases he traveled under were not. Getting their hands on both these men's identity papers would be huge.

But there was more.

Even more important, the upstairs safe was also believed to contain al Sayika's master plan for the development and deployment of a highly lethal bioweapon, rumored to be some kind of horrific hybrid of an Armageddon virus. Avian flu, swine flu, smallpox, anthrax, Ebola. Take your pick. All equally deadly on their own. A mixed combination would be hell on Earth. Literally. It was crucial to stop the weapon before it got started.

Tonight Marc and Quinn were tasked to reach the embassy safe, open it, and photo-digitize all of the al Sayika documents without making a ripple. Thus insuring the two leaders would be caught, the bioweapon neutralized, and al Sayika's growing power in the terrorist world stopped before it gained any more momentum.

CIA Barbie—aka Darcy Zimmerman—was supposed to pass them the combination to the safe—obtained from an enterprising embassy cleaning lady who'd gotten the deal of a lifetime, compliments of the U.S. taxpayers. Marc wondered how Zimmerman had managed that coup, especially looking like she did. After all, most conservative Muslims would be highly suspicious of any woman who was unmarried, showed so much skin, and interacted so freely with men. Frankly, he'd been expecting their contact to be a short, frumpy fortysomething old-maid type with sensible shoes. But tall, golden blond, and model-gorgeous Darcy Zimmerman broke the mold on all counts. The Company must be raising their standards.

Speak of the devil. Zimmerman was coming toward them on the arm of the Dumani agricultural attaché. She laughed at something the old roué said in her ear—he had to go practically on tiptoes—just as she spotted them.

"There you are!" she called with a cheerful wave, as if they'd actually met before. "I thought you two had left without me!"

Without missing a beat, she answered Quinn's welcoming

smile with one of her own and slid into his arms for a hug, kissing him on the cheeks, Euro-style. "Darling, meet Sheikh Asood." She introduced them, using code names they'd been given for the op.

She was smooth; Marc had to give her that.

And so was Quinn. One smarmy smile and *he* ended up as the boyfriend, *le tayau*. Not that Marc was interested. *Bon*, she was beautiful, but not his type. He preferred women who had nothing to do with the world he worked in. And unlike Quinn, he never mixed business and pleasure.

As they made meaningless chitchat with Asood, Marc studied what he could see of the embassy's structure. He knew from blueprints supplied by STORM that the building was an old converted Ottoman palace. Complex mosaic décor adorned the carved stucco walls and high ceilings; intricate marble arches and gilded scrollwork were everywhere, the perfect backdrop to the luxurious furnishings, rugs, and tapestries. Pretty impressive stuff.

The good news was because of the palace's age and historical value, very little renovation had taken place inside—including even the most rudimentary security features. No cameras, alarms, or motion detectors. The bad news was guards had been liberally sprinkled around the main staircases. It would be tricky getting past them.

"Shall we visit the buffet?" Zimmerman suggested, looping her wrists around each of their elbows after Asood saw which way the wind blew and excused himself.

"I'm Bobby Lee, by the way," Quinn said, pulling her closer to his side than was strictly necessary.

She smiled up at him. "Yeah. I know. You guys ready for this?"

"You've got the combination?" Marc asked, trying to move things along as they casually strolled from the salon toward the opulent dining room. They had to wade through three smaller rooms crushed with people to reach it. He instinctively scanned faces and body language, looking for anything suspicious. So far, so good.

"Just follow my lead," she said.

They grabbed plates and selected a few morsels from the overflowing buffet table, slowly making their way down the line. She obviously had a plan, so he and Quinn just went along, ready for anything. Marc already had a plan, but what was he going to do about it, stamp his foot and demand his was better? Besides, maybe his wasn't better. *Semper Gumby.*

"How do you like Istanbul so far?" he asked Zimmerman, to fill the silence. Ah, *merde*. She and Quinn were already making goo-goo eyes at each other over the hors d'oeuvres. Marc barely resisted rolling his. *Get a room.* Please. *After* the op.

"Amazing place," she answered, still looking at Quinn. "Gorgeous city."

"Aren't you afraid?" Quinn asked. "Being a young woman alone and all. Dangerous place, Istanbul."

She gave him a dazzling smile. "Worried about me?"

He grinned. "Wouldn't want anything untoward to happen."

Not until he got her back to his hotel room, anyway, Marc thought. *Salleau prie.*

She reached up and touched Quinn's chin with a finger. "Hell, no fun in that."

Marc was just about to clear his throat and suggest getting back to business when she winked at him and suddenly melted back through an arched opening he recalled seeing on the blueprints. Hidden by a beaded screen, it blended in perfectly with the line of marble arches marching along the back wall of the room. But this one opened discreetly into a darkened hallway leading to the kitchens in the back.

She'd timed her exit to exactly when the guard was looking the other way, distracted by a serving spoon clattering onto the marble floor like a firecracker. A setup?

Alors. Not bad. Marc slipped through after her, followed by Quinn.

She deposited her plate on a cart sitting in the shadows, and they quickly did the same. She beckoned, hurrying down the hall until they reached a narrow flight of stairs.

"This is the servants' staircase," she whispered. "It goes all the way up. You know where the safe is hidden, right?" She glanced between the two of them, her gaze finally landing on Marc.

"Third floor. Second office, east wing," he recited.

"Exactly. Here." From a low hall table drawer she produced a red-patterned kaffiyeh scarf of the type worn by Saudi-aligned Arabs, along with the distinctive bronze knotted *agal* of the Dumani security guards to hold it in place. "You'll blend in better than Quinn," she said.

Considering Quinn had short, white blond hair and striking blue eyes reminiscent of an Alaskan husky in the dead of winter, and Marc was typical Cajun dark, yeah, you think?

"I'm also lead on this one, me," he informed her dryly.

"Pretend you're a guard," she said, ignoring the gentle barb. "You speak Arabic, right?"

He nodded. "Some."

"Good. However, there's been a complication."

Naturellement. It wouldn't be a typical joint-CIA goat-fuck without one. And here he'd thought he'd gotten off easy, with just Quinn's flag waving in the air.

"The stairs between the second and third floors were varnished today," she said. "They're still wet."

Which meant he'd leave permanent footprints. Yeah, *mal pris*. Not good.

"*What?*" Quinn exploded under his breath, his face clouding with anger. "Why didn't you tell us this in the—"

"It'll still work," she insisted to Marc. "You'll just have to come around to the front staircase and sneak past the guards to get to the other wing. There's an old *harim* staircase that leads up to the third floor."

They already knew that, but had dismissed it as unnecessarily dangerous. The staircase spilled out into the ambassador's private living quarters rather than the hallway. *De foutre*.

Quinn looked ready to strangle her. "And how the *fuck* is he supposed to get by the guards without being—"

"He'll look like one of them. And you and I will create a diversion," she said impatiently, then turned back to Marc. "Just be in position and ready to roll in five, okay?"

It sounded crazy. But crazy had worked before.

"What the hell." He grabbed the kaffiyeh from her and wound it expertly around his head and shoulders. They *had* to get what was in that safe—the al Sayika identity papers and bioweapon plans—at all costs.

Besides, what was the worst that could happen? Firing squad at dawn? No big deal. Standard occupational hazard.

"Safe combination?" he asked.

She rattled it off and he committed it to memory. To his surprise, she reached up and gave him a kiss on the cheek, too. "Good luck." Then she was off, hurrying back toward the dining room.

Quinn shook his head, obviously not pleased. "Still time to call it off, buddy. Or switch back to our own plan."

"No worries, *boug*. But that diversion? Make it a good one. Anything goes wrong, see you back at the rendezvous point."

"Sure. Right after I kill that chick."

GRINDING his teeth, Bobby Lee Quinn strode double-time after the CIA babe. Sweet fucking Jesus. He and Lafayette should have bailed while they still had the chance. Wet *floor varnish*? Shit on a freaking brick. This thing had clusterfuck written all over it.

Well, what did he expect from the Company? That they'd actually be able to find their ass from a hole in the wall? Christ.

And here Bobby Lee'd had visions of trying to establish closer relations between their two organizations . . . *Much* closer.

He snorted silently and followed the babe back through the beaded screen into the dining room. Darcy Zimmerman was hot as a Tuscaloosa afternoon in July, but if her lack of seasoning and preparedness got his friend killed—

Bobby Lee had worked with the Cajun Lafayette off and on over his five-plus years at STORM and liked him a lot. Marc was the kind of man who expected the best from people and usually got it. Like now, for instance. Dude. What planet did he live on to think this plan could actually work?

The long strands of beads clicked closed behind Bobby Lee, and to his momentary surprise Darcy Zimmerman greeted him with an "accidental" brush of her lush body as they rejoined the buffet line. He had to white-knuckle the plate in his hands so he didn't drop it. The under-the-lashes look she gave him was pure, unadulterated, walking sex. She'd even managed to mess up her hair so it looked like he'd had his fingers in it just seconds ago.

Well, okay, then.

He readjusted his thinking. *This* part of her plan . . . Well, hell, it worked just fine for him.

He'd caught on immediately, of course: they'd just slipped back from a steamy tryst in the hallway, which explained their sudden emergence from an off-limits area. The guard over by the archway was shocked to see them. But at that sizzling look from Zimmerman, he gave them a salacious grin and let it go. Bobby Lee waggled his eyebrows.

Just call him Stud Lee.

His plate suddenly disappeared from his hands and he found himself being steered through the crowd toward the front foyer with just enough casualness not to attract attention. But that full-body contact had already gotten his unwavering attention.

And God, that dress. The floor-length gown she wore was a true work of art. Blue like the Prophet's paradise, slinky like pearls running through your fingers, and without straps or any visible means of staying up, it hugged her curves like a man begging for more. And just about any man in the place *would* be begging for more, given half a chance. Including him. Hell, especially him. His breath was virtually backed up in his lungs waiting for her drapey blue bodice to come sliding down off her breasts. Her very amazing breasts. Full, ripe breasts that were pert and high and just the right size. Breasts a man could lose himself in completely.

Maybe CIA wasn't so stupid after all. Talk about Mata Hari potential.

And okay, this diversion thing might work. It could happen.

They got to the foyer and he tore his eyes off her long enough to do a quick survey. The evening was still early, but a few departing diplomats and their companions milled around, waiting for limos to be fetched by chauffeurs.

He checked out the room itself. Despite having no furniture and no function beyond serving as the main entrance to the old palace, the massive octagonal gold-and-marble foyer was bigger than the whole stinkin' house Bobby Lee had grown up in. Which admittedly wasn't tough, since that had been a two-room backwoods shanty. Unlike that bad memory, this space was all done up fancier than a whore's wedding cake with a series of deep, fussy alcoves around the perimeter that contained giant potted palm trees and aromatic flowering shrubs. The place smelled like jasmine and oranges.

Or was that Darcy Zimmerman?

She looped her arm through his and tilted her head a fraction toward the centerpiece of the foyer, the grand staircase that ascended like a gilded stairway to heaven. The one Lafayette would have to get across at the second-floor landing—past three armed guards—and reach the other side unseen before continuing up the *harim* stairs to the floor where the safe was located. Those guards looked big, mean, and no-nonsense, dressed in traditional Arab garb, complete with flashing scimitars hanging at their sides. Oh, yeah, and AK-47s.

This could get ugly.

"All right. Now what?" he asked under his breath, speaking into Zimmerman's cloud of golden hair.

He was six feet four, but he didn't even have to bend over. Man, she was tall in those heels. And she smelled damn good, he couldn't help but notice as she tipped up her face to answer. Not jasmine and oranges, but some exotic blend of—

"You carrying a condom in any of those pockets?" she murmured, taking hold of his tux lapels and easing into him like a lover. Her fingers started to trail south.

Whoa. Hold on, there. *What?* "Um—" What the *fuck* did she just say?

Not that he wasn't all over it.

"Just in case you want to forget about the op and go back to my place," she added with an amused wink.

He felt his lips curve up. Very funny, ha-ha. Okay, point taken. She'd focused his wandering attention. But obviously, she had no idea she was playing with fire here.

Far be it for him to warn her. Where there was smoke, fire wasn't far behind. And the woman was insanely smokin' hot.

Distraction? He'd give her a stinkin' distraction.

He put his hands on her waist and leisurely ran them over her hips and down onto her ass. Like her lover might. He held her gaze as he gathered her in his fingers and press-ground her into him. Yeah, *him*. Center to center. Right where he was dying to have her.

The room's chatter suddenly dropped to whispers—some giggling, some disapproving—and he knew without a doubt that every person in the foyer was watching them.

He tilted his head down again, murmuring, "There's no 'just in case' about it, sugar. Later, you're all mine."

Her eyes widened, as though his calling her bluff caught her slightly off guard. Hardly surprising. She was a real firecracker. Probably most men she encountered out in the world either wilted like a linen suit in all that heat, or turned tail and ran screaming from her kind of strength and audacity.

Him, it just turned on all the more. He liked a woman to be his equal. Which she most assuredly was.

Ignoring everything and everyone around them, he leaned down and languidly trailed hot breath over her cheek, down to her lips. She gasped softly as he covered them with his. And kissed her. Like he had every intention of following through on his threat, but right then and there.

This was highly inappropriate behavior for an embassy party, especially with a Muslim country as host. He figured that outrageous kiss would earn him a resounding slap on the cheek. As part of the diversion, of course.

But somewhere along the line his bold strategy backfired. Because she kissed him back. Like she had every intention of taking him up on that little dare.

Christ on a fuckin' cracker.

From the second his tongue touched hers he was hard as the marble columns that surrounded them. Sweet mercy, she tasted good.

But he couldn't. Not here. Not now. *The guards*, he re-minded himself. Distract *them*, not himself.

He grasped her head in his hands and managed a glance upward at the second-floor landing as he changed the angle of the kiss. At least it was working. The three Dumanis were stunned by the sight of a beautiful woman's very public kiss with a man obviously not her husband.

Bobby Lee caught a glimpse of Marc taking a careful step out from the shadows of the east-wing hallway.

This is it.

He needed to be absolutely sure those guards would stay distracted, shocked motionless, so absorbed by what he and Zimmerman were doing that Marc could glide past their backs in perfect safety.

And that was the *only* reason he spun her around and walked her backward one deliberate step at a time, kissing her to within an inch of her life. Honestly it was.

He aimed for the short wall between two of those fancy archways and kept going until her backside hit mosaic tile. Which finally roused her. She jerked out of his arms, took a second to regroup, then shoved him away with an embarrassed giggle, playing the enamored junior embassy staffer belatedly trying to salvage her job. "Darling, stop! People are staring!"

But her eyes said, "Just wait till I get you alone, boy."

Real, or part of the charade?

Both?

One could only hope.

"Okay," she murmured, taking a deep breath. "Marc made it to the other side."

Thank you, Jesus.

Bobby Lee straightened his jacket, joining her where she leaned her back against the cool wall. He was breathing hard, his body thrumming with need. *Damn*, he wanted her.

"So, are you always this creative in your operations?" he asked, pitching his voice to barely audible. Suddenly he was insanely jealous of all the other operators she might have done this with in her short but no doubt illustrious spook career.

"Oh, you'd be surprised," she said.

Oh, he doubted it.

"But it seems to me *you're* the one who took it up a notch," she pointed out.

Possibly.

He looked at her. Wondering. *Was* this personal? "You

didn't seem to object." He shrugged, playing it cool. "Got the job done."

"Yes," she agreed. "It did."

He stuck his hands in his trouser pockets so he wouldn't grab her again. "By the way, you're one hell of a kisser."

She smiled. "I know."

He barked a laugh. "That mouth of yours gonna get you in real trouble someday."

"Tell me something I *don't* know."

"Okay." He made a quarter turn to face her, dead serious. "When they fire you tomorrow, come work for me."

She blinked, and stared at him. "Don't be absurd. They won't fire me."

"Maybe not tomorrow. But I'll bet you a thousand bucks that within two weeks you'll be suddenly transferred. To somewhere not nearly as glamorous as Istanbul. And they're gonna ask you to do things you won't want to do." He hoped to hell she didn't want to do them. "When that happens, give me a call."

"I'll take that bet," she said. "Because you're crazy."

"Maybe. But I've been in this game a long time, sugar. I know how your bosses operate."

Her look turned incredulous. "All this because I let you kiss me?"

"Hell, no. It was the *way* you let me kiss you."

She obviously didn't understand. And he had to know.

He stepped in close, as though whispering licentious suggestions in her ear. "My kissing you had nothing to do with this job. You and I both know that. But *they* don't. They won't understand that I'm an irresistibly sexy guy and you want me naked. They'll think you'd do this with anyone they order you to."

He held his breath, waiting for her reaction.

"Oh. My. God." Her mouth went crooked. "You really *are* insane."

Fuck.

"Just remember, STORM Corps. We're in the D.C. book."

"Look. I appreciate the—"

But he didn't give her the chance to finish the thought. He cut her off and in an instant was back to business.

"It's Marc. He's back on the landing, giving the signal that he has the package. We better do something quick."

DARCY Zimmerman had seen some massive egos during her short tenure at CIA, but STORM operator Bobby Lee Quinn really took the cake. Banking her amazement at the sheer conceit of the man, along with her incredulity over his presumptuous job offer, she prepared herself to continue their mock-seduction-slash-pantomime-diversion.

They were still leaning with shoulders against the wall, face-to-face, when he grabbed her and pushed her right into the nearest alcove.

She yelped. "What are you—"

His mouth crashed onto hers. Apparently the provocative but fairly harmless kissing she'd expected was not what Bobby Lee Quinn had in mind. Now, there was a shock. The man was simply unpredictable.

Taken by surprise, she didn't have the presence of mind to resist. And after about three seconds, okay, call her fickle, but resisting was the *last* thing on her mind.

Sometimes unpredictable was good.

Good *lord*, what a kiss.

Everything about the man was hard. His body was hard against hers. His muscles were hard pressing into her. His lips and tongue were hard as they took her mouth in a blinding, grinding assault. His cock was huge and hard as it rocked into her belly, telling her it wanted her *now*. He practically vibrated with sexual power and virility.

Did she say *mock* seduction? If this was acting, Bobby Lee Quinn deserved a freaking Oscar.

She moaned, unable to stop her body from responding to the onslaught. Her nipples tightened. Her pulse throbbed. Her limbs weakened—along with her mental capacity.

He might have an ego the size of Canada, but he was ridiculously, totally, to-die-for sexy. In college she would have done Quinn in a hot second. She'd like to think she had more sense now, having managed to avoid men altogether since her last disastrous relationship. Talk about a train wreck. That one had actually had the audacity to propose marriage and babies while seeing someone else on the side.

But this man . . . This man made her stomach zing and that sweet spot between her legs ache with a breathtaking need for his touch.

She might just have to let him have her.

She completely melted under his hands as they claimed her, touching her body, caressing her breasts. Dipping into her strapless bodice with bold fingers.

Sweet mercy. "Quinn!" she squeaked.

"Distraction," he muttered.

She sucked in the cry of utter protest that leapt to her lips. But his fingers found her nipples and squeezed, hard, and she cried out loud, for real.

Except it didn't sound like her. The cries sounded male. But not Quinn's. His mouth was still too busy kissing her.

She ripped her lips from his.

The guards. It was the *guards* shouting. At *them*.

For the second time that night, she forced herself to break out of Quinn's sensual web. How did he keep *doing* that to her?

Her neckline had slipped down precariously close to indecency. She attempted to yank it back up, but the guards were on them too fast. Yelling. Waving guns. Pulling them apart. Dragging them out into the public foyer.

"Damn it, let me go!" she screamed at them.

His expression appalled, Quinn struggled to get free, to get to her. Apparently *not* what he'd had in mind. That was a relief.

"Leave the lady alone! For chrissakes, let her cover herself!" he shouted. Among other choice, anatomically impossible suggestions.

As a diversion it was pretty damn good.

She was half naked. Quinn's vocabulary was amazingly imaginative. Deadly AK-47s were pointing at their heads. Everyone in the place was mesmerized with shock.

Except the third guard.

This was the night in her fledgling career that Darcy Zimmerman learned an important lesson: there's one in every crowd—the inevitable *one* member of the enemy camp who is actually alert and good at his job.

The third guard wasn't staring at her almost bare breasts. Or aiming his weapon at Quinn. Even though he was standing in the middle of the melee, he was watching the stairs like he was supposed to be doing. Which was where he spotted Lafayette. Sneaking down. She cursed under her breath. Where were Marc's kaffiyeh and *agal*? He must have decided to take a shortcut and try blending into the crowd.

"Halt!" the guard shouted, rushing over to intercept him before he jumped the banister and got away. "Stop or I shoot!"

The sound of a half dozen guns being locked and loaded echoed like shots off the marble.

Lafayette froze. And was instantly surrounded by three more guards.

Darcy's stomach plummeted.

Oh, *fuck*.

They were so screwed.

TWO

Five years later
December, present day
Lower St. Martin Parish, Louisiana

BODIES lay scattered on the wet ground in an unholy tangle of bones and rotting flesh. Swamp mist swirled in wispy drifts through the chilly morning air, making the scene seem almost surreal.

Marc Lafayette waded slowly through the still, green waters of Bayou Creche, taking in the putrid jumble of remains scattered above the low bank. It was real, all right. All too real.

Rage exploded within him. *Dieu*, it was bad. The worst kill yet.

In the distance, the *plink-splash*, *plink-splash* of a paddle dipping in water echoed through the silent morning. He halted to listen intently. Had the terrorists come back to inventory the lethal effects of their latest bioweapon experiment?

He couldn't possibly get so lucky.

Marc quickly scanned the area and ducked under cover of a dense clump of swamp oak, grateful he'd left the pirogue moored farther upstream. With the practiced ease of a lifetime hunter—both of creatures and of men—he melted into the verdant foliage, making himself invisible.

A canoe glided slowly past him, with a lone occupant.

The boat was one of Charlie Thibadeaux's rentals. Marc

didn't recognize the woman. Late twenties maybe? Soft, sable brown hair pulled back in a thick braid. Interesting face. *Très joli*. Very pretty.

But she lost all appeal the second he spotted the unmistakable gold "LSP" on the back of her blue Windbreaker. Louisiana State Police.

De merde. What the hell was—

She suddenly gasped, spotting the carnage. Clamping a hand over her mouth, she let the prow of the canoe run up onto the muddy shore below the kill site, staring in horror at the largest of the carcasses: a mature black bear. There were also birds, nutria, and even a bloated gator floating nearby. All poisoned by a specially genetically altered, weaponized virus.

All clues to a bioterror threat the likes of which had never been experienced on American soil.

Until now.

Of course, a local cop had no way of knowing that.

He assumed.

"My God," the woman murmured aloud, her words whispering through the thick cypress and Spanish moss like a troubled prayer.

What the hell was she doing here, anyway? Although technically the whole state of Louisiana fell under state police jurisdiction, and Bayou Creche was only about a mile into the wilderness from Highway 70, usually troopers never ventured even this far into the swamp. Not in a canoe. Certainly not without a good reason. Which meant she'd come out here deliberately.

Putain de merde. This was all they needed. A *foutu* nosy cop on their six.

For fifteen minutes Marc remained silent and still, watching with growing agitation as she photographed the scene, then brought out a series of small specimen tubes and collected evidence from the carcasses. What was she, some kind of goddamn CSI?

The boss was not going to like this. Not one damn bit.

Since when had the LSP started concerning itself with animal kills? Wasn't there some damn traffic jam somewhere that needed unraveling?

The female trooper finally got back in the canoe and started paddling in the direction of the highway. Marc was going to have to have a talk with Charlie Thibadeaux about renting out to *étrangers* who had no business in the swamp. At least not without telling Marc about it. He made a mental note to put Charlie on the payroll, then pulled out his PDA-style cell phone and sent a quick text message to the STORM field HQ, located for the moment in a remote fishing camp about twelve clicks north.

Within seconds the response came back. He swore softly under his breath.

Neutralize her. Any means necessary.

GINA Cappozi stood in front of the portable fan at her work-table and let the breeze dry her tears; she refused to let any more fall.

Tears were useless. She knew that. From long, bitter experience she knew that. Sometimes they even made things worse. Her captors did not like weepy women. Actually, her captors did not like women at all.

In any case, tears were for those who had hope. And Gina Cappozi had pretty much lost all hope nearly two months ago.

She could remember the exact moment when it had happened. For weeks after being taken prisoner by these disgusting terrorist extremists, she had expected someone to burst through the door of this sick excuse for a lab, riding a white steed with guns blazing, and rescue her. So naïve. So freakingly, bitterly naïve. That day the door *had* slammed open, she'd jumped up, praying it was the police, or the FBI, or the CIA, or Wade her ex . . . or, in the darkest, bleakest, most hidden recesses of her heart even that scum-fucker, Gregg van Halen.

But of course it had been the lead bastard, Abbas Tawhid. Again. As always. It was always Tawhid who came through the door when Gina most needed it to be someone else. Anyone else.

He took special pleasure in tormenting her with stories of his past victims. Bragged about the special-ops agent he'd helped break through a year and a half of torture, to the point where the man had actually thought his name was Pig, and answered to it, groveling on command, rolling in his own filth. Tawhid had laughed then. And looked down at her with his flat, empty eyes. The ones where she could read he intended to do it all over again, this time with her, if she didn't cooperate. Hell, probably even if she did.

But it was the laugh that had finally done it. Cold. Emotionless. Without mercy.

That was when she'd known for certain. No one would ever come to rescue her. Her life was over. She would die in this hellish place. Probably sooner than later. If she was lucky.

Coming back to the present, she took a deep breath and switched off the fan.

So be it.

But would she help that devil with his evil plot to bring down the country she loved?

No.

Never.

SHE wasn't scared.

Honestly.

But good flipping grief.

Shivering in the falling darkness—from the *cold*, not fear—Louisiana State Trooper First Class Tara Reeves looked up at the badly painted sign over the dilapidated, rambling wooden shack perched on a rickety deck that overhung the bayou. She then looked down to double-check the name on the bit of paper in her hand.

Au Chien.

A match. Oh, joy.

The seedy roadhouse bar was sandwiched between a mud parking lot overflowing with Harleys, ancient Fords, and dirt-caked trucks of all sizes and description on one side, and the obsidian black waters of a bayou whose name she couldn't pronounce on the other. In the middle of goddamn nowhere. And despite it being eight p.m. on a Wednesday night, music blared from every orifice of the structure, which virtually pulsed with activity.

God help her. Was she really going to have to go *into* that place?

Tara knew exactly the greeting her uniform—complete with standard-issue SIG-Sauer sidearm—would get her. More of the same cold shoulder and rude comments she'd been treated to all afternoon.

Afraid? Hell, no. Just sick and tired.

But she could not shake a feeling of unease. Not from the roadhouse. But because she was being followed. *Followed.* She was almost sure of it.

She'd been getting the same creepy feeling all day. That tickle on the back of her neck, that hum of nerves that for no apparent reason rushed down the length of her spine. Her inner alarms had been going off ever since finding those poor dead animals.

Poisoned. By some kind of über-toxic chemical being illegally spewed into the swamp. *That* she was 100 percent sure of. She was all too familiar with the deadly symptoms.

Whoever was doing this environmental damage would pay, and pay big. She'd make sure of it. Because if the pollution kept up at this rate, it was only a matter of time before *people* started dying, too. If they hadn't already.

And that was unacceptable. She wasn't about to let some other innocent kid's mother die because of unchecked corporate greed. No one should have to go through what she did.

But to shut down and punish the bad guys, she had to *find* them first. Along with the actual source of the pollution.

She crossed her arms in frustration. Why would none of the locals help her? *They* were the ones who'd be dying. Hell, all she needed was a guide to take her farther into the swamp than she dared venture by herself. She'd do the rest.

A guy and a boat. One day. Maybe two.

Was that too much to ask?

But, *noooooo.* Every official and unofficial guide she'd approached all afternoon had been "too busy" or "not interested." The guy she'd rented the canoe from had nearly run her off with a shotgun at first. Could she help that the last big-city morons he'd rented his favorite boat to had totaled it by trying to haul a heavy propane air-conditioner and fridge to the wilderness outpost where they were staying? Only her

LSP uniform had saved her getting a backside full of buck-shot. An ironic switch. That same uniform—along with her Yankee accent—had gotten the door slammed in her face by every other guide she'd approached. Talk about instant con-versation killers.

So anyway, now she was down to the dregs—the unem-ployed and the weekend moonshiners who might do a spot of guiding for a few extra bucks to spend on beer—even from a Yankee female in uniform.

Suddenly a twig snapped behind her. She spun to a crouch, reaching for the SIG under her jacket.

A tall man sauntered out of the shadows beyond the park-ing lot. "Easy, *cher*," he drawled. "Since when is goin' for a drink against the law?"

She let out a breath, bristling to cover the heat creeping up her cheeks. Jumpy? Her? "It's TFC Reeves to you," she ground out, "and if you don't want to risk getting shot, don't sneak up behind a police officer." She reholstered her weapon.

He grinned and gave an unconcerned shrug. "I'll keep that in mind . . . TFC Reeves." His slow Cajun accent coated the deliberately drawled-out letters with pure Acadian molasses, making them sound more like sweet-talking than her rank.

He oozed to a stop in front of her. The man was big. Broad shoulders and at least six-three. Good-looking, too. In that swarthy, bad-boy way that Cajun men seemed to carry off so effortlessly. Except for the angry scar radiating back from his temple into his thick black hair. That made him look a shade . . . menacing.

He glanced around the parking lot. "There a crime goin' on here I'm not aware of, TFC Reeves?" He looked back at her, his black eyes glittering from the colorful lights strung willy-nilly around the roof of the roadhouse. The corner of his mouth curved up. "Or . . . maybe you've come for some-thin' else . . . ?"

Oh. Subtle.

She pushed her Smokey hat up with the tip of her forefin-ger and leaned closer to him, beckoning with a tilt of her head. He scootched down to meet her halfway, so their faces were mere inches apart.

"You soliciting me, *cher*?" she asked softly, infusing the mirrored Cajun endearment with a liberal dose of threat.

His gaze slipped lazily down to her lips. "*Mais non*, officer." Then he just grinned wider and met her eyes. "I doubt you could afford me."

With that, he sidestepped her and sauntered off, continuing on his way to the Au Chien's front entrance, located up a narrow wooden gangplank and across the low deck the rambling shack crouched on.

She slammed her eyes shut and ground her jaw.

Yeah. This was going to be *rea*-lly fun.

She waited until Mr. Sweet-talker disappeared through the door, added an extra minute or two, braced herself, then strode up into the joint.

It was like in the movies, when John Wayne walks into the saloon and everything stops and everyone stares at him for a really long second. Well, the Au Chien was too big for that to totally happen, but it did in waves. As she walked, big concentric circles of silence followed along in her wake.

Just like John Wayne, that didn't bother her. She was used to it. Same thing happened wherever she went. Out in the world, it was the gun and uniform caused it. On the job it was her gender. Female troopers were few and far between. The males either resented her completely or considered her their personal plaything. A notion she quickly disabused them of. But it made for a lonely workday. Again, she was used to it. Didn't matter. She wasn't there looking for friends.

Carefully pasting a friendly smile on her face, she walked up to the polished wooden bar. The grizzled old bartender smiled back, but his eyes were wary. "Kin I help you?"

She came straight to the point. "I'm looking for a good wilderness guide. I was told this was the place to come."

The bartender nodded sagely. "Well, now. Dis here is sort of a waterin' hole for our local outdoor types. What kinda guide you needin'?"

"Someone who knows the swamps well. I'm looking into the animal die-offs that have been happening recently around here."

She didn't elaborate. Mention the words "toxic runoff" and people started fighting. Especially in Louisiana. Tree huggers and do-gooders versus those who liked the high-paying jobs the big, dirty industries brought to people who needed them badly.

Tara kept out of the controversy. Her only interest was in enforcing the law and saving people from dying unnecessary and painful deaths and creating motherless children and widowers.

"Well, now, lessee." The bartender glanced around the crowded establishment. He pointed out two men sprawled in a wooden booth. "You try dem *fils* for starters. Dey not available, dey prob'ly recommend you some other *fils*."

The two men looked more like overfed gorillas than boys. But at this point beggars couldn't be choosers. She only had until Monday to wrap this up. That was all the time the captain let her take off from work. Unless, of course, he found out what she was doing. Then she'd have all the time in the world. "Don't you worry your pretty little head investigatin'. Jest some ol' dead animals. Don't mean a thang."

She wrestled with her conscience, broke down, and bought a beer—for show—before saying thanks to the bartender and going over to the gorillas' table.

Her luck didn't improve. After talking to them, plus two other so-called guides they recommended, all of whom turned her down with one excuse lamer than the next, she actually took a sip of the beer.

When she was turned down flat by another three bozos, she drank half of it and went back to the bar.

"No joy, eh, *fille*?" the bartender asked.

She took a last disgusted swig, then set the beer aside. "Don't know if it's me or the uniform scares them worse."

Chuckling, he leaned a forearm on the sticky bar. "Well, now. You might jus' ask dat guy over dere. He don' scare so easy." He jerked a thumb at a man bending over the pool table, getting ready to take a shot. *Hel*-lo. His back was turned toward her. Okay, his *butt* was turned toward her.

And a very nice butt it was. Tight. Lean. Muscular. A pair of well-fitting jeans stretched over it as he bent even further, affording her a back-row seat. As it were.

Oh, *ma*ma.

"Now, dat boy, he grew up here in da bayou, but ain' been around for a while. He know da swamp real good, though."

That boy. Yeah. The man was on the downside of thirty if he was a day. Not that his age mattered.

"Is he trustworthy?" she asked, noting the big Ka-Bar hunting knife strapped to his thigh.

The bartender grinned. "Well, I heard talk of some jail time, but dat prob'ly jus' some ol' story. He always pay his tab and leave a good tip."

A ringing endorsement. "There's no one else?"

"I think you hit everyone, *fille*."

Ho-kay, then. Mr. Perfect Butt it was. "Give me another of whatever he's drinking," she told the bartender, and left him a ten-dollar tip when he handed her an icy bottle of Stella.

All righty, then. Do or die. If she didn't get a guide for tomorrow, she wasn't sure what she'd do. Probably go into the swamp by herself, get lost, and never come out again. Her captain would be thrilled.

She stood back and waited patiently, admiring the guy's fine backside while he finished his shots and cleared the table, leaving his opponent in the chalk dust. Then she stepped forward, offering the Stella up to him as he turned around to face her for the first time.

She froze.

Oh.

Shit.

The guy from outside. Mr. Perfect Butt was Mr. Sweet-talker.

Her miserable day was now complete.

Without missing a beat he took the beer from her and grinned that supremely irritating grin of his and said, "Had a feelin' you'd change your mind, *cher*. Glad to see I haven' lost my touch."

She almost sputtered. "Yeah, well, you've lost your *mind* if you think I came over here to . . . to—"

But he ignored her stuttering, tipped the bottle to his mouth, and took a long pull. With lips that were full and sculpted, and looked like they could—

Ho-boy.

"So, what have you come for, then?" he asked, dark bedroom eyes all innocence, like he hadn't noticed her staring at him.

She snapped her mouth shut. Okay. This was a bad idea. A *really* bad idea. She hadn't come here looking for a date. Or . . . anything else he seemed to have on his mind.

Tara didn't do men. Not for *that* stuff, anyway. She'd given up dating shortly after she'd started carrying a gun for a living. Guns and men did not mix. When they spotted the SIG, they either got all defensive and macho, or they got waaay too turned on—which gave her the heebie-jeebies.

She was here looking for a swamp guide. Nothing else. No way was she getting within ten feet of *this* guy's pirogue.

She cleared her throat. "Uh, nothing," she answered. "Just wanted to apologize for drawing down on you out there in the parking lot. See y'round."

She'd started walking away when he called, "Hey, *cher*. Heard you were trying to hire yourself a guide."

Of course he had.

"Know anyone good?" she tossed back over her shoulder.

"Oh, I'm real good," he said with that infernal grin.

"Yeah?" She stopped and pretended to consider. Shook her head. "Nope. Can't afford you, remember?" She kept on walking.

He caught up to her just before she reached the door, wrapping his fingers around her arm. "Hold up."

She whirled and gave him a death-ray glare.

He let go and raised his hands in the air. "Sorry. Meant no disrespect, TFC Reeves. Listen, can we talk?"

"About what?"

He tipped his chin at the door. "Outside."

Bad idea, Reeves.

But then again, lately, she'd been having nothing *but* bad ideas.

What. Ever.

She stepped out the door, and he followed her across the deck and down the gangplank to the parking lot. After the roasting-hot, deafeningly noisy bar, the December night air was chilly but soothingly quiet. He led her around to the side of the structure where the water of the bayou lapped softly against the reedy shore.

She pulled her jacket tighter around her. "So. What?"

"You need someone who knows the swamps, and I know them better than anyone around these parts."

She shook her head again and started for her cruiser. "Sorry. I'm not interested in hiring you."

"You would have taken on any one of those losers in there. Why not me?"

She gave him a withering look. "You know why."

He came around and stopped in front of her. "Because you're attracted to me? *Cher*, that's just a bonus."

She laughed. And poked him in the chest. "You. Are delusional." She tried to sidestep him.

He got in her way again, folding his arms across that mile-wide chest. "I'll level with you. I could really use this job. I thought flirting would help. But if you don't like it, I'll quit."

"I *don't* like it."

"It's finished, then."

He looked so sincere, and he was being so reasonable. Almost too reasonable. She narrowed her eyes. "Why do you need the job?"

His shoulder lifted. "The usual reasons."

She thought about what the bartender had said. Tried *not* to think about that Ka-Bar strapped to his thigh. "When were you in jail?"

There was a pause. "Define jail."

"Right." Don't *think* so. "Thanks anyway." She stepped to the side again.

He blocked her. "Okay. I was a POW for a while. Well, more like political prisoner, I guess. Sort of."

That stopped her dead. A POW? Looking for a job. If she were her ex-army-sergeant father, she'd hire him on the spot, no more questions asked. But as her dad constantly reminded her, she wasn't him. Not remotely.

"Where?" she asked.

Another pause. "Istanbul."

She regarded the handsome Cajun evenly. As far as she knew the U.S. hadn't been at war with Turkey during his lifetime. He couldn't be telling the truth. Plus with that long hair and smart-ass attitude and pirate scar, he looked more like a drug smuggler than a military man. She wouldn't be at all surprised if he'd been in a Turkish prison for that. And yet . . . his muscular body, proud bearing, and those eyes . . . eyes that missed nothing, that radiated confidence and ruthless determination. *Dangerous* eyes. All things a man picked up during a long stint in the military.

Yeah, or running drugs.

But she felt instinctively he wasn't lying. About *that*, anyway.

His lips curved impishly, making all that danger morph into even more dangerous charm. "There was also a little incident in junior high landed me in some hot water. Involved a fast car and an older woman."

God. She waved her hands in front of her face. "Don't want to know. Seriously."

"That mean I'm hired?"

Jesus. What was she *think*ing? This was the last man on the planet she should be sharing a confined space with in a strange wilderness where she had no idea where she was. With no escape.

But it was him or nothing—admitting defeat.

And Tara Reeves *never* admitted defeat.

"Fine," she said reluctantly. "One day only. Meet me here with your boat at eight a.m. A minute later, don't bother coming."

She went around him and this time he let her pass.

"I'll be here," he called after.

She let out a sigh.

Yeah.

That's what she was afraid of.

MARC waited until the *jolie* state trooper had threaded her way halfway across the parking lot before he ducked down and followed her.

The woman was a troublemaker through and through. Okay, he wouldn't kick her out of his bed. Surprisingly. She was a cop. Not the kind of woman he ever went for. He preferred his women not to be packing heat—of the bullet-shooting variety. But this one was packing a different kind of heat. They definitely had chemistry. Which in his book was the very worst combination for trouble.

Oh, he enjoyed a feisty *joli fille* as much as the next man. Naked and under him. Where she belonged. *Not* interfering in his job. Which this one was. Big-time.

The woman had yanked his chain but good. On several levels. Frustration swirled in his chest—frustration that had nothing to do with her rejecting him sexually. *Donc*, that stung. Just a little. She certainly got his blood pumping. Which in this case was *not* good. *Dieu*. Look how she was already fucking with his head.

But what made him really nuts was being ordered by his team leader to waylay and misdirect her highly inconvenient dead animal investigation by any means necessary. Hell, this gig was tantamount to babysitting. He knew what the STORM acronym stood for, and it wasn't "Swamp Tours R Me." His job was to catch terrorists and save the world. Not play native guide to some too-nosy cop.

He'd been combat-ready for weeks. But his commanders at STORM Corps had been treating him like an invalid ever since he'd landed badly parachuting into the Sudan three months ago. Four broken ribs and a shattered arm were just not that big a deal. Besides, he was all healed now. Good as new, except for a scar or two and a couple of aches in his bones.

Hell, even if his reactions were a bit slow—which they *weren't*—he was no damn babysitter. This reconnaissance team was small and each member had a vital part to play on this op. Time was ticking like a dirty bomb, and the team was relying on Marc to pump the locals for any information he could glean to narrow down the possible location of the al Sayika cell that was here perfecting a horrific bioweapon, then help execute a plan to take them down.

And that's what he was chafing to do. Without being side-tracked by some damn female cop and her interfering investigation.

Or her sexy mouth.

Merde.

Tamping down his irritation, he jumped in his truck and tailed Tara Reeves to her room at a cheap motel a few miles down the road. He watched her window until the light went out, then slipped the night receptionist—who happened to be a distant second cousin—a twenty to call him if she made a move before morning.

At the sit-rep meeting tonight he intended to have a serious talk with his team leader.

And tomorrow, he'd get rid of the pesky state trooper. Somehow.

One way or another, he was done with babysitting.

THREE

HER name was one of life's perfect little ironies.

Because FBI Special Agent Rebel Haywood was probably the least rebellious person on earth.

Rebel hated her name. She wore it like a cross to bear, along with all the other fun neuroses her parents had loaded her down with at birth. Not that she blamed her parents. Not really. They were equally burdened. Their biggest rebellion in life had been to name their only girl-child Rebel. How pathetic was that?

In hopes of a change? Or as a final homage to the last gasp of their dear, departed Southern aristocrat ways? Who knew.

But today Rebel actually felt like making some waves. Big ones. She wanted to jump up and down and yell, and smack some much-needed sense into her friend Alex Zane.

She wouldn't do it, though. Aside from the fact that he'd been yelled at and smacked around far too much over the past two years, it wouldn't do any good. The man's overactive sense of honor would drive him to do the "right thing" all the way to the bitter end.

Didn't he see it? Didn't he see that Helena Middleton was completely and totally wrong for him?

"Aren't you happy for me?" Zane asked Rebel now. He'd just announced that he and Helena had finally set a date for their ill-conceived wedding.

Just swell. Rebel had made the two-hour drive upstate after her shift ended, and it was nearly midnight. She was exhausted. Too exhausted for this particular argument.

"It's great," she lied, walking over to the window and gazing down over the night-dark, manicured sanatorium grounds so she wouldn't have to meet his eyes.

To think she had actually introduced them. That's what was most maddening about the situation. Helena was a childhood friend from Charleston who'd moved to New York around the same time Rebel had graduated from the FBI academy and been assigned to the New York City field office. Housemates. How perfect. Zane had belonged to a covert-ops team run by CIA—Zero Unit—to which Rebel was the liaison for her first couple years on the job. Sometimes she and Zane had gone out for a drink after hours to discuss the spec-ops business—strictly unclassified stuff, of course. One time, vivacious, picture-perfect Helena had tagged along, and the rest, as they say, was history.

"I'm thrilled for you, Alex, really."

"You don't sound thrilled."

She sighed. "Marriage is a big step. Especially . . ." She let her words die because she didn't want to have *that* argument again, either.

When Alex had been brought back from the dead three months ago, he couldn't walk, could barely see, and didn't remember a thing about his life before his sixteen-month hostage ordeal. It had been a long and rocky road back. But one thing was patently clear. He was just as stubborn now as he'd ever been before being taken prisoner by terrorists.

"Especially what?" he demanded. "Because I'm still a head case? Because I still wake up screaming in the night? Because I still can't get it up unless—" Now *his* words cut off, his frustration thick enough to slice.

She felt her cheeks go hot. She didn't want to talk about his problems getting it up. Didn't even want to *think* about that particular bit of his anatomy. He'd tried to tell her about it once, right after he'd been rescued from certain death in the

Sudan and brought home. But she hadn't let him. Not her place. They didn't have that kind of relationship. Business. *Just business.* And Alex Zane was taken. Engaged to marry her good friend Helena Middleton for the past two and a half years—Helena, who had waited faithfully for him the whole sixteen months he'd been presumed dead, and unflaggingly—if a bit remotely—stood by him for the endless weeks before his memory returned.

Helena was the one he should talk to about his sexual problems. Not Rebel.

She cleared her throat. "I just think you've been through a lot. Maybe you should slow down before you make decisions that affect the rest of both your lives. Have you talked to your therapist?"

"Damn it, Rebel, I don't want to talk to my fucking therapist. I want to talk to *you.*"

"Language, Zane."

"Sorry."

She turned around to look at him. He was sitting up in his hospital-style bed, on top of the covers, wearing nothing but sky blue scrub bottoms. Sky blue, like his eyes. One knee was bent and he'd rested his forearm on it, picking impatiently at the remains of a dinner tray. He was still thin, but not as painfully emaciated as he'd been when they first brought him in, broken and sick as a dog.

But even thirty pounds underweight, he was by far the most beautiful man Rebel had ever met. His blond hair was like spun sunshine, and the days spent outside in the Olympic-sized heated pool had restored a hint of his former wide shoulders and six-pack abs, and endless walks around the outdoor gardens had coated his face with a hint of golden winter tan.

Before, he'd been big and broad and dangerous as a Viking warrior, but now, even with the new scars marring his arms and chest, he looked more like an ethereal faerie king.

She really wished he'd put his scrub top on. It was all she could do to keep from climbing onto that bed and wrapping her body around his and licking his flat bronze nipples just to see what real temptation tasted like.

Man. She really needed to find herself a boyfriend.

"Rebel?"

She jerked her gaze up from his chest and realized he must have said something needing an answer. "Sorry—what?"

"Are you sure there's no other reason you don't want me to get married?"

She gathered herself and looked him in the eye. "Yes, there is another reason."

His pupils widened and his body froze in place for just an instant. "Really?"

"You know there is. We can't go on ignoring it forever, Zane. We have to deal with it sometime."

He didn't move an eyelash. "Okay."

"Are you ready for this? You realize what it means?"

He unfroze, his gaze locking onto hers. "Yeah, I . . . God, yes. Angel, I . . ."

At the endearment, a genuine thrill went through her tummy. Before his capture, he'd always called her "Haywood" and she'd called him "Zane." But that had changed when he got back. They'd switched to first names. And he'd also taken to calling her "angel" occasionally. She wasn't sure why he did, but it made her feel dizzy with joy and terribly guilty all at the same time. He should be calling Helena that. Not her.

She tamped down the tingles and focused on reality. "Your friend Kick Jackson called me again yesterday. Said he was wheels up on that al Sayika op he'd been expecting. I'm surprised you didn't mention it."

Zane halted again, looking momentarily confused. "What? Oh. Yeah. That. Oh. *Christ.*" He pressed the heels of his palms into his eyes. They'd been terribly infected when he came home. Even now they bothered him. "Right. That." He took a deep breath and looked up at her, his face transformed into a familiar portrait of stubbornness, with a dash of guilt thrown in for good measure. "I've already told you, I don't want you involved in any of that."

"I'm already involved. My transfer to the Gina Cappozi case finally came through, and—"

"*What*? God*damn* it, I told you not to get within ten miles of that case!"

"Oh, and what am I supposed to do? Tell my SAC, sorry, sir, but I can't take the case because I don't really care about a missing scientist believed to have been kidnapped by al Sayika terrorists? Not to mention my career?"

"There have to be other cases—"

"And what do I tell your best friend? That I refuse to help track down the fanatics he's sure are involved in the Cappozi kidnapping? The same people, I might add, who may have done this to you?" She gestured to his scars. "No, Zane. I'm on that case, and I'm staying on it whether you like it or not."

He glared at her. Actually glared. Then he grabbed her hand and pulled her down to sit on the edge of the bed. "Goddamn it, Rebel. I'm fucking serious. I—"

"Language, Zane."

"If swearing is the only way to get your goddamn attention, I'm fucking well going to swear!" He grabbed her shoulders. "You don't seem to understand how dangerous this thing is. Kick thinks we were both betrayed, *twice*, by someone within CIA—maybe even Zero Unit—working with al Sayika. In Afghanistan, and again in the Sudan. We're talking a mole inside *CIA*, Rebel. Not some ignorant home-grown survivalist misfit."

"If that's true, it's doubly important to find Gina Cappozi so she can expose the traitor!" Rebel argued.

His fingers tightened on her flesh. "A man in that position will do anything—*anything*—to eliminate those who try to expose him. Why do you think they tried to blow up Kick in the Sudan? Why do you think STORM Corps has hidden me away in this godforsaken sanatorium? You really think my health is still that bad?"

His face came so close to hers she could smell the cinnamon from the apple pie he'd eaten for dessert. And a whisper of citrusy shampoo wafting from his hair. She swallowed.

"I would fucking kill myself if anything happened to you because of me. I swear to God I would."

She tried vainly to pull back. "I'm an FBI agent, Zane. This is my job. And you mustn't say things like that. You don't mean it. Think of Helena. You want your future wife to be safe from this terrorist threat, don't you?"

His green eyes were on fire. "Yes," he gritted out. "I do."

"Well, then." She finally managed to pop out of his grip and scrambled back to her feet. "The sooner I find Dr. Cappozi and those who kidnapped her, the sooner we can all sleep better at night."

The grimness of her tone snapped his head up. "Why? What's happened?"

"I told you. Kick has been called up."

He gave her a penetrating gaze. "And?"

She didn't want to tell him, but he deserved to know the truth. Even if it made his nightmares worse. "Zane, it's Abbas Tawhid."

His face went sheet white. "Tawhid? What about him?"

"Kick says they've tracked him here to the States, to an al Sayika cell in Louisiana. And he's planning a new attack. Some kind of bioweapon. Right here. On U.S. soil."

"Sweet fucking Jesus."

She didn't bother scolding his language. He wouldn't hear her anyway. The sadistic leader of al Sayika was one of the two men responsible for the horrible torture Alex had endured during his captivity. Although the other man, Jallil Abu Bakr, known as the Sultan of Pain, had been the one to actually carry it out, it was believed Abbas Tawhid was behind the orders to break Alex.

"The weaponized virus that almost killed Kick?" he asked.

She nodded. "I believe so. STORM has sent a team to find them. Kick's part of it. He didn't have time to come and tell you that particular detail himself so he asked me to."

Alex slashed his hands through his hair, clenching his jaw. "But if al Sayika's got a plant in CIA, as we believe, Kick's team could be walking right into a trap!"

"Security's at top level. Besides, CIA doesn't even know about this operation. It's strictly STORM."

"You know about it, don't you?"

"Trust me, I haven't told a soul."

"Doesn't matter. The Sultan of pain has his ways. He knows everything," Alex said hoarsely, his eyes focusing inward, filled with a terrible past she didn't even want to guess at.

"The Sultan's dead, Zane," she reminded him. Sometimes the PTSD took over and he forgot. "Kick shot him, far away in the Sudan." She squeezed his hand. "They'll get Tawhid, too. I promise. *Kick* promises."

"You better hope he does," Alex said, swallowing. "Before it's too late for us all."

* * *

THE STORM team sit-rep meetings were being held in the largest of the eight or nine cabins in the fishing camp they'd chosen as Op HQ just twenty-four hours ago. The same cabin's kitchen was where the team ate their meals. Sometimes the two activities were combined. Tonight, of the six-member team, four were present, coffee cups in hand. Marc made five. The last spot was still waiting to be filled.

This STORM operation was a top-secret contract originating from the highest levels of the Department of Homeland Security, brought about when a local veterinarian reported several swamp birds had died from what he believed was avian flu. Tests revealed it to be a new, much more insidious cocktail consisting of a resistant form of anthrax that had been vectored into a virulent and incredibly fast-incubating strain of the deadly influenza A virus, using standard gene-therapy methodology already common in treating genetic diseases such as cystic fibrosis.

As it happened, that same cocktail had been injected into one of the team members, Kick Jackson, three months ago when he was on a mission in the Sudan. Thankfully, he'd survived, and Jallil Abu Bakr, the al Sayika leader he'd been sent to kill, hadn't.

But according to CDC scientists who'd analyzed the Louisiana animal kills, someone had done some more genetic tinkering, and every indication was they were in the final stages of weaponizing it. That was making it possible to release the lethal mutant virus by spraying it via an aerosol mist into a crowd of people, ensuring its swift spread to millions within days. Possibly hours, if the terrorists had succeeded with their modifications.

The other problematical part was that the only way to produce a vaccine to counter its effect would be for someone to copy and generate the same live attenuated virus for use in the inoculation. Unfortunately, the 1972 international biological weapons moratorium forbade the government from doing that legally.

Which was another reason STORM had been called in. Not only could a small, independent spec-ops team move more quickly and easily to seek and destroy the terrorists themselves, but STORM scientists could do the initial replication work on the vaccine and give the government plausible deniability from violating the treaty.

Anyway, since the discovery of the first dead birds, three more group animal kills had been reported, along with the one from this morning that had since been cleaned up and sent off to the CDC.

Which all jibed with recent Internet chatter NSA had intercepted hinting that the large-scale bio attack that had been rumored for years now was finally happening. And it was happening right here in the U.S., by a transplanted al Sayika fundamentalist cell, led by the fanatic terrorist Abbas Tawhid. The same bioweapon and the same terrorist Marc's team had tried to expose five years ago, and failed.

This time he wouldn't.

A Department of Homeland Security strategic response unit was being hurriedly assembled to deal with the biological threat. But until the STORM team pinpointed exactly where the cell was hiding, and their secret laboratory located, no one dared move in any closer.

Marc was a little late when he strode into the midnight strategy meeting, which was held every night to keep one another informed of progress made that day. He nodded to the others, already seated around the table. Everyone looked up at him with stupid grins on their faces. All except the team leader, whose expression was more like expectant. *Dieu.* Nice to inspire such confidence.

"So how'd it go with the cute cop?" the op's team leader, Darcy Zimmerman, asked.

A grainy digi-print of himself talking with TFC Tara Reeves in the Au Chien parking lot, taken from above, was circulating around the table. STORM had deployed the company's UAV, or unmanned aerial vehicle, to assist in the mission. The compact model UAV was the newest weapon in STORM's growing arsenal of high-tech surveillance gear, acquired from the military. The high-flying, slow-moving spy plane came equipped with broad-area, long-distance optical and infrared capabilities, all-weather radar, and streaming video, all of which could be observed and controlled from a manned mobile ground unit hundreds of miles—or even continents—away.

Mon Dieu. Marc knew the UAV could photograph and identify the species of fly on the nose of a tango from fifty thousand feet up, but he was always freaked-out when the subject was himself. And naturally in this photo, he was checking out Tara Reeves like a man who hadn't had sex in two years.

Which, unfortunately, he hadn't.

His own fault.

He dropped into the chair opposite Zimmerman, tempering his response before he answered her question.

After a somewhat rocky start—she'd also been on the team that had failed to secure al Sayika's bioweapon plans—in the five years since being recruited into STORM, Darcy Zimmerman had grown into an exceptional operator, a whiz-kid computer specialist, and a damn good leader. In spite of Marc's half-dozen-plus-years' seniority over her, because of her proven skills he had no problem working under her command.

The fact was, that was the *only* way he'd work with her—with her as team leader. When he was in charge of an op, he had a strict no-women rule. Sure, he had a general policy of not disrespecting women, ever. But he'd grown up watching over his mama and five sisters. He didn't need the responsibility at work, too. He knew how females operated—all batting eyelashes and promises to do as he told them . . . and then doing whatever they damn well pleased.

Don't get him wrong—he dearly loved women, him. Loved his *maman* and sisters like crazy. But females had no place on the job. Politically incorrect? *Mais,* yeah. But there you go. Women needed protecting, and this job was all about the danger.

However, he'd stopped thinking of Zimmerman as a woman a long time ago. Despite her Barbie-doll looks, she could kill you in twenty different and creative ways with her bare hands if she so desired. Anyone who'd been with STORM more than a week went out of their way not to piss her off. Except Bobby Lee Quinn of course—the man who'd recruited her. Among other things. But he was a special case and halfway around the world at the moment, *merci Dieu.*

Thanks to his *maman* and five sisters, Marc knew better than to argue with a woman. However, after tonight's frustrations he was feeling just a tetch grouchy. He needed to redeem himself for that fiasco five years ago. Help stop this terrible threat to his country. But to do that, he *had* to get out of this babysitting gig.

"Yeah, I'm all set up as her guide," he answered Darcy, ignoring the "cute cop" jab and allowing his displeasure to shine through as a deep scowl. "But I still don't like it. She'll get in my way. Waste precious time. Why can't we bring in a contractor to take care of her?"

Zimmerman clamped her jaw in what Marc had come to think of as her God-Give-Me-Patience-With-Imbecilic-Men look. She did that one a lot. Especially around Quinn. "We've already been over this, Lafayette. Your personal knowledge of the locals is invaluable to this op, and we need you out there asking questions. But you are not at a hundred percent yet. You agreed to take it easy."

"Not this fucking easy," he muttered. "Babysitting Reeves is going to hold me back. I can't do my job and we're under the gun here."

"We've already contacted her superiors to get her to drop her investigation. But we have to be careful. If the local constabulary gets wind of a serious terrorist threat in their jurisdiction, you know what'll happen."

Yeah, they'll want in and the whole stealth operation will go balls-up in a massive goatfuck.

"If she's been pulled off, I shouldn't need to show up at all in the morning," he suggested.

"Please, just hang in there until we're sure she leaves." Zimmerman jetted out a breath and glanced around the table at the others. "A little help, folks?"

Rand Jaeger, communications specialist and the team's UAV pilot and sensory operator—filched four years ago from the Air Force Seventeenth Squadron—sat next to her. Originally South African, terse, and somewhat mysterious, for a comm spec he rarely spoke, just fixed it so others could. Regardless of the situation, he'd find a way for the team to communicate with one another and with STORM Command.

Electronically, yeah. In person, not so much. Rand just shrugged.

"If she doesn't scram by morning, you could scare her off." That suggestion came from JC Kowalski, the team's bioterror expert, who looked and sounded more like an enforcer for the Russian mob than a brilliant research scientist. Marc didn't know Ski that well, had never worked with him before. But he seemed a decent enough guy. Other than the fact that he always sided with Zimmerman. Probably because she was the only one who understood his geekish ways. "Rand did a background on Reeves," Ski continued, "and she's a city slicker, from up north. Like me." He grinned. "Show her a few big gators and trust me, she'll run screaming back to her trooper buddies. Maybe even all the way to New York City."

That strategy might have worked on Ski, but obviously he'd never met TFC Tara Reeves.

"She doesn't strike me as the running type," Marc observed, hanging on to his irritation by a thread. "Seemed pretty damn determined, in fact." To pursue her investigation, as well as to keep him at arm's length. Shame. That two year stretch was no doubt a major contributor to his general tetchiness.

"All the more reason for you to stick with her," Zimmerman argued. "You've got to keep her under control until she gets yanked. If she starts asking questions all over the parish, the tangos are going to hear about it and pull up stakes. If they get away and release that Armageddon virus in a populated area, it's game over."

"Which is why I need to help find the bastards," Marc argued right back. "Not waste my time babysitting some damn female." *Oops.* "Cop," he amended, too late.

The men looked amused, but Zimmerman looked like she would pop a gasket any second.

"Avian flu crossed with anthrax, Lafayette. This is the nightmare scenario the world has been dreading for years," she reminded him somberly. "And lest you forget, we screwed up and let these bastards slip through our fingers once before."

"Like I need reminding," he growled.

Thanks to the disastrous op five years ago, Marc, Darcy, and Bobby Lee Quinn had totally blown the best chance the West had ever had to nail the two infamous al Sayika leaders and stop their reign of terror. Instead, Marc had ended up in a Turkish prison for four long months, Zimmerman had been fired from CIA for conduct unbecoming, and Quinn . . . Well, Quinn had gotten laid. As usual.

But Marc was now determined to make up for his mistakes.

"It's up to us to stop them for good this time," Darcy said. "There's no way in hell I'm letting your misplaced machismo or wounded male ego jeopardize this mission, Lafayette. The whole country is depending on us."

Marc took a calming breath. She had him all wrong. He wanted to *help*, full-speed ahead, not be relegated to the sidelines.

"She's right," Kick said quietly next to him.

"*Et tu*, Jackson?" Marc muttered.

Kick Jackson was the team sniper. If anyone would be his ally, Marc had thought it would be him. They had some recent, fairly intense boots-on-ground history together in the Sudan, that's where Marc had received his injuries. Jackson had been taken prisoner by al Sayika over there—and injected with an early version of the deadly virus they were now trying to stop. He'd barely escaped with his life. Even so, he'd managed to kill one of the leaders, Jallil Abu Bakr, during a STORM air strike on the camp. Unfortunately, Abbas Tawhid, Abu Bakr's coleader, had escaped the bombing.

Only Marc and Kick had survived that particular mission, along with Kick's new wife, Rainie—which was a story in itself—and his best friend, a poor slob by the name of Alex Zane who was now tucked away in some mental hospital somewhere, no use to anyone.

Kick's main mission in life was to put al Sayika out of business for good. And Marc was right behind him in line.

"You know how smart Tawhid is," Kick said now. "And how paranoid."

Yeah, Marc knew. And now it seemed *le connard* had slipped into the U.S. in order to wreak revenge for his coleader's death by setting loose the dreaded Armageddon virus.

"It wouldn't surprise me if Tawhid has paid informants among the locals," Zimmerman said.

"I'm a local," Marc argued. "Someone will tell me if he's been spreading money around."

"Exactly," she agreed, pushing the photo of TFC Tara Reeves in front of him. "Which is why we need you on this cop like white on rice. If you're with her, she won't be seen as an outsider, and hopefully word of her investigation won't reach Tawhid. Meanwhile keep your ears open for anything useful."

Yeah, that white-on-rice image really helped. He flipped the photo facedown on the table, then shot his fingers through his hair in sublime frustration. *Rien à foutre.* He knew when he'd been overruled. STORM encouraged dialogue between team members, but the team leader always had the final say in what went down and how it happened.

"Fine. I'll take care of her," he ground out.

But unless *he* got laid, too, he sure as hell didn't have to like it.

BOBBY Lee Quinn rolled off the back of the flatbed truck that had carried him from Houma up to Bumfuck, Louisiana, and hefted his field pack onto his back.

"You sure dis da right place?" the driver asked, leaning out of the window, his cigarette glowing in the midnight darkness. There'd been no sign of civilization for miles. Just swamp and more swamp. With a little swamp on the side.

But Bobby Lee was sure. He'd found his way through the deepest, darkest jungles and across the flattest expanses of sand on the planet with nothing more than the stars to guide him. This place was a piece of cake. Hell, there was even a road and warm transpo.

But the old man's concern was touching. It was the cammie, natch. Everyone fell over themselves to help a soldier. Not like in the old days after 'Nam; his daddy still talked of that time with bitterness.

Of course, Bobby Lee wasn't exactly a soldier anymore. Not in the official sense.

Details.

With a wave of thanks, he flipped up his collar against the chill and struck off down a deserted dirt road that branched off from the highway. Skirting bullfrogs and mud puddles, he picked up speed like a snowball going downhill. Because he knew what waited for him at the end of the road.

Darcy Zimmerman.

The bane of his days and the wet dream of his nights.

Dang. She was *not* going to take kindly to his being here. Not after tomorrow morning, any rate.

Tonight, he hoped, would be a different proposition. Proposition being the operative word.

Half an hour of brisk walking brought him to the perimeter of the fishing camp where the team was bivouacked. All looked quiet. Deceptively so, Zimmie was nothing if not thorough. She was also a true genius with any kind of computers. Including setting up electronic countermeasures. She'd have this place wired up tighter than a virgin's knees.

He grinned, swatting at a mosquito that landed on his neck. Hell, this should be fun.

QUINN was back in her dreams. The jerk.

She could smell him. Even over the rank stench of the swamp and the cloyingly musty odor of the canvas mattress she slept on.

Quinn always smelled the same. Toe-curlingly, arousingly good. Like a real man. Like a man to the extreme. He could be straight off a seventy-two-hour forced march through the jungle, covered in sweat and dirt and camo grease, and crawl right into her bed and he'd still smell so good she'd practically come before he even touched her. And then afterward, after he'd rolled her and fucked her and covered her in his own unique scent, marked her with it on every inch of her body, embedding that unique male spice deep into her pores, she'd smell him on her skin for days after he'd gone.

It wasn't fair. *She* washed right off of him.

She'd asked him about it once, if her scent lingered on him after he left her, and he'd just laughed and said a bar of Ivory soap took care of all his unwanted odors.

Which had told her way more than she'd wanted to know.

Not that she was sweet on Bobby Lee Quinn. *Hell*, no. She refused to be sweet on the bastard. But that had hurt. Just a little.

And yet, she continued to welcome him into her bed. Even when he wasn't really there. Like tonight.

The musky, spicy smell of him filled the tiny fishing cabin and she sighed in her sleep, wanting him so badly she could taste him. He might be a goddamn bastard, but he was a magician with his cock. And his fingers. And his tongue . . .

Thankfully, her dream-Quinn was as hungry as she was. She could feel it now, that talented tongue, trailing up her thigh, wet and velvety warm. *Oh, yeah*. She moaned softly. Opened her legs. And he made that sexy sound she loved, a kind of gravelly groan that rumbled deep in his throat whenever she did something to almost make him lose that iron control of his. Almost. He never quite lost it completely. Not even when he exploded in climax. With Quinn, there was always some kind of control in place . . . usually him gripping her hair or another body part hard enough to leave bruises.

Probably just as well. She lost control enough for both of them.

But no more . . . At least in person.

But in dreams . . . what would it hurt?

She moaned again when his hands glided over her hips and tugged down the panties she'd worn to bed along with a T-shirt. She lifted up to help, sighing with pleasure when the barrier disappeared and his lips nuzzled her inner thigh. He kissed between her legs. She spread them wide. There came that gravelly groan again.

And then his tongue was on her like a tempest. Lashing and laving and swirling, drenching her with pleasure and turning her world upside down with the intensity of its onslaught.

She panted, crying out Quinn's name in the darkness, wishing he were really there with her. Thankful he *wasn't* there to hear the desperate need in her voice as she called out to him. It would scare him. It sure as hell scared *her*.

Because she *didn't* want him that badly. Refused to need him.

She *didn't* need him.

She didn't need *any*one.

This was just about the sex. That was all. Nothing more.

No matter how desperate her cries sounded.

His tongue swirled expertly and she gave herself over to it, swept up in a tide of agonizing want and need. She was safe within her dreams, safe to surrender, safe to let the sharp, swift pleasure engulf her and throw her whole body into sweet, endless convulsions of release. Safe to cling tight when, afterward, he climbed up her body and scythed into her. And to give voice to the pure drunken joy of having him thrust deep, deep, deep into her and fill her with the insane sense of completion she always felt when he was inside her.

Which she would never, ever dare let herself feel if he were there in person. Because to him, she meant nothing.

Her dream-Quinn held her close, moving above her like a hot steel piston, saying things in her ear between gulped breaths, things that alternately made her melt and made her blush. And ultimately made her come again. And then he came, too, roaring out his climax, strangling her wrists in manacles of calloused fingers.

She savored the weight of him crushing her into the stiff, lumpy mattress as he recovered, savored the erotic smell of him, the scent of their sex that filled the bed, relished the temporary sensation of happiness and fulfillment she felt in his arms. Moaned contentedly when he rolled her on top of him and draped her body over his, and sighed when he stroked her skin and scraped the tangled hair from her face to kiss her long and deep.

"Damn, girl, I've missed you," he whispered.

And it wasn't until she fell asleep nestled in his embrace and started to dream for real that she realized . . .

Oh. My. God.

He really *was* there.

FOUR

HE felt her trying to slip away from him.

Bobby Lee came awake immediately and tightened his arms around the woman sprawled on top of him without bothering to open his eyes. It was the same deal every time. Darcy Zimmerman had issues about sleeping with him.

Oh, not about the sex. That she was fine with. Willing and enthusiastic. Ever since the first night they met, they'd been jumping each other's bones every single time their paths crossed. No, it was the actual sleeping part she objected to. Don't ask him why. It bugged the crap out of him. When he worked so hard to please a woman, the least she could do was give her a nice cuddle for his effort. Some skin-to-skin time.

He loved the feel of a naked woman in his arms. Loved waking up in the middle of the night and sliding back into her while they both were half asleep. Sometimes just falling back asleep like that without doing anything else.

It was *nice* passing the night in a woman's bed. There were so few women he trusted enough to do it with, so it happened infrequently. This woman was by far his favorite. No contest.

But Darcy Zimmerman had issues.

"Go back to sleep," he ordered.

"What the hell are you doing here?" she demanded in a hushed voice. Yeah. Like everyone in camp hadn't already heard them having monkey sex.

"Trying to get some shut-eye," he answered. "I had a long trip over."

"Find somewhere else. I don't want—"

"I'm not done fucking you yet. Just taking a little break."

She gasped. God, she was easy. "Maybe I don't *want* you—"

He sighed. And in a single motion rolled her under him again, spread her legs with his knees, and thrust into her. He didn't have to check that he was hard. He was always hard around her. It was the perpetual state of being that Darcy Zimmerman put him in. Hard and ready. And she wondered why he didn't bother to find another bed.

She gasped even louder. "Quinn! No condom!"

He was very aware of that. It felt really, really good.

"Stop wiggling and maybe I won't come," he told her. Not that there was any danger of it. He was in total control. Always.

"You are such a fucking"—he gathered her thighs in his hands and pushed in deeper—"*Ohhh*. Damn it, Quinn."

But there was no real heat to her anger. She knew he was clean, and he knew she wouldn't get pregnant. The condom was a symbolic thing. Like sleeping in the same bed.

He pulled out and thrust back in, gratified when she gave a reluctant moan. "Will you let me sleep with you?" he pressed.

She tried to squirm away. "This is blackmail."

Holding on tight, he nuzzled her ear and gave her a lingering kiss below it. "Oh, yeah."

"You realize this stupid bed is narrower than a twin."

"Then we'll be real cozy." He gave another leisurely thrust. "Do we have a deal?"

A jet of air hit his throat. "Fine." Another jet. "But only if I get to be on top."

Oh. Oh. Twist his arm. He grinned in triumph. "Well. Just this once."

He flipped them again so she straddled him and reached

for one of the packets he'd left in a small pile on a folding canvas stool next to the bed. Held it up for her.

Her brow raised as she glanced at the pile. "A little ambitious, even for you, Quinn."

"Oh, y—Ahhhh—" He groaned when she rolled the rubber slowly over him with deft fingers. "—ye of little faith," he croaked.

Da-*amn*, it had been *wa-ay-ay* too long.

She reached between them and gently grasped his balls. Kissed the groan from his lips and began to squeeze. And squeeze. And squ-*eeze*.

He popped his eyes open. And found her watching him, a menacing little smile on her face as she squeezed some more.

"Hey!" he squeaked. *Shit*. He'd actually *squeaked*. "What the fuck?"

"Now, Bobby Lee Quinn," she said when she had his complete, utter, and undivided attention. "You are going to tell me *exactly* what you're doing here."

OKAY, breathe.

She could do this. Oh, yes, she could.

Tara Reeves ignored the uneasy roil of beignets and coffee making her stomach feel like a carnival ride and concentrated on looking businesslike and indifferent as Marc Lafayette ambled across the deserted Au Chien parking lot toward her cruiser. On time. Of course. Shoot, five minutes early. Clearly he had no intention of giving her a reason to jettison his services.

He looked bright-eyed and well rested and just as ridiculously attractive as last night. Unlike her, no doubt. She'd spent the intervening hours tossing and turning and trying desperately not to think about his sexy smart-ass grin and dark bedroom eyes, and consequently got no sleep whatsoever and probably looked like something a swamp rat dragged in.

Not that it mattered how she looked. To him. Not a whit.

"TFC Reeves," he drawled in greeting when she grabbed her backpack and got out of the police car. "How are you this morning?" He was wearing that Ka-Bar knife strapped to his thigh again. Nervous? Her?

"Mr. Lafayette. I wasn't sure you'd make it."

He smiled. "Marc, please. 'Mr. Lafayette' is such a mouthful." His gaze dropped to her mouth for a second, but to his credit he didn't say what they both knew he was thinking.

At least she thought he was thinking it.

Or maybe it was just *her* thinking it.

God.

"Anyway," he added when she was too upset by *that* thought that she didn't respond, "why wouldn't I make it?"

She blinked. Gave herself a mental kick. "No reason." She glanced down to the bayou. "You have a boat?"

"I do." He didn't move, but tipped his head at her jeans and ZZ Top T-shirt under a fleece jacket. "No uniform to-day?"

"It seems to put people off for some reason. Besides, I'm not on the clock. This isn't an official investigation."

His brows flicked up. "It's not?"

"No. Look, can we go now? We have a lot of area to cover."

"Sure." Before she could object, he took her backpack from her, then gave her a rueful look when her jacket flapped open. "The gun on the hip kinda spoils the casual image, though."

"Yeah, like I'd really get in a boat with you and go ten feet into that swamp unarmed," she said evenly, starting for the short dock protruding into the bayou behind the road-house.

Instead of being insulted, he grinned, falling into step. "Is it the swamp, or is it me you're so afraid of?"

"Does it matter?"

His grin went lopsided. "Uh. Maybe."

She followed his gaze to a long, thin boat floating just under the dock. Except . . . Oh, crap. It wasn't a boat at all. It was a tandem kayak.

She stared at the seating arrangement in dismay. It was like that bobsled ride at Disney World she'd gone on one spring break with a high school boyfriend. Where one person sat between the other's legs with no barrier between them. She'd been a virgin at the time, and wow, had that been an education. Way too much information about that guy. She'd been mortified for the entire ride.

Okay, this was *so* not going to work. If Lafayette thought he could—

"No," she said.

"Don' worry. I—"

"No!"

"It's just a kayak, *cher*, not a bed. I'm not flirting, or—"

"What part of *no* don't you get?"

"Yeah, well, what happened to wanting to cover a lot of ground today? With a kayak we can go places even a two-man pirogue can't go, like shortcuts through the shallows. And it goes real fast." He shrugged. "But if you're so afraid of touching me, we can take the pirogue."

"I'm a Louisiana state trooper," she ground out, "and I'm wearing a gun. Don't flatter yourself I'm afraid of you."

"Shy, then?"

What he found so damn funny was beyond her. "Yeah. Let's go with that."

"Well, then. Good thing the front seat moves forward." She narrowed her eyes. "So I can paddle. And in case you were, uh, shy, and the backrest wasn' enough."

Backrest?

She glanced at the kayak again and she saw the row of indents where the seat could be moved. And sitting under the front apron along with a dry bag was a loose padded seat with a thin curved back.

Okay, now she was just plain embarrassed. He'd actually thought about it and decided she'd be too much of a priss to get in without a backrest between them, even with the seats separated by at least two feet.

Jesus. Was she *that* easy to read?

And when had she turned into such a frigging old maid?

"Great," she said, inwardly cursing at how prim she still sounded.

"*Bon*. Shall we?"

Her pulse suddenly rocketed.

Okay, what was *wrong* with her? The man was a total hunk. Who the hell cared if she sat right in his lap? Who would even know? It wasn't like the guys at the station would find out and accuse her of . . . whatever their dirty little minds could come up with. Or worse, her father and his overly strict sense of propriety—and low opinion of her personal strength. Even if she spent the entire day flirting with Marc Lafayette, not a soul would ever have to know.

Not that she was going to. Flirt with him. Why start something that was so obviously doomed from the word go? Aside from which, Mr. Sweet-talker seemed like a one-night-stand kind of guy. *Definitely* no interest in that.

She straightened her spine and followed him down to the water. "Do you know where the four animal kills were found?"

He didn't seem to notice the abrupt change of topic. "I figured you'd want to see them, so I made some inquiries."

She had to give him points for being prepared. Call him Mr. Sweet-talking Boy Scout. "Right. That's where we'll start."

"Yes, ma'am."

She cringed. And said, "I guess you better call me Tara."

He looked up from pulling the nose of the kayak onto the muddy bank. And gave her The Grin. "Guess that makes us friends now, eh, *cher*?"

My God, how could anyone so unrelentingly obnoxious be so damn charming? "Don't push it, Lafayette," she warned, watching him stuff her backpack into the dry bag and stow it under the aft apron.

"*Mais non, cher.*" He stepped into the kayak, settling himself onto the rear seat at the back of the low, narrow craft. All innocence. "I'm not pushing it, me."

God, were her hands *shaking*? She stuck them under her armpits. "Good."

Grabbing the extra seat, he positioned it between his thighs, adjusting it so he'd have enough space to breathe and she'd have enough space to get in. *God.* Too close.

He offered her his hand. And suddenly she desperately wanted to change her mind again. Back to being the prissy old maid afraid to let him near her. Because she realized she *was* afraid to let him near her. Irrational, stupid, but there you go. Issues? Thanks, Dad.

The bold challenge in his eyes dared her to back down.

He was *expecting* her to chicken out and run away. Waiting for it.

The ancient, familiar churn of inadequacy in her stomach nearly made her give in and do just that. But this time she wouldn't let it defeat her.

No. Way.

Determined, she grasped Lafayette's warm, strong hand and somehow managed to slide into the seat without obsessing over how his thighs were pressing into her hips, or how she could feel his knees close over hers under the apron where she couldn't see a thing, or that their feet were in one big tangle at the front, or that God only knew what else he was doing under there.

Oh, sweet *Jesus*.

And then, just as she thought her heart would thunder out of her chest, he bent his head down to hers and whispered in her ear from behind, "Believe me, *cher*, when I push it, you'll know."

DARCY was being a big baby and she knew it.

Guess what? She didn't care. She was so mad she could spit nails.

How dare STORM Command remove her as team leader? And especially in favor of that . . . that . . .

Ugh!

"It should be coming through now, Darce," Rand said, pointing at the special laptop set up in front of her. Sure enough, the distinctive shape of the earth's curve popped into focus on the screen. "The UAV should be finishing up its first pass within the hour."

"Thanks," she clipped out. She picked up the zoom joystick and navigated the image being streamed from the UAV, which had been routed in a grid pattern over Louisiana.

But it was no use. All she could see was Quinn's face as he'd broken the news to her last night. Brave man. She'd been gripping his balls in her hand, threatening to tear them off if he didn't tell her why he'd shown up in her camp like a thief in the night bypassing all her security like it had been a kindergarten and not a highly classified secure base camp.

He'd honestly thought he could just give her a good roll in the hay and everything would be hunky-dory.

After they'd replaced her with *him*.

The lousy little shit.

Okay, maybe not so little.

"Throttling back to dwell," Rand said.

She took a cleansing breath and forced herself to concentrate on zooming further in on the UAV image and finding their fishing camp among the myriad small yellow dots glowing on the monitor.

She loosened her death grip on the joystick. Hell, if anyone should be replacing her around here, it should be Marc Lafayette. He had both seniority and the experience. *And* he was already here. Why not him?

Why replace her at all?

Quinn claimed her computer skills were needed full-time on the op, and that Command thought doing both jobs would be too much for one person—*any* person—to handle. Therefore they'd brought in Quinn, a ground strategy specialist who just happened to have finished up his previous assignment OCONUS at exactly the right time to take over her leadership duties.

How convenient.

With a growl, she focused back on the screen. Starting at the Gulf, she located the mouth of the Atchafalaya River, followed it up past Morgan City, found Stephensville, and turned northwest. Highway 70 took her up to the turnoff, and she zoomed in on ultra-high mag. Yep, there they were. The distinctive pattern of nine cabins and the vehicles parked next to them, along with a speedboat on a trailer and the UAV ground station mobile unit—affectionately dubbed the Moby—in the clearing. She hit a button and the screen turned green, with black outlines and four orange blobs moving inside the structures.

"Get up and walk around, Rand," she ordered. He did, and one of the orange blobs followed his movements. She clicked a series of buttons on the keyboard. "Okay, got us tagged."

One of the other blobs caught her attention. *Quinn*. What was he still doing in her cabin? Making himself at home, no doubt. Well, if he thought he was moving in with her, he had another thing coming.

In the first flush of anger she'd mentally accused STORM Command of being sexist. That she'd been replaced because this was turning into an über-important assignment and she was a mere woman. But the more rational part of her knew that wasn't true. Plenty of über-important ops had been led by female team leaders in the past.

So it must just be Darcy Zimmerman who was lacking.

So much for her skyrocketing career.

Quinn had tried to assure her that wasn't the case. But he would, wouldn't he? His balls had been turning a pretty shade of blue by that point.

She grabbed the joystick angrily and zoomed out on the image, so she could see about a fifty-mile square around the camp. Just freaking great. There were at least a thousand more glowing heat blobs, any one of which could be the terrorists' hideout.

Or none of them.

There was no possible way a team of six could search all those dots. If Lafayette didn't come up with any useful leads from the locals, she'd have to figure out a way to narrow down the odds using some other means.

But how?

And how the hell would she be able to take orders from the one man in the universe who invariably made her lose her concentration, her temper, her common sense, and her panties all with a single look from those deceiving blue eyes?

Oh, yeah. This was going to be a real hoot.

GINA'S hands trembled as she removed a vial of deadly dried viral isolate from the rack containing six identical vials of powder. Quickly she slid it back into the rack and shook her hands out.

Holy Mother of God.

She couldn't believe she was touching this stuff without a hazmat suit. *Again.* The flimsy Home Depot dust masks and painting gloves they'd supplied her with were as good as useless.

She sent up her hundredth silent prayer of thanks for the compulsory anthrax vaccination the university had made all the researchers get . . . and her thousandth prayer that the hasty, jerry-rigged inoculation she'd dosed herself with during her first weeks of captivity had taken. During those early weeks she'd deliberately sabotaged all but one of the vials of live virus they'd given her to work with. At first she'd fooled them, working diligently at her instruments every day, making vaccine instead of the deadly cocktail they wanted. Stalling until she could be rescued.

That's when Tawhid had sprung a surprise test on her. He'd taken a vial and had one of his men sprinkle it on a couple of birds they'd caught in the swamp outside the lab. Days later, the birds still hadn't died. Hadn't even gotten sick.

Tawhid had been very, very angry.

Nearly two months later, her cuts and bruises had healed. But not the memory of the intense pain he'd inflicted. She'd known then that she shouldn't try to fool him. She should just do what he asked of her. No one would blame her. She was a scientist, not a spy trained to withstand torture.

But she couldn't do it.

She'd started working on developing a self-destruct gene to embed in the virus, so if it was unleashed, it would not be able to reproduce itself . . . thus preventing its spread from person to person. Though there was no guarantee it would succeed. The lab was so rudimentary it would be a miracle if it *did* succeed. Therefore, she also had to find a way of foiling the terrorists' plans. Or she would die trying. She was going to die anyway. She knew that.

Gina was not afraid to die. If she had to sacrifice her life a bit sooner to stop this madman from attacking her country, killing her friends and neighbors, she would gladly do it.

But she so badly wanted to live. If for no other reason than to find that rat bastard Gregg van Halen.

This was all his fault—Gregg and his gorgeous body and his edgy, kinky sex. Sex that had her doing things with him she'd never done before. Things she'd never even dreamed of doing, with any man. Sex that *still* had her waking up in the throes of orgasm just dreaming about it. About him. Gregg van Halen.

Even now, knowing what he was, her body craved him. Craved his touch. Even knowing he'd done this to her. That he'd sold her out, his own lover, to his country's worst enemies.

How could he? How could he have turned traitor like this?

If by some miracle she was still breathing when this was all over, she would find him. Oh, yes. She would.

Gregg van Halen had better run. As far and fast as he could.

Because she was coming after him. And when she was done with the fucking bastard, he'd be begging *her*. And this time, it wouldn't be to come.

But to live.

If it was the last thing she ever did, she'd find him. And then she'd plunge a knife right through his black heart.

The same way he'd done hers.

FIVE

"**YEAH,** baby. I'm okay. Just missing you lots . . . I know. Just please stay safe. Don't even think about leaving Haven Oaks, okay, sweetheart?"

Bobby Lee waited politely while Kick Jackson finished his hourly phone conversation with his new bride, Rainie. Normally such sugary affection in a grown man would make Bobby Lee ill, but he could tell the guy genuinely felt all that mush pouring off his tongue into the phone. The man was stone-cold in love, and that was a damn fact.

Poor fuck.

Kick shot him a glance with a goofy smile that made Bobby Lee want to be tested for rapid-onset diabetes. Yikes.

"Okay, baby, love you . . . Love you more. Think of me when you're in the shower."

Oh, jeez. Definitely too much information. It was all Bobby Lee could do not to start tapping his foot for the man to get over it already.

"Sorry," Kick said unapologetically when he snapped shut his PDA, still smiling. "Newlyweds."

Newlyweds. The thought gave Bobby Lee hives.

Nevertheless, he slapped the tall, lanky man on the back and they started walking toward the big cabin. Bobby Lee had taken a couple of hours after breakfast to read through all the op files . . . and to let Zimmie cool off a little longer before their inevitable confrontation. Kick had been familiarizing himself with their substantial arsenal of weapons in his cabin when his wife had called.

"Better you than me, buddy. Better you than me," Bobby Lee observed.

"You should be so lucky. So. How're things with Zimmerman?"

Bobby Lee sighed philosophically. "The night started out pretty well."

Kick barked a laugh. "Yup. Hard to miss that part. But the tone of . . . uh, conversation . . . sort of changed around four a.m. What happened?"

"She woke up."

Kick shot him a look, then dissolved in laughter. "Ouch, man."

"Yeah."

"So, STORM Dog Six, how you gonna get back in her good graces?" Kick was a former marine, as were many of the guys in STORM. Dog six was military-speak for commanding officer.

Bobby Lee was only the team leader, which didn't warrant the "dog," but he saw where it was going and gave the other man a wry smile. "God knows. Any advice? You know, from a card-carrying romantic newlywed and all?"

Kick's lip curled in return. "Advice, eh."

"Yeah. Dog six with privileges sounds a lot better than the doghouse."

The jokester coughed back a grin. "By that I assume you're not willing to give her back her command."

Bobby Lee shrugged philosophically. "What can I do? Orders."

"Uh-huh. Just following orders. That one always goes over *real* well."

He shot the other man a withering look.

Kick chuckled. "Okay, here's my advice. Throw yourself at her feet and beg for mercy. Tell her you'll be her slave for life."

Yeah, right.

It wasn't that the thought didn't have a certain appeal . . .
Especially that last part . . . But . . . "A bit extreme, maybe?"

"You might try chocolate—it releases endorphins, you
know. Great for sex. And, oh, yeah, apologizing works pretty
well, too."

"But I haven't done anyth—"

Kick's eyes rolled. "Whatever, dude. Apologize anyway.
But whatever you do, *don't* sneak into her cabin tonight and
expect any action unless she invites you. That'll only make
things worse."

Bobby Lee sighed again. So much for *that* strategy.

God, all this for a little hot sex.

Was it even worth it?

He wanted to say no. *Hell*, no. No woman was worth
jumping through this kind of hoop for.

Except . . . she was.

He'd wanted to cry like a two-year-old when she'd stalked
out of the cabin last night and left him alone in her bed with
just the scent of her to keep him company. After coming
halfway around the world just to see her.

Jesus in a boat, did he have it bad.

Note to self: in future stick to meaningless one-night bim-
bos. Much less complicated. And much more his style. He
didn't know what had gotten into him about this particular
woman.

Shit. "What the hell," he said resignedly. "I'm here to
catch terrorists anyway, not get laid."

"I hear ya," Kick said, sobering. "Loud and clear. Nothing
in the world could have taken me away from Rainie except a
chance to kill Abbas Tawhid."

Zimmie had been too furious to read Bobby Lee into the
unwritten operation directives yet. She'd just dumped the
printed files onto the bed with him, then stomped out of
the cabin.

"That the op mandate?" he asked Kick. "Kill him?"

"That's *my* mandate. Frankly, I don't care what STORM
wants." The other man's eyes went cold and deadly. "Honest to
God, Quinn, when we find him, don't ask me not to take the
shot. I'd rather spend the rest of my life in prison than let that
animal live. After what he did to my friend Alex."

Bobby Lee had rarely seen such intense hatred as he read now in those eyes. You had to respect that kind of raw emotion in a good man. It came from a place well beyond official mandates. It came from a place of personal justice.

He nodded. "I understand."

Okay. So now all they had to do was find the fucker.

"Look," Kick said, "there's something else you need to know."

"Shoot."

They were fast approaching the big cabin. Kick slowed to a stop. "I don't know how much is in the STORM files about this, but you know that scientist who was kidnapped up in New York a few months back?"

Bobby Lee nodded. "It's now suspected al Sayika may have her. Right?"

"Yup. I'm pretty sure they do, and I'm pretty sure it's my fault."

Hold on. This was news. "*Your* fault? You were being medevaced out of the Sudan at the time, as I recall, hanging on to life by a thread."

"Yup, but after we got back to New York and were told Gina had disappeared, Rainie was really worried."

"Wait, Gina? As in Dr. Cappozi? The kidnapped scientist?"

Kick nodded. "The same. She and Rainie are best friends. How's that for a coincidence?" The look on his face said he didn't think it was a coincidence at all. "Anyway, I did some digging on my own about her disappearance. Used my old contacts."

"And . . . ?"

Kick paced away agitatedly, then turned back. "Let me backtrack. It's a long story, but the gist of it is, when my old CIA black-ops unit—you know, Zero Unit?—shipped me over to the Sudan, through a series of unfortunate choices on my part, my wife, Rainie, was secretly sent along with me. We didn't actually know each other at the time—"

Okay, wait. "*What?*" Bobby Lee interjected in surprise.

"Like I said, long, sordid story. Anyway, when Rainie just dropped off the face of the earth, her best friend—Gina—launched an all-out campaign to find out what CIA had done with her."

"How the hell did she know CIA was involved? Nobody off-grid knows about their connection to Zero Unit."

"Rainie was able to phone Gina before we got shipped out. Gave her an actual name to check out. At CIA."

Bobby Lee made a face. "I'll bet that went over well."

"Like a lead balloon. She started calling them, and an operator from Zero Unit was eventually sent out to . . . mitigate her. Man name of van Halen. He's the one who found out what she did for a living—splicing genes and making aerosol inoculations for some kids' disease. The kind of bio specialty terrorists salivate over and would pay big money to get hold of."

"Christ." Bobby Lee regarded Kick with growing guardedness. "And you think . . . ?"

"And I think the coincidence of Gina's job was too much to resist. Someone didn't."

"What the fuck, Kick. Are you saying what I think you're saying?"

"What I'm saying is, a few days after meeting this Zero Unit operator van Halen, Dr. Gina Cappozi disappeared, too. Through back channels and a lot of bribes, I was able to track her last movements. You'll never guess where she was grabbed."

Bobby Lee was almost afraid to ask. "The file said from somewhere in the Bronx. No one knows why she was up there."

"Oh, they know. Zero Unit pulled her in. To their top-secret northeastern headquarters. In the *Bronx*. And by the way, ZU-NE headquarters was moved the very next day."

Jesus. If all this was true . . .

"Kick, I need to be one hundred percent certain of what you're telling me. You believe Zero Unit—in other words CIA, our own government—orchestrated Dr. Cappozi's disappearance?"

"Officially and unofficially they're denying everything, and I don't want to believe it was a sanctioned action. But I *do* think someone on the inside—probably the same traitor who betrayed at least two of my own missions, someone possibly within Zero Unit itself—turned her over to Tawhid. I think she's being held captive here in Louisiana, and that she's the one weaponizing the virus that's been killing the animals in the swamp."

"Against her will."

"Very much so."

"Can she do it? Finish the job?"

"She definitely has the skill set."

Which meant the team really did have a ticking bomb on its hands.

Bobby Lee took a deep breath, sorting through all Kick had told him. Christ on a cracker. "Does STORM Command know? About this CIA traitor?"

Kick nodded. "Marc Lafayette was on the Sudan op with me, and I told him my suspicions back then. Luckily I'd made a deal to quit Zero Unit if I completed the mission, and they actually honored it. So Lafayette encouraged me to join up with STORM so we could burn the bastard. We told two members of STORM Command when I signed on, and my friend Alex Zane because he was part of the betrayed missions and his life could also be in danger. And Rainie, of course. But no one in Zero Unit."

No shit. "Understandable."

"Anyway. I thought you should know about that situation. But one op at a time. Before we can find the traitor, we have to neutralize Tawhid and this new threat."

"And hopefully find Dr. Cappozi before they eliminate her."

"I promised Rainie I'd bring her back, Quinn. Alive."

Yeah, about that. He had a bad feeling. "You should know better, buddy. Never make promises you aren't completely sure you can keep."

"Oh, I plan to keep it, Quinn. You can take that to the bank."

DARCY had managed to avoid Quinn since storming out of the cabin early this morning, but the respite had come to an abrupt end fifteen minutes ago. He'd walked into the big cabin with Kick and immediately come over to her for a report. All puppy-dog eyes and leaning over her shoulder.

The good news—so far she hadn't killed the man.

In fact, she was being very professional. Cool. Objective. Outwardly accepting of being demoted. *Undeservedly* demoted. In other words, being a good team player.

She could handle this. She could.

"Damn, you're fast. Great work, Zimmie," he told her now. "I can see why they wanted you on computers full-time. It's like watching friggin' *Numb3rs* or something."

Darcy didn't want or need Quinn's praise. She was just doing her job. She accepted she was no longer team leader, but she'd be damned if she'd let him mollify her with such transparent positive reinforcement. Talk about Management 101. Or Parenting 101. Yeah, her parents had said the same thing when they'd replaced her, the child they'd adopted in desperation, with the much-wanted real children that came after. She'd seen right through them, too.

"Thanks," she said. And waited. Biting her tongue on the orders that chafed to come out. *Split into teams. Divide up the list. Check out the buildings thoroughly and stay in touch. Let's go, people, we've got tangos to catch.*

"How did you come up with these addresses?" Quinn asked instead of jumping up and getting a move on.

A complete waste of time. But he was watching her like he wanted an answer. "It was Rand's idea to narrow down buildings according to their heat signature on the UAV images, combined with their actual electricity consumption," she told him impatiently. "Ski figured out what kind of laboratory someone would need to use to—" She looked over at him for the correct verbage.

"To replicate a pandemic flu strain mutated with anthrax," Ski filled in, "using the latest methods, but stripped down to minimal production, and then weaponize the virus's distribution through an intranasal gelling powder mechanism."

She resisted a smile. The geek-speak was his way of telling her he was on her side. Quinn was a ground fighter, not a brainiac like them.

"Yeah, that," she continued without pausing. "Anyway, after doing an analysis of the UAV images, we hacked into the electric company records and, after eliminating legit businesses, we compiled a list of customers who fell within Ski's projected range. Then we narrowed it down by comparing current usage versus usage four months ago. Buildings with a corresponding jump went onto the A-list. There are only a couple dozen addresses on it."

Quinn nodded. "Excellent work. Time to take it to the ground." He tapped a finger on the map of the parish spread out on the table. "I assume you have coordinates?"

She handed him three pages, the list divided up by geographical location: villages north and south, and the outlying bayou areas.

Finally he stood up. "All right. Rand, you're with me. We'll start with the villages." He handed a page to Kick. "You're with Ski in the bayous. Okay, let's go find these assholes."

Uh.

"Ex*cuse* me?" she said pointedly and loudly. Everyone halted in mid-motion. "Where do *I* go?"

Quinn looked surprised. Everyone else looked uncomfortable. "Nowhere. Stay here and come up with another scenario," he said. "Generate another sort of list. We can't count on getting lucky the first time out."

"Are you fucking *kidding* me? You want me to sit here twiddling my thumbs while you four macho men go out and bring down the bad guys? I don't *think* so."

"You're the computer specialist on this op now, and—"

"If you must know, I've already sent out inquiries about online sales of the needed lab equipment and supplies, especially the specialized gelling powder. There's nothing I can do here until answers come in."

"Then I need you to—"

"I don't give a *damn* what you need, Quinn. I'm a field operative just like you and a damn good one. I have no intention of staying at camp like a good little girl playing it safe."

Of all the unmitigated nerve!

"Listen, Zimmie—"

"Don't you fucking Zimmie me, Quinn—"

"All right! All right! But even if I approved, Marc is occupied with that cop, so we're an odd number. There's no one for you to partner wi—"

"I can go out by myself," Kick interrupted. "I'm used to working alone. Might even run into Lafayette out there."

"Thank you," she said to him, reaching for the village pages before Quinn could. "Then I'm with Ski."

He snatched them away from her. "No." He handed one list to Rand. "You and Ski take these. Kick, can you handle the bayous on your own?"

"Sure thing, boss."

Freaking great. Which meant . . .

He turned to her. "You're with me, Zimmerman. Want to change your mind?"

She sent him a glower. "Makes no difference who I'm with. Let's go."

SPECIAL Agent Rebel Haywood balanced her delicate teacup and saucer on her knee and quietly did the Snoopy dance inside her head.

Whoo-hoo. Paydirt!

It was amazing. Someone friendly in New York City, who actually knew their neighbors and was willing to talk. What were the chances?

Rebel was out digging for leads in the Gina Cappozi case. From a different angle. The other three FBI agents on the task force were concentrating on identifying Gina's terrorist kidnappers, thought to be an al Sayika cell run by Abbas Tawhid. Alex's friend Kick was convinced she was being held by them in Louisiana. But until his STORM operation found the location where they were hiding her, there was no proof.

So, Rebel thought it might be useful to track Dr. Cappozi's disappearance from the other direction—from Gina's end. In nearly three months, no one had officially figured out how, of all the scientists who did what she did, she specifically had come to be targeted.

When Zane had first gotten home, Rebel had heard the story of how his old friend Kick Jackson had needed to get off an addiction to OxyContin while he was on the run. Rainie, who was an ER nurse, had helped him and ended up accidentally shanghaied onto a deadly Zero Unit spec-ops mission to the Sudan. Where she and Kick had subsequently rescued Zane from imprisonment in a notorious al Sayika training camp.

Kick's wife, Rainie, was sure she'd come to the attention of the terrorists because of the trouble she'd caused at CIA when Rainie had gone missing a few months back. Kick was convinced there was an al Sayika mole working in the government. But who?

There had to be a clue hidden somewhere in her movements of those last few weeks. If Rebel found it, she'd be that much closer to figuring out exactly where Gina was being held, and who, if anyone, had sold her out.

"So you were good friends with Dr. Cappozi, Mrs. Duluth?"

"Oh, yes," the considerably older lady replied, nodding vigorously. She was probably pushing eighty, spritely and silver-haired, and if Rebel's luck held, she knew everything about everyone on the whole block where Gina Cappozi had lived for six years. "She often dropped by for a cuppa on the rare days she wasn't working. So sweet. She would never say so, but I knew she was keeping an eye on me. Making sure I hadn't fallen and couldn't get up, you know?" Her eyes twinkled with humor.

Rebel chuckled. The police and FBI had already talked to the people living on both sides of Gina Cappozi's brownstone, to the ends of the block. But Mrs. Duluth lived two blocks away. Next to a small flower shop. Rebel had noticed an abundance of vases on Gina's shelves and dropped into the florist on the off chance that was where she filled them, and had run into the talkative senior buying camellias for the neighborhood co-op garden. What a break.

"Dr. Cappozi sounds very nice."

"Oh, she is. Loves gardening, though lord knows there's little enough opportunity in the city. I water her ferns and African violets while she's away," she added. Her smile faded. "I'm so worried. Three months is a long time to be gone, even if she had things to sort out. I do hope nothing bad has happened to her."

The fact that the government suspected Dr. Cappozi of being kidnapped by terrorists was a closely guarded secret. If it leaked out, Gina could be in even more danger than she already was. To the general public, the case was being treated as a routine missing person with suspicious circumstances.

"Was she away often?" Rebel asked.

"She didn't travel nearly so much anymore," Mrs. Duluth said with a frown. "Not since . . ." She sighed.

Rebel stifled an impolite yawn. She'd gotten home from visiting Zane just after three this morning. Even being late for work, she'd only had four hours of sleep. And she was due to meet the new SAC on the case this afternoon—the previous SAC had had a sudden heart attack yesterday, and would be out for weeks. Fine way to make a great first impression.

She forced herself to focus. "Not since when, Mrs. Duluth?"

"Since she broke up with her fiancé."

Rebel's stomach pinged. *Fiancé*. Her brand-new least-favorite word.

Okay, so four hours of sleep might be a slight exaggeration. She'd probably stared at the ceiling for a solid hour before finally falling into fitful dreams. Thinking about what could possibly be driving Alex Zane to go ahead and marry Helena Middleton.

Other than her flawless beauty and bubbling personality. Her thoughtful nature. Oh, yes, and her *Mayflower* lineage and immense trust fund.

Not that those last two things would matter to a man like Alex Zane, Rebel scolded herself. It was his damned sense of honor driving this marriage, and she knew it.

Forget about Zane.

She glanced at Mrs. D. What were they talking about? *Fiancé*. Right. How could she forget?

"Gina was engaged?" she asked, making a mental note to check with Rainie about that. She would certainly know about a broken engagement. "Did you meet him?"

"Once or twice. *Such* a nice man." Her face perked up. "Why, he's an FBI agent just like you! Maybe you know him? Oh! He must be the one who sent you!"

"No, I don't think so. Do you remember his name?"

"It was Wade. Wade . . ." The older woman thought. "Something with mountains."

Rebel wrote the information in her notebook and put a star next to it. An ex-fiancé always shot to the top of her suspect list when it concerned a missing woman. Interesting that he worked for the Bureau.

She wondered briefly why Kick hadn't told her Gina had an ex who was still somewhat in the picture. But then, Kick hadn't told her a whole hell of a lot—and what he had, she'd had to pry out of him using Gina's relationship with his wife, Rainie, as inducement. The man was as tight-lipped as a two-year-old in front of a plate of broccoli. Worried no doubt, despite her solemn oath that she would not pass on anything to another living soul, that whatever he told her would never find its way to the traitor he and Alex suspected was helping al Sayika from somewhere within CIA, or possibly another agency with ties to Zero Unit, their old spec-ops outfit. Thereby getting him dead. Possibly along with Alex, Rainie, and Gina.

Suddenly Rebel had a terrible thought. The FBI was a government agency. Could this fiancé be the mole?

No. He couldn't be. Kick and Alex were fairly certain the traitor who betrayed them was lurking deep inside CIA. Not the FBI.

Then again, there was no hard proof of a mole, or terrorists, or indeed even that Gina had been kidnapped, other than circumstantial. Gina Cappozi could have disappeared, or even been murdered, for entirely different reasons than the work in viral genetics everyone on the task force assumed had caused her to be targeted.

An FBI agent would certainly know how to make a person disappear, for whatever reason. So, why hadn't this ex-fiancé been investigated? Or mentioned in the files?

"Wade was devoted to Gina. But a little too old-fashioned in his ways for her, I suppose. He wanted her to quit her job and move to Washington, D.C. to be with him. Gina preferred to continue her career here in New York. Macaroon, dear?"

"Thanks." Rebel took a cookie and nibbled. Her mind wandered once again to Zane. What would *he* do once he was married? He'd already quit Zero Unit. Obviously, given his weakened physical condition, any similar job would be out of the question. He'd probably live on the beach and go fishing for the rest of his life. Being pampered by his perfect, perky wife and her trust fund.

God knew he deserved it after enduring sixteen months of torture.

She shook off the hollowness in her chest. "Was it a bad

breakup? Did they fight, Wade and Gina?" she asked Mrs. D.

"Oh, no. Nothing like that. He was obviously hurt by her decision, but not vindictive. In fact, when that business with Gina's best friend, Rainie, happened a while back, Wade helped track her down."

Rebel sat up and blinked.

Neither Kick nor Zane had ever mentioned this Wade person in connection with Rainie's disappearance.

"Really?" she asked.

"When Rainie disappeared, Gina was frantic," Mrs. Duluth said. "Wade apparently tracked down who Rainie was with and gave Gina the phone number." Her face creased with a disapproving scowl. "And that's how she met that latest . . . gentleman . . . of hers."

Rebel frowned, suddenly lost. "Who? Rainie?"

"No, Gina. He was some sort of military man." The older woman gave a delicate shudder. "Awful person. Downright frightening if you ask me, in those camouflage pants and combat boots." She leaned in and lowered her voice. "Drives a motorcycle, too."

Rebel resisted a smile. Actually, he sounded pretty attractive to her. She'd always had a thing for camouflage and motorcycles. In fact, Zane used to—

She clamped her jaw. *Not going there*.

"So," she clarified, "Gina got this new man's phone number from Wade? And the new guy was somehow tied into Rainie's disappearance?"

"That's right—about the phone number, anyway. But Rainie hadn't disappeared at all, of course. She'd just gone off with this third fellow, something Jackson. Rainie is married to him now, you know."

"Yes, I do." Zane was Kick's best man at the small wedding, so Rebel and Helena had attended. The ceremony had been held at the Haven Oaks Sanatorium because Zane's doctors wouldn't let him out of bed yet. It had been truly lovely. So incredibly romantic. And embarrassing. For some unfathomable reason, Rebel had cried the whole way through. Rainie had cried, too, thinking about how her best friend, Gina, wasn't there with her. That was when Rebel had first thought about transferring to the case to help find her.

The personal connections were too close not to feel a real stake in the outcome. Especially given the fact that the same sadists about whom Zane still had screaming nightmares were the ones suspected of kidnapping Gina. Zane didn't approve of her involvement, which was why it had taken her so long to ask for the transfer. He'd clammed up whenever she brought up the subject. But that was just too bad. It was something she had to do.

"In any case," Mrs. Duluth said, "Gina met up with this man, and I guess they hit it off at first, because he started showing up at her door at all hours. And she always let him in."

Okay, wait. "Which man, again?"

"The camouflage man with the motorcycle. I know because he always parked it in front of the flower shop and walked all the way down two blocks to her place. Very odd, if you ask me. More tea, dear?"

"No, thank you."

Hmm. That *was* odd.

Rebel set her teacup on the bedoilied table next to the old-fashioned tapestry sofa where she sat. Excitement began buzzing in her veins. Odd, and all new information. There'd never been mention of a fiancé Wade, or of any recent boyfriend, or anyone with a motorcycle, in the files. Nor had Kick said anything.

"Do you know the man's name, by any chance?" she asked hopefully.

"Oh, yes. Gregg. Two g's. I remember because I have a nephew called that. But I don't believe I ever heard a last name."

Rebel wrote it down, her radar going off. *This was it.* The lead she was looking for. She knew it was. "You said they hit it off *at first*. Did something happen?"

"Well, the day after she left, I was out doing my marketing and came home to find a note under my door from Gina, saying she was going to visit family for a few weeks, asking if I could look after her plants until she got back. I assumed they'd had a fight."

Rebel sat even straighter. "Why's that?"

"Her next-door neighbor had told me she'd told *him* she would only be gone for the day. That had been the day *before*. Why else would she have come back without this Gregg person, and then gone off to visit family a day later?"

The hair on the back of Rebel's neck stood up. "Came back without him? You mean she was *with him* when she first went away?" Nowhere in the files had there been mention of Gina going anywhere the day of, or the day before, her disappearance. With anyone. And anyone could have written that note . . . or made her do it at gunpoint.

"Oh, yes. She was with him that first day." Mrs. D nodded, pouring herself another cup of tea. But she didn't elaborate.

"What makes you think so?"

Mrs. Duluth blinked at her like she was slower than molasses. "Because, dear, the day before I got the note, I saw her drive off on the back of his motorcycle!"

SIX

THIS *wasn't* working.

Marc watched Tara observe a seven-foot alligator float by the kayak without even blinking. Ha. He'd told Kowalski she wouldn't scare easily, and that assessment had been dead-on. Why had he even attempted this stupid idea?

"Awful lot of gators out today," she remarked, holding her paddle loosely, like she planned to whack it on the nose if it got too close. He wouldn't put it past her.

Still, he had the shotgun ready anyway, tucked under the dry bag behind him, and his Beretta strapped to his calf. The Ka-Bar hung at his thigh as always, if it came to that. No sense taking chances, regardless of his scare tactics.

"Always a lot of gators in the swamp, *cher*," he returned.

"Snakes and giant spiders, too, I've noticed."

"*Mais*, yeah." And he'd made sure to point out every single one of them. For all the good it had done.

Another gator floated past—this one smaller—and she darted Marc a knowing look over her shoulder. "Almost like you've been deliberately steering us through the biggest colonies of nasty critters you know of."

Whoops.

"Now, *cher*, why would I do that?"

"Good question. You wouldn't by any chance be trying to, oh, say, frighten me?"

The woman was too smart for her own good. "Again, why would I do that?"

She faced front again, scanning the dense wilderness surrounding them. She'd been vigilant all morning, scrutinizing the black waters and low-lying islands and clumps of vegetation they passed for any sign of what she was looking for—a chemical dump or other source for the pollution she thought killed those animals. And for more dead animals, of course. They'd revisited all the kill sites and now were headed to talk to the first of the backwoods hunters who'd reported them.

"Why, indeed?" she said. "Maybe to have some fun with the li'l Yankee gal? Hoping I'll panic like a wuss, so you can gleefully tell all your friends what a wimp I am?"

Attends. She'd made the suggestion light and casual-like, but her voice was just a little too grim, her tone a little too brittle for it to be a joke. And there'd been too many occasions Marc himself had been the brunt of the same kind of narrow-minded thinking to miss the implication.

"That what they do to you?" he asked, disgusted. "The male troopers you work with?"

She speared him with another over-the-shoulder look. It was not a happy one. "What makes you say that?"

He gave a humorless chuckle. "Take a good look at me, *cher*, then take a wild guess."

She did, giving his upper body a long, thorough perusal. His chest and shoulders, the muscles of his arms, the line of his jaw. "Sorry. You don't look like the kind of man anyone in their right mind would dare mess with."

For an operator, it was the ultimate compliment. His body stirred, knowing she admired it. Even if she didn't get what he was saying. He tried to nudge her closer to the truth. "Now imagine a skinny little Cajun kid instead, and guess again."

Understanding dawned. "Ah. I see." Her head tilted. "So that's why you joined the military? To get more of the same thrown at you?"

She was darn good at that, deflecting questions from herself. But he decided to answer anyway. "Nah," he said with a straight face. "It was to get away from my five sisters." At first, anyway. Being away from them and home, ironically missing the responsibility of caring for them, and seeing how other young men were treated by their families—that was when he'd learned to appreciate them and love them all the more for their nurturing and loving—if willful—ways. Unfortunately, when he joined spec ops, he'd had to stay away from them . . . for their own safety. He missed them like crazy, for all they drove him nuts.

She laughed in surprise. "Don't tell me. You're the baby of the family."

"*Non*. The oldest." He grinned. "Why? Do I look like a baby?"

She scanned his body again. This time he let himself enjoy the full impact. It went straight between his legs, hot and heavy. Who said she wasn't his type?

"No," she said and turned around again.

He wasn't sure which question she was answering, the spoken or the unspoken.

Too bad. He really could use a good, hard, tension-relieving fuck. He'd been up and down like a *foutu* drawbridge all morning. And he could have sworn her cheeks flushed just now. She wanted him. She just wouldn't admit it. To him or herself.

A copperhead swam by, its long serpent body wiggling sleekly through the bright green duckweed floating on the surface of the still, black water. She barely glanced at it. She was right; he *had* steered the kayak through the worst gator country in the parish and pointed out every poisonous snake and huge spider he could find lurking in and over the murky bayou.

He gave up.

"So you're a Yankee, eh?" he asked.

"Like you couldn't hear that."

"What brought you to Louisiana, then?"

They paddled silently between the thick trunks of the towering cypress, dodging hanging strands of Spanish moss. Birds cried out in alarm as the kayak invaded their territories, some flapping away on giant wings, others jumping from branch to branch squawking.

"Hurricane Katrina," she finally answered. "I came down to volunteer. Never left."

Interesting. "Pretty bad, huh."

"Yep. Pretty bad."

"Came down from where?"

"Small town in Pennsylvania."

He steered them under a spreading oak covered in colorful orange and green bromeliads. "So what are *you* running away from?"

Her shoulders stiffened. "What makes you think I'm running away from anything?"

Did she never answer a question straight on? "Aren't you?"

"No."

Uh-huh. Other than from him. "*Bon.*"

"How much further to this hunter's place? We have a lot of people to interview today."

"Another mile or two. Then about five miles to the second guy. The other two will be easier. They live in town. But they're probably at their jobs and won't be available until tonight." Which meant he might actually get some real work done this afternoon. Providing he got rid of her first.

She turned and sent him a frown.

He lifted his hands. "Sorry. Can't be helped. I could drop you off at your motel and—" He stopped when she shook her head. "What?"

"Are you forgetting I hired you for the day? The *whole* day?"

Dieu. The woman was nothing if not persistent. But then, so was he.

He raised a brow. "Well, now. What did you have in mind for us to do all afternoon?"

For a second she stared at him, just long enough for him to tighten his legs against hers a tiny bit as they sat in the kayak, just enough so she'd notice. Those two years loomed. Work could wait a spell, he reckoned.

Color streaked her cheeks. "You're incorrigible, you know that?"

So that would be a no. "I will take that as a compliment."

"Why do you keep doing this when you know you aren't going to get what you want?"

"Aren't I?"

She jetted out a breath. "No."

Alors. He smiled. "But that all depends on what it is I want, now, doesn' it, *cher*?"

BLOOD sprayed across the room in a graceful arch.

Her blood.

The part of Gina's mind that was still objective struggled desperately to concentrate on the elegant curve of the spray, the delicate formation of the bright red droplets as they sailed through the air almost in slow motion, and the artistic distortion and burst of the liquid bubbles as they splattered against the wall in a picture-perfect textbook pattern. Not the excruciating pain exploding through her.

She barely had a chance to suck in a breath before the next blow smashed her face, sending an equally elegant arch of blood cascading in the opposite direction. And even worse pain.

She'd really screwed up this time.

And she was paying the price for it.

Every nerve, every muscle, every cell of flesh and bone throbbed with pain; every breath burned like the fires of hell. She could feel her jaw crack as Tawhid's fist hit her again, and her eyelids begin to swell shut from the blows.

Her eyes rolled up and she prayed for unconsciousness. But her mind was too filled with self-recrimination to allow herself that small comfort.

She had thought she was being so clever. But the fiend was diabolical. Tawhid must have suspected all along what she was doing. Had let her believe she was succeeding in her sabotage of the bioterror weapon he was forcing her to finish perfecting.

Oh, she'd finished it, all right. It was now ready. Modified to his specifications and dried to a powdered form. Easy to use. Lethal. It hadn't been that difficult to replicate the deadly anthrax-vectored, fast-incubating influenza A virus some previous scientist had developed for them. Drying it for use with a powdered spray-delivery system had been trickier, but not impossible. But for the past two months, ever since that first beating she'd taken, she'd been playing Penelope to Tawhid's suitor, secretly unraveling the day's accomplishments and modifying her work when the guards weren't looking. Splicing in her self-destruct gene so the strain would die instead of becoming contagious. And evolving the virus so it would not be able to survive the outside winter temperatures, thus rendering it impotent as soon as it left the climate-controlled temps of the lab.

She'd had a ridiculously short time to make those genetic changes. But apparently she'd managed at least the latter. Unfortunately, she had not been prepared for the surprise test they'd sprung on her this morning. After all, they'd tested it just two days ago. So when Tawhid had marched into the lab early and demanded she prepare a small spray canister with the virus she was working on, she hadn't been able to substitute a vial of the original strain to fool them with, as she'd done in his previous tests. Today, the wild swamp animals the terrorist had tested it on had not died. And his suspicions about her sabotage had been confirmed.

Tawhid did not like being defied. He'd warned her once.

He did not give second chances.

She crashed to the floor, her head bouncing off the hard cement. A spangle of stars burst across her vision, and for a second her body went tingly numb. She tried to curl into a protective ball but wasn't fast enough. Rough hands jerked at her. Her side danced with electric pain as the hard toe of his boot buried itself in her ribs, drew back, and struck again.

In that distant, objective part of her brain she knew he wouldn't kill her. He couldn't. Not until he was 100 percent certain his evil weapon would work as planned.

She only had to endure this. The pain. The humiliation. And the grinding fear that she could be wrong and this was the day she would die. But she *wouldn't* die. It only felt like it. She would get through this.

She had to. For the sake of all those millions of people who really would die if Tawhid won. It was up to her to save them.

The blows finally stopped and a thick, heavy silence hung over the room. She dared to take a breath. But not to move. Let him think he'd gone too far . . .

"Don't pretend with me, whore," he said coldly. "I know

you are conscious."

She touched her tongue to her lips. They were wet with blood, thick and coppery tasting. Her lower lip was split, her upper lip swollen into her cheek. She didn't dare answer.

Hot tears and warm blood trickled down her face. *At least it was over.* And she hadn't screamed. She hadn't given him the satisfaction.

"You take your beating like a man," he said, his flat, icy voice insinuating itself into her skull, like a disgusting disease.

She pulled in a shuddering breath. Didn't dare say thank you. It hadn't sounded like a compliment.

"Maybe you *are* a man," he said. "Perhaps we should check."

She froze.

Oh, God.

Then twisted away. "No!"

He jerked her onto her back and ripped down her pants. Exposing her.

She tried to fight. But didn't stand a chance. Her body was too battered. Too weak. The guards too strong as they held her down and laughed at her degradation.

Tawhid made an ugly sound. "Just as I thought. You are no man, but a useless woman. A woman designed by God to obey. Your pride is an insult to Allah. You must be taught your proper place, American whore."

He grabbed her top and ripped it down the middle. She let out a sob. *Sweet Mary, Mother of God, help me.*

His weight crushed onto her; his cruel fingers wrenched her legs apart.

She couldn't help it. She screamed in despair.

No! Oh, God. No!

SEVEN

MARC stacked his hands behind his head and watched as
Tara paced down the length of the rickety old jetty hanging
off a derelict hunting shack where they'd pulled in to eat
their lunch. At the end she turned and paced back again.
She'd been doing that for the past ten minutes, stopping
only when he got out the collapsible mini-cooler and
handed her a po'boy, which she ate while pacing, then a
sweet tea, which she drank while pacing, and then paused
for half a minute deciding whether or not to take the beer
he offered her. Which she finally waved off.

Damn, she needed *some*thing to calm her down. He was
getting tired just watching her wear ruts in the old jetty
boards.

"*Cher*, will you please sit down and talk to me? What is
the problem?"

He was sprawled on the sun-warmed wooden slats, doing
his level best to appear relaxed when in fact he was jumpy as
a grasshopper in a frying pan.

Except for the acute sexual frustration he was feeling, the
morning had gone better than anticipated. Yeah, he'd done
his damnedest to implement Kowalski's idea of scaring her off
the investigation—to no avail. But when they had no luck

picking the brains of the first two men who'd reported the animal kills, she'd asked Marc to find some other random people who lived in the swamp to interview before going back to town. Naturally, he'd deliberately picked the most reclusive gun-toting Cajuns he was personally acquainted with—so he'd be sure they'd receive a hostile reception but wouldn't actually get shot at, though she had no way of knowing that. Still, not once all morning had she batted an eyelash or shown the least sign of fear, even staring down the double barrel of a shotgun.

Luckily, she didn't speak Cajun French, so he'd taken the opportunity to plant the idea that the state police thought it was an illegal meth lab releasing the chemicals that killed the animals. It had also been the perfect setup to ask his own questions. Talking to that last hunter, he'd gotten a couple of good leads on *étrangers* renting area buildings suitable to running a meth lab—or a makeshift genetics lab—in.

Now he was anxious to get out of there and track them down. Or at least call Zimmerman . . . er, Quinn, and let the team investigate. But there was no cell service out here and it wasn't like he could just pull out the satellite phone from the dry bag. Might look a tad suspicious for a jailbird wilderness guide to be using a thousand-dollar comm device.

Tara came to a halt in front of him. "Maybe we should tell them we're together," she said.

He blinked. Pulled himself back into focus.

"We *are* together," he pointed out, taking a sip from his own beer. He normally didn't drink on the job, but he had to keep up his Cajun bad-boy image, didn't he? Besides, he needed something to calm *him* down. *Foutre de merde*. She was driving him slowly but surely out of his mind. And for the record, it was *not* the close proximity to her amazing body in the kayak all morning and his increasing-by-the-second horniness making him insane.

Okay, *bon*. It was.

Partly.

Along with the need to get moving. Time was slipping away and he was still no closer to finding Tawhid. He had to follow those leads.

"No. I mean *together* together," she explained.

Wait. Wait. *Quoi sa dit?* "Say what?"

"Everyone talks to you," she said exasperatedly. "You're friends with *everyone* around here."

Not strictly true, but okay, it *was* true that everyone in the parish was friends with one or another of his many relatives. His social-butterfly sisters, especially. Therefore he was greeted as an old friend as soon as he was recognized. *Mais . . .* "So?"

"So no one will say a word to *me*. Maybe if people think I'm your girlfriend, they won't clam up when I ask about the dead animals and possible sources of pollution."

His high blood pressure took a left turn. Just as high, but for a different reason.

Bon Dieu.

His *girl*friend?

He took an extra-long draught on his beer, stalling. The possibilities were tantalizing.

His respect for the woman had gone up considerably over the past hours. Which, unfortunately, had just made her all the more attractive. Completely bizarre. Since gun-toting danger-junky females had never appealed to him. And women in uniform generally turned him off completely.

Of course, she wasn't in uniform today.

She'd also put away her gun a while back, relenting to his suggestion she stow it in the dry bag to allay suspicion in her interviewees. He supposed he should feel happy she trusted him that much.

And now she wanted to play his girlfriend.

Salleau prie. This was so wrong. She was handing him a way in on a silver platter. And damn if he didn't want to grab it.

Merde. How to turn this around?

"*Cher.* I already told you," he said lazily. "You can't afford me."

Her expectant expression turned to scandalized. "You'd make me *pay* you to pretend you're my boyfriend?"

"Hell, yeah." He stretched out his legs and took another deep pull. "Unless . . ." *Whoops.* Better stop right there.

"Unless what?" She stood over him with fists planted on

her hips, trying to look like he couldn't take her with both hands tied behind his back. He had to work not to grin. Or break out in a cold sweat.

He had to figure out some way to shake her off so he could get away from there. Jump on those leads. No time for jumping on *her*. More's the pity.

She was watching him warily.

"Here's the thing," he said, clearing his throat. "No one would actually believe you're my *fille*."

"Why?" she demanded. "I'm not *that* bad, am I?" Suddenly she glanced away.

Great. Now he'd offended her.

"*Mais non, cher*, you're not *bad* at all. That's kind of the problem."

She looked back at him, her *joli* mouth thinning. "In other words, I'm not . . . I'm too . . . I'm not the kind of woman you'd ever get involved with."

Despite the unexpected attraction sizzling between them, she was right. He always preferred soft, ultrafeminine women, like his sisters. Someone he could keep safe and protect. Who needed him. A woman who swooned at his touch would be nice, and who wanted nothing more than to please him, to—

And just like that it hit him. The solution was staring him right in the face.

She was terrified of getting close. Physically. She'd proven it over and over all day.

He could use that.

"Aw, honey, I'm not sayin' that at all." He gazed up at her and allowed all the heat he was feeling to fill his eyes. "I'm just sayin', everyone around here knows my family. We're a very demonstrative bunch, us. For anyone to seriously believe you're my woman, you'd have to be all over me, and me you. Touching-wise."

Her lips parted. Then closed. "Oh."

"So unless you're willing to let me take substantial liberties with your person, and you mine . . . the idea just won't work."

For a second she had a look on her face he couldn't begin

to decipher. She took a step forward. His pulse took off. *Bon Dieu* . . . Then she stopped and shook her head.

"Wow, Lafayette. Very good. For a minute you almost had me going there."

TARA rolled her eyes. Give the man major points for creativity, she thought, barely holding back a snort.

"Going where? I can't imagine what you mean," Marc protested with an unrepentant grin.

"Seriously," she said. To think she'd almost *fallen* for that line. "Nice try."

Take away about a thousand points of her own for coming up with the lame-brained idea in the first place.

Jeez Lou*ise*. Had she really suggested he pretend to be her *boy*friend? Like, (a) that would ever happen in this lifetime, or (b) if it did, she would ever have the guts to follow through and actually touch the man.

Hell, she *was* a wimp and a wuss. A sorry-ass excuse for a—

No.

Tara closed her eyes for a moment and banished her father's harsh voice from her head. She *wasn't* a wimp, or an excuse for *anything*.

There. *Gone.*

"I think we're done here," she said and started gathering up their lunch things.

Marc checked his watch as he rose to his feet. "Sure. Like I said, I can drop you at your hotel until—"

Annoyance raked through her. "You have somewhere else to be, Lafayette? Is that why you're so anxious to get rid of me?"

He glanced up sharply. "*Mais non*, I just—"

A surge of illogical pique joined the annoyance. "Or maybe you're worried I'll change my mind and agree to your terms? Since it turns out I'm not to your taste after all, despite your relentless—and apparently empty—sexual innuendo."

His eyes narrowed. "Careful, *cher*."

"No, no. It's okay. I realize I've been a total bitch today.

Hot and sweaty, too, and God knows not that attractive to begin with. So who could blame you for not—"

Suddenly his hands were wrapped around her upper arms. "Shut up."

She gasped as he dragged her up against his chest. "Hey!"

And then his mouth was on hers. His lips covered hers in an explosion of wet heat, erotic taste, and . . . anger?

She was so stunned she couldn't think, couldn't react, as he banded his arms around her, pulled her close, and kissed her. Kissed her like she'd never been kissed before.

A shock of pleasure burst through her body like a lightning ball. His hands were on her back, her backside, trapping her against him as his mouth ravaged hers, merciless and insistent. He bit her lip and sucked at it until she gasped again, and then his tongue shoved between her lips and he was inside, licking and claiming her mouth as his own property. She shook, frozen and helpless against the onslaught.

His fingers shot through her hair, gripped it savagely, holding her fast for his taking. His other hand spread across her bottom, pressed her firmly into the Y of his thighs. Where he was rock hard. And huge.

She was boneless. Trembling. Her mind dizzy with the impact.

Without letting up the pressure, one hand slid between her legs. The other pulled her head back, tearing her lips from his.

He glowered at her, his breath rough.

"Don't ever," he growled, pressing his fingertips up into her like he wanted to break through the solid denim of her jeans and breach the swollen flesh just beyond his reach, "mistake me being a gentleman"—he withdrew, grabbed her arms again, and firmly set her away from him—"for not wanting you."

She just stood there panting, confused and brainless, barely able to stand and—amazingly—aching for him to finish what he'd started.

"Okay," she managed. Though her voice cracked like a teenaged boy's. "Okay."

He swiped up their trash and the empty cooler and

smashed it all into the dry bag. Stalked over to the kayak and loaded it up. Then turned to her.

"So, *cher*. This afternoon. What's it going to be? More pointless questions? Or your hotel room and bed?"

EIGHT

OH, God. What should she do?

Tara had never experienced such painful indecision in her entire life.

How could she want him this much? A man she'd barely met? A man who obviously had no more in mind than a quick fuck and then to get away from her as fast as he could. Marc Lafayette had been embarrassingly transparent in his efforts to rid himself of her all day.

And yet, she now yearned for him with every fiber of her being. For his touch. For what he would do to her. With her. To her body.

Her desire must have shown in her face, because his expression slowly turned from angry to surprised, and then to . . . something predatory and uncivilized.

"Rien à foutre," he growled.

And in two steps he was on her again. Instantly his mouth was back wreaking havoc on hers, his hands all over her—holding her face, tugging out her ponytail and digging into her hair, under her T-shirt, tunneling into her bra.

This was all wrong. But, oh, God, just once, she wanted to experience the total abandon of surrendering to something so completely, utterly wrong. And in this, at least, she trusted him.

She moaned and let go all sense of time and control. Allowed herself to fall into the pure screaming pleasure of his tongue and his fingers, the solid measure of his tall, demanding body pressing into her, the feel of his hot skin and powerful muscles and his long, thick hair under her hands. Oh, the taste of him. The flavor of his hunger. *So good.* So male. So arousing. Her flesh was sizzling with pleasure, slickening, blossoming, rushing toward an implosion of sensation from the instant he touched her.

He shoved her jeans and panties down to her knees and his hand snaked between her thighs. This time there was no barrier to shield her from the assault. His fingers circled and prodded and coaxed her, higher and tighter and—

"Oh, Marc," she moaned into his mouth, "Please don't stop."

"*Jamais, beb.*"

The sexy, gravelly spoken words and his relentless demand sent her careening over the edge of reason and restraint. She cried his name aloud. Pleasure detonated at his fingertips and spread through her like a bomb going off. She cried out and shuddered, sobbing with the exquisite sensations that pulsed through her, clinging to him so she wouldn't collapse from the sudden fiery weakness in her limbs.

But they did give out and he caught her, lowering her down, and all at once she was on her hands and knees, panting, gasping, gripping the warm, smooth wood for purchase as he positioned himself behind her. She heard a quick snap of latex and then—

Oh, God. Oh, *God*, and then he was inside her. Thrusting hard, banding his other arm around her middle to hold her at exactly the right angle so he could plunge deep, deep, deep into her.

Again she cried out, inarticulate pleas for more, for harder, for him to fill her with his thick, ravening cock and drive her to a sweet, staggering oblivion of pleasure she'd never experienced before. Not like this.

He took her.

He took all of her. Every last morsel that she gave, willingly and not.

He ripped another orgasm from her, rough and without

apology, without letting up. No time for second thoughts, no time for any thoughts at all . . . save the one that burned through her consciousness at the last possible moment before she dissolved once again under his ruthless insistence and surrendered to him completely. Surrendered everything buried deep inside. Everything she'd safely hidden from the world—and herself—for all these years.

And that last thought was, dear God in heaven, how would she ever let this man go?

DARCY cringed at the outfits Quinn had picked out for them at a thrift store in Stephensville. It had been his idea to dress "in character" before they started knocking on doors.

"Trust me, it'll work," he said as they changed clothes in the cab of their truck, which he'd parked on a side road in the out-of-the-way industrial park where the first address on their list of possible terrorist hideouts was located. "Nonthreatening. That's the image we want to project."

The look Quinn was going for was typical nerdy bean counter, complete with clipboard and pocket protector. Darcy was his ditzy assistant. His cover story idea was that they were conducting a cellular provider survey to pinpoint holes in coverage. Brilliant, really, she hated to admit. Everyone liked to bitch about spotty cell reception to anyone who'd listen. Closemouthed bad guys would stick out like a sore thumb.

"I get it, Quinn. I've taken Spying 101, too," she muttered. She'd also done the distracting female thing before. With him, in fact.

And just look where *that* had gotten her.

She tried to block the memory of the first time they'd met, five years ago in Istanbul, practically devouring each other both during the op and after. Not an easy task with the scent of him still clinging to her skin after last night. Once again a shower hadn't begun to banish it.

"Didn't want you thinking I had ulterior motives," he said with a knowing grin, "for picking out that skirt and sweater."

Yeah, right. Ulterior Motives was Quinn's middle name. But she was determined to treat this like any other op with any other partner. "Not to worry. I often go for the naughty schoolgirl look when undercover. It's so classic."

"For good reason," he said, apparently missing the sarcasm. He watched a little too closely as she peeled off her T-shirt, exposing the lacy pink push-up bra she wore underneath it. What? It wasn't like he'd never seen her naked before. Recently.

He shifted in his seat. "Jesus, Zimmie. You are so fucking hot."

She evaded his reach. "Don't even think about it," she warned.

His gaze latched longingly to her breasts. She was vaguely surprised he didn't start drooling.

In a swift move, he drew off his own T-shirt. Leaving his broad, ripped chest temptingly naked. Unwillingly, her gaze skated over the expanse of tanned flesh and downward, drawn by the arrow of hair on his concave belly down to the provocative shadows in the denim that hugged his waist and cupped his obvious hard-on.

Not fair. Not fair.

"Don't suppose we could declare a truce for, say, half an hour?" he drawled, jerking her focus back up to his face. He was watching her steadily, a flush of arousal coloring his throat and deepening the polar ice of his eyes to cerulean blue.

He was so ridiculously attractive, for a second she actually considered it.

Damn. She had no spine at all around this man.

"Not a chance in hell," she answered crisply. "Things to do. Bad guys to catch."

He just smiled, unzipped his jeans, and peeled them off. Okay, *so* not fair.

But she would *not* give him the satisfaction of knowing how much she still wanted him. She pushed out a breath and nonchalantly took hers off, too.

Naturally, he picked that moment to say, "This cold-shoulder thing. It's not about me being team leader. Is it." Not a question.

For someone who'd been in her company maybe six weeks total over the past five years, most of which they had *not* spent talking, he knew her well.

Scary well.

"Of course it is," she refuted, careful not to phrase her reply in the form of a question like, "What makes you say that?" She *really* didn't aim to break precedent and start meaningful conversation with the man now.

Make that *ever*.

"You've never had a problem taking orders from me before," he said, watching her grab the tight, powder blue sweater he'd picked out for her and pull it over her head.

She shot him a narrow look. "Nor you, me."

He sighed. "Which can only mean you're angry with me over something else."

"Don't flatter yourself, Quinn."

"Is it Fiji? I told you I was sorry about missing our rendezvous."

Not going there, she singsonged in her head. This was so not about Fiji.

Much.

Okay, fine. It was.

"Apology already accepted. Now, forget about it, okay?"

"Darcy—"

Uh-oh. Use of first name. Red alert.

"Please, Quinn." She held up a palm. "There's no time for this now. We have an urgent job to do." She slid on her skirt and zipped it.

He looked so deliciously frustrated she almost felt sorry for him. Almost. But then she thought about what a fool he'd made of her. She didn't like being replaced. Professionally or personally. Sorry? She didn't think so.

He'd been a real shit. Not only had he not shown up at their planned romantic getaway on Fiji last year, he hadn't even bothered with a phone call or an e-mail. But later? She'd found out he'd spent that same week in Paris with another woman. A job, he'd insisted.

Sure it was.

The worst part? Fiji had been *his* idea. A deserted island, nude sunbathing, spectacular diving, umbrella drinks, making love for a whole long, undisturbed week. And she'd fallen for it like a sixteen-year-old with her first crush. For months she'd looked forward to their tryst. Had splurged on an incredibly sexy wardrobe for the occasion. Well. A *non*-wardrobe, really. Even made up a lovely fantasy in her head that she actually meant something to the jerk.

Remembering the whole episode mortified her. To think she'd been so freaking easy. Shame on her. She knew better.

Yeah, she'd gone that whole pathetic route before—let her heart and her expectations get all tangled up in someone—and been crushed so badly it had taken her years to overcome.

This time, never again. She'd learned her lesson too many times to ignore the basic truth.

Love was seriously not worth the pain.

Sex? Sure. Sex was great. The more, the merrier.

But love? Ha. Maybe when hell froze over.

Until then, she was just fine the way she was. Happy and independent. No strings. No commitment. No risk. No worries.

Bobby Lee Quinn could just go find himself some other heart to break.

"I really am sorry," he said as he pulled on his nerd slacks and strapped a holstered Beretta onto his ankle. "She was an assignment. I swear it. And I couldn't risk—"

"Stop. Honestly. I believe you. And I. Don't. Care."

He shoved an HK in the back of his waistband and pulled an ugly brown sport coat over it. "But—"

"Quinn. We're not exclusive. Never have been. Never will be." She fastened the Velcro wrist sheath of her OTF blade and tidied her sweater cuff over it. "Come on, let's go kick some terrorist butt."

With that, she jumped out of the truck, straightened her short skirt, and adjusted the Glock gartered to her thigh. He climbed out after her.

"You can pretend all you want," he said, joining her in a quick strut up the litter-strewn street to the first address on their list of possibles, a warehouse in the run-down industrial park. "But I know the truth. You *do* care. And you still want me."

She managed a convincing laugh. "Wow. You go psychic while I wasn't looking, Quinn?"

They approached the warehouse entrance, and he pushed his fake glasses up the bridge of his nose with a finger.

"Don't need to be. I was there last night. Remember?"

All too vividly. "Well, you *won't* be tonight."

He grabbed her arm as she reached for the buzzer, swung her around to face him. God. How could any man look so damn handsome dressed in that goofy getup? Maybe it was knowing he was armed to the teeth under it. In more ways than one. The contrast was . . . oddly arousing.

"Why not?" he demanded in a dangerously low growl. "If you're so damn indifferent to me, why not just enjoy the great sex? You certainly seemed to last night."

"Sorry, my bad," she said, steadfastly ignoring the bite of his fingers on her flesh and the sudden pain zinging through her heart. "It won't happen again. There'll be no more sex from now on."

"And why not?"

"Do I have to spell it out? We're finished, Quinn. It's over."

WHOA, there. "*What?*"

Pure confusion spun through Bobby Lee's head. Unfortunately, by the time he got his mouth in working order to ask her what the *hell* she meant by that, Zimmie had already mashed the buzzer and voices were approaching the other side of the warehouse door.

So he was forced to shift mental gears and ask probing questions about cell phone coverage of two high school dropouts who'd just started a pimp-your-truck business that hadn't made it into the phone company business roster yet.

Obviously not terrorists.

But it took ten minutes to extract themselves from the conversation.

"We might just be *too* convincing," Zimmie muttered when they finally got back to their own truck. "Maybe we should switch to hawking religion instead. I had no idea there was so much anger out there about cell phone reception."

Speaking of anger . . . His own had built up quite a head of steam by this time, growing and roiling inside him. Sure, he'd expected to pay for his careless inattention to the Fiji debacle, but this was going too far.

He threw her a hard look. "Talk to me, woman."

Her eyes avoided his. "I thought I had."

"Is there someone else?" he demanded, surprising himself as much as he surprised her. Her mouth dropped open, taken aback by the question. Or maybe by the vehemence with which it had been asked.

"Huh?"

"Another guy. You're sleeping with." For some inexplicable reason, the thought of her getting down with another man churned through him like an acid wash. Funny, it never had before.

Or maybe he'd just never thought seriously about the possibility before.

Christ. Was he that egotistical?

He fired the truck's engine to life and burned rubber toward the next address on their list.

"I thought we had an agreement," he said. "An arrangement."

She raised a brow. "To what? Fuck like minks every time we see each other and then walk away without another thought until next time? You mean *that* arrangement?"

He clamped his jaw. Okay. So, put that way, it didn't sound very . . . well, very romantic.

Romantic?

Jesus, had he really just thought that?

"Yeah, that one," he said, grinding the truck into third. "I happen to like our arrangement. I don't *want* us to be over."

Great. Now he sounded like a petulant child.

"There *is* no us, Quinn. Never has been."

He jetted out a breath. "Can you please, just once in your life, call me Bobby Lee?" Using his last name when they were alone together was another of her distancing maneuvers that made him crazy. Like the condom and sleeping thing.

She scrunched down in her seat and crossed her arms. "No."

"Goddamn it, Zimmie—"

"I could call you Quinnie if you like."

"Cute." He cut her another look. She retreated like a hermit crab if he called her Darcy, so years ago he'd started using the nickname from an old Dylan song. "You are such a fucking punk."

She showed him her teeth.

He ground his to stubs. "Why are you doing this, sugar? I don't know what else I can say to apologize. If you want me to get down on my knees and—"

"Now you're flat-out scaring me. Please, Quinn. Can we maintain a little dignity here?"

"No. *Hell*, no. Baby, I don't want to lose what we have."

"*Have?* Did I miss something somewhere? The sex, you mean? The guilt-free, no-strings, twice-a-year sex, you mean?"

"It's more than that, and you know it," he gritted out.

"Three times a year?" she deliberately misinterpreted.

"Damn it, woman, you . . . I . . . We have a relationship!"

Lord have fucking mercy. Had the R-word really left his lips?

She stared at him wide-eyed. "You can't be serious. You can't possibly believe we have an actual—" She held up a hand. "No. Don't answer that."

He stared back.

They didn't?

"Watch out!"

He slammed on the brakes just before crashing into a chain-link fence running next to the road. And suddenly the realization hit him right in the gonads. Oh, sweet Mother of God.

"You want a fucking commitment, don't you?"

SOMEHOW Darcy managed to restrain herself from pulling out her Glock and shooting the big jerk right then and there.

Instead, she calmly—*very* calmly—smoothed her skirt over her thighs, exhaled a calming breath, and said oh-so-calmly, "No, Quinn, I do not. Even after that most eloquent plea. And let's see . . ." She pretended to think. "No, not if you were the very last man on earth." Then she smiled sweetly at his rigid face.

He exhaled just as slowly. And said, "So. That's how you're going to play it."

"Yes," she affirmed. "Yes, it is."

"All right. Fine."

Was that the slightest spike of disappointment she felt at his easy capitulation? God, no.

She gave a quick nod. "Good. I'm glad you are able to see reason."

Okay, maybe not so easy. The look he sent her was anything but an admission of defeat. More like gearing up for round two.

An absurd, shimmering breath of hope whispered through her. Was it possible he . . .

No. *Get real.*

She was doing this for a reason. The cleaner the break, the better for both of them. Well, her, anyway. Incredible as it sounded, even to her, her heart was getting in too deep. And she knew very well what happened when you put your trust in a relationship, let it go beyond casual. As soon as you did, the other person got tired of you and you were replaced. And this man was a player. Even if she wanted to—which she didn't—he would never settle down. Certainly not with one woman. When they first met, she'd firmly believed they were cut from the same cloth. And for three or four years they'd been perfect for each other. But then unwillingly, and to her supreme shock, her emotions had begun to get involved, not just her body. *God, so dangerous.* She'd started thinking about him at the oddest moments. Dragged her feet just a little when leaving their all-too-fleeting hookups in the far-flung corners of the world. Had felt herself slowly start to go mental picturing him with his other women.

Oh, and there *had* been other women. He'd made no secret of that from the beginning. She'd said the same thing to him regarding other men. How was he to know she'd never actually followed through? And gradually she had started fearing their informal arrangement was taking on far too much importance in her heart.

She'd wanted to break it off then. But her traitorous heart, filled with foolish hope caused by his invitation to Fiji, had refused to release its hold on her head. And she'd started thinking . . . dreaming . . . that maybe this relationship could be different from all the rest. They'd been together so long . . . There had been other women, but he'd always come back to her. Always made her feel like she was the most important woman in the world to him.

She'd decided it was time to make a decision, one way or

another. Either she had to take the leap, give it one last try, and find out if they could be a real couple or she had to stop seeing him for her own good.

Fiji had been the watershed. But they'd landed on different sides of the continental divide.

He'd failed the test. Miserably. Chosen another woman over her. *Replaced again.*

That had hurt.

Even so, she'd given some serious thought to just confronting him with her growing feelings. In case it really *had* been a job. And maybe . . .

But yeah. If nothing else, the look of abject horror just now on his face as he'd said those fateful words, "You want a fucking commitment, don't you?" was more than answer enough.

Better to save herself the humiliation and infinite heartache.

Better by far.

So from now on, they would be strictly coworkers.

Teammates. Not bedmates.

As difficult as that would be.

"I just want to give you fair warning," he said, bringing her back to the present with a jerk. "I don't agree to this bullshit. Not remotely. And I do not intend to go away just because you got your panties in a twist about a job I had no control over. We had amazing sex last night, and I see no good reason we can't continue to share a bed as long as we're in the same damn place on the same damn op."

Such a romantic. She opened her mouth to retort, but he cut her off.

"However, you're right. We're here on a mission. We've got to concentrate on getting these bads put away. So that's what we're going to do. For now." He tapped his finger on her chin. "But later? When the lights are off? Sugar, so are all bets."

With that, he ground the truck into gear and pulled back onto the road with a squeal of tires.

She wanted to laugh in his face. To tell him he had no right to question her decisions. That if she was done with him, there wasn't a damn thing he could do about it.

But she restrained herself. The man had a definite stubborn streak. If she challenged him that forcefully, he'd feel the need to prove himself. Using any means necessary. And she wasn't sure she could withstand an assault on her will-power. Not here, not now, alone, with no means of escape. She knew herself. And she knew this was the only man in the world who could wrap her around his finger with one little word.

Okay. Maybe three little words.

But that wasn't going to happen anytime soon. And even if it did, she couldn't trust he really meant them. She'd been fooled before. A lifetime's worth.

So she'd wait to set him straight. Tonight, she'd cut him loose for good. Tell him she really *didn't* want to see him anymore. Not as lovers.

And with any luck, her heart would survive the ordeal.

NINE

OKAY, this was unexpected.

Bon Dieu.

Marc sure hoped there wasn't some sort of law against seducing a state trooper . . .

What there *should* be a law against was a state trooper being so damn sexy a man couldn't possibly resist her, or stop himself from creating a worse disaster than the one he'd already landed in.

Merde.

And on top of everything else, she'd *cried*.

After he'd fucked her to within an inch of her life, then flipped her over and did it all over again looking straight into her eyes. . . Afterward TFC Tara Reeves had actually broken down and cried. Not from shame or regret, she'd assured him tearfully, *merci Dieu*. But from . . . Well, he wasn't exactly sure what from. She'd mumbled something about relief and letting go and . . . her mother? The woman seemed to have some major issues. Not that he hadn't suspected as much.

Good thing he had so many sisters and was used to this sort of irrational female behavior and could see it as endearing, or the whole deal would have freaked him out mondo.

And yet . . .

He peered down at her, nestled on his chest asleep, his arms around her to keep her from sliding off onto the old, uneven jetty. She was so damn pretty. Her face looked so young, so innocent as she slept, her long lashes brushing her cheeks, her thick chestnut hair spread over his chest like a cloud of whipped mocha. He could smell a hint of her perfume, or shampoo—distinctive and nuanced, like the woman who wore it—over the ambient earthy blend of sex and swamp.

Locked in his embrace, she stirred, letting out a contented sigh that blew across his heartstrings. He tightened his hold a bit more, feeling oddly protective. She was such a tough little cookie. Or tried to be. So brave and obstinate and mouthy. But now she just looked like a *petite fille*. *Donc*, a naughty little girl. Her jeans were still down around her shapely knees. As were his. He'd attempted to pull them up after she fell asleep but was afraid to wake her, so he'd left them both at half mast. Him, he'd probably have a butt full of splinters when he got up. Which was just fine. Their good bits were bare and fitted intimately, and his hand had found a soft, sweet pillow to rest on.

He caressed the smooth curve of her backside, and unbelievably, his body began to respond again. How long had it been since they made love? A half hour, hour max. Damn, he hadn't had this kind of visceral reaction to a woman in years. Wouldn't you know it would be someone like her. Someone completely incompatible, who'd as soon fight with him as look at him, and who'd near given him a complex bursting into tears after having sex with him. *Merde*.

Not that he was interested in steady company. *Mais non*.

Hell, just see what Kick and Rainie were going through in order to be together, trying to figure out where they'd live and who'd quit their job. Not to mention the danger Rainie'd put herself into by choosing to be with someone in the spec-ops world. Loving an operator was not easy. Emotionally or logistically.

Marc loved his family dearly but deliberately kept his distance from them so as not to expose those he loved to any fallout from his work. You never knew when some crazy *foutard* would get it into their head to take revenge on your loved ones for something you may or may not have done.

He'd learned long ago to avoid having anyone you cared about within grabbing distance.

For any length of time, anyway.

Tara made a humming noise and snuggled closer to him. He sure wished they didn't have all these clothes on. He wanted to feel their bodies sliding up against each other, skin to skin. Be able to look at her. *All* of her. And take his time lazily tasting and exploring every inch of her soft curves and hidden places.

Putain, he was turning himself on just thinking about it. And his lengthening hard-on was like a heat-seeking missile, zeroing in on its target instinctively.

Tara's eyes fluttered open. He could tell she had no clue where she was. At first. Then her head shot up and her gaze met his. His cock picked that exact moment to find her moist opening. Her face turned bright red.

"Hey," he said gently and gave her a wink. Down below, his rogue arousal nudged at her impatiently.

"Oh, God," she whispered, squeezed her eyes shut, and groaned. Tried to roll off him.

"Hey, now." He held her firmly in place. "What's the hurry, *cher*?"

His cock nudged a bit harder. Her body shivered. He hoped in a good way.

She didn't open her eyes. "We really did this, didn't we?"

"Oh, yeah."

She stuttered out a breath. "Sorry I fell asleep on you."

"I dozed a little, too. Guess we both needed it."

There was something else they both needed. Before she ran scared. He slid his fingers between her legs and spread her apart, then pushed in a few inches. A low groan escaped him. She was still hot and slick from last time.

"Damn, you feel good, *cher*."

She moaned softly, then suddenly let out a small gasp. "Marc, protection!"

Foutu Dieu. He abruptly halted his slow slide into her. No wonder it felt so freaking good. "Don't s'pose you have any on you?" he asked between gritted teeth. "I'm out. Wasn't really expecting to . . . uh, get lucky."

"Funny enough," she said with a strangled laugh, "me, neither."

At least she still had a sense of humor.

Wishing he did, too, he swore in sublime frustration. And pushed in just a little farther. She sucked in a breath, but he just couldn't help himself. If she was going to get pregnant, it was probably already too late. As for anything else— "Just so you know, I was in the hospital last month. Got a clean bill of health. All counts."

She swallowed. "I, um . . ."

He cut her off with a long kiss. A big part of his job was to read people. He wasn't worried about her. At all.

He was more worried about how he was going to make himself pull out of her sweet heat. Luckily neither of them could move much because of their constricting jeans. He kissed her again, letting her know how much he wanted her. Her fingers clutched at his shoulders as she opened to him. Apparently, the feeling was mutual.

"Marc," she groaned when he finally let her up for air.

By now he was as far into her as he could go. But still he wanted more.

Foutre de merde.

Before he weakened further, he grasped her hips and pulled her off him, rolled her onto her back on the deck, and cursed long and hard at the sky. Battling for control.

Okay, *that* was probably the stupidest thing he'd ever done in his life—the part where he pushed into her unprotected in the first place. Which was exactly the sort of selfish stunt that could get a man into deep trouble. Because he shouldn't *have* to fight the overwhelming urge to throw caution to the wind, launch himself on top of her, and push in all over again regardless of the consequences.

"Why were you in the hospital?" she asked after a few long moments of tense silence.

Quoi sa dit?

Oh. Right.

He opened his mouth to tell her the story and caught himself just in time. *Dieu.* The hair stood up on the back of his neck at the huge mistake he'd nearly made. Where had he left his brains today?

"A wreck," he said. "Broken arm."

"Lucky," she replied, trying to make her voice sound normal. Not succeeding. "Most car crash victims sustain far worse injuries. You were fortunate to walk away."

Especially since it hadn't been a car wreck but a plane exploding in midair. And he'd more crawled away than walked. Well. Dragged himself. But he had been lucky. His broken ribs hadn't punctured a lung. And he'd survived. With a little help from his friends.

Anyway. That had sounded like a canned speech from her. She was doing it again. Deflecting attention. No doubt because—

He turned his head to look at her. *Mais*, yeah. She was freaking out all right. Even worse than he was.

"You know, that just about killed me," he said. .

She carefully studied the Spanish moss blowing in the breeze above them. "A broken arm?"

Like she didn't know what he was talking about. "Not being able to finish what we started."

"What, twice wasn't enough for you?" Her eyes squeezed shut for a second. "Sorry." She lifted her bottom to pull up her jeans. "We should go now."

He quickly did the same, wincing as he zipped over his hard-on, then caught her around the waist as she tried to sit up. He rolled on top of her, pinning her down. She wriggled under him, trying to get away. *Dieu*, so tempting.

"Don't," he warned gruffly.

She peered up at him, agitated as hell. "We should go," she repeated.

"Yeah. But first I've got something to say."

"Don't bother. I've heard it all before. This was fun," she recited in a monotone, "but don't get any ideas about doing it ag—"

He cut her off with a kiss. "No. Hardly." Little wonder the woman was gun-shy. "And I don't particularly appreciate being compared to whatever low-life *connard* said that to you."

She blinked up at him.

"What *I* want to say is, we'll finish this later, us. At your motel, where I can make love to you properly. With no clothes and an unlimited supply of condoms."

For a law enforcement officer, it was amazing how often she blushed. And yet she said, "I don't think so. This was clearly a mistake, and—"

He snorted incredulously. "You mean, it's been fun, but don' get any ideas about doing it again?"

She had the grace to blush even redder. "Don't push it, Lafayette. You know what I mean."

"Do I?"

"Oh. I'm supposed to believe you've all of a sudden done a one-eighty about me for a reason *other* than the sex?" she accused.

Bon. The answer was more complicated than he wanted to get into. "Would you believe me if I said yes?" He brushed his lips over hers to cut off her retort. "Hell, would it even matter? There's something wrong with great sex?"

"Yes!" She made a face. "No. It's just . . ." She jetted out a breath.

She was too damn easy to read. "You don' do this kind of thing," he completed for her. "Right now you can pretend I seduced you. But inviting me back to your motel room would force you to admit you wanted this to happen as much as I did. Am I close?"

"No." Her mouth thinned. "All right, maybe. A little. But that's not the point."

"And what is?"

"The point is, there's no point. Marc, we don't even like each other."

He smiled. "Oh, you are definitely growing on me."

She rolled her eyes. "Yeah, and you're really going to want to see me again tomorrow."

"Sure, why not?"

"But why?"

"I'm a man, *cher*. Great sex is a pretty damn good reason for a man to want to see a woman."

She actually smiled. A wry, unwilling smile, but nevertheless, there it was. A hell of a lot better than tears. "You really are a prick," she said, but there was no malice in the words.

He grinned. "Been called worse. Look—" He opened his mouth to tell her they should play it by ear, go with what felt right, but then suddenly he remembered. And the unexpected happiness he was feeling caved right in on itself.

He was in the middle of an op. There was no *way* he could play *any*thing by ear.

Her brow raised. "Yeah?"

And his job was to *get rid* of the woman. Not start a damn affair with her!

Merde. What was *wrong* with him?

When he remained silent, her expression darkened. A few moments before, her arms had crept up around his neck, but now they recoiled and she shoved at his chest. "Off," she said.

"Tara, wait."

"*Now.*"

He wanted to argue, tell her he really did want to see her again. But if he fulfilled his assignment, that would be impossible. She'd be gone, and he'd be fully occupied hunting tangos.

Merde. Merde. Putain de merde.

He rolled off her again, scrubbing his face with his hands as he lay on the jetty and listened to her jump to her feet and march over to where the kayak was tied up.

"Are you coming?" she asked tightly.

Unfortunate choice of words, he thought idly.

"Apparently not," he muttered under his breath, and with a quiet curse, he got up, too. And wondered if there was any earthly way to turn this situation around and make it work.

Because the hell of it was, she really *was* growing on him.

TARA was used to not measuring up.

Her army sergeant father was a cold, hard man with uncompromisingly high standards of both behavior and performance. Growing up, she'd never quite managed to meet those impossible standards. He'd just shake his head and walk away after barking out his displeasure. Her state police captain felt much the same way about her.

But they were both wrong.

The captain was nothing but a mean, chauvinist good ol' boy relic from a bygone era when women were expected to keep a man's house and have his babies, nothing more. Certainly not become a cop. Her father was a military lifer who'd pulled himself up from the depths of poverty by his bootstraps through ruthless discipline and sheer orneriness. Hardly surprising he held everyone else up to his own yard-stick.

Including Tara's mother, in whom he'd also been persistently disappointed. But her mama's unconditional love for Tara had been living proof of the unreasonableness of her father's opinion. And convinced her with its steadfast warmth and approval that she was worth loving. She still believed that with all her heart. Other than maybe in the deepest, most hidden part of it, which was what compelled her to keep trying after so much bitter disappointment. It was a daughter's duty to please her father.

But to Marc Lafayette she owed nothing. Not a blessed thing. She'd already given him more than he was entitled to.

So she shut off the hurt at his rejection and concentrated on the task at hand.

Or tried to.

She felt him come up behind her as she untied the kayak's line from the mooring post at the end of the dock and stand there, looming over her, like her father had so many times in the past. Lafayette didn't say a word, either. Just loomed, his shadow falling over her as her fingers fumbled with the knot.

Seconds stretched out, and finally it came undone. She dragged the kayak up alongside, stalling. She'd have to stand up now. Despite the fact that he was too close. Body-brushing close. But it was either stand and possibly let her body touch his or fall into the swamp trying to avoid it.

Before she could decide which would be worse, he knelt down behind her and took the rope from her hand.

God help her.

"Turns out," she told her reluctant lover without looking at him, "I won't be needing your services for the rest of the day, after all. Just drop me back at the Au Chien and you can go."

He hesitated, then cupped his hands on her shoulders. "Can't do that, *cher*."

She stiffened. What was he playing at? "Don't make this harder than it is, Lafayette."

"You still have two interviews to do. I promised to take you."

"That's not necessary. Besides, you said those guys probably wouldn't be around until after work."

He didn't prevent her when she stood up, but followed along, then turned her, keeping hold of her arms. "That's true," he said. His dark eyes were somber as he met her gaze. So different from the burning heat that had simmered in them just an hour before. An hour that now seemed like a lifetime ago.

She looked away, not wanting to remember.

"Tara, there's something I have to do."

"And now you'll have the rest of the afternoon to do it," she told him evenly. Keeping it together.

He cleared his throat. "Okay. You were right. I *was* trying to get away from you earlier. But just for an hour or two, I swear. And only because there are some buildings I need to take a look at," he said.

Buildings. Yeah. Did she *look* like an idiot?

"Like I said," she reiterated, extricating herself from his grasp, "you're free to go."

"Come with me," he said.

She shook her head. "No time." Or interest. Whatever his game was, she was done playing.

"One of the places is pretty close by," he persisted. "It won't take long, I promise. You can keep an eye out for more dead birds along the way."

"Why?" she asked testily.

"I don't want to leave you like this."

Oh. Please.

"No," she corrected. "Why do you need to see these mythical buildings?"

As an excuse, it seemed pretty lame. Why not just take her up on her offer to leave? Something was going on here, but she couldn't for the life of her figure out what. For some inexplicable reason, her cop instincts started going off like rockets.

"Investment," he said with a totally straight face.

She took in his long hair and stubbled jaw, his well-worn clothes. Remembered his comment about needing a job.

"Yeah. I believe that." *Not.* "Try again."

He pursed his lips. Met her look with one of his own. "Sorry. I can't tell you why," he finally said. "It's just something I need to do. Can't you just trust me?"

Hello? Had he *been* there for the last ten minutes?

His face had gone completely neutral, his black eyes devoid of . . . of anything at all.

More rockets went off. My God. The man was keeping secrets! Big secrets, by the look of it. From a *cop.*

She narrowed her eyes. "Lafayette, are you into something illegal?"

No change. Not an eyelash flutter as he said, "No. I'm not."

She was a pretty good judge of lies, and to her mild surprise, this didn't feel like one. Which left . . . what?

She looked at him again. Really looked. At his tall, proud bearing, his straight shoulders, the hard, tight muscles of his perfectly toned body, his absolute stillness as he waited for her reaction.

And got the most peculiar feeling in the pit of her stomach.

It started out as a niggle, but almost immediately burst into full Technicolor certainty.

Marc Lafayette is not who he is pretending to be. He sure as hell wasn't a down-on-his-luck wilderness guide.

How could she have been so blind?

Her pulse kicked up. Damn.

Okay, okay. *Stay calm.*

Possibilities?

Undercover cop? Or some other kind of law enforcement, investigating the same thing she was?

But that made no sense—he would have just told her, so they could work together on it, instead of at cross-purposes.

So, then . . .

The first trickle of fear sifted through her when she suddenly recalled how he'd deliberately pursued her, using all his considerable charms to talk her into hiring him for this job. Then tried his damndest to scare her into abandoning her investigation.

Was he still trying to charm her, even now?

Was *that* what the sex had been about? The next tactic on his list?

She backed away from him slowly, wondering what in hell she'd gotten herself into.

Who *was* this guy?

And more important, what did he want with her?

TEN

GINA was floating in a sea of pain, buffeted by waves of shock.

It was a sea of oranges and reds, and blacks and blues; liquid hot and sticky sweet, and so cold she shivered uncontrollably. It smelled like fear and her own urine.

She wanted to sob, to scream and pound her fists in rage against what had been done to her. Miraculously, she'd been spared the unspeakable violation she'd been led to expect. But she had paid dearly for the evil bastard's inability to follow through on his lewd threats. He'd used his fists and his boots instead. She could barely move, even to breathe.

Warm fingers touched the moisture on her cheek. She flinched away, cried out.

"Hush," said a masculine voice. Her ears hummed and gurgled, and the word came to her muffled, as though wrapped in cotton batting.

"Don't touch me," she pleaded, her voice a fragile thread in the vast and endless ocean.

"He's an animal," the deep voice said, its disapproval clear, even through the mounds of cotton.

Odd . . .

"I am sorry," it said.

And then she felt a tiny prick in her arm. Or was it her imagination? How could she feel anything at all over the terrible sea of pain . . .

But then, bit by bit, the sea swallowed her. And all sensation slowly ebbed away, became unreal.

Oh, thank you.

Thankyouthankyou.

Suddenly she was flying, soaring above it all, leaving the memories behind in a jumble of nothingness. Blessed peace. Soothing masculine voice. She wanted to sleep. Sleep and sleep and sleep, forever and ever.

With a last effort she forced her eyes open. To see the man who had delivered her from the awful nightmare of pain.

Oh, thank you!

But . . .

But she was so very sleepy. Her arms and legs were leaden, her blood thick and slowing in her veins. Her mind numb and dizzy. Her vision blurred.

"Hush, now," he said again, his voice low and comforting, his fingertips gentle against her bruised cheek.

Who was this man? Did he sound familiar? Did he?

She fought to keep her eyelids open, but they were falling, falling, as though weighted down with heavy stones.

It was no use. She lost the battle. And her mind emptied into the great, blank void of nothingness.

"JUST forwarded those phone LUDs you asked for, Special Agent Haywood."

Rebel glanced up distractedly from the disorderly scatter of files that covered her desk and smiled as the office newbie, a kid fresh from the Academy a few weeks back, took a step into her office. "Thanks, Chip." She glanced at the clock: 4:53 p.m. "Any news on when the new SAC for the Cappozi case will be in?"

"Word is, his plane was four hours late. He's wheels down now, but stuck in traffic somewhere between here and La-Guardia."

"Excellent." She turned back to quickly type a few strokes on her keyboard, downloading the computer file Chip had sent her.

The kid smirked. "Excellent he's stuck in traffic? Or excellent he's finally arrived?"

"Both," she said. "I think I'm on to something big, but I need to nail down a few things before reporting." She opened and scrolled down the file of LUDs—or local usage details—which was the list of phone numbers Gina Cappozi had dialed and received over the month preceding her disappearance. Not a very long list. Mostly calls to and from the Columbia U. lab she where worked and the hospital where she volunteered a couple days a week. A few take-out restaurants. Her friend Rainie. Not much else. Dr. Cappozi didn't have much of a social life, it seemed.

Hmm. What was this?

Rebel frowned. "Why doesn't this number have the owner's name listed?" she asked Chip, pointing to one. The same number appeared again farther down. Three times.

He shook his head. "Throwaway cell. We're trying to trace it, at least to point of sale, but so far no luck."

"No luck?" She glanced at him incredulously. "Chip. We're the FBI, for Pete's sake. We can trace anything."

He shrugged. "Hey, I'm just the gopher."

"Not even where the phone was purchased?"

Again, he shrugged. "They're still working on it."

Wow. What was with *that*?

After he left, she rolled back in her office chair and stared at the numbers on the computer screen. In addition to the unaccounted-for phone number, one other familiar number jumped boldly out at her from the list.

CIA.

Well, naturally it wasn't actually listed as Central Intelligence Agency, but she recognized the name of the front used for one of their covert units. Because she'd been their liaison for two years.

Zero Unit.

And wasn't *that* interesting?

In her head she did a victory dance. Oh, yeah. Oh, yeah. Corroborating proof that the information old Mrs. Duluth had given her was dead on target.

Gina Cappozi's ex-fiancé, Wade last name–unknown, who

was an FBI agent, must have given Gina the phone number of Zero Unit when she'd become frantic about her friend Rainie—who in fact *had* been detained by Zero Unit, as attested to by Rainie herself.

And Mrs. D had also said Gina met her latest boyfriend, Gregg-with-two-g's last name–also-unknown, by calling that same phone number and talking to him about Rainie's disappearance. The camo, the boots, the motorcycle that Mrs. Duluth complained about—it all fit.

The new boyfriend was an operator. A ZU operator.

And he was the last person to see Gina Cappozi before her abduction.

Rebel swiftly made some notes so she would sound coherent to the new SAC when she reported it to him. Then she went back to her keyboard. The first question the SAC would ask was, what is the FBI agent ex-fiancé's name? Didn't Mrs. D say something about mountains? She needed a more precise answer. She wanted to growl in frustration—and smack Kick Jackson for not telling her about this guy. She didn't have Kick's direct number. The few times they'd spoken about the Cappozi case, she'd had to ask Alex to have Kick call her. So she put in a call to his wife, Rainie, instead.

There were a few minutes of polite chitchat and listening with her teeth gritted while the other woman—a nurse who had been hired by STORM to be Alex's nurse at Haven Oaks Sanatorium—talked cheerfully about how well he was doing and how nice his pretty fiancée, Helena, was.

"Speaking of fiancés," Rebel gratefully seized the opportunity to change the subject, "I'm calling to ask if you know what Gina Cappozi's ex-fiancé's name is. I need to get hold of him."

"Why, sure. It's Wade Montana."

Hallelujah. Didn't get much closer to mountains than Montana.

"What do you need him for?" Rainie asked.

"Just a quick question about that last phone call Gina made to him," she said.

"Ah. About my disappearance," Rainie murmured guiltily.

"Don't go there," Rebel told her gently. She knew Rainie blamed herself for Gina's kidnapping. "This isn't your fault."

Rainie sighed unhappily, but didn't argue. "But what if she's—"

"She isn't. They need her alive. And we're going to find her."

She thanked Rainie and promised to say hi next time she was up at Haven Oaks. *Hopefully not anytime soon.*

She was adding the name to her other notes when a knock came on her door. Chip stuck his head in again. "Special Agent Haywood? The new SAC is here. Conference room, pronto."

"On my way."

Excited, she gathered her materials and swiftly made her way to the conference room located three floors down. There were five people on the Cappozi task force, six counting the new special agent in charge, who'd been brought in from another field office to take over for the previous SAC who'd suffered an unexpected heart attack two days earlier.

She took a seat at the big black table just as the bureau chief entered and strode straight to the front of the room, followed closely by a good-looking fortyish man dressed in standard FBI uniform—dark blue suit, white dress shirt, striped tie, with a pair of dark sunglasses hanging out of his breast pocket and a briefcase in his hand. His brown hair was short but stylish, and his ski tan gave him an athletic, all-American look, as did his square jaw and clear blue eyes. If he was the least bit frazzled by the day's airline delays, it didn't show.

While the bureau chief stepped behind the podium, the other man snapped open his briefcase and extracted a pile of manila folders.

"Good afternoon, people," the chief said, gathering everyone's attention. "Apologize for the lateness of this meeting." Chip came in and handed him and the other guy each a cup of coffee, then put a full carafe on the table. "Thanks. I have a feeling y'all are going to need that." He turned to the second man. "Ready?"

He stepped up beside the chief. "Yes, sir."

"All right. NYFO is extremely lucky to be able to borrow one of D.C.'s most outstanding agents. Folks, I'd like to introduce you to your new boss on the Cappozi case. Special Agent in Charge, Wade Montana."

ELEVEN

THE sun was precariously close to setting. Already the glowing orb was well below the treetops, filtered into a dappled quilt of yellows and greens, shadow and light, covering the lush junglelike Louisiana foliage.

Over the past two hours, Tara's heartbeat had managed to slow down from a charging locomotive to merely a fast trot.

She'd agreed to come along with Marc Lafayette to check out his mysterious "buildings" because her professional instincts had gone on red alert, temporarily overshadowing her concern for personal safety. She'd wanted to know who this man was, what he was up to, and exactly what he was hiding. Enough to swallow her sizeable misgivings and let him paddle her even farther into the depths of the swamp.

Now she was questioning the wisdom of that move. She might be a cop, but she was alone with no way to call for backup if things turned ugly.

But they hadn't. In fact, Lafayette hadn't done a thing that was threatening. Not even slightly. Hadn't raised a hand to her, or his voice. Certainly not a weapon.

So why did she have the distinct feeling she was being held hostage?

Because (a) he hadn't answered her questions, either, and (b) he was behaving suspiciously.

He'd checked out his buildings, all right. Two of them. Like a pro. Hell, like a freaking SWAT guy in full stealth mode.

At the first place, he'd pulled the kayak to shore a few hundred yards from a large scrap heap of a pumping station surrounded by piles of salvage metal and junk, located on the edge of the swamp along a remote section of private back road. A track, really, which she could barely see for the trees and vines choking it.

From somewhere in the hollow depths of the kayak behind his seat he'd produced a double-barreled Mossberg shotgun. Oh. My. God. How had she missed seeing *that* before?

"Stay here," he'd admonished her quietly. Then he'd grabbed the dry bag and slithered over the side of the kayak like a water snake into the shallows and disappeared.

Totally freaked-out, Tara's first thought after seeing that shotgun had been to ditch him. Fast. Hightail it down that overgrown path calling itself a road and get the hell out of there. He was *armed*? Enough was enough.

But then she'd looked around. She had no clue where she was. He'd taken the bag containing their few supplies . . . including her SIG-Sauer. Even if Lafayette didn't kill her outright, without him to guide her back to civilization she'd probably get lost and die out there anyway. Or have her throat slit by whatever low-life scum was occupying that pump station. The place didn't exactly look welcoming.

So, yeah. That's why she'd stayed put in the kayak, hidden from view.

Self-preservation.

Ha. Talk about terminally misplaced trust.

Natch, she'd searched the kayak as soon as he'd gone. Every last square inch of it. Found nothing. Big surprise. He'd taken the dry bag and along with it any incriminating evidence. The man was definitely not stupid.

Seizing the bull by the horns, when he returned she'd asked him point-blank, "What the hell are you looking for? And don't tell me it's investment property. I know you're after something else."

He'd just given her one of his killer smiles. *Yikes. Bad choice of words.* "Now, what would that be, *cher?*" Then he'd distracted her with a kiss.

Like she couldn't see right through *that* well-worn tactic.

Though admittedly, it *had* chased the whole what-was-he-doing question right out of her head. At least until he'd winked and started paddling again.

The second building he'd checked out had literally been in the middle of nowhere. Surrounded on all sides by nothing but black water and massive trees, they came suddenly upon a small country store built high on stilts, with a veranda full of crab traps and a newly hand-painted sign in bright yellow that read *T-Garou's Bait and General Store. Night Crawlers! Faut Carot! Sea Bob!*

Marc left her behind again, with instructions to stay put. Again he took the dry bag. And disappeared for twenty long minutes. Which was a lot of time for her to think.

The man was obviously on a hunt. For what, she couldn't guess. But one thing was clear. The pressure he'd put on her last night to hire him had nothing to do with their attraction or him needing a job. He'd been worried she would interfere with his plans—whatever they were—so he'd put himself directly in her path and tried to deflect her.

The setup was obvious now: sexy Cajun guide leads the clueless statie on a wild-goose chase, doing everything he can to scare her off so he can return unhindered to his *real* agenda. And when that didn't work, he'd seduced her with his amazing body and skills as a lover, so she wouldn't question him when he boldly pursued whatever it was, right under her nose.

She definitely wanted to know what that agenda was. And if it was against the law.

Could he be working for drug dealers searching for a new place to cook? Gunrunners looking for a remote place to stash stolen weapons? Or even the people responsible for the deadly pollution she was investigating, searching for a new dump site?

That thought raised goose bumps on her arms but good. Along with the thought that until now, she'd been so thoroughly misled about his motives that she'd actually had sex with the man. Twice.

Jesus.

A violent shiver worked its way down her spine, radiating out to her arms, raising more gooseflesh in its wake.

She was in such deep shit.

She had to find out the truth about him. And what his plans were for her once he found whatever he was looking for. Soon. Before it was too late.

Now they were paddling to the third building on Marc's short list, and she was having a very hard time staying calm.

The sun was about to disappear completely. No way did she want to be out in the swamp with this man after dark. Her imagination was coming up with all sorts of scenarios. None of which she particularly wanted to experience firsthand—none of the ones that were likely to happen, anyway.

"What are you thinking about, *cher*?" he interrupted her burgeoning panic from behind her, breaking the tense silence between them. "Your back is stiff as a week-old baguette."

The kayak slowed and shifted, and she felt him slide his seat up close behind hers. Her pulse thundered. He touched her upper arms and her whole body jumped.

"Hey, hey." His fingers tightened on her briefly. "What is it, *cher*? You're acting like you're suddenly afraid of me." He paused, then asked, "Are you?"

She looked at him over her shoulder. "Should I be?"

His eyes were dark and shuttered, unrevealing of whatever was going on behind them. Long-lashed, lean-cheeked, stubble-jawed. He was the epitome of a bad, bad boy. Despite the danger, her heart sped faster. Or maybe *because* of it. A bad boy could still be a good man.

Or not.

Oh, God.

Her throat ached with desire just looking at him. What was *wrong* with her?

"Tara, you're my lover. A man protects his lover."

"Not all men," she murmured. In her job, she'd seen plenty who'd done the opposite.

He cupped her face and angled his head around to meet her gaze. "This one does."

He kissed her, his mouth gentle at first, then his tongue slowly going deep and thorough. An unwelcome surge of

need swept through her body. Her nipples hardened painfully, and between her legs a desperate want coiled like a
tight spring.

Pulling away, she shook off the unwanted response.
"Then tell me what's going on."

"Nothing's going on, *cher*."

She gripped her paddle and faced forward again. Nobody
should be that good at lying. And he was. Lying. She could
feel it. "Take me back to the Au Chien. It's getting late and I
need to do those interviews."

"All right," he said. "After I check out this last place."

She let out a measured breath. "Marc—"

His warm breath spilled along her neck, sending a tin-
gling shiver across her pulsing nerves. "And when we're
done with those interviews, we can go back to your place and
I'll show you you've got nothing to be afraid of."

She swallowed down the urge to turn around and give him
a big piece of her mind. Best not to piss him off. But, like,
hello? *Can you say no way in hell?*

The only thing she'd be doing after making it back to the
safety of her police cruiser was to radio in and have someone
from the department run a thorough check on him. He
seemed to forget she was a police officer. You couldn't go
around acting like a criminal without invoking suspicion. No
doubt he thought having sex with her would make her forget
about doing her job.

Fat chance.

When he slowed the kayak a short while later and steered
it up to the shore, she made a decision.

She had to stop being a wuss. He was never going to vol-
untarily tell her what he was doing. She had to use her own
skills and ingenuity to find out if he was up to something
illegal.

So this time when he went to check his "building," she
would follow him.

That was the plan, anyway.

But the man was like a ghost.

After he left her in the kayak, she counted to thirty, then
took off in pursuit. Ten seconds later, she'd lost him in the
junglelike vegetation. There was barely enough daylight left

to walk without tripping, let alone follow anyone.

As it happened, he was heading away from the bayou on a spit of land surrounded on three sides by water, so it wasn't hard to figure out which way he went. And the moon was coming up, so it should get a bit lighter soon. She decided to keep going.

Almost right away she passed a dense flowering shrub with an isolated scattering of dropped flowers around the base—a lot more than the neighboring bushes. A childhood spent in the woods of Pennsylvania had taught her that usually meant the flowers had been knocked off by an animal.

An alligator? Big cat? Or had it been brushed by an animal of the two-legged variety . . . ?

She stopped, turned back, and studied it. Picking up a long stick, she cautiously lifted the lower branches. And wouldn't you know, there it was. *The dry bag.* Stashed beneath the bush.

Damn, she was good.

She knelt down and quickly opened up the bag, digging around for her SIG. Instead, she found something hard and rectangular. She pulled it out.

What the—

A walkie-talkie? Except larger. Like some kind of military communications device. She glanced up through the dense trees at the nearly dark patches of sky. Cell phones didn't work out here in the bayou. A satellite phone would.

But why would he have one of those?

Most likely because (a) whatever he was involved in was big enough to warrant serious equipment, and (b) there were other people involved.

Oh.

Shit.

She contemplated the satphone for a long moment. Was anyone on the other end of this thing? Waiting for Lafayette to check in? Maybe she should find out.

Pulse hammering in her fingertips, she turned it on. And pushed the call button. After a short burst of static, it didn't make a sound. For about ten seconds.

Then a voice—a *female* voice—said, "STORM Alpha Zulu here, go ahead STORM Mike, over."

Military-speak? She'd thought earlier this morning that he might be ex-military. Damn. No one better to run guns than a group of disillusioned ex-grunts.

"STORM Alpha Zulu to STORM Mike, come on back, over."

Okay. Mike stood for the letter M. Obviously meaning Marc. So he and the woman on the other end were on a first-name basis. Who was this zulu chick?

She sounded young.

And pretty.

Tara silently groaned. *Wow.* So much for objectivity. Jealous of a *voice*? How screwed up was *that*?

She took a deep breath.

Hell, being jealous at *all* was so far beyond screwed up she was completely appalled at herself.

She switched off the satphone and replaced it in the dry bag, giving one last grope for the SIG. No joy. But she did find a Kel-Lite. At least she could use that.

He must have taken the SIG with him. Was he expecting trouble? She thought about the shotgun he'd kept hidden. Or was he expecting to *be* the trouble . . . ?

Rubbing her arms against a growing chill, she stashed the dry bag, switched on the flashlight, and took off again in the direction he'd disappeared.

And prayed she didn't live to regret it.

"SPECIAL Agent Haywood?"

Rebel glanced up from gathering her notes from the table. It had been a stressful briefing. And endless. Two hours and change. The whole time spent wishing she were anywhere but there.

All because the man Rebel had just put on her Top Two Suspects List in the Gina Cappozi disappearance had unexpectedly—and hair-raisingly—turned out to be the new SAC on the case.

She had to think about this. Hard.

Not a single word had she spoken during the entire briefing. Terrified if she opened her mouth the accusation would come hurtling out. But without proof, there would go her career, just as fast. Her stomach felt like she'd swallowed nails.

Nuts on thinking about it. Even if she didn't have proof, she needed to *tell* someone. Preferably Chief Jansson. He'd yank that poser off the case so fast he—

"Special Agent Haywood? Is everything all right?"

She came to with a start. SAC Wade Montana was standing right behind her. Her heartbeat took off at a gallop.

"Yes," she blurted out, spinning around so fast the papers in her hands flew all over the place. "I'm fine."

Montana's brows rose as he watched the snowfall of notes. "Sure?"

She felt her face go crimson. She didn't answer, but dropped to her knees to gather them from the floor, praying her stockings didn't run.

"I couldn't help but notice you didn't say anything during the meeting," he said.

Of course he had. Dealing with sixteen unfamiliar agents, including the five other Cappozi task force members, all new faces in a new office, with a new chief and on a new case, he *would* notice every detail. Obviously his reputation was no accident.

"It's my first week on the task force, sir," she said. "Just getting my bearings. Better to listen than talk, and all that."

"Commendable." He watched her stuff the papers into her notebook and rise. "But complete bullshit. Walk with me to my office."

Just kill me now. She swallowed. "Sure. Sir."

"Please. I'm not one for formality. Call me Wade. I assume I may call you Rebel?"

"Um. Yeah. Of course, sir. Um . . . Wade. Sir."

He chuckled. "How long have you been with the Bureau, Rebel?"

She had the creepiest feeling he already knew the answer. "Five years."

"Mm-hmm. And before that?"

"University of South Carolina. Masters in criminal justice."

He nodded. "Good."

They arrived at his office and he opened the door, indicating she should go in before him.

Which was the last thing she wanted to do. "It's late. I'm sure you have things to—"

"Yes, I do. And one of them is to talk to you. Please have a seat." He held the door and gave her a hard look.

Help.

She went in and sat down in the visitor's chair. He perched on the corner of his desk so his knee was almost touching hers.

Oka-ay.

She risked a glance up at his face. What exactly was going on here?

Wade Montana was handsome, no doubt about it. Probably at least ten years her senior, but the kind of forty-something that made a man look affluent, sexy, in his prime—fit, tanned, tailored, and financially sound. Any female in the office would be drooling all over him. *Had* been drooling all over him since he arrived. Every female except her.

Because she knew the truth about him.

"So. Rebel. What am I going to do with you?" he said conversationally.

A shiver tingled up her spine. "What do you mean, sir? Wade." She caught the look in his eyes. "Sir."

"I mean, you *know*. About me. Don't you." Not a question.

She didn't insult either of them by pretending not to understand. It was crystal clear in his expression: she was *so* busted. "What gave me away?"

He smiled wryly. "Your poker face could use work." He sobered. "Have you told anyone else?"

Her pulse took off faster than Jeff Gordon at the pole, but she kept it together and regarded the SAC coolly. "Is this the part where I tell you I've left a letter with my attorney to be delivered to the chief if anything bad happens to me?"

Again he chuckled. But there was no humor in those sharp eyes. "Let's cut to the chase, shall we? How much do you know?"

"Everything."

He sighed. "Oh, I doubt that very much."

"Then, enough," she amended. "Enough to know you shouldn't be the SAC on this case. You shouldn't even be working on it."

He glanced at the floor for several heartbeats. "It's true I have history with Gina Cappozi," he admitted. "We were engaged, and she broke it off. Which means anyone with half a brain will automatically shoot me to the top of their suspect list."

He looked up and studied her, but she kept her mouth firmly shut. He was doing perfectly well without her input. Her poker face might need help, but her interrogation technique was just fine, thank you very much.

"Here's the thing," he said somberly. "I may be responsible for setting off a chain of events that led to a woman I care deeply about being kidnapped by God knows who and made to do God knows what. *Me*." He closed his eyes and took a breath. Opened them. Drilled her. "Do you understand? *I* may have done that to her." His voice cracked and he rose abruptly from the desk, turned away, and plunged his hands into his pockets. "I've got to find her, Rebel. If it's the last thing I do with the Bureau."

She stared at his back for a long moment. He stood straight and tall, uncompromising. Yet the heavenward tilt of his head, the tenseness of his shoulder muscles radiating through the fine cloth of his suit jacket, it all made him seem incongruently vulnerable.

God help her, she wanted to believe him.

She thought about her own involvement in the case, being so determined to solve it simply because of a tenuous connection to Gina through Alex Zane's friend Kick. How must this man be feeling?

"Okay," she said at length. "I guess I do understand."

Visibly relieved, he exhaled. Faced her. "Then be my assistant. Work with me. Help me get her back. Watch my every move, if you must. So you know I'm not trying to cover up anything."

It all sounded so reasonable.

Almost *too* reasonable.

Not really joking, she said, "Looks like I'll have to give one of those letters to my attorney, after all."

He smiled anyway. "Whatever you need to get the job done."

She stood up. "Let me sleep on the offer."

His smile dimmed. "I could order you to do it."

"And I could rat you out."

He held her gaze. But she didn't intimidate that easily. He nodded once. "Fine. Let me know in the morning."

"I will."

Assuming she lived that long.

Good grief. The man was personally involved with Gina Cappozi, and he had just confirmed setting in motion her kidnapping. Exactly as Rebel had theorized. The question was, had it been inadvertent? An unforeseen outcome of trying to help her find her best friend, Rainie? Or had he done it deliberately, as revenge for Gina having jilted him, or for some other unknown reason . . . ? Like a hefty payoff from a terrorist looking for a scientist with skills matching hers? Maybe a little of both?

Either way, bottom line, he shouldn't be on the case. But Wade Montana's reputation was spotless. Before she reported him and possibly ruined his career, not to mention hers, she needed more solid evidence than the say-so of a ditzy octogenarian and her own paranoid instincts.

The first thing she needed to do was talk to Kick Jackson. Tonight.

TWELVE

SOMEONE was following him.

One guess who.

Fils du putain. He supposed it had been inevitable, but hell of a time for Tara to go commando on him.

Jetting out a sigh, Marc racked the Mossberg. Just in case he was wrong. Back at T-Garou's Bait and General Store, he'd casually asked about this last place on his informant's list—a crumbling, deserted cotton mill. Been warned to give it a wide berth. Some *bien mauvais drigaille* had squatted in what was left of the building and were supposedly using it as a meth lab. Garbage who would shoot first and never bother to ask questions.

Just the kind of scum Marc was looking for. He wouldn't put it past the al Sayika terrorist cell to masquerade as drug dealers.

And he was pretty sure this was no meth lab. There was no trace in the swamp-scented air of the distinctive putrid odor of chemicals cooking. *Non*, this was something else. Like a secret bioweapons lab?

Raising the thermal imaging night-vision binoculars he'd taken from the dry bag, he did a visual sweep, looking for any sign of a guard or the occupants. Dense trees were like a curtain surrounding him, so all that popped were a few birds and lizards, and something furry on four legs, possibly a possum or squirrel.

He could hear Tara snapping twigs underfoot a few hundred yards back. *Foutu Dieu.* He didn't want her anywhere near this place. Why couldn't the woman just do as she was told?

The burned-out carcass of the old cotton mill loomed in front of him. Seemingly deserted. NVBs couldn't see through walls, even crumbling ones, but he'd see anything alive and breathing on the outside. If he were alone, he'd put on the headgear so he could go hands-free and not get surprised by one of the bads. Marc didn't like surprises. But if he was all rigged up like an extra for *Generation Kill*, when Tara caught up to him it would be just one more thing he couldn't explain.

Not that she wasn't already convinced he was up to no good. Asking him questions he couldn't answer without outright lying. He hated lying to a woman he was sleeping with. His mama had brought him up to be a better man than that.

Which possibly explained his previous two-year dry spell.

Merde. Tara Reeves was one complication he did not need right now. And yet, not only had he had sex with her, he hadn't been able to bring himself to get rid of the woman once and for all when the opportunity presented itself. *Mais non.* Instead he'd asked her to come along with him. On a mission reconnaissance. *Co fou.* How stupid was *that*?

Suddenly, a subtle noise up ahead made him halt in his tracks. He cocked an ear. From along the uneven brick wall of the cotton mill, footsteps sounded—careful, furtive.

He melted into the heavy greenery, making himself invisible. Slid on his headgear and snapped the NVB eyepiece down in front of his left eye. Better to be alive and have to explain than dead and sorry.

Sure enough, a bright green figure flashed into focus. Someone was creeping along the wall. Too tall for Tara. It was a man. Carrying some kind of submachine gun.

Bingo.

This could really be them—the terrorists.

Which meant he had to get Tara the fuck out of there.

As he turned and crouch-ran toward her position, he saw the unmistakable signature of two people about a hundred yards out. *Tara.* And another man with a gun. *Closing in on her.*

"Tara, behind you!" Marc shouted, taking off at a run toward her through the underbrush.

She whirled around just in time to avoid her assailant's jerky grab at her arm. She yelled, but Marc couldn't hear her words.

He sprinted through the trees to reach her, branches whipping across his face, his boots feeling like they were made of lead.

"Touch her and you're a dead man!" he shouted, slinging the Mossberg onto his back by its strap and whipping out his Beretta. If he had to shoot the fucker, he didn't want her caught in the shotgun's blast.

Behind him, he heard the first man exclaim and start to crash blindly through the foliage in pursuit, shouting obscenities. Somewhere in his mind it registered they were *Cajun* obscenities.

Therefore probably not the tangos.

Half of him was relieved—fewer opponents to deal with—but the other half was furious that he couldn't just blow these two assholes away with impunity. *No*body put hands on his woman and got away with it.

In the NVBs, Tara's bright blob merged with her attacker's in a ball of thrashing limbs and more yelling. *Fils du diable.* He pointed the Beretta at the sky and squeezed off a couple of warning rounds.

"*Arrête!* Get off her or I'll blow your damn head off!" he roared as his boots ate up the remaining ground between them. The guy had Tara's arm twisted up behind her back and was screaming in her ear—

Except—

Marc came to a skidding halt.

Quoi?

It was *Tara* who had the man's arm twisted up behind *his* back. And she was holding a gun next to his ear as he jerked and twitched. *She* was yelling at the guy to stay still or she would blow his damn head off.

Mon Dieu. She'd overpowered *and* disarmed the man?

Marc didn't know whether to laugh or raise his hands over his head and surrender himself.

Suddenly her gun was pointed at him. "Get back!" she barked, peering at him through the darkness.

"Don't shoot, *beb.* It's me," he called, raising his gun hand and flipping up the NVBs with the other so she could see his face. Her expression was filled with suspicion as she lowered her aim to the ground.

"What the hell's going on here, Lafayette?"

"Not sure, but I think we're about to find out."

In two strides, he'd relieved her of her prisoner, stashed her behind his back—despite her squawk of protest—and yanked the bad guy in front of them both as a shield, just in time.

The first man came barreling up waving an Uzi. "You got thirty seconds to get outta here or I'll—" Uzi-man halted in confusion. "Dat you, Chaz? What da—" The machine gun wavered and the man took a step backward, his wide eyes skittering to his friend, who was dangling from Marc's hand by the collar. Both of them were twitching like frog legs.

Obviously tweaking. In other words, paranoid and unpredictable.

"Put the weapon down. *Now,*" Marc ordered Uzi-tweaker. When he didn't move, Marc tightened his grip, cutting off ol' Chaz's air so he made gurgling noises.

"Do it, Jacko!" Chaz choked out. "He crazy! Gonna kill me!"

Suddenly, Tara appeared out of the darkness behind Uzi-man and jammed her gun into his back. "That's right, jackass. Do as my friend says before I arr—"

"Before she gets *really* mad," Marc cut her off. Way to go, letting them know she was a cop. And god*damn* it! He should have known she wouldn't stay put behind him. He gave her a tight scowl, then focused on the two men.

They were younger than he'd first thought. Late teens, early twenties. Both unkempt and scrawny as beanpoles, yellow-eyed and twitchy as hell. No doubt about it, the ruined mill must be a drug establishment of some sort. Disappointment threaded through Marc as he lowered Chaz's feet to the ground.

"No need for things to get messy, boys," he told them. "We're just looking for a little information. Nothing more. Now, put down the hardware."

Jacko proved he had at least half a brain left in that jack-o'-lantern head of his. After only a short hesitation, he did as he was told.

"And you." Marc jerked the Beretta at Tara in annoyance. "Get the fuck back over here and stand behind me."

She actually snorted.

Pumpkin-head's gaze bounced back and forth between them. He wiped his nose. "Ain' sayin' nothin' without my lawyer, *boug.*"

Marc gave Chaz a push so he stumbled over to his pal. "Do we look like we give a *foutu* rat's ass about your *foutu* drug business? You'll answer my questions or severely regret it."

Four sallow eyes regarded him nervously. Took in his rig. His bearing. The weapons strapped to every limb. Then darted to Tara. Registered the way she stood and held the gun she'd so easily taken from them. And flinched at the barely restrained fury in her expression.

Of course, they had no way of knowing that particular fury was directed at *him*, not them. Still, it worked in his favor at the moment.

"Please don't kill us," Chaz whined, his dusky skin blanching pale in the moonlight.

"I told you—"

"*You* murdered those people!" Chaz blurted out hoarsely. "Don' deny it!"

Marc frowned, his long-honed internal red-flag meter pumping alarm through his veins like a double shot of adrenaline. "What people?"

Jack-for-brains shook his head. "No one. It nothin'! Chaz, he don' know what he's talkin'—"

"*What* people?" Marc took a threatening step toward them.

Jacko's beanstalk frame spasmed violently. "Dem over at Bayou Morreau!"

"Dead? You've actually seen these dead people?"

They both nodded jerkily.

Marc did a quick mental map. Bayou Morreau was several miles southwest of their present position. Far into the swamplands. As isolated as it got. "How many?"

Jacko's shoulders hunched together, like he was trying to make himself invisible. "Five. Mebbe six."

Marc briefly met Tara's horrified gaze. *Dieu.*

"How did they die?" she asked.

Both kids looked like they were going to puke. "Dunno."

"How?" Marc demanded.

"Seriously, *boug.* No idea," Jacko rushed to say, the words cracking like dry kindling underfoot. "All's I know is dey looked sick, dem. Like dey'd choked on their own vomit or somethin'. An' covered in black blisters."

Tara's hand flew to her mouth. Marc's stomach dropped. *Symptoms of anthrax and avian flu.* "What made you think they were murdered?" he asked.

"'Cause," Jacko said, crossing his arms and pressing them into his gut, like it hurt, "dey's all shackled together in leg irons. Like a *foutu* chain gang."

"**STORM** Alpha Six, this is STORM Mike, over."

When Lafayette's call came in on the satphone, Bobby Lee grabbed it off the truck dash before Zimmie could reach it.

"STORM Mike, this is STORM Alpha Six actual. You all right, buddy? Over."

"Affirmative, over." Marc sounded far away but fine.

"What's going on out there?" Bobby Lee asked. "Got a dead-air transmission from you earlier and haven't been able to raise you since. Over."

Bobby Lee heard a colorful swear word, then there was a half minute of static. "Sorry about that," Marc said when he came back. "I'll explain when you get here. We got a tip on a possible crime scene containing five or more DBs. Sounds like our tangos' handiwork, over."

Holy Jesus. *Five dead bodies?*

"What the hell happened, over?" Bobby Lee asked.

"From the description, same kind of biologicals as the animal kills. Looks like the weapon-testing has escalated. Recommend you alert STORM Command and the Homies to arrange biocontainment while we get eyes on the situation. Stand by for details, over."

STORM Command and Homeland Security could probably have boots on ground within the hour. There was already a hazmat point team mobilizing in Baton Rouge to assist in the takedown of the lab when Bobby Lee's team located it. With any luck they were good to go.

He made a writing motion to Zimmie. "Go ahead," he told Marc.

Zimmie scribbled down information as Quinn spun the truck around on the highway and gunned it toward home base to fetch the speedboat. He didn't care for traversing the swamp at night, but the UAV would help navigate, and he didn't want to lose a single minute.

The hair rose on the back of his neck as Lafayette described what the informant had told him about the scene. Jesus. Abbas Tawhid really was a complete psychopath.

"Copy that. We're oscar mike," Bobby Lee said with a grimace, and floored the gas. "Don't even think about going near that place until we get there with the hazmat gear, Lafayette. Rendezvous in"—he glanced at his watch—"thirty. Over."

"Copy that," Marc came back. "Yeah, and STORM Alpha Six? There's one other minor detail, over."

Quinn groaned inwardly. With Marc, details were never minor. "What's that, over?"

"I, uh, seem to have acquired myself another prisoner, over."

Okay, *prisoner*? Bobby Lee blinked. Glanced at Zimmie, who seemed equally perplexed. Marc sounded more chagrined than worried or heated, so it couldn't be a tango.

"Besides the *witnesses*?" he demanded, semi-alarmed.

"Um, yeah."

WTF?

And that's when it hit him. Ah, *shit*. Tara Reeves!

"Lafayette. *Please* tell me you did not put a Louisiana state trooper in handcuffs."

The sound of a clearing throat came over the satphone. "Flex-cuffs, actually. Hell, she's yelling at me about calling in the LSP and the county sheriff. Damn lucky I don't gag her, too."

Sure enough, in the background Bobby Lee could just make

out a very angry woman yelling all sorts of suggestions, not all strictly limited to law enforcement procedure.

Jesus, Mary, and fucking Joseph.

"Tell her the fuck who you are!" Bobby Lee ordered in exasperation.

"She doesn' believe me."

So of course the solution was to fucking *kidnap* her. A goddamn law enforcement officer. How many felony counts was *that* worth? Shi-yit.

Lafayette had always been way too good at UC work. Fooled everyone nearly 100 percent of the time. At least he had since coming off those four months in a Turkish prison. Those months had changed him. Made him harder. Edgier. Put a look behind those black eyes that could freeze a guy to his very soul, or charm him like the devil himself. The man was lethally, insidiously dangerous, a werewolf in sheep's clothing, and Bobby Lee was very glad he drew his line on the right side of the law. Most of the time.

Anyway, no surprise Trooper Tara Reeves hadn't believed Marc when he finally told her the truth about himself. He'd probably totally convinced her of his cover story earlier.

"She'll believe you when Homeland Security shows up, over," Bobby Lee said, not looking forward to the lecture they were both in for from Command.

"I'm not taking any bets, me. Meanwhile the cuffs stay where they are, over."

"Whatever you need to do to keep us off the radar," Bobby Lee agreed resignedly. "Just do it. Over and out."

"Wow," Zimmie said when he put down the satphone.

"Yeah. A real goatfuck." He jetted out an angry breath, dismissing Lafayette's predicament. There were bigger things to worry about than a disgruntled LSP trooper. "Five or six DBs. *Damn.*"

"You know what this means."

"Tawhid is about to make his move." And it was all on Bobby Lee. He should have figured out a way to catch the bastard before he killed a single innocent person.

As if sensing the direction of his thoughts, Zimmie said, "You can't blame the team for this, Quinn. Or yourself."

He disagreed. "We spent the entire day talking to people

about fucking *cell phone* reception! And came up with exactly *nothing* relevant."

"We had nothing go on," she reminded him logically. "We were looking for a lead. That's why they call it *reconnaissance*. And why we split into teams. This time Marc came up with something solid. We'll get the bad guys now."

"Too late for those dead people."

Zimmie shook her head. "Tawhid has been eluding law enforcement for years, Bobby Lee. You can't expect to take down him or al Sayika overnight."

She was right. In his mind he knew that. But it still felt wrong in his gut. People were dead and he'd been playing games, thinking as much about how to get into Zimmie's pants as how to stop the worst terrorist threat to the country since 9/11.

And she was right about another thing, too. That was what happened when you mixed business with pleasure. When you let yourself get too personally involved in a working relationship. It messed with your concentration. Fucked with your judgment. Robbed you of focus. All sure ways to get innocent people killed.

Even if there were days, every once in a while, when that particular relationship was the only thing kept you going in this lonely, dirty business . . . and gave you a reason to live.

The irony didn't escape him.

But today, there was no doubt which choice was the right one.

"No. I *am* going to find the motherfucker overnight," he vowed in a low growl. "I swear, I'm not letting any more innocent people die. Not on my watch."

And if it meant giving up the comfort of Zimmie's warm arms, that was just the price he'd have to pay.

TEARS seeped down Gina's cheeks, wetting the seam of her swollen lips with their warm saltiness, then slid to the bare mattress she lay curled up on. She wanted to pull her torn clothes closer around her battered body, but it hurt too much to move. Whatever drug The Voice had given her had worn off while she was out cold.

Remembering that soothing masculine voice worked to calm some of the trembling that had shaken her body since waking up a few minutes ago.

Who had he been? Would he be back? She had a dim memory of him holding her hand and lightly stroking her hair as his deep voice murmured the words of comfort. Was he here to help her? Rescue her?

She sighed. More likely she'd hallucinated the whole thing. Or dreamt it. The way she'd been dreaming about Gregg van Halen and his traitorous charm. She couldn't believe the man continued to hold a kind of sensual spell over her. He'd been rough with her when they were together in bed. Demanding. Even frightening at times. But for all he'd tied her up and spanked her and taken his pleasure in her body, she had never felt violated. Never unsafe, or disrespected as a woman.

Not until he'd turned her over to be mercilessly used by terrorists.

Obviously her judgment was for shit.

A ravenous thirst clawed at her throat, bringing her unhappily back to the present.

How long had she been unconscious? With all the windows to the outside covered by plywood, no clocks, no point of reference, it was impossible to say. It could be minutes. Hours. Days, since . . .

Well, maybe not days. New bruises were still coming in on her pale skin, starting to bloom in the livid blue black of freshly pounded flesh, not the violet or green of older wounds.

See? Being a doctor was good for something besides helping terrorists create weapons of mass destruction.

That depressing thought brought on a new wave of tears.

Stop.

She hadn't felt sorry for herself yet during this entire three-month ordeal. Furious, yes. Terrified, resigned, determined, desperate, anguished, all yes, yes, yes. But self-pity, no. She wasn't about to start now.

Not even after that devil had nearly—

No.

Not going there, either. Not. Not. Not.

It hadn't happened, and it wasn't going to. She'd kill herself first.

And she was definitely not lying here defeated, like some kind of wounded animal. She refused to give the bastard the satisfaction.

Slowly, Gina forced herself to move, experimentally unfurling her body from its fetal position. Testing her mouth and limbs for broken teeth and bones, her ribs for fractures, her private areas for abuse.

She felt two cracked teeth under her split lip. The rest of her was bruised and battered, but miraculously, not broken. *Thank you, merciful Jesus.*

Gingerly she wiped her eyes. Shuddered out a sigh. And with excruciating slowness, pulled herself to a sitting position. She held her sides and caught her labored breath when she was finally upright. Damn. Even her hair hurt.

But she would make it through this. She would.

Suddenly, there was a quick snick of the lock and the door opened wide. She sucked in a breath of panic when *he* stepped into the room. The author of her life's worst torment.

Please. Not again.

Anger welled up inside her, bursting to come out. She'd thought she wanted to kill Gregg van Halen for betraying her. But that desire was nothing—*nothing*—compared to how badly she wanted to take a surgical blade to this man's gullet.

Horrified at her own bloodthirstiness, she swallowed down the rage, hating the person she'd become because of it. The person *he'd* made her.

Tawhid's eyes were empty as he gazed at her for an endless moment. There was no gloating in them. No pleasure. No hatred. Not even a spark of memory of what he'd done to her lingering in his eyes. Nothing. A blank wall.

But then he smiled. The expression looked so wrong on his face. What should have made it pleasant instead distorted his cheeks and made his black beard stick out comically to the sides. That alien smile was far worse than anything he could have said or done.

Because she knew exactly what it meant.

"I have good news, Dr. Cappozi," he said. Confirming her worst fears. "Your aerosol mechanism worked perfectly."

Oh, God. Had they killed someone with her handiwork? Sprayed an innocent with the virus and watched another human being die?

The possibility was too sickening to bear.

Because if they had, it was over. She'd lost the fight.

Her heart thundered painfully in her chest. She fully expected him to pull out a gun and kill her.

Nausea filled her throat, nearly choking her, but somehow she managed not to show her anguish. *She deserved it.*

She'd stayed alive by deluding herself into thinking she could actually stop this devil and his demonic plans. Her failsafe gene would never work. It had been cobbled together with the genetic equivalent of duct tape and baling wire. How naïve could a person be thinking something that unstable could work?

She stared silently down at her hands, twining and untwining them in her lap. Hands that had helped design a weapon that would kill millions of people. Possibly her own friends. Neighbors. Loved ones.

She was a damned coward. She should have killed herself long ago. Before the harm had been done. But it was too late now.

Or was it . . . ?

The human spirit was an amazing thing. Defying him would mean her certain death. But at last she accepted the inevitable, the end of life, and embraced it. Better that than living with the terrible guilt of seeing the consequences of her cowardly actions. Better by far.

The moment drew out. No shot came.

Of course not. He wouldn't make the end so easy for her.

"Just one more job to do," he said, as though understanding her despair. Relishing it. Wallowing in it. "Then you will receive your reward."

Her just reward, no doubt. "Thanks anyway," she said, her voice quavering from the pain in her body and her soul. "Not really in the mood for another party."

His expression didn't waver. "Then I suggest you do as I say. *Exactly* as I say. No more feeble attempts at deception."

At last a wonderful peace settled over her soul. *She could do this.*

She prayed whatever he wanted would take her back to the makeshift lab one final time. So she could destroy the deadly vials of virus before he could use them to destroy her country.

"What do you want me to do?" she asked.

"Prepare five aerosol units," he said. "Fill them with the weaponized virus."

She looked up into the face of the devil himself, trying to control the sting in her eyes and the shaking of her limbs.

"Why are you doing this?" she asked. She knew better than to ask. But she had to. "Why are you planning this mass murder of innocent people? Doesn't your faith forbid killing? Or have you lost your faith as well as your humanity? Is that why you kill? To prove you are God's equal?"

His face twisted, became mottled and ugly, his eyes flashing with the first real emotion she had ever seen in them.

"Get on your feet, whore! You will do as I say! Now!"

"Or what?" she asked defiantly. "You'll kill me?"

"No," he said. "I'll kill you *slowly*."

THIRTEEN

TARA did her best to contain the anger and frustration roiling in her blood over Marc Lafayette's pigheadedness . . . along with the bead of fear riding just below the surface.

She couldn't be*lieve* he had gotten the drop on her so quickly. In her defense, it had been totally unexpected when he'd slapped *her* in flex-cuffs along with those two druggies. One second he was helping her secure her two suspects—or so she'd thought—and the next, *she* was the one being taken prisoner. Just seconds after she'd told him she was going to fetch his satphone and call her captain to report the homicides. She should have known . . .

"What the hell!" she protested, taken by surprise.

"Don't make me tie your ankles," he warned. And meant it, too, because he'd already trussed up the tweaker boys like Thanksgiving turkeys. At least he'd only cuffed her hands in front of her.

"What is going on?" she demanded between gritted teeth, tugging at her restraints.

He just shook his head. "You'll find out soon enough."

She ground her jaw and fumed as he wordlessly untied the boys' flat-bottomed, motorized fishing boat, which he'd found hidden near the abandoned mill, and herded her into it.

After stuffing the druggies into the kayak and tying it like a trailer behind the boat, he started the motor and chugged out into the eerily still, thick-as-black-velvet night. Despite her running catalogue of verbal objections to her treatment, he was as silent as the swamp for most of their strange midnight excursion.

Jacko reluctantly pointed the way to the place where he and Chaz had encountered the bodies. When they arrived fifteen minutes later, it turned out to be a weathered but cozy-looking typical backwoods family house on stilts. Tara was tempted to ask what they'd been doing there to begin with, but the grim look on Marc's face congealed the words in her throat. Okay, fine. This was his show. For now.

They pulled in at a small, dry island several hundred feet shy of the small dwelling.

"We need to keep our distance," he said evenly. "Possible contamination." Then he pulled out the satphone and radioed their position to that alpha zulu chick, or whoever picked up on the other end.

Tara thought about just grabbing the thing and running. Sending out a desperate 911. Then sighed. Too bad there was nowhere to run.

Instead she muttered, "Contamination to us, or to the crime scene?"

He scowled at her. "What do you think?"

"You don't want to know what I think."

Unfortunately, her money was on the former. Marc had obviously called for someone to take care of cleanup detail. She absolutely had to stop them from destroying evidence, or the perpetrators would get away with murder.

Lord, was this what he'd been sent to do, all along? Find the bodies and destroy the evidence? No wonder he'd wanted to get rid of her.

As he helped her out of the boat, she glanced back at the tweaker boys, wondering what would become of them. A shudder traveled up her spine. Frankly, she trusted Jacko and Chaz even less than she did Lafayette and was glad he'd taken them out of the equation. Temporarily, at any rate. He'd left them parked in the kayak sans paddles, secured to a tree trunk out in the chilly water.

The moon was high in the sky, but the thick canopy of trees choked off most of the moonlight, so all she could see of them were occasional glimpses when the bobbing kayak drifted through a patch of brightness. She bet they must be jonesing pretty bad by now. She could hear them out there, snapping curses and blame at each other, paying no attention to her and Lafayette as he prodded her up the spongy bank of the island.

She turned to face off against her captor. "I want to know what the hell is going on, Marc," she ground out for the umpteenth time. This time she meant to get an answer.

"Not authorized to say," he responded, infuriatingly calm. "Sorry about the cuffs. I had to make sure you didn't contact anyone before Homeland Security gets here."

She halted. Rolled her eyes in disbelief that he was actually sticking to that outlandish story. "You're telling me the U.S. Department of Homeland Security is on the way. Here."

Oh, sure. Like she really bought *that*. Any more than she bought that he was working for the government on a top-secret mission—the cockamamie story he'd given her after slapping cuffs on her.

More likely some drug lord or crooked factory owner was on his way. Maybe a rival to whomever those two losers worked for. Or someone from the manufacturing plant responsible for the toxic chemicals she suspected had killed those people along with the animals she'd come out to investigate.

Whichever side Marc worked for.

Homeland Security. Jesus. He really must have a pair of brass ones to play a law enforcement angle on her. Too bad he'd picked the wrong agency. DHS dealt with customs and terrorism. Nice try, boyfriend.

"I'm pretty sure," she nevertheless pointed out, playing along angrily, "DHS would *want* me to report five or six suspicious deaths and a possible drug lab to the proper authorities."

"Normally, they would," he agreed.

"So, what does Homeland Security have to do with this, anyway?"

"I told you—"

She cut him off. "I know, I know. Not authorized to say. And I'm supposed to believe that?"

"Yeah," he said, looking at her somberly. "Please. Try to trust me, *cher*."

"And to think I'd actually started to." She looked away, more disgusted with herself than with him for *that* gargantuan lapse in judgment. She lifted her cuffed wrists. "Look where it got me."

He took a step toward her. "Keep an open mind a bit longer. Can you do that for me?"

"Trust works both ways, Lafayette."

"But I do trust you, Tara."

She let out a huff. "Yeah. I can tell."

"I do. I trust you are an ethical person and a dedicated police officer. I trust you'll do anything in your power to call in and report this situation—and me. Which is why I have to restrain you."

Oka-ay. Indictment or compliment?

A ray of moonlight broke through the trees and for a few moments caught Lafayette in an ethereal column of light, illuminating his square-jawed face in a slowly shifting portrait of silver and shadow. His expression was oddly regretful.

Suddenly, her certainty wavered with the shadows.

Damn.

Could he be telling the truth?

She exhaled slowly. Regrouped. "So I'm really supposed to believe you work for the Department of Homeland Security?"

He hesitated before answering. Concocting a lie? "Not for them. With them. For the moment."

He looked utterly serious. Not a trace of his usual charming ambiguity.

Her heart stuttered. God, how she wanted to believe him. Did she dare? She hadn't realized how badly she needed him to be one of the good guys.

"Why didn't you tell me this before?"

"I couldn't. No one can know."

"And yet, you told me now."

"No choice. You're in too deep. And time is of the essence if we're going to catch the scumbags who did this."

Catch them.

She stared hard at him. He wasn't lying. She felt it clear to her bones. Slowly, her stubborn suspicions melted away. Jesus. He *was* a good guy. Which meant . . .

There was only one logical conclusion. She'd been right all along. "These murders are connected to the animal kills."

He nodded. "I believe so."

Which still didn't explain DHS being involved. DHS, who dealt with customs and . . . Oh, shit . . .

Suddenly it all fell into place. "My God. *Terrorists* did this?"

"That's what we believe."

"It's going to get worse, isn't it? There are going to be more deaths, aren't there?"

"Not if I can help it."

For a split second she forgot about her restraints. "What can I do?"

"Tara . . ." He sighed. "Nothing. I'm sorry." He watched her with an apologetic look. As though expecting—

She sucked in a sharp breath, the brutal realization crashing in on her. *Oh, God.* For some reason it had been excusable when she'd theorized he was a bad guy, before she'd had sex with him. But— "You really *were* sent here to sidetrack my investigation. To get rid of me. Weren't you?"

His regretful expression told her she was right. "This situation isn't what you think it is, *cher.*"

Conflict raged in her mind. On one hand, a bizarre kind of giddy euphoria that her instincts had been right about him. That she hadn't given herself to a criminal. That she hadn't started falling for a man on the other side of the law, a man her conscience would never condone being with.

On the other hand . . .

She took a deep, steadying breath to ease the pain razoring through her heart. "So what you're telling me is that everything you've done, every word you've uttered to me since the minute I met you, it's all been one big, fat lie."

Wow. And who'd have thought *that* would hurt so much?

It must have shown on her face. He reached for her. "Ah, *'tite cher*—"

She whirled away. "Don't!"

This was ridiculous. She'd spent the whole day wishing he weren't just a *bon-temps* Cajun wilderness guide who spent his days either in jail or out drinking and hunting. Hoping against hope he hadn't been sent by some dirty big business to use his considerable charms to derail her investigation. She should be *thrilled* he worked for the government, even if his objective was the same. *Homeland Security*, for crying out loud! You couldn't find a more dependable, straighter arrow than a fed.

Yet here she was, *disappointed*?

But there you go. She was. Hugely. She told herself it was because of his lies. A bad boy's lies were expected, but a good man didn't lie to a woman and then seduce her, then lie some more.

But if she were really honest, she knew it was because deep down, that love-starved little girl locked inside her had been hoping, hoping, hoping he'd taken the guide job because of *her*. That regardless of his agenda, sticking around today had actually meant he wanted to be with her. That he'd made love to her because he'd fallen for her as hard as she was falling for him . . .

Finding out the cold, hard truth was like a knife blade to the gut.

What a damn fool.

His hands grasped her shoulders from behind. "*Cher*, don't do this. It *wasn't* all lies. Some of the words may not have been true, but what happened between us was real." His lips brushed her neck. "That was the real me wanting you." Warm breath trailed up to her ear, and he murmured, "The real me inside you." His arms came around her. "The real me asking you to wait to judge me."

She swallowed. Tried not to let herself weaken at his plea. It sounded so sincere. But she was so confused, he could tell her anything right now and she'd probably believe it.

She disentangled herself and turned to face him again. Over his shoulder she saw pinpoints of light on the distant bayou and heard the faint buzz of an approaching boat motor.

"Well," she said, echoing his earlier words. "Whatever the truth is, I guess I'm about to find out."

* * *

THE bodies weren't so bad.

Even with the rapid decomp caused by the swampy envi-
ronment, Darcy had seen a lot worse. The fact that the victims had been shackled together made for unpleasant
scenarios running through the head, but they hadn't been
brutalized or tortured. Well, except for being deliberately
infected with a deadly virus and left to watch one another die
horrible, painful deaths with no means of remedy or escape.

Yeah, that was pretty sick.

Darcy glanced over at Trooper Tara Reeves, wondering
how she was taking the scene. State police usually dealt with
traffic, not homicide. She looked upset, but not unduly traumatized. Maybe all those bloody car crashes had inured her
to violent death.

Of course, it was hard to tell 100 percent under the
hazmat gear. They'd all suited up before approaching the
crime scene, looking like a troop of invaders from the Sci-
Fi Channel. All Darcy could see behind the visor of the
other woman's full helmet mask were her eyes and cheeks.
And the upset just might be from being handcuffed and
forcibly detained by a man who turned out to be someone
vastly different than he'd pretended to be. Someone she'd
obviously trusted.

Darcy'd insisted they take the flex-cuffs off Trooper
Reeves, and she'd been shown enough credentials by the
DHS commander to satisfy her they weren't as big a sham as
Lafayette. But still. The whole experience had to be some-
thing of a shock for the poor woman.

Darcy jerked her head at Reeves to follow her outside the
shack, away from the bodies and the beehive of forensic activity being conducted by the DHS PIADC forensics team.

"You okay?" she asked through the ventilator mic when
they'd walked together to the end of the ubiquitous boat jetty
that seemed to stick out from every house in Louisiana into
some alligator-infested bayou or other.

Reeves nodded wordlessly.

It was freaking dark out here in the swamp. Lately, most
of the ops Darcy had been on were either in a city—Munich,

Riyadh, Cairo—or out in the endless deserts of the Middle East. Places where a million electric signs or a billion brilliant stars brightened the night with sparkling neon or twinkling faerie lights.

Here it was just plain stygian.

She watched a couple of fireflies flit around Kick Jackson's head, attracted by the green glow of his NVGs. Being the team sniper, Kick had pulled guard duty. He was silently working a pattern around the perimeter of the scene while keeping one eye on the two witnesses secured out on the water. Marc and Quinn were still inside the shack doing a careful search for possible leads as to where the terrorists' lab might be located. Rand and Ski had the farthest to come and were still en route by land in the Moby, the UAV's mobile ground unit. Rand insisted on driving it everywhere, even though it wasn't necessary to be anywhere close to the actual UAV to control the plane.

Probably just as well. Pressure would really be on the team now to find these tangos. Once they were done here, they'd likely be pulling twenty-hour days, trying to tighten the search area on the lab.

"Who would do something like this?" Tara Reeves asked, interrupting Darcy's thoughts.

"I, um . . ." How much to say?

Reeves saved her the trouble, holding up her gloved hands. "Never mind. I forgot. Top secret."

Darcy heard her frustration and sympathized. "I expect DHS will read you in, Trooper Reeves." May as well. She already knew too much to cut her loose.

"I hope so. I'd like to help catch these people, whoever they are."

Darcy didn't comment. She'd long since given up trying to understand how the federal alphabets doled out clearance and didn't want to second-guess them regarding Reeves.

"I knew there was something very wrong about those animal kills," the trooper murmured.

"You have good instincts," Darcy told her, meaning it.

A breath jetted through the other woman's ventilator, sounding like Darth Vader's death rattle. Reeves was watching the house, where Lafayette was visible through a window, moving around inside. There was a peculiar expression in her eyes.

Kind of like a lovesick puppy who'd just been kicked in the backside by its beloved master.

*Hel*lo.

Darcy had thought she detected a weird undercurrent going on between the two of them when she and Quinn had first arrived. Darcy had been very surprised to find Marc had broken protocol big-time and told Reeves enough about their mission to compromise it, should she manage to get away and tell someone. Like the local constabulary. Which would be a disaster.

Now it was obvious why he'd done it. To keep her from thinking badly of him.

Sweet Jesus. The man finally had a crush.

And by the look of things, so did Tara Reeves. Damn, that was quick.

Suddenly, their incongruous behavior clicked in her mind.

"Oh. My. God," Darcy exclaimed softly.

Reeves glanced at her. "What?"

"I do not believe it. He's already fucked you!"

What she could see of Reeves's face turned beet red. "I don't think that's any—"

She waved her hand. "Hell, no. None of my business." But just then Quinn came into view in the shack's window, bending over something with Lafayette. Darcy's own heart skipped a beat, then squeezed with regret. "But woman to woman," she felt compelled to add, "I want you to know what you're getting yourself into."

"Look, I—"

"Don't get me wrong, unlike some men I could name," she plowed on determinedly, "Marc Lafayette is a great guy. Sensitive. Considerate. But he's also one of our best operators. Gone eleven months out of the year, in meetings for the twelfth. Not to mention any minute he could wind up dead in some shithole country, never to be heard from again. If you're looking for steady, or even for tomorrow, I highly recommend you look elsewhere."

Reeves cleared her throat, her face still scarlet behind the mask. "I'm not." The declaration sounded thin and breathless. But that may just be the respirator.

"Okay." Darcy turned away from the house. "Anyway. I'm just saying. Because he seems to like you. *Really* like you. He must, if you've already had sex. Not something he usually does. *Ever* does. With someone he just met. Especially after he—"

Oops.

"After he what?"

Unfortunately, Reeves didn't miss a thing. Undoubtedly an outstanding investigator. Why she was wasting her time as a traffic cop was a damn mystery.

"Yeah, well. He wasn't exactly thrilled with the assignment," Darcy admitted. "Of babysitting you."

Reeves winced. "Wow. Babysitting. Nice."

Darcy shrugged. "Nothing personal."

"That does explain a few things."

"Obviously he changed his mind," Darcy hastened to add. She didn't want to hurt Reeves's feelings. Just warn her. She seemed like a decent person. "Which is probably a good thing, you know, considering."

Reeves frowned. "Considering what?"

Darcy pressed her lips tighter, half amused, but more than half irritated. "He didn't tell you, did he?" Now, *there* was a shock. The big shit.

The other woman regarded her. Even through the hazmat suit Darcy could see her tense up. "I'm not going to like this, am I?"

She wrinkled her nose. "Prob'ly not." But if Lafayette thought she would save his sorry butt covering for him, he was dead wrong.

"Tell me," the other woman insisted.

"I'm sorry, Trooper Reeves," Darcy said, "but for national security reasons we have no choice but to detain you until the operation is complete. And Marc Lafayette has already requested you be remanded into his custody."

FOURTEEN

IT took some doing for Rebel to actually get a call through to Kick Jackson. Alex knew how to get in touch with him directly, but for security reasons she wasn't allowed to contact Alex by phone. It had been a huge hassle just for Alex to get permission to tell her the location of Haven Oaks. Even his fiancée, Helena, was forced to use STORM-provided transportation with blacked-out windows to visit and had no idea where she was taken. Thank goodness Rebel worked for the FBI.

Tonight, she'd been forced of necessity to make the long drive upstate to the sanatorium to ask him to get in touch with his best friend and leave a message to call her ASAP.

Of course, ASAP on mission time could be anything from thirty seconds to thirty days or more. She crossed her fingers Kick would get back to her soon. She needed to talk to him before she had to report for work in the morning—with her answer for SAC Wade Montana about being his "personal assistant."

It was well after midnight and Alex was asleep when she arrived in his room. She felt a pang of guilt over waking him. But no choice. Aside from contacting Kick, she desperately wanted Zane's opinion on what to do.

After only two sentences of her hurried request, he stopped her, needing no more than those few words to prompt him to action. Propping himself up against his pillows in bed, he made the phone call to Kick. It was nice to be trusted. Respected. It made her insides all mushy and gooey.

As did the looks of him on that bed.

Lord help her, he looked so lusciously rumpled and sleepy-eyed. His golden hair was mussed as though from a woman's touch, sending a dart of jealousy through her. Had Helena been there earlier?

Stop it. Chill!

Rebel forced her gaze away from him. Once again he wasn't wearing his scrub top. The bare skin of his chest radiated the rosy warmth of slumber. The flimsy bottoms were loosely tied, slung low on his lean hips, molding the intriguing anatomy beneath the thin fabric into stark relief.

Ho-boy.

Far too great a temptation.

"So. Tell me what's going on," he said when he hung up. "Why do you need to talk to Kick?"

Mind on business, Special Agent Haywood.

"I found out some things. About the Cappozi case," she said and turned to pace around the room as she launched into a detailed description of what she'd learned from Mrs. Duluth, for starters.

She'd gotten as far as the part about Wade Montana giving Gina Cappozi the phone number for Zero Unit, and that one of their operators had likely become Gina's latest boyfriend, when from the corner of her eye she noticed Zane was acting a bit squirrelly.

She halted in midsentence and spun to him. Yep. He was definitely squirming. A tell, if ever she saw one. He never had been able to lie to her.

"Okay, Alex Zane, what are you not telling me?" she demanded.

His gaze darted to her in surprise, then chagrin. "Damn it, Rebel. Anyone ever tell you you're too damn good at your job?"

"Language, Zane. And no, an FBI agent can never be too good at her job. Now, spill."

He pushed out a breath. "You know how I feel about you being involved in this case at all."

She planted her hands on her hips. "Whatever you think you're protecting me from, don't. A woman's life is at stake here. Maybe even mine."

He looked stricken. She knew he was terrified that the same terrorist organization that had held him prisoner for sixteen months was involved in the Cappozi case. That Abbas Tawhid would somehow reach out to hurt Rebel, too. Or worse.

"Angel, please, don't even joke about that."

Refusing to be distracted by the endearment, she concentrated on the fact that he might know something about her case and was actually considering not telling her.

But then he held out his hand to her, and her wavering concentration fell apart completely.

Normally she was able to resist him, to keep her distance, as she knew she must. But tonight she was so tired from being up for far too many hours and stressed-out about this whole Wade Montana thing. And Alex's expression was so full of concern . . . or something . . .

She broke down and put her hand in his. His grasp was firm and strong as he tugged her to sit on the bed next to him. He'd been working out more and more, slowly regaining his former strength; even if she wanted to, she doubted she could pull away. Merciful heaven, she didn't want to. He'd been such a mess when she first came back from his ordeal as a prisoner overseas. Both physically and mentally. She was so proud of the way he'd dug himself out of it. So very proud.

He touched her face with his fingertips and she fought back a shiver.

"I'll tell you what I know," he said. "But you have to swear it won't leave this room."

She nodded, hypnotized by his long-lashed, green-and-gold-flecked eyes. "You have my word."

She barely noticed when he didn't continue, just gazed at her with those wonderful, expressive eyes that had come so close to being closed forever. "God, I love your hair down," he murmured.

For a second what he'd said didn't register, then her hand went self-consciously to the mass of red curls she'd set free on the ride up. Her standard work hairdo—a bun at the nape of her neck—gave her a headache after too many hours up.

"I dreamt of your hair at night," he murmured.

Oh, dear. From his faraway expression she knew instinctively he meant when he was a captive. He'd told her that before, but she'd always cut him off, not wanting him to have to relive those terrible days and nights. But now, something in his expression made her hold her peace.

His fingers reverently touched a curl. "Dreamed about the color of it . . . the scent of it . . ." He sighed. "Of you."

. Her cheeks warmed. She knew this was wrong; she shouldn't listen. Shouldn't, shouldn't, shouldn't. But to save her life, she couldn't tear herself away or make him stop.

"I dreamt of you," he said as though dreaming even now, like he was in a kind of trance, "and you talked to me. At night you would come to me and we would talk. About home. About what I missed most. About how I could escape. For sixteen months you were the only one who said a kind word to me. You saved my life. My own angel."

Surely, he meant he'd dreamt of Helena, not her. Pretty, vivacious, talkative Helena.

"My own beautiful, red-haired angel."

She swallowed. Vivacious, talkative, *brunette* Helena.

"Do you want to know a secret?" he whispered, his dreamy gaze dropping to her—

Oh, no.

"In my dreams you were always naked."

She gasped softly. Shocked to the core. The moist rush of excitement in her center shocked her even more.

"You never let me touch you," he murmured sadly. "Not even a kiss."

Thank goodness.

His hands trailed down the arms of her suit jacket, his eyes sliding up to her mouth. She tried to ease backward. When had he pulled her so close? *Or had she leaned in toward him?*

Apparently her dream self had more willpower than she did in real life.

"Alex," she whispered. A soft plea.

"Angel," he whispered back, and she could no more move a millimeter than sprout heavenly wings and fly away. *Which was exactly what she should be doing.*

His lips paused a hairsbreadth from hers.

Far away.

Right now.

Please, oh, lord, please.

Suddenly, her cell phone shrilled loudly through the room.

"Oh!" She jumped two feet in the air.

Zane started, his face registering incomprehension, like someone had just snapped him out of hypnosis.

He jerked back from her. "Jesus. What— My God. Sorry!"

She scrambled to her feet, away from the bed.

She had almost *kissed* him! An engaged man!

What had she been *think*ing?

Zane grabbed her cell, oblivious that it wasn't his room phone. "Hello? Kick! Hi. Yeah. I'm— Nothing. Everything's fine. Yeah, she's right here."

Rebel wanted to sink through the floor and disappear forever. This was exactly what she *didn't* want to happen. What *couldn't ever* happen. Never, ever.

No use torturing herself even dreaming about it.

Had he really said she was naked in his dreams?

She clung to the windowsill, struggling to pull herself together. Purge the unwanted desire that pulsed through her body. For a man she couldn't have. *Couldn't ever have.*

"Rebel!" Zane said. How many times had he called to her? "Here. Take the phone. It's Kick."

She inhaled a cleansing breath, shook off the trembling in her limbs, and walked over to take it from him. Desperately scrambling to remember why she needed to speak with Kick Jackson.

"H-hey, Kick," she stuttered. Right. The Cappozi case. "Thanks for calling back. Did Alex explain?"

"Yeah." Kick's voice was loud and clear despite the distance, if a bit hesitant. "Tell me what you have and . . . I'll fill in what I can."

She forced herself to collect her thoughts. There was no question she could trust him. The question was more if he would trust her with the information she needed. But she had to try. So she sat down in Zane's visitor's chair and told Kick everything, including about Gina's last boyfriend and what she had theorized about Zero Unit, as well as her reservations about SAC Wade Montana.

"Hmm," Kick said. "I can't say for absolute certain about Montana, but I doubt he's involved in Gina's disappearance. Evidence is pointing in a different direction."

"Al Sayika?"

"Yup."

Relief spiraled through her at his assurance. "What about Zero Unit? Have you found a connection?"

There was a long silence on the other end.

"Kick?"

"I shouldn't be telling you this."

"Don't *you* start with me," she scolded. "You want me to help find your wife's friend, I need to know everything."

"You have *got* to promise me this information won't go any further than you. Not in a file. Not to the task force. Or even whispered in Montana's ear. I'm deadly serious, Rebel."

"I know. And I swear." Though the last could be tricky.

"We were right about the ZU connection," he said reluctantly.

"I *knew* it."

"They sent out an operator by the name of Gregg van Halen."

Gregg-with-two-g's. The name Mrs. D had given her for the boyfriend. Hallelujah. Finally, she was getting somewhere.

"He'd been assigned to reassure Gina," Kick continued. "Get her to drop her attention-drawing inquiry into Rainie's disappearance. They were afraid she'd go to the press as threatened. My informant said they saw each other several times, and Gina did in fact stop calling CIA to ask questions."

"Were they seeing each other romantically?" she asked.

"Hadn't heard that. But I wouldn't be surprised if van Halen used sex to get her to trust him. SOP for that kind of honey op."

Rebel made a noise of disapproval. "Slime."

"Yup, well, here's where it gets scary. I couldn't find out who or why, but they pulled her in. On the day she disappeared."

Rebel was stunned. Surely, she'd misunderstood. "*Zero Unit* pulled her in?"

"To ZU-NE, their northeastern headquarters. And guess where it was at the time? The Bronx."

"*That's* why she was in the Bronx that day?"

"Remember, not a word to anyone, Rebel. On your life."

Slowly it dawned on her what he was really saying. "Wait. You're telling me *Zero Unit* kidnapped her? You're serious about this information?"

"As cancer."

"Good heavens," she murmured in total disbelief. "But why would they do that?"

Again he hesitated, and she could almost hear him debating with himself over how much more to tell her.

"Kick, please, for the love of God. If our own government has abducted an innocent woman, we have to *do* something!"

A few more seconds ticked by. Then, "I don't believe they have," he finally said. "It's still my belief she's being held by the al Sayika terrorist cell somewhere here in Louisiana."

Rebel's mind was spinning. "But if she disappeared at Zero Unit, even with a traitor's help, how did al Sayika get her away from them?"

"I don't know. I don't even know if she ever made it to the meeting in the Bronx. The timing could just be a coincidence."

Rebel didn't believe in coincidences. "Or," she said somberly, "it could be that van Halen had a hand in it."

"It's possible. I tried to find him earlier, to question him, but he's gone off-grid. No one's saying if he's OCONUS on an op, or in the wind."

She let out a low whistle. "Could *he* be the mole? The one who betrayed you and Alex in Afghanistan, and again in the Sudan?"

"He's definitely high on my suspect list. Be careful, Rebel. *Very* careful. I know you have history with Zero Unit, but they are completely ruthless, even with one of their own. Believe me, I know."

She glanced at Alex, who was watching her steadily from his place on the bed. "Yeah," she said grimly. "I got that."

"Listen, about al Sayika," Kick said. "There've been developments. I'm hoping we'll have the exact location of the cell within a day or two." There was a short pause, then, "You'll be my second call if we spot Gina."

The first being Rainie. "Thanks, Kick. I really appreciate all the info. It helps me a lot."

"And Rebel? I wouldn't worry too much about Wade Montana. From what Rainie says, he seems like a decent guy. Still carries a torch for Gina, but not bad enough to do her harm. At least in Rainie's opinion."

Rebel gave her thanks and hung up, feeling more than a little shell-shocked. She turned to Alex, who was still watching her, an inscrutable look on his face.

She summarized what Kick had told her. "Did you know?"

"About the connection to Zero Unit?" He shook his head no. "Looks like Rainie isn't the only one Kick is protecting."

She gave him a sympathetic smile. "Rightly so. You have enough to deal with."

He shifted on the bed, his thigh muscles flexing with the movement. Drawing her eye. Bringing the memory of what had happened earlier between them rushing back through her body in a hot torrent of shame and desire.

She jumped up from her chair. "Well, I have a long drive so—"

At the exact same moment, he said, "Rebel, about what happened—"

"*Nothing* happened," she said quickly. Too quickly, and they both knew it. "Have you and Helena set a date yet?"

"I believe I told you that last night," he replied, his gaze almost accusing.

"Of course. Sorry, I forgot." *More like blocked it from her mind.* Why on earth had she brought *that* up? To make herself feel even more ashamed and guilt-ridden, no doubt. "June, right?"

"February. Fourteenth."

How could she have forgotten? Helena had giggled when Rebel called to congratulate her this morning. "That way he'll never forget our anniversary," she'd said. Thanks for that, Helena. Now Rebel would never be able to celebrate another Valentine's Day without thinking of *him*, Dudley Do-the-Right-Thing. Because—what could be more perfect?—Helena had then asked her to be maid of honor at the wedding. How could Rebel get out of *that* without exposing her highly inappropriate feelings?

What a total, colossal cliché.

The maid of honor hopelessly in love with the groom, whose brain must *really* be made of honor and nothing else, because he couldn't, or wouldn't, see he was doing exactly the *wrong* thing by marrying Helena Middleton.

Beautiful, perfect Helena, who had waited faithfully for him for sixteen long months, all while he was presumed dead.

Of course, Rebel had waited, too.

But no one had asked *her*.

Nor, three months ago when, to everyone's stunned surprise, Alex had returned from hell alive, and they made a big fuss and glorified Helena's virtuous devotion and self-sacrifice to pedestal status. Rebel had always thought there was something vaguely wrong with that scenario. Helena *had* been faithful, never even looked at another man . . . but she hadn't seemed all that heartbroken, either. She'd gone out partying constantly with her high-society girlfriends.

Oh, well. Anyway, Rebel had stopped celebrating Valentine's Day a while back—the year Cupid had thoughtlessly given away her heart's only desire. Maybe it wouldn't be so bad being reminded of that over and over and over and over.

Yeah.

"I have to go now," she said, determined to stop torturing herself with these midnight visits. From now on, she would *not* see him unless she came in the limo with Helena. "Take care of yourself, Zane."

And she would redouble her efforts to find herself a *real* boyfriend to take her mind off this impossible situation.

"Rebel!" he called after her.

But she'd already closed the door behind her. She leaned

her forehead against it, exhaling a long, painful breath of finality.

And knew with an aching in her heart, tonight was the closest she would ever get to kissing Alex Zane.

FIFTEEN

BOBBY Lee knew there was going to be trouble about the sleeping arrangements.

Seven people. Nine cabins and the Moby. It should be real simple. Yeah, simple as petting a fucking porcupine.

It had taken the DHS forensics team three long hours to process the bodies and the small house where the victims had died. Marc's two tweaker witnesses had been packed off for interrogation, and toward the end of the night, there'd been a short but intense debate as to what to do with Trooper Tara Reeves. The DHS commander had wanted to take her into "protective" custody for the duration of the op, but Marc insisted he'd gotten clearance from higher up to keep her with the STORM team—under his recognizance.

Say *what*?

Though a bit surprised, Bobby Lee wasn't worried. He'd known Marc long enough to trust his judgment. And one look at that Cajun, and Bobby Lee knew better than to stick his nose into whatever the hell was going on between him and the feisty LSP trooper. But he couldn't resist poking him a bit, and had pretended to object at first, with the resulting remarkably reasonable argument from Marc that she was a trained law enforcement officer, and as long as she'd stumbled onto their covert operation they may as well make use of her skills.

Uh-huh. Bobby Lee had a pretty damn good idea which of Trooper Reeves's skills Marc wanted to make use of. Possibly already had, from the heated looks passing between them. Though he wasn't quite sure whether that heat was sexual or some kind of silent personal battle they were engaged in. Probably both.

But hey, Bobby Lee was the last one to be pointing fingers.

Anyway, the issue had ultimately been decided in Marc's favor. STORM Command had been called, DHS orders had been issued, and shortly thereafter, custody of the pretty little trooper had been turned over to Lafayette. And that—aside from throwing her into a fuming hissy fit—had resulted in another hour being lost to retrieve her police unit from a seedy roadhouse parking lot before the team made it back to camp to grab showers and an hour or two of much-needed sleep before throwing themselves into the hunt again. By this time it was going on 0300.

As soon as the SUV pulling the boat, followed by Reeves' unit, drove into camp, Bobby Lee announced that the usual midnight sit-rep meeting would be postponed until 0600. With a grateful wave, Rand did a U-turn back to the Moby. Usually he bunked down there. Ski and Kick made beelines for their respective cabins. Smart boys.

"You're with me," Marc said to Tara as they climbed out of her unit—which Marc had insisted on driving. It had been a real good thing she'd been in handcuffs again, at the insistence of the DHS commander.

To Bobby Lee's amusement, Marc started walking toward his cabin thinking she'd just follow. Lord, what planet did that boy live on?

She let out a rude noise. "I don't *think* so." She turned to Bobby Lee, obviously still mad as a damn yellow hornet. "Isn't it against the Geneva Convention or something to make a prisoner sleep with her captor?"

Bobby Lee stifled a grin. The woman was exhausted, splattered with mud, and angry as any woman he'd ever seen, but he could definitely see why Marc was so clearly smitten. She was a real firecracker.

Before he could answer, Marc announced irritably, "Don't worry. There are two beds. You don't have to come near me if you don't want to."

"It's not *me* I'm worried about," she returned.

Zimmie was also watching their byplay with amusement. Bobby Lee caught her eye and winked. Which made her smile switch off like a light.

Well, hell.

"She can share my cabin," Zimmie said, giving him a cool dismissal.

He thought briefly about his earlier decision to give up sleeping with her in favor of better concentration and not ending up dead because of some stupid, lust-induced mistake.

A wave of pure regret washed through him. He was doing the right thing. He was convinced of it. But hell on a stick.

She was so damn fine. And talk about a firecracker. He loved their frequent clashes—almost as much as he loved it when they came together afterward.

"No chance," Marc said at the exact same time Tara said, "Thank you."

"She's in *my* custody," Marc said to Zimmie. "If she escapes and blows this op, it'll be my hide on the line."

"Why would I do that?" Tara insisted, pulling at her arm, which Marc had clamped between his fingers. "I swear I won't tell anyone."

"Like you swore to stay in the kayak?" Marc shot back with not a little exasperation. "Do I *look* that gullible? *Non.* I know how you operate and I'm not taking any chances."

"And I know how *you* operate," she retorted, jabbing him in the chest with a finger. "I am *not* sleeping with you again, Lafayette."

All righty, then. Settled *that* question.

Tara suddenly remembered they had an audience and snapped her mouth shut, blushing to the roots of her pretty brown hair.

Marc looked about ready to boil his crawdads. "Whatever you like, *cher.* Stay up all night. Me, I'm going to get some sleep. Now, come on, you." He put his other hand on the small of her back and propelled her toward his cabin.

"Are you going to let him get away with this?" she appealed to Bobby Lee over her shoulder, still struggling. "I thought you were in command here!"

He shrugged. Menfolk had to stick together. It was the only way to survive. "Marc's right," he said. "You're his charge. But he lays a finger on you that you don't want, just yell. These cabin walls are paper thin."

He slanted Zimmie a glance as the two lovebirds—still arguing—disappeared down the path to Marc's cabin. Zimmie was glaring at him. Now, didn't *that* just figure.

He held up his hand like a stop sign and headed for their cabin. Well, hers. But all his stuff was still in it. "Baby, I already know what you're going to say, so don't even bother."

Unfortunately for her, that morning he'd been the last one out of their cabin, and he still had the key. So, yeah. *Theirs*. Leaving his dirty boots on the stoop, he unlocked the door and walked in. Then headed directly for the microscopic shower tucked into a corner of the postage-stamp-sized bathroom, shedding his clothes along the way.

"Hey!" Zimmie yelled, charging after him. He could hear her boots plop on the wooden deck as she hastily drew them off. "What do you think you're doing?"

"Washing the stink off." He hopped on one foot, then the other, to peel off his BDUs. "Feel free to join me if you like. No guarantees there'll be any hot water left when I'm done."

An unladylike bellow of outrage followed him into the bathroom.

The woman liked her creature comforts—never was one for cold showers. One time on an op high in the Andes, she'd made him heat water in an old lard can on the engine of their Jeep so she could wash her hair without her teeth chattering. He'd indulged her with wry amusement—but the gesture had been amply rewarded, he recalled with a surge of yearning in his nether regions.

Not that he intended to do anything tonight but wash. No siree. She'd made her wishes good and clear, and he'd made up his mind to honor them. For his own fucking good.

His body, on the other hand, hadn't quite gotten the e-mail. Just being in the same room with her, let alone stripping to the skin, made his cock quicken and pulse with need.

He grabbed the soap and shampoo from his kit, turned on the water, and stepped under the meager, icy spray. He let out a Bama yell at the first shock of cold on his bare flesh. Folks thought of the South as being hot and sultry, but in winter it was anything but. He well remembered shivering through many a subfreezing night in the unheated backwoods shack he grew up in. "Make a man out of you," his daddy used to say. But it only succeeded in making his mama cough blood till she died and killing his baby sister with the pneumonia before she turned three. Daddy was right though; now the frigid jolt of water barely fazed Bobby Lee.

He shook his head like a happy hound, spraying droplets all around before soaping up. Through the transparent shower cubicle, he caught sight of Zimmie standing in the door of the bathroom, leaning against the jam, arms folded across her front.

Now, Bobby Lee was no exhibitionist. And lord knew it wasn't the first time she'd looked at him naked. But there was just something about having a woman stand and admire your body that got a man's blood pumping in a certain direction. And she was admiring him, all right. No doubt about that. No matter the scowl crinkling her pretty blue eyes or that downturned shit-smeller moue.

"Come on in, the water's fine," he invited, leisurely scrubbing himself. If she accepted, she'd get the shock of her life when he didn't so much as touch her. So would he, come to that.

She saved him the battle of temptation. "No, thanks. I'll wait."

"Suit yourself. Don't blame me if there's no hot left."

She tilted her head. "Not too worried. You seem to have forgotten to turn it on."

Hell, she wasn't a spy for nothing, that one. "Yeah, well, hot's for sissies and girls anyway."

He washed his hair till it squeaked, then rinsed off. Putting his nose to his arm, he tested the smell. That crime scene had been rank, and he didn't want it clogging his nostrils for the next two days. Even through the hazmat suit, a subtle trace of death had permeated his skin. He decided to give himself another quick scrub.

And all the while she wordlessly watched him. Because the water was cold, no steam rose from it, leaving the cubicle crystal clear and giving her an unobstructed view.

Quite the little voyeur.

Not that he objected. A taste for the mildly edgy was something they shared and had enjoyed exploring together.

But by the time he rinsed off again he was hard as a steel pipe.

"Are you finished yet?" she asked, pretending she wasn't just as turned on as he was.

What the hell. He'd never get any sleep like this, anyway.

He curled the corner of his lip. "Not quite."

Fisting his cock in his right hand, he ran his thumb up the thick shaft and squeezed the swollen head so an electric buzz of pleasure coursed through him on a shiver. His throat caught in a jolt of sexual hunger. Her gaze faltered at his actions, but to her credit her eyes didn't widen or display any hint of shock. Not that he figured she was. Surprised maybe. Hopefully jealous. *Real* jealous. Of his hand.

Pressing his fingers deep into the throbbing vein on the underside, he dragged them slowly down, then up again, making his toes curl with an urgent physical need for release. His breath came harder.

Her eyes darted uncertainly to his. He captured her gaze, kept it firmly locked with his as he began to work his cock. He wanted to look into the depths of her eyes as he pleasured himself, wanted her to know he was thinking of her as he did it. Imagining in his mind all that his body wanted to do to hers.

How he wanted to tug her under the water with him, naked, and lather the silken skin of her lush curves with the soap, using that as an excuse to touch every exquisite part of her. He wanted to kiss her using his tongue as his thumbs slid over the peaks of her nipples, back and forth, back and forth, making her writhe and pant for him. He wanted to drop to his knees and find the tender flesh between her legs, slip his fingers into the furrow of her moist folds, spreading them for his mouth and tongue to explore, bringing her to a quivering, helpless state of need. *For him.* And then he would surge up, drive himself into her, reveling in the exquisite tight heat as he gloved himself in her sex and pumped, pumped, pumped.

Aw, *fu-uck*.

He shattered in an explosion of pleasure, squelching his roar of completion with a low growl torn from his throat.

He slapped a hand on the cold wall to steady himself, and finished off to the last drop, ending up with a long, measured exhale.

Zimmie stood rooted to the spot, unable to look away, her cheeks flagged with the dark pink flush of arousal he knew so well. God, she was beautiful.

And done with him.

He turned away, toward the shower stream, to wash away the essence of his desire for her. He snorted silently. As if it were that easy. Even now, the echoes of pleasure he was feeling were hollow, empty; already he hungered for the real thing. With her.

But that was not to be. Not now at any rate.

After this mission was over, then he'd see what could be done to change her mind. Maybe. Or maybe it would be better all around just to let it go, as she insisted.

Meanwhile he seriously needed some z's.

He shut off the taps and grabbed his towel off the rack.

"All yours," he said with a wink, sliding past her as he dried himself.

Then he collapsed on the bed. Before his head hit the pillow, he was asleep.

"TARA? Please, *cher*. Come over here with me."

The man had to be out of his ever-loving mind.

"No," she said.

At least she felt perfectly safe, if nothing else. He wouldn't come over to her bed, no matter how much he wanted to. Marc Lafayette wasn't the kind of man to force his attentions on a woman.

No matter how much she might want him to.

No. She *didn't*. She needed this time alone. Relatively alone. To sort through the events of the past few hours. Figure out what everything really meant. Figure out how she felt about it all. About him.

Except she already knew how she felt. She felt out of control and powerless. Dismissed.

How she hated that all-too-familiar state of being! It had been that way with her from the time she was too small to remember, through her whole life. First with her father, then, after her mother died, with the boarding school teachers who'd ruled her days and nights with close-minded iron fists, all the way up until now, with the jokester coworkers and chauvinist commanders who made her life a constant struggle against the inequities and prejudice on the job. She'd thought becoming a cop would bring a measure of respect and self-determination over her life. How wrong she'd been.

The only part of her life she'd ever been able to control was her own reactions to what was going on around her. The only real respect she'd earned was her own self-respect. Personal relationships? She'd always been determined not to get involved with anyone who didn't treat her as an equal and grant her the control she needed.

But now Marc had invaded both her personal and professional lives like a marauding army of one, leaving only chaos and uncertainty in his arrogant wake.

"Come on now, talk to me, *cher*," he said.

They were each lying on their own narrow bed, at opposite ends of the tiny cabin. Even so, they could probably touch fingers if they stretched out their arms. She kept her fingers tucked resolutely under the blanket, folded over the T-shirt he'd reluctantly lent her to sleep in. After a thorough shower using his soap and shampoo, and the toothbrush and comb he'd scrounged for her, she'd made it perfectly clear that what he'd had in mind next was not an option.

She laced her fingers together so she wouldn't do something stupid like reach for him anyway. She was more torn than she wanted to admit.

"What would you like me to talk about?" she asked.

"Why you're mad."

"I'm not mad," she said. Tired, vulnerable, confused, frustrated, yes. But she'd gotten past her anger. Mostly.

"So that steam coming out your ears, it's just from being too hot, yeah?" he said dryly.

Inside the cabin it was maybe fifty degrees.

"Very funny."

"I only want to hold you," he pushed softly. "Nothing more."

Okay, that was just a bald-faced lie and they both knew it was.

"I'll consider it," she lied back, "if you tell me what this DHS operation is really about."

Even though DHS had effectively taken her into custody, and technically deputized her by making her sign some secrecy papers—though no one had fallen for *that* transparent ruse, certainly not her—no one had told her the reason, either, only mumbled something about national security and need to know. When she'd become angry over their blithe dismissal of her rights, they'd told her this wasn't about her rights; this was about her duty as a law enforcement officer to keep her mouth shut and do as they ordered.

What. Ever.

Marc sighed, and after a while she assumed he'd dismissed her as well and fallen asleep. But at length he said, "It's about terrorism. On our own soil." And then he started to talk about his mission, and by the time he'd finished, for the first time in her life she was really, truly frightened.

"My God," she whispered. "You think this madman, this Abbas Tawhid and his terrorist cell are close by, preparing to attack our country with this lethal virus?"

"These deaths today confirm their intent," he answered quietly.

She squeezed her eyes shut, trying to banish the awful possibilities that swirled through her mind, amplified by the memory of those bloated, shackled bodies.

"We'd hoped we had a little more time," he continued. "But this tells us they're further along in weaponizing the virus than we anticipated. We have to find them. Soon."

Or else. Marc didn't say the words aloud but they were there, implicit in the grim determination of his voice.

She remembered the feeling of helpless rage she'd felt after 9/11. The rage everyone had felt so powerfully. America had never recovered, the country changed forever. What would happen if she were forced to endure another horrific attack, this time even worse and more far-reaching than the Towers had been? This deadly virus could kill millions, literally wiping out entire cities if it was let loose unchecked. It would be Armageddon.

That poor scientist, Dr. Cappozi, whom Marc said Tawhid had probably kidnapped and forced to help develop the bioweapon. What terrible fate had she been forced to endure over these past three months? What overwhelming pain, laden with enormous guilt? Or was she already dead? Sick, tortured, or her life ended by her own hand rather than go along?

In the face of such overwhelming horror, Tara's own fears and concerns dwarfed by comparison.

She drew in a shuddering breath, pressing the heels of her hands to her eyes.

"Cher?"

Suddenly she needed Marc. Needed his safe, secure arms wrapped around her. Needed the steady, unflappable strength she'd witnessed in him all day, to lean against. Needed the searing release of pent-up emotion his big, hard body would provide if she but let herself accept his offer.

Before she could think, and possibly stop herself, she slid out of her bed and padded to his in the darkness. He reached for her. Pulled her down next to him. And then she was cradled in his embrace, surrounded by his reassuring warmth, protected by the solid wall of his powerful frame shielding her against the outside world.

Warm tears trailed down her cheeks, falling onto his bare skin.

"Shhh," he crooned. "It's okay."

"No," she murmured. "It's not. But with you I can almost believe it will be."

She wanted him. She wanted him to do all those things to her he'd promised this afternoon when he'd pushed himself inside her, then had to withdraw, almost killing both of them.

She wanted him to make her forget the awful world around them. The hurtful past. The uncertain future. Just for a little while.

She realized he was already nude. And hard. So hard. She reached between them and touched his long, thick arousal, to let him know she wasn't there just to be held.

He groaned and thrust his erection against her hand, encouraging her touch. She obliged, wrapping her fingers around its iron-hard, satiny girth. Exploring the expanding column of flesh. God, he was big. No wonder he had felt so amazing inside her. She wanted to feel him there again.

His mouth sought hers as his body canted over her. He slipped between her legs. "Are you sure?" he asked, his voice strained along with every muscle as he held himself several inches above her.

"Yes." She shivered with a need so potent it scared her. "Very sure." And even more so because he'd gifted her with the power to deny him. "Make love to me," she whispered.

Wordlessly, he lifted off her sleep shirt and set it aside.

She sighed at the feel of him lowering onto her, his body hot, vital, demanding. The response she'd been holding in all afternoon exploded through her, taking her breath away; her nipples spiraled painfully, her throat ached, her sex blossomed with slick, throbbing heat. Her hand convulsed around him desperately, and he shuddered as if struck.

He tore his mouth free and let out a growl, yanking her hand away. "It's okay, *cher*. I'm not going anywhere. We have the rest of the night." He put her arms around his neck, then deepened their kiss with a moan, thrusting his tongue into her mouth in a graphic hint of what would come. She drew him down, holding him closer, grasping handfuls of his thick, long hair. Needing him. Needing him so much.

He shifted down her body. And his mouth found her breasts.

For long moments he pleasured them with his tongue and his teeth, suckling, licking, drawing on them till she trembled with desire.

She arched, reveling in the feel of his skin against hers, molten, sprinkled with coarse masculine hair. Soaking up the weight and the smell of him. The urgency of his want for her.

She lifted and tightened her legs around his hips, opening herself to him. Wanting him more than she'd ever wanted anything on earth.

"Wait," he ordered hoarsely. "Wait." His hand swept under the pillow and emerged with a crinkle and tear of plastic.

Seconds later she felt the insistent nudge of his hard flesh furrow into her soft folds.

"Marc," she whispered, the sound cracking with emotion.

"Yeah, *cher*." His voice was thick, needy, too.

"I'm glad you're one of the good guys."

He groaned softly, and then he was in her, to the hilt. She cried out in pleasure, digging her nails into his back at the stretch and the pressure, the unbearable rightness of his invasion. He pulled out partially and thrust in again, bringing a guttural moan to both their throats. He gave a little grind, letting loose a glittering shock of sensation that blazed through the small sensual nub just above their joining. She gasped.

His eyes swept to hers and he made a male noise of satisfaction. He did it again and she lost control.

"Please, Marc," she begged.

With a growled curse, he began to thrust, pounding heavily into her, driving her further and further from her conscious self, making her wild with abandon. She was on fire, meeting the savage force of his hips, excitement and tension coiling violently in her center, her whole body given over to the frantic pleasure of their joining.

His arm was under her shoulder, his hand gripping the back of her hair, the other wrapped around her thigh, holding her, changing the angle of their pistoning bodies until she panted and writhed and cried out in mindless, helpless bliss.

His mouth sealed over hers, stealing the cry from her lips, feeding her with his tongue and groaned Cajun curses as he hammered into her faster and faster. Harder and harder.

She quivered violently, gasped, and the tight knot of exquisite tension within her shattered. Shards of sensation tore through her body, lifting her from the bed in a perfect arc of pleasure.

He thrust hard into her, once, twice, and on the third he bucked, throwing his head back with a masculine roar of completion.

SIXTEEN

DARCY squinted bleary-eyed at the computer screen. She was scrolling through an e-mail attachment that contained a list of laboratory equipment, broken down by order, recently purchased from a medical supplier in Birmingham. One of the three dozen or so suppliers she'd queried yesterday. Surprisingly, many of them had answered by the end of business. Amazing what a little threat from the Department of Homeland Security could do.

"Oh, yeah, come to Mama," she murmured, growing more hopeful as she read. This was the third order from different suppliers that contained important items the terrorists would need to set up their makeshift bioengineering lab, according to Kowalski, the team expert on the subject. The three orders fit together perfectly without overlap, as though someone had split their list of purchases and spread them around, so as not to arouse suspicion. True, the buyers' names on the purchase orders were not the same, but that was to be expected. Terrorists might be lunatics, but they weren't necessarily stupid.

This could be the lead the team so desperately needed.

"Something good?" Kowalski asked, looking up from what he was doing.

"Maybe." She sent it to the printer, then handed him the

three papers. "Please tell me I'm not so exhausted I'm hallucinating." Truthfully? She wouldn't be surprised; she was that tired.

She hadn't gone to bed at all last night. After embarrassing the crap out of herself watching Quinn jerk off—and hadn't *that* been a freaking study in self-restraint—there was no way she could even have thought about sleeping in the same room with him, knowing he was lying just five feet away, naked as a jaybird and horny as a bear in heat.

Yeah, he'd once told her that bears *really* liked to fuck. They'd been known to do it for hours and hours without stopping. Just for fun, way past the point of civilized behavior. Kind of like him. They'd laughed at the image, and that long-ago night pretended to be bears. Good thing they both liked honey, because they'd gone through an entire—

"Hot damn," Kowalski said, interrupting her heated visual as he scanned the orders. "I think you may be on to something."

She blinked away the vivid memory and pushed out a breath, going back to her computer screen. "Then I'd better get started tracing the buyers."

"What buyers?" asked a deep voice from the doorway.

Ah, hell. She'd known it was too good to last. He'd had to show up sooner or later—and knowing Quinn, sooner. She glanced at her watch and was shocked. Almost six a.m., time for the team sit-rep meeting.

She ignored Quinn's approaching boot steps and let Kowalski handle him. Or tried to.

"Answers to your e-mails?" Quinn asked, not getting the hint. He came up right behind her.

She unclenched her jaw. "Yes. I think a few are worth looking into. Kowalski has the printouts." *Hint, freaking hint.*

Putting a hand on her shoulder, the oblivious dolt leaned over her and typed in a few keystrokes, bringing up the e-mails on the screen. She stiffened at his touch. But all he did was read, nod, and say, "I agree. Good work, Zimmie."

Then he was off, heading for the kitchen area. Easing out her breath, she flexed her shoulders and listened as he poured himself his usual mug of coffee and bowl of Frosted Mini-Wheats with milk. Breakfast of champions, he always said

when she teased him about it. Then he'd grin and say a light
meal in the morning helped him keep his girlish figure. Ha-
ha. But she suspected it was a habit born of a childhood
where, more often than not, it was eat light or not eat at all.

Anyway. At least he hadn't gotten all touchy-feely on her.

Which, come to think of it, was totally unlike him. He *always* got touchy-feely with her. What was going on?

Last night when he'd pulled his little shower stunt she'd
figured it had been some kind of twisted retaliation for her
ending their sexual relationship. To show her what she was
missing in a graphic way. And tempt her back.

But now she wasn't so sure. He'd been uncharacteristically
standoffish ever since she'd told him of her decision. Almost
like—shock of shocks—he'd accepted it and moved on.

Had he?

If so, that was a good thing.

Honestly.

Because she didn't *want* him to put up a fight.

The danger was too great that she'd cave and let him talk
her out of it.

Or worse, that she'd let slip how she *really* felt about him.
Then things would get genuinely awkward. Too awkward to
work together ever again. Not good. STORM Command
didn't like operators letting their personal lives interfere with
the job. Especially if it involved another STORM agent. The
minute a relationship became a problem, one of the parties
was gone. Instantly. And neither Quinn nor she wanted to
quit STORM anytime soon. She'd already been through one
humiliating change of employment—when CIA had fired her
ass after that disaster in Istanbul five years ago. Quinn had
rescued her dignity and her career that time by bringing her
on board with STORM Corps. Obviously, his days as her
personal white knight were over.

Ah, well. The price she had to pay.

She didn't get the chance to digest that bit of depressing
insight, because just then Rand and Kick strode into the
cabin, followed a few moments later by Marc and Trooper
Reeves. Darcy'd have to think about her situation with Quinn
later. Much later.

While everyone grabbed some breakfast before the meeting started, Darcy quickly logged in to the main STORM database and entered the names of the companies listed on the three suspicious purchase orders. She wanted to run them through the extensive system, which included data imported from a dozen national and international databases—STORM had done missions for every major government in the world, and inclusion in the country's security data pool was a non-negotiable condition of their services. With any luck she would have an answer before the meeting was over as to whether the companies were legit businesses or fronts for illegal activity—such as Abbas Tawhid and his al Sayika terrorist cell.

She rolled her shoulders again, went to grab another cup of coffee, then joined the others at the kitchen table. To her consternation, the only chair open was the one kitty-corner to Quinn, who sat at the head of the table.

"Have a seat," he admonished her, his face perfectly neutral.

But his eyes were another story. She knew those arctic blues so well—well enough to spot the veiled shadow of some emotion lurking deep within them . . . but unfortunately not well enough to know what it was. However, one thing it definitely *wasn't*—desire.

All righty, then.

"Let's get started, shall we?" he said. "Postmortem on yesterday. Kick, you're up."

Darcy shook off her cloying fatigue and made herself listen carefully to the various reports. But there was nothing new, except Marc's more detailed account of what he and Trooper Reeves had done yesterday, finishing up with how they'd located the shack with the bodies.

The pretty state trooper looked uncomfortable the whole time Marc spoke. They sat next to each other, and Marc held her hand under the table. Which apparently embarrassed her. Sweet, Darcy thought. And so foolish. The woman should cherish the moment, instead of wanting to end it.

God. Darcy barely resisted the urge to roll her eyes. Listen to her.

She rose abruptly and went for more coffee while Quinn quizzed Kowalski on what had been learned from the CDC scientists and from the human tissue samples he'd sent to the STORM forensics lab along with those Tara had taken the day before from the kill site. "Is it the same virus as killed the animals?" Quinn asked.

Kowalski nodded somberly. "Definitely. The same highly contagious influenza A virus, which has a resistant form of anthrax vectored into it. But this time it's been dried and combined with chitosan, a carrier powder used in nasal inoculations."

Suddenly Darcy's coffee tasted like sawdust in her mouth. You didn't have to understand the science to comprehend the implications of *that* loud and clear.

The terrorists had succeeded in weaponizing the virus.

"*Fuck.*" Kick's troubled curse gave voice to everyone's reaction. "We've got to find these bastards *today*. If we don't, it could be all over."

"Unfortunately, I concur," Kowalski said. "My guess is this was their final test. They're ready to launch the attack anytime."

"*Jesus,*" Quinn swore, slashing his fingers through his short hair. He pinned Darcy with a look. "Anything on those equipment orders yet?"

She hurried over to her monitor and scrolled through the results of her database search. "Two of the three purchasers don't appear anywhere. Still working on the third."

"That's it," Marc said, jumping up. "Fictitious identities. It has to be them. Where was the lab equipment delivered?"

Frustration surged through her as she scanned the forms. "Both picked up in person."

Marc sat down again, hard. "*De putain.*"

"What do you bet the suppliers have video surveillance?" Rand suggested.

Quinn was already on his cell phone calling the DHS commander to request copies be obtained.

"Tell them to route it all to the Moby," Rand said. "I can run the mainframe's facial recognition software from there."

This time, Kick shot to his feet, slamming his chair to the floor in the process. "Meanwhile we do what? Stand ready? No fucking way!"

Quinn had gone into thinking mode, pressing his fingers

to his temples, elbows on the kitchen table, staring down at the multicolored Formica dots. "No. We're close," he said. "I can feel it. We just need to think. Bring over the UAV image printouts. Let's look at them again."

Marc and Kick dragged over the easel where they'd mounted a patchwork of blown-up aerial photos, which Rand had isolated from yesterday's UAV footage of all the surrounding parishes. The photos sported a sprinkling of yellow pins for the animal kills, green for the buildings the team had already investigated, red for yesterday's dead family.

"Lose the green pins," Quinn ordered, and Kick yanked them out, leaving just the sites with hard evidence.

They all stared at the blow-ups.

"I want to hear everything. Every idea, no matter how far-fetched," Quinn said.

"All right," Marc started. "I still think the tangos have to be holed up somewhere in the bayou. The pattern of kills doesn't fit in relation to any one city, or specific village."

"You don't think the kill sites were simply random?" This from Kick.

"Nothing's ever random," Kowalski said. "Even when the selection is deliberately random, it's not random."

Everyone stared at Kowalski.

"If that's true," Darcy said, seeing his point, "you should be able to extrapolate the origin of the pattern."

He nodded slowly. "Theoretically."

Kick looked lost but hopeful. "Can you write a program?"

"No need. There are a dozen programs already that can do it. The real problem is entering all the variables, so in the end it spits out what you're actually looking for."

"Variables?"

"Such as topography, defensibility, the unknown factors of what is important to the terrorists in selecting locations both for their lab and the kills. A million things."

"Can you do it?" Quinn asked, ever the pragmatic leader. "Make an educated guess? So Rand can get the UAV focused in to take a closer look for possible structures?"

Kowalski swiped a hand across his mouth. "It's a long shot. But I'll try."

He scraped back his chair and went over to his laptop, already lost in thought. Good freaking luck. Darcy knew the haystack that particular needle was hidden in was enormous.

"Good. Next?" Quinn looked around the table.

More ideas were tossed out in rapid succession and dismissed just as quickly. It seemed the only thing they could do was go over the same ground again and again until the surveillance video from the three medical companies arrived. Maybe it would show something new.

"Come on, people," Quinn burst out in frustration. "What are we missing? There has to be *some*thing we've overlooked."

After a few moments, a tentative voice said, "A boat."

All eyes turned to Trooper Reeves. Instead of studying the map like the others, she was examining the three purchase orders Darcy had printed out.

Marc reached for her hand again and opened his mouth to say something, but Quinn cut him off.

"Talk to me," Quinn snapped.

A spurt of pride stole through Darcy, that he hadn't dismissed the other woman's comment out of hand. Damn. He really was a good leader. Not that there'd ever been any doubt. Just an overdose of Darcy's wounded pride.

Trooper Reeves glanced over at Marc. "You're positive these terrorists are holed up somewhere in the swamp?"

After a brief hesitation, Marc nodded. "I'd stake my career on it."

Not that he wasn't already, literally. Darcy had the distinct feeling they all were. But she agreed with him. A populated area would pose too many risks for terrorist kidnappers being sought by every federal agency in existence, especially when experimenting with a lethal bioweapon.

"Then it seems to me," Trooper Reeves said, "what with all this heavy equipment they ordered, if they picked it up themselves, they'd need a way to transport it back through the swamp to their camp." She looked up. "Like a boat."

A second of silence was shattered by a chorus of curse words and a general scrambling for file, phones, and computer keyboards.

She cleared her throat.

Everyone halted in mid-motion, looked back at her.

"And I think I know where to find it."

* * *

FIVE armed men wearing gas masks stood against the walls of the lab. As Gina was pushed into the room, their guns jerked up. Hatred flowed from their brown eyes. And contempt.

Terrified, Gina kept her own eyes cast downward. A wave of despair washed through her. If there'd been only one guard, or two, she might have a fighting chance to sabotage the canisters of virus Tawhid had ordered her to prepare. But a lone woman against five men? There was no chance.

Her whole body shook with fear. There was little doubt what they'd do to her if she tried anything, because she'd already endured it. But that had been just one man. This time it would be far worse. Killing her would be an act of mercy.

But how could she possibly destroy the virus with them watching her every move?

Stay calm, she told herself. *Go along for now*. Something would present itself. It had to.

Pain shot through her ribs and limbs from the ordeal this morning, slowing her steps to a shuffle. Her captors didn't seem to mind the snail's pace. Impatience was a Western fault. In their part of the world, events were measured not in minutes, but in centuries ... millennia ... a concept Western politicians did not begin to grasp. How could a leader whose term lasted forty-eight short months fathom a mentality that kept blood feuds alive for five hundred years? Time was on their side. They simply had to wait for the West's short memory to move on to other things.

So she took her time, too. Fighting the trembling in her hands, she pulled the empty spray canisters and measuring beakers from a shelf and lined them up in a tidy row on the laboratory work counter; she retrieved the chitosan powder from the cupboard, the compressed air tank from its place under the sink, and the half dozen other things she'd need to complete her task and placed them in orderly fashion on the high counter.

Before fetching the final ingredient from the climate-controlled unit it was stored in, she turned toward her attacker. Tawhid had appeared there, and now stood in the doorway, watching her from a distance. *Fucking coward.*

"Don't I get a mask?" she asked, voice shaking, not able to look at more than his feet. *Fucking bastard.*

Even so, a searing image of his brutal violation bit through her mind, and the ghostly feel of his filthy hands on her curdled her flesh. She wanted to double over with the nausea of the memory, but fought to stay upright. She would not give him the satisfaction.

He didn't answer, just kept watching her impassively, as a bird might idly watch an insect.

It didn't really matter. She harbored no illusions that she would survive to see tomorrow. She just wanted it to happen before he put his disgusting hands on her again. And if she could take these pigs with her, so much the better.

She walked to the fridge and opened it. Saying a silent prayer for fortitude, she reached for the metal rack holding the six remaining containers of death.

Instantly, one of the guards whisked the rack from her hands. She yelped, jumping back in fear.

"You don't seriously think I would let you touch those vials again?" Tawhid said with smug disdain from his place by the door.

She struggled to keep it together, not to fall apart where she stood. *Oh, sweet God.* Now what? Had she lost her last chance to destroy the deadly avian flu–anthrax cocktail before it destroyed everyone and everything she loved?

"Fill the canisters," the bastard ordered. "One at a time."

She took a fortifying breath. Let it out slowly. *Okay, girl. This is it.* Time to show what she was really made of.

"No," she said. "I won't."

REBEL felt like death warmed over. She was exhausted from the stress of the Cappozi case, as well as her consecutive midnight excursions upstate to see Zane . . . not to mention the sleepless nights that inevitably followed those excursions. Especially after what almost happened . . . Last night she'd dreamt she sprouted wings, let down her hair, and was flying around in *his* dream.

Naked.

Heaven give her strength.

She tucked in several stray curls that had escaped her untidy bun because she'd been too freaked-out by that dream to fix it right this morning, then took a deep breath and knocked on SAC Wade Montana's open door.

He glanced up from his desk, as handsome as she remembered—though not half as handsome as Zane, of course—looking fresh as a daisy. No guilty conscience there, apparently.

"Rebel. Come in." He smiled, bringing out the clefts in his cheeks that made his face so distinctive and attractive. Well, that, and his meltingly blue eyes. Too bad he was her boss—and a suspect. Otherwise she might seriously consider going out with him. "Close the door," he ordered.

Back to reality.

Maybe she really *should* have taken the time to write and deposit that incriminating letter with her lawyer. If only she had a lawyer.

Nah, she was just being paranoid. How could she consider him boyfriend material one minute and be afraid of him the next? Talk about mixed signals.

She walked into his office and closed the door behind her. But instinctively kept a grip on the doorknob. "So, I've decided to take your offer," she said, cutting to the chase.

"Excellent." He checked the wall clock. The task force meeting was set to start in six and a half minutes. "Before we get going, I want you to take a look at this." He handed her a printout, which meant she was forced to let go of the doorknob. *Paranoid.* The printout was Gina's phone LUDs—the list of phone numbers from Gina's home and cell that Rebel had gotten yesterday from Chip. Montana studied her reaction. "You've seen them before."

She'd really have to work on that poker face.

"Yes," she admitted. And waited for his response. Just because she was paranoid didn't mean he wasn't out to get her.

"Recognize any of the phone numbers?"

He had to know she did. Her assignment as liaison to Zero Unit must be in her file. "Sure," she said noncommittally. He had to recognize the number, too. He was the one who'd given it to Gina in the first place.

"I think it's time we paid them a little visit," he said.

Wait. "Zero Unit?" She was surprised by the suggestion, though she'd been thinking the same thing.

"Don't you?"

"Absolutely. I'll set it up. Where do you want the meet?"

He shook his head. "No. I mean knock on their door. In person, no advance warning."

Her jaw dropped. "Seriously?" In all those months she'd served as ZU liaison, she'd never actually been to ZU-NE, their northeastern headquarters here in NYC. She'd always met her counterpart—usually Zane in those days—at some public place like a downtown bar or café to exchange information. Zero Unit was fanatical about security. Never let anyone into their headquarters who didn't belong. "Do you even know where it's located?"

"I do," the SAC said but didn't elaborate. He rose from behind his desk, grabbed a thick file, and motioned for her to precede him out of the office. "After the meeting," he instructed her, "be ready to roll."

MARC strolled up to Charlie Thibadeaux's boat rental place with a brand-new fishing pole over his shoulder and a grin on his face.

"Hey, you ol' coonass!" Charlie greeted him with an answering grin and slap on the back. "Where da hell you been keepin' all dis time, you?"

He and Charlie had grown up together, gone to the same grammar school—on the rare days they'd both shown up. Back then, Marc hadn't yet seen the value of a good education. Charlie still didn't.

"Oh, here and there," Marc answered, shaking his friend's hand. "Brought you a present." He handed him the fishing pole.

"It's a beaut." Charlie's delight was mixed with obvious confusion as he hesitantly took it. "But what dis all about, *boug*? Wife make you give up fishin' to get out da doghouse?" He glanced at the SUV, where Tara sat in the front seat. Bobby Lee and Kick were also there, in the back, waiting for his signal. But he knew what Charlie was thinking. A good guess, if you were talking about a bayou man.

Marc laughed. "*Mais non*. Not married, me. Not yet any-way," he added for some incomprehensible reason. "*Écoute*. Got a favor to ask you, Charlie."

"Anything for an old friend. Jus' name it."

"I understand one of your boats got messed up pretty bad a few months back. By some tourists hauling stuff they shouldn't have been."

Charlie's face clouded with anger. "*Foutu étrangers*. Dey left my boat in da swamp to rot. I ever see those jackals again, dey won' be comin' outta no swamp alive, dat's for damn sure."

"Well, now." Marc put a solemn promise into a grim smile. "How'd you like some help with that, *mon ami*?"

SEVENTEEN

WITH the map spread out on Charlie Thibadeaux's wooden dock, Marc, Charlie, Quinn, and Kick narrowed down the most likely search area, based on the route the tangos were following when the boat carrying their equipment sank. The terrorists had gone to some trouble to make sure the ruined boat wasn't found, but a hard rain had jarred the craft loose from the stones they'd used to hold it underwater, and a friend of Charlie's had recognized the drifting remains when out fishing several weeks later.

Marc drew a tight circle on the map with a pen. "I just talked with Ski, and he says according to his random site analysis, this is the area we should be taking a closer look at." There was a large overlap with the circle they'd just drawn based on navigable boat routes. He drew a heavy line around the overlap. "It fits. The tangos should be holed up somewhere inside this perimeter."

"All right. We're oscar mike. Let's go find these fuckers," Quinn said and jumped to his feet, followed by Marc and the others. "Y'all get the boats in the water and gear up. I'll confirm our search coordinates with Rand, so he can run point with the UAV." Quinn waved at Charlie, who'd been told they were tracking a wanted felon. "You're with us, yeah?"

"Wouldn't miss it," Charlie confirmed.

Marc turned and ran smack into Tara, who'd been standing silently behind him during the discussion. "Can you find your way back to the cabins on your own?" he asked, steadying her so she wouldn't fall backward into the water.

Hell. He should have known better.

"What are you talking about?" she said. Her chin took on a stubborn tilt. "I'm going with you."

Over his dead body. "*Non*. Tara, *cher*, you aren't, and it's not up for dis—"

"You *still* don't trust me," she accused, sounding mondo insulted.

"How can you say that? Of course I trust you. We all do. That's not the issue—"

Her eyes narrowed. "Then what is? The fact that I'm a woman?"

"You're *my* woman," he corrected fiercely. "And I don't want you putting yourself in—"

"Oh, my *God*." The words were colored with patent disbelief. "I sleep with you, and suddenly I'm not supposed to do my job?"

"This *isn't* your job," he pointed out. What was the big deal here? He just wanted to keep her safe. He didn't want her within a hundred miles of those insane tangos and their Armageddon virus.

"I don't need or want you to protect me, Marc! And oh, yeah, I'm *not* your woman."

If she'd slapped his face, she couldn't have gotten his attention more thoroughly. He frowned down at her, unsure how he should feel about that fervent declaration.

He mentally counted to ten, but only made it to five.

"All right," he said heatedly. "So maybe I was dreaming and that *wasn't* you all over me in bed last night."

Her chin jerked up higher. "That doesn't make me your woman. That was just . . ." She glanced around.

He raised his brows.

She lowered her voice. "Just sex."

Oh, really. It sure hadn't felt like "just sex" to *him*. It had felt more like . . . well, like nothing he'd felt before. Closer, deeper, more emotional, more . . . *connected* than "just sex."

Quoi sa dit? Suddenly, the hairs rose on the back of his neck. *Emotional connection?* What the hell was he thinking?

"And I *wasn't* all over you," she added insistently, checking around for eavesdroppers. But Kick and Quinn were unhitching the team's cigar boat from behind the SUV, and Charlie was down the dock launching one of his bateaus, well out of earshot.

Still, Marc stepped back in close to her, invading her space again. "You *were*," he said, leaning down into her face. "And I want more. But that means you have to stay a*live* for me. So you *aren't* comin—"

"Wow." She stared up at him incredulously. "You are so out of line it's not even funny."

"*Cher*—"

"Listen to me, Lafayette. Okay, I'll admit I was feeling vulnerable last night. And you were . . . there for me. I'm grateful for that."

Grateful? He opened his mouth to issue a scathing retort about where she could put her *foutu* gratitude, but before he could clear aside his tangled outrage and form the words, she held up her hand.

"Don't get all huffy. You know I'm attracted to you. More than attracted, obviously. But if you think that's going to influence how and when I do my job, you're nuts. Jesus, Marc. I want these bastards as much as you do. I'm a *cop*, for chrissakes! I'm in this now, and I intend to be part of bringing them down. I don't *need* your consent."

Actually, she did. She was officially in his custody and technically had to do whatever he damn well told her.

Why wouldn't she just let him protect her?

He ordered himself to take a calming breath. This wasn't about sex, or gratitude, or even his bruised feelings. This was about the mission.

Besides, the stubborn glint in her eyes told him it would be a battle royal if he tried to impose his will on her. Once she'd sunk her teeth into a decision, she'd hang on with the tenacity of a *foutu* wolverine. He'd known *that* from word one. Tara Reeves was definitely not the kind of woman he was used to—the soft, pliable kind of woman who would demur to his wishes just because he asked. The kind of woman he much preferred.

No, she was exactly the opposite of his sisters. Opinionated, ornery, and obstreperous. All the things he judiciously avoided in females. He just couldn't understand his out-of-control attraction for *this* irritating woman.

Dieu. He could not deal with this right now. His frustration and protective instincts were running amok in his stomach like a cayenne pepper brew, wanting to roar out of him in a burst of flames.

Best to go chill down.

"*Bon*," he said, and backed off her. "Whatever you say, *cher*." He turned, intending to go help Quinn and Kick with the boat. Get his head screwed on straight.

"Marc."

The catch in her voice stopped him, but he refused to turn around. Childish? Maybe. But he didn't trust his mouth right now. Her hand touched his biceps. She tugged at his sleeve.

Ah, hell. He let go of his stubbornness and looked at her. To his surprise, her arms slipped around his neck and her body pressed against him. She reached up and kissed him.

For a split second he held himself apart. But he couldn't keep it up. God knew he couldn't help himself. He wanted her too damn much. Groaning in unwilling surrender, he sank into her mouth.

The kiss was deep and wet and clinging. The taste of her strafed through him, detonating memories of last night in his head. And his body. He was helpless to fight the onslaught. How could a woman like her bring him to his knees like this?

"Please, Marc," she pleaded softly, long moments later, still planting tiny kisses all around his mouth and cheeks. "Don't make this hard."

"Too late," he murmured with a sigh, and he didn't just mean his cock. But she didn't have to know that. With his hands on her bottom, he pressed her up against his full-blown hard-on, so she wouldn't guess at the chaos running rampant through him.

She let out a little noise, half laugh, half frustration. "You know what I mean."

Unfortunately, he did. "Yeah," he said. "I lose." At least this battle. They'd see about the war.

"No." She brushed another lingering kiss over his lips.

"Those terrorists lose. That's all we should be thinking about today."

He jetted out a breath. *Damn*. The present came rushing back, pushing away the uncertain future. "I know. You're right. But if you get hurt—"

"I won't. I'm good at what I do, Marc."

What? Writing tickets? he wanted to ask. She was a state trooper, for fuck's sake, not a spec operator. But he stopped himself from saying it out loud. He was in enough trouble as it was. On all levels.

"*Bon*," he said. "You can come." He'd just have to make sure she didn't get anywhere close to the real action. Protect her as best he could.

"Thank you." She beamed up at him. "You won't regret this. I swear you won't."

Hell, he already did.

She kissed him one last time, then tried to let him go.

Some perverse streak deep inside made him hang on to her. Tight. "But I want you to know one thing, *cher*. You're wrong. Dead wrong."

She frowned. "About what?"

"About being mine." He caught her face in his hand, held it between his fingers, and drilled her with a look. "You're my lover. My woman. Like it or not, Tara Reeves, you *are* mine."

EIGHTEEN

ONCE Rebel arrived at the task force meeting with the SAC, the whole thing didn't take much more than an hour. Montana heard reports, then dished out assignments—along with a box of cannoli; yes, the man definitely had style—then dismissed everyone with an admonition to check in before jumping on any major leads.

He did not mention Rebel's assignment as his assistant, she noted. Should that make her nervous? Or just relieved she wouldn't have to endure the petty jealousies of the other female agents . . . ? Tough call.

Good grief. No, it wasn't. Wade Montana had *not* murdered Gina Cappozi. He'd already convinced Rebel of that. And Kick agreed. Why was she being so ridiculous?

After the meeting, he crooked his finger at her, grabbed his Burberry raincoat from the rack outside his office, picked up two steaming go-cups that were waiting on his secretary's desk, and handed her one as they strode down the hall to the elevator. "Coffee," he said. "Double cream, no sugar. Right?"

Should she be flattered? Was this more of his subtle flirting? Or was she just imagining the whole thing? Coffee preference was easy enough to find out. He'd probably asked Chip. Or, more likely, his secretary had.

Montana barely slowed as they sped past her cubicle. "Coat," he reminded her.

She blinked, ducked in and grabbed it, then chased after him, juggling the coffee cup as she put her raincoat on over her suit. With his long-legged stride, she practically had to run to make the elevator before the doors closed. Not easy in a skirt and heels—but no time to change into the sneaks she kept in her desk drawer. She hated the things, and refused to wear them in the office. Totally spoiled her look.

After catching her breath, she took a big sip from the sloshing go-cup. "I hope this is decaf," she said.

He snorted. "When you start getting some sleep, I'll start getting you decaf."

How on earth did he know *that*? Her gaze strayed to the elevator's mirrored wall and her reflection. Okay, never mind. Those black smudges around her eyes were not just from her kohl eyeliner.

"Yeah, that's why they pay me the big bucks," he said wryly, reading her mind. Again.

She made a face at him and took another slug. "So where are we going, boss?" she asked.

He gave her a look. "You know where we're going."

"I mean where. As in what address do I program in the GPS?"

"That's classified. And I'm driving."

A superior who drove himself. That was a first.

She hiked a brow. "What do you plan to do? Blindfold me?"

The very corner of his lip curled up. "Would you like me to?"

Hello. She almost choked on her coffee. Okay, *that* was definitely flirting. Or . . . something. She felt her face go hot. "That won't be necessary."

They got out on the garage level. He clicked his key remote and a nearby car beeped. A Beemer. Blue. Like his eyes.

"My credit card gives points," he said when she whistled appreciatively. At the *car*. "I upgraded my rental."

Must be nice. Her own credit cards could probably sue her for neglect lately.

They got in, and Montana headed north to Canal, turning left, toward the Holland Tunnel.

"Jersey?"

He didn't comment. But it made sense. There were a lot of places across the river where a covert paramilitary training facility would blend in unnoticed. Forty-five minutes later they were in scenic Bayonne, taking the potholed road into the port district with its scattered jungle of dirty warehouses, giant rusting storage tanks, and foul-smelling container facilities.

It occurred to her that maybe she *should* be worried. Or at least a little nervous. Flirting aside, coming to a place like this with the man who himself admitted that anyone with half a brain would consider him the prime suspect in their investigation . . . Well, maybe it wasn't very smart. Especially since no one knew where they'd gone. He hadn't said anything to the task force. Hadn't stopped to speak with his secretary before leaving the office. Heck, even Rebel didn't know where they were going. Not precisely.

Surreptitiously, she touched the grip of her Glock .40, holstered as usual at her hip. It was right where it should be, within easy reach. Nothing to be nervous about.

Besides, he was innocent. She truly believed that. Otherwise she would have reported him to the chief right away. And not even driven to Starbucks with the man, let alone here.

"How do you know where ZU-NE is located?" she asked, making careful note of the circuitous route he was taking, regardless of her conviction he wasn't guilty. Paranoid? Nah. Just prudent.

"I have my sources," he responded.

"Care to share them?" she pressed.

"Nope."

The Mr. Mysterious routine was starting to wear thin. "You know," she said, "if I'm supposed to be your assistant, don't you think you should be a bit more forthcoming? Especially since it hasn't been completely ruled out that you were somehow involved in Dr. Cappozi's disappearance."

He glanced over at her, his expression wry. "You still think I'm the bad guy?"

"Doesn't matter what I think. What matters is the evidence."

"And you think the evidence says I'm involved."

"Big-time."

He pulled into a potholed alley behind a group of deserted warehouses. "And yet," he said, "here you are. Alone with me in a place where it could take years for your body to be found."

Her pulse spiked. Instinctively, her hand crept to the Glock again. "Don't forget I have—"

He rolled his eyes. "Yeah, yeah. Sent a letter about me to your lawyer."

Despite the tension, she chuckled. How could a man with such an irrepressible sense of self-irony hurt anyone? "I was going to say a gun. But whatever works."

He drove nearly to the dead end of the alley, then stopped and turned in his seat to regard her.

"Yeah, about the gun," he said, unperturbed. "They'll probably want to take it. These guys tend to get antsy about armed strangers in their midst."

She met his steady gaze. "Then it's a good thing I'm not a stranger."

This time *he* chuckled. "To them, a stranger is anyone who doesn't have the tattoo or know the secret handshake."

Ah, yes. The infamous ZU tattoo. The whole time she worked as liaison she'd thought it was a myth. But then, during one of her first visits after Zane's rescue, she'd accidentally seen his. He'd been unconscious at the time, and the nurse was giving him a sponge bath, the creamy suds trickling down over the elaborate design . . . onto an embarrassingly intimate bit of his anatomy. So okay. Maybe it hadn't been an accident. She'd been curious. Wow. Talk about an eyeful, even in repose. She could still feel the coil of heat in her belly at the memory of seeing—

Ho-boy. *Never mind.*

"Who says I don't?" she said, flustered, banishing thoughts of tattoos.

She realized SAC Montana was staring at her with a mixture of amusement and . . . interest?

"Really," he said, his eyes dipping to her lap, then back up again. "I wouldn't mention that if I were you. They might demand to see it."

She slammed her eyes shut. *Oh, brother.* "I meant the handshake," she muttered.

Suddenly, she felt a soft touch on her cheek. She opened her eyes and found him pushing one of her unruly red curls behind her ear.

"What are you doing?" she asked, her breath catching.

"Waiting until you're ready," he said gently.

She swallowed. Okay. This was so not good. She *definitely* didn't want to ask ready for what.

"We're here," he said. "I just need to beep the horn. Say when."

Here?

In front of them was the solid brick of a warehouse. No doors. No openings. No other exit.

Oh, *here!*

Of course it would look like this. Run-down. Deserted. Uninviting. Well hidden. Zero Unit didn't exactly want visitors dropping in.

She shot out her hand and gave the horn a couple of good blasts. After the sound died, the graffiti-covered walls rang with silence.

Suddenly, a square section of the grimy building began to rise like a lumbering garage door, exposing a gaping maw of blackness beyond. Despite the neglected outward appearance, the place looked steel-reinforced and impenetrable without some major explosive power.

Okay. Now she really *was* nervous.

Montana put the Beemer in gear and urged it forward through the opening. Once the car was completely inside the warehouse, the garage door glided down again, cutting them off completely from the outside world. An overhead light blinked on, instantly flooding the bay like a klieg light, nearly blinding her.

"Out," a gruff voice called.

As they climbed out of the car, two armed guards ran up to them, weapons raised.

"Hands in the air," they ordered. "Reach for that gun and you're dead."

Belatedly, Rebel thought about Gina. She'd also been brought to Zero Unit headquarters. And by a man she trusted.

But that had been a ruse, her summons a trap.

Gina hadn't been seen since.

A word Rebel had never used before streaked through her mind. Her stomach clenched.

Had she just fallen for a similar ruse? And walked into exactly the same trap?

IT was quiet.

Too quiet.

And yet, Bobby Lee had a bad feeling about this place. His skin was crawling. Which was good. *Real* good. Maybe they'd finally found the motherfuckers.

The stubby cement building that squatted on a built-up spit of land had a tall fence around it, and held a sign that read: Field Station 5, Property of Louisiana State University, Department of Biology. No Trespassing!

A *research* station. WTF?

"I vetted that building myself," Zimmie protested when he asked her over the sat comm why the *fuck* they hadn't investigated it before. Why it hadn't even made their list of fucking possibles? "Damn it," she exclaimed over the static, "I called the chairman of the LSU biology department and spoke to him personally! He said it's currently being used by a group of graduate students working on a project involving marsh birds. They check in regularly, and he assured me there's nothing unusual going on there."

"Someone's lying. This is the target. I can feel it in my bones."

"Sorry." Angry sincerity rang in her voice, even over the comm.

Hopefully that professor really hated his job, because Bobby Lee had a hunch he wouldn't be in it much longer, either way.

"Don't beat yourself up, Zulu," he told Zimmie. "Romeo, do you have eyes on the situation, over?" Rand had been monitoring their sortie and putting the UAV in position from the Moby back at camp, since there was no way to drive it into the swamp.

"External only."

Fucking great. "We're going in for a look-see. Apprise STORM Command to have the Homies standing ready, over."

"Copy that."

"Take care of yourself out there, Alpha Six, over," Darcy said.

Yeah, because she cared so much what happened to him. *Fuck.* Didn't need to be thinking about *that* right now. "Over and out," he muttered.

Once they'd approached, using hand signals, Bobby Lee motioned Kick around to the right of the building. He'd take the left. The two of them were doing a sneak-and-peek while Marc, Charlie, and Tara drew attention, motoring past on the bayou in Charlie's flatboat, pretending they were having a good ol' time drinking beer and fishing. Marc hadn't looked real happy about the division of labor but hadn't actually protested. Which told Bobby Lee louder than words how preoccupied he was with his sexy state trooper. Jesus. The whole team was losing it.

Just one more argument in favor of the decision Bobby Lee had made regarding his involvement with Darcy Zimmerman. To let her go. Because love had absolutely no place on a spec-ops missi—

Whoa! Love? No, no. Sex. *Sex* had no place on—

Shi-yit. This was not helping.

He gave himself a mental boot in the ass as he slithered up and over the fence and dropped inside the compound, rolling to a ready position behind a clump of bushes, weapon trained on the structure.

Nothing moved, except for the party boat floating by on the bayou. No alarms. No guards. No one even stuck a nose out the front door to see what all the commotion was about.

Well, hell. Maybe these doofuses really were studying marsh birds. Nervous tangos would have shown their faces by now for damn sure.

Either that, or the team had arrived too late. Had Tawhid already broken camp and gone on to phase two of his terrorist attack?

Damn it to hell.

Using cover as best he could, Bobby Lee crouch-ran over

to the building, all the while keeping an eye out for booby traps and trip wires. But it was smooth sailing. For every silent minute that went by, his nerves jacked up higher. If they were too late . . .

With his back to the wall, he stole a peek in the window closest to the corner. Inside appeared to be some kind of dormitory. Unmade camp beds littered the room, along with two dressers. A few items of clothing hung out of the drawers. An ancient TV occupied a metal stand. A couple of beat-up suitcases were sprawled open on the floor in the corner like they'd been hastily ransacked and dumped.

No people. No weapons.

Tension coiled tighter in his chest.

Warily, he stuck his head around the back corner of the building, just in time to see Kick do the same from his side. Kick looked madder than a stepped-on rattler. With a few hand signals they traded intel. So far neither of them had found a fucking thing. *Damn.* He'd been *so* sure.

Bobby Lee suddenly noticed the three rear windows. All were boarded up tight as a drum with thick slabs of plywood, the edges of which were sealed shut with some kind of gloopy grout. Recently.

It wasn't hurricane season. His blood pumped faster as he signaled to Kick and they exchanged a troubled glance. If the barriers weren't there to keep out the weather, they might just be to keep someone *in*.

Like a kidnapped scientist.

Kick's jaw clenched and he gave Bobby Lee an urgent signal to go back around and meet him up front.

Bobby Lee agreed. No more pussyfooting around. He wasn't getting the vibe this was a trap waiting to spring. The knot in his stomach screamed they were too fucking late for a trap. *Shit.*

He hurried back along the side wall, checking through the windows as he went. First the dormitory—still no sign of life—then a narrow kitchen—no one visible—and last a common room with sofas, chairs, and a dining table up against one side. Not a peep.

He scooted around the corner and met Kick at the front stoop. "Anything?" he asked in a voice barely audible.

Kick shook his head. "Just more boarded-up windows. God*damn* it," he growled under his breath.

They regarded each other for a brief moment. Bobby Lee knew Kick well enough by now to be certain they were both thinking the same thing. The mission was to *find* the terrorists. Not to engage them. But what the hell.

"Feel like disobeying a direct order from STORM Command *and* DHS?" Bobby Lee murmured.

"Thought you'd never ask."

Just then a scuffle came from inside the building. Followed by a muffled scream. A *woman's* scream.

Kick reacted instantly, winding up a leg to crash the door down. Bobby Lee grabbed the radio just as fast.

"This is STORM Alpha Six actual. Possible hostage situation. We're going in."

GINA couldn't believe she was still alive.

Barely. But alive.

She was locked in her room again. Sprawled broken and bleeding on the bare mattress.

But alive.

What had happened? Why had she been spared?

After refusing to do Tawhid's final dirty work, he'd hit her. Hard. She must have passed out. Who knew how long or what had happened then. She vaguely remembered the sensation of being dragged by one of the gorillas and dumped on the bed. How long ago was that? Impossible to tell with the outside windows battened down and the lights off.

She tried to shift her burning, aching body, to see if she could even think about getting up to turn on the overhead. A soft moan slipped from her throat. *Jesus, she hurt.* No freaking way she could move.

So she listened.

The place was silent. More silent than she'd ever heard it before. No TV. No incomprehensible chatter. No loud prayers being chanted. Had they all gone? Left her alone to die in the icy darkness? She was almost grateful.

Suddenly, she heard a noise; barely perceptible, but definitely there. *Breathing*. Heavy and even. Someone else was in the room!

Oh, sweet God.

Why couldn't they just have killed her?

Because she had disobeyed. Tawhid had warned her what would happen. The other cell members must have left to execute their appointed tasks of terror, everyone except this last man. His task was surely to execute her. Slowly and painfully, as Tawhid had promised.

Why hadn't she killed herself?

In the darkness, the man said something unintelligible in a young, harsh voice. She recognized that voice. It belonged to the most youthful of the terrorists, a kid of maybe eighteen. The most fanatical and zealous of the lot. And violent. What was it about youth that made a person so cold? She'd seen the hatred in his eyes and the bloodlust. To think not too long ago she'd preferred younger men.

He spoke again, louder this time. To her? She didn't understand his words, but their meaning was clear. She'd been a gift to him. He'd waited for her to regain consciousness, and now it was time to open his present.

A mewl of desperation escaped her. *This was not going to happen*. Not again. She'd force him to kill her first. Or she really would do it herself.

Suddenly the light switched on, blinding her stinging eyes.

Then he was on her, his body reeking of foul sweat, the stench of his breath overwhelming. She gagged and struck out with all her might, kicking and clawing. Ignoring the pain in her body, fighting with every last ounce of strength. Her knee connected with the soft sac between his legs. He cursed, fury sweeping across his face. A knife appeared from nowhere in his hand. He raised it high above her chest.

She screamed. It was useless, hopeless, she knew. But she screamed anyway, flailing, kicking, fighting him with all her might. Something crashed loudly; he yelled and swore at her, but for each blow he struck, she landed two.

All at once there was a loud *bang!* He froze above her with a surprised look on his face. She squeezed her eyes shut as once again a shower of blood rained down on her. But mercifully, this time it wasn't hers.

Before she could react, his weight was lifted and men suddenly surrounded her, shouting. *In English.*

She felt a sob rise within her. A trembling cry of hope. It lodged in her throat, unable to pass the lump of burning emotion growing there.

Dare she believe?

Amidst the chaos, someone gently took her hand. "Dr. Cappozi?"

She didn't dare open her eyes. In case it was all just a hallucination or a cruel joke.

Please don't let it be a cruel joke.

"Gina?" the man's voice said softly. Almost tenderly. "It's okay. You're safe now. We've come to take you home."

NINETEEN

THEY hadn't told Tara about the hostage. The *female* hostage.

Peering up at them, she was trembling violently, curled in a tight ball on a blood-soaked mattress. A curved, gleaming knife lay on the floor next to it, testament to how close a call it had been for her.

Tara moved aside as Marc and Quinn dragged the woman's struggling attacker from the room. He was screeching at the top of his lungs, bleeding like a stuck pig from a stump of wrist, his hand hanging by a thin strip of flesh where it had been severed by Quinn's well-aimed shot.

The hostage looked terrified, cringing away from the armed male commandos and their prisoner. Kick was kneeling at her bedside, holding her hand, trying to calm her fears and get her to focus on him. But it was obvious to anyone with eyes that the woman was in shock and not hearing a word he said. Tara slid past him to get to her side.

"Let me try," Tara said, squeezing his shoulder. "Do we know who she is?"

"Dr. Gina Cappozi," he answered, reluctantly moving aside. "A scientist from New York. She's my wife's best friend."

Tara's eyebrows flicked in surprise at that last part, but

she didn't ask. That could wait. "See if you can scare up a washcloth and some warm water," she told him. "And a blanket."

"We need to question her," he said, not without sympathy. "If she knows where Tawhid's gone, how long ago the others left, we could—"

"I understand. But first she has to trust us."

After a brief hesitation, he gave a quick nod. "You're right. I'll get the blanket and water."

Tara turned to Dr. Cappozi. Gina. And did her best to keep her horrified reaction to the brutal injuries on the woman's face and body from showing on her own face. It wasn't easy. Dr. Cappozi must have gone through hell and back at the hands of those monsters.

She knelt down. "Gina, my name is Tara. I'm a police officer. Hang in there, okay? Medical help is on the way."

Large brown eyes, ringed with bruises, stared back at her. But the fear in them ebbed, just a little.

"Is there someone we can contact? To tell you're safe?" No reaction. "Kick says you're his wife's best friend. Is that Rainie? Rainie Jackson? We can phone her if you like." Tara didn't know if that was strictly kosher, but she needed a way in past the shock.

Gina's throat worked. Her head shook a fraction back and forth. "Rainie . . . not . . . married."

A response. Relief washed through Tara. "Ah," she said, wondering if she'd misunderstood what Kick had said. Although, how many women were named Rainie? "Well, maybe—"

"They just got married a couple months ago," Marc interjected from the doorway. He was holding a blanket, cloth, and a pan of steaming water. "May I come in?"

Gina's eyes shot back to Tara's, panic filling them anew. The woman was terrified of men . . . or maybe just men with black hair and olive skin. Who could blame her?

"It's okay," Tara assured her. "He's with me. American through and through. Marc won't hurt you, I promise."

He came far enough into the room to hand her the things he'd brought, along with a bottle of water, then backed away to the door again. "I was in the Sudan with Rainie," he said.

"That's where she was . . . taken . . . back when you were trying to find her. But she's home now. Safe and sound. Like you will be soon."

Gina's gaze went to him, filled with conflicting emotion. She swallowed, lips trembling, as though she wanted to say something but couldn't. Tara cracked the water bottle and fed her a sip.

"She saved my life over there," Marc continued, his voice quietly intense. "Kick's, too. I've never met a braver lady. *Donc*, not until today, anyway."

A tear seeped from the corner of Gina's eye and dropped onto the mattress. Tara's own vision swam out of focus. She didn't know the story, but the warmth and sincerity in Marc's confession touched her heart.

These men she was with—Marc, Kick, even Quinn and the others—were unlike any men she'd ever met before. Tough and macho to the max, each one could kill a man swiftly and efficiently without a second thought when necessary, she was quite sure. And yet, none of them seemed to be afraid to let his emotions show when it really mattered. To allow himself to be vulnerable and sensitive to another human being's needs.

She thought about how tender Marc had been with her last night, when she'd been shocked and terrified by what he'd told her, desperately needing someone to hold her. He'd gently soothed her fears, then given her a night she would never forget as long as she lived. She'd been horribly embarrassed this morning by her weakness, her neediness. She'd tried to withdraw from him, pretend it had never happened. Yet, he'd refused to go along. He'd openly shown her how much he still wanted her, in front of the others. Even when she wouldn't acknowledge him in return.

What was wrong with her?

"Five," Gina softly rasped.

Tara whipped her gaze from Marc to Gina, and he took an involuntary step forward into the room. "What?"

"Five . . . spray canisters," Gina said, her voice shaking with the effort. Tara gave her another swallow of water. "Virus. In the lab."

"Five canisters. That will help us a lot, Dr. Cappozi,"

Marc said, taking another cautious step in. "Can you tell us about the men? How many? Who they were?"

Her body suddenly jerked and started shaking again. Tara grabbed the blanket and spread it over her, gingerly tucking it in. "Marc, she's in no shape to talk yet."

"Yes," she protested. "Want to. Tawhid . . ." She halted.

"Abbas Tawhid?" Marc prodded, coming to full attention. "Leader of the al Sayika terrorist organization? Are you sure that's who it was? You saw him yourself?"

Gina's eyes shut, her face crumbling. She sucked in a stuttered breath. "Yes. Plus four more. Five . . . maybe. Or a dream . . . nightmare . . ." She stopped again, squeezing her eyes even harder.

Tara gave him an imploring look. "You're okay, Gina," she said to her. "No one can hurt you any more. I promise."

After giving her a moment, Marc persisted. "All men?" he asked. "Any women?"

"No," Gina whispered. "He hates women. Kept telling me I would die in pain like all the other whores."

More tears seeped down her cheeks. Okay, that was a good sign. It meant she wasn't completely numb, her emotions not shut off totally by the experience. Marc was right. She was an incredibly strong woman.

"Do you have any idea where they were going when they left here?" Marc asked. "Any hint at all?"

"No. Sorry."

"Transportation?"

She licked her lips, and Tara gave her more water. "Boat. Brought me in a boat."

"Okay. *Bon.*" He nodded. And apparently decided there was no more information to be gleaned at this point. "We're going to get these *fils du putains*, Dr. Cappozi. On that, you have my solemn word."

"Kill them," she rasped, her voice choked with feelings Tara couldn't even begin to guess at. "Please. Kill them all."

Looking at Gina, Tara agreed completely with the sentiment.

"I'll probably have to fight Kick for the privilege," Marc said somberly. "That man is definitely on a mission of vengeance."

"Kick," Gina said haltingly, uncertainly. "Kidnapped Rainie . . . and married her?"

"*Mais*, yeah. Fell crazy in love, him." Marc sent her a gentle smile. "He's phoning her now. To let her know you're okay."

Tara saw Gina's tense muscles slowly start to ease as her eyes brimmed over in earnest. Trust finally taking hold. "Thank you. Both. For . . ."

"No need. My pleasure, ma'am." Marc started to back out the door. He shifted his gaze to Tara. Paused. "STORM is on the way with an evac helo. We've got to get her out of here before DHS arrives. Can you stay with her? Make sure that happens?"

"Of course. But why?"

"For her own safety. They'll explain on the helo."

Alarm suddenly sang through her. "Wait. Where will you be?"

"Not sure. I'll let you know."

She came to her feet. "You're going after them, aren't you?"

"We don't know that yet."

The truth suddenly slammed her in the gut. "You're going without me." And this time he really would.

She didn't know why this time it felt different. Worse. Like a razor slashing through her heart. This morning at Charlie's she'd practically bitten his head off, after he'd treated her so sweet last night. Actually told him she was *grateful* for his lovemaking. So cold . . . Had he finally had enough?

She struggled not to let her eyes bleed the pain she was feeling. Not to fling herself into his arms and beg him not to leave without her.

"*Cher*, it's not like that. Someone needs to stay with Dr. Cappozi until—"

Screw it. She ran to him and wrapped her arms tight around his waist. "I'm sorry, Marc. I'm such a fool. I *am* yours, just like you said."

His eyes softened. "I know, *mon cœur*. But for now, take care of Gina. I'll call you." He kissed her. "*D'accord?*"

"But . . ."

He kissed her again. Then he was gone.

Leaving her feeling the slightest bit frustrated and desperate. And not a little uncertain.

I know?

Thank God she hadn't said, "I love you."

"He seems like . . . a good man." Gina's strained observation interrupted Tara's bout of acute self-doubt.

She let out a ragged breath, turned, and knelt down by the bed again. "Yes. He is. It's me that's totally screwed up."

For the first time, a glimmer of a smile flitted over Gina's cracked lips. "Join the club," she whispered. Then she closed her eyes and issued a pain-filled sigh. "At least he didn't seduce you, make you fall in love with him, then sell you out to terrorists he knew would use you and kill you."

She frowned. If what Gina was implying was true, that really sucked. Tara's life had been no bed of roses, but she couldn't even imagine such an unforgivable betrayal.

Suddenly, she realized what the other woman was saying. "Gina, you *know* the person who did this to you?"

Gina's body gave an uneasy shudder. "Yes. At least who delivered me to the kidnappers."

Good lord. "Who was it?"

She swallowed heavily. "Gregg van Halen. Works for CIA. Black ops."

"My God. Someone from *our* side?"

Now Tara understood why Kick had been so adamant about getting Gina out of the research center before DHS arrived.

"Who'd have thought." Gina's bruised eyes leaked tears from the corners. "We were lovers," she whispered, her voice cracking.

Jesus. "You must really hate him," Tara said without thinking.

"You have no idea." But the expression on Gina's face didn't look like hatred. It looked more like utter desolation.

Tara carefully took Gina's battered hand in both of hers, anger surging through her on the other woman's behalf. "Please don't tell me you still have *feelings* for the bastard?"

The rescued hostage turned her head slowly, gazed up at Tara, eyes swimming. "How could I possibly still have feelings for a man who's so heartless and evil?"

Ho-boy. The poor woman was in far worse shape than

Tara had thought. Physical injuries would heal in time. But how could anyone ever get over such a badly broken heart? The goddamn *bastard*.

"You *don't* love him," Tara told her firmly. "You're just confused. In shock. Not yourself yet. Ever hear of Stockholm syndrome?"

Gina smiled bleakly. Weak, but at least it was a smile.

"Yeah," she whispered. "Stockholm syndrome. That must be it."

THEY were trying to intimidate her.

But Rebel refused to be intimidated. Seriously. The Zero Unit goons would have to do better than to keep her cooling her heels for more than an hour in a nasty sectioned-off room guarded by two armed-to-the-teeth apes in camouflage. To her, that was a normal day at work. Well. If you switched the camouflage for bad polyester suits.

Besides, it was hard to be intimidated when the guards kept ogling her legs. She might not be able to take them both down, but she could sure embarrass the heck out one of them if she chose to display some of her martial arts skills. But nah. No sense antagonizing the apes. She didn't mind the ogling that much. And she'd much rather bring their commander down a peg or two instead, when he appeared.

She continued to pace, high heels clicking on the bare cement floor, until finally the grimy steel door slammed opened and a man strode in. Wiry, compact, but all muscle, he was older than the apes—pushing fifty or more. Definitely the zookeeper. They straightened instantly, eyes front, morphing into tough-guy mode. Apparently *she* didn't warrant the macho posturing. What. Ever.

After curtly introducing himself as ZU commander Colonel Frank Blair, he asked, "Aren't you frightened, Miss Haywood?"

You had to pick your battles, so she chose to ignore his deliberate slight in not using her FBI creds to address her. "Should I be frightened?" she asked sweetly, looking directly into the colonel's bleached-out hazel eyes.

He stepped closer, trying to tower over her, but her three-inch spikes foiled that attempt. He had a stern, weathered face, and a head dusted with silver that was buzzed in a Marine cut so short you could see more skin than bristly hair. His thin lips looked more accustomed to shouting orders than cracking a smile. She didn't recognize him from her days as liaison, hadn't ever heard the name Col. Frank Blair. Not surprising, as Alex had been even more tight-lipped then than he was now. He had, however, occasionally mentioned a piss-and-iron unit commander she would put good money on was none other than this man.

"Do you have any *idea* what kind of shit storm I could bring down on you for coming here without a top-secret CIA clearance?" he barked.

"Like you did for Gina Cappozi, you mean, sir? Except, oh, wait. You summoned her here yourself. Didn't you?"

His gaze sharpened. "What exactly do you know about Dr. Cappozi?"

Aha. No denial, therefore a direct hit. "Why? Afraid you'll be implicated in her kidnapping?" she baited.

She could trade questions with him all afternoon without giving away a damn thing. Unlike him—who was obviously a field man, not an interrogator. He'd just admitted he knew Gina. Rebel had *not* called her *Dr.* Cappozi.

She saw exactly when he realized his mistake. *Too late.* He gave her a death-ray glare.

Temper, temper.

"SAC Montana and I are in charge of the FBI investigation into Dr. Cappozi's disappearance," she said, matching him toe-to-toe for authority. Then she deliberately softened her tone. "You should tell us what you know, Colonel Blair. We're not after Zero Unit. Unless it's somehow involved, of course . . ." She let the sentence hang. An invitation to come clean.

Not that she expected him to. And he didn't disappoint. Instead, he glared at her for a full minute. Maybe two. Nice try, bucko. She didn't flinch. Didn't look away. She occupied the time counting the sun crinkles around his angry eyes. She'd reached twenty-three when he broke the silence with a growl.

"You are a very stupid woman, Miss Haywood. You have

no damn clue who it is you're dealing with. If you so much as whisper that my unit had anything to do with—"

She interrupted his saber-rattling. "You should have thought about that before you had your man contact Dr. Cappozi."

"I didn't."

"Funny, ZU's dummy phone number is on her LUDs. And before you consider hacking into phone company records and removing it, that information is already in every FBI file having to do with the case."

A muscle ticked in his jaw. Guilt?

"I'd like to speak with the man who was sent to deal with her," she told him.

"I know nothing about—"

"His name is Gregg van Halen. *That's* in the FBI files, too."

The muscle ticked again. "Captain van Halen is unavailable."

Oh, what a shock. But a captain, eh? She tucked away the new morsel of information. "In that case, you tell me. Why was Dr. Cappozi summoned here to Zero Unit, Colonel Blair?"

"Don't be absurd," he barked. "Outsiders are not welcome at ZU-NE, let alone summoned. You of all people should know, Miss Haywood, if we need to speak with nonops, it is done elsewhere."

"I have a witness who says otherwise," she informed him.

A lethal edge crept into his eyes. "Then they're wrong."

Rebel hadn't really expected to get the truth about anything from anyone here. But it was still frustrating. Except in the sense that a cover-up seemed to confirm there was something going on. Zero Unit, or someone in the unit, *was* involved in Gina's disappearance. If not in more nefarious activities.

The question was, was it just one individual, or the whole unit? A chilling question.

"Associating with known terrorists is a serious offense, Colonel," she observed. "How does a charge of treason sound?"

The guards stirred. Blair went deathly still. "Seems to me, Miss Haywood, it's your friend Alex Zane who's been associating with terrorists for the past year and a half. Why don't you ask *him* about Dr. Cappozi's disappearance?"

At the deliberate insult, she came dangerously close to punching the two-faced creep. *Careful*, she ordered herself. This was just a clumsy fishing expedition, designed to make her lose her cool and betray Alex's whereabouts. "He's *your* operator, Colonel Blair," she said evenly. "Tell me where he's hiding, and I will ask him."

Blair's eyes narrowed. "Strange how he seems to have dropped off the face of the earth, but the FBI is not investigating *his* disappearance."

So Zero Unit *was* looking for Zane. Out of concern? Or to eliminate a loose end, as his friend Kick Jackson feared?

She folded her arms over her jacket front. "Alex Zane is a black-ops operator for CIA. I assume disappearing is what he does." She allowed her brows to arch, feigning curiosity. "Why? Can't you find him, either? Is he really missing?"

He didn't answer. Getting smarter? Nah.

"Anyway." She reached into her jacket pocket. Instantly, the two apes' guns were racked and pointing at her. Since hers had been taken away—just as Montana had predicted—she gave the colonel a withering look. "Oh, please. Tell your creatures to chill out." She pulled out a business card and extended it to him. "Here's my number. If you decide to cooperate, or if van Halen shows up, give me a call."

He didn't take the card.

This was getting really old. She jammed it into his camo T-shirt pocket. "By the way, what have you done with SAC Montana?"

Not that she was worried. Blair had almost certainly interrogated her boss first. The colonel was obviously an old-school military lifer. God forbid Blair see a mere woman as any kind of threat to himself or to the ZU.

He ignored her query. She got the distinct feeling the old buzzard was miffed at her. Sure enough, he turned on a bootheel and marched out of the room without another word.

The two guards hustled her out after him, one in front and one behind, leading her back along the same angled corridor as they'd initially come in through. She glanced around, peering down several other passageways they passed by on the way out. The cavernous warehouse had been divided up into a rat maze of rooms and narrow passages, but the metal walls reached only halfway to the two-story ceiling. There was little furniture, less equipment. Only a distant echo of men's crude laughter and the hum of electronics echoing off the steel-beam rafters.

It all struck her as somehow wrong. Temporary. Thrown together. Totally unlike the streamlined, well-stocked headquarters Rainie had described being held in before getting shipped out on her harrowing adventure with Kick. Even Alex's vague, oblique remarks about where he'd been based for several years did not remotely resemble this place.

Well, ZU-NE had moved locations since both those two had seen it. Maybe this space hadn't been fixed up yet to the ZU's usual specs.

"You all right?"

She spun toward the demanding male voice. It was Montana. They had arrived back in the bay where the Beemer was parked.

As she broke ranks and strode over to him, Montana pushed away from the front fender and put his hands on his hips, sweeping a furious look over her before narrowing his anger on her guards. He opened his mouth.

"Worried about me?" she interrupted before he said something that got them both in trouble. And earned them even one more minute in this hellhole. She wanted out of there.

"Of course I'm worried," he ground out. "It's been two fucking hours. God knows what they could have—"

"Language, sir," she told him with a relieved smile. It was amazing how good it felt to see him again. "I'm fine. Reall—"

To her shock, his hand cupped her shoulder and he leaned in and kissed her cheek. "Thank God," he muttered, herding her into the Beemer as he called out to the guards, "Open the damn bay!"

Okay, *that* was unprofessional.

But . . . not unpleasant.

A brief thought of Zane flashed through her mind, followed by a tiny spike of guilt.

Which was, of course, ridiculous. Being kissed on the cheek by Wade Montana was not cheating. Besides, Rebel was *not* romantically involved with Alex Zane. Never would be.

If Wade kissed her, on the cheek or anywhere else, she had

absolutely nothing to feel guilty about. He was handsome, intelligent, and darn sexy. In fact, if she had a lick of sense, she'd encourage him to do it again, and not on the cheek.

Except, of course, he was also her SAC.

Yikes. Not a good idea. Kissing was not something you did with your boss.

So not.

Even if it could take her mind off Alex Zane.

The car did a squealing U-turn, shot outside into the bright afternoon sunshine, and the huge warehouse bay door lumbered down, sealing them out with a final metallic death rattle. *Thank goodness.* The whole place gave her the definite creeps.

Rays of sunlight poured in through the Beemer's windshield like liquid gold. After the hours spent in the cavelike warehouse, Rebel squinted against the light, shaded her eyes, and looked around to get her bearings. Apparently, Montana's eyes had trouble adjusting, too. As soon as they reached the mouth of the alley, he abruptly pulled the car to a halt and put it in park.

"Jesus," he muttered.

"Lang—" she started to say.

"Shut up and come here," he said and grabbed her.

Her eyes popped. "Wha—?"

His arms banded around her, and his lips crashed down on hers, warm and urgent.

"Oh!"

And suddenly she forgot all about his bad language.

TWENTY

MARC hadn't liked watching Tara take off on the evac helo. But he'd had no choice. His orders were to go after Abbas Tawhid. No way could she come along on the deadly hunt. No way Marc *wanted* her along. She'd be better off taking care of Gina Cappozi, under the close protection of STORM.

Until Marc could get back to her.

As soon as the Homeland Security team arrived at the research station, the STORM away team sped back to their base camp to pack up and go. Where, he wasn't sure. The only things they'd found at the scene had been a few abandoned clothes and a stack of various sports magazines. Were those magazines a clue? Maybe. Or maybe it was just a houseful of bored men following the scores, because whoever was in charge of the TV seemed to have kept it on CNBC. Wasn't that a business channel? Definitely not sports. In any case, the magazines were the only lead they had of a possible target, or at least a type of target. Maybe. Gina hadn't been much help in that regard.

Marc whipped through his cabin at the base camp, hastily throwing things into his duffel bag. But as he swiped a shirt off the bed, he stalled in mid-motion.

It was the T-shirt he'd given Tara to sleep in last night.

The one he'd peeled off her incredible body before making love to her, when she'd come to him hurting, needing his arms and his comfort.

The memory nearly took his breath away.

Or was it simply panic he was feeling?

He *did* want to get back to her . . . didn't he?

Or maybe he should just stay away . . . Let her go, despite this overwhelming sense of rightness, this uncharacteristic and irrational inner certainty that she belonged to him. *Dieu*, he'd practically forced her to acknowledge his right to her affections. That was not like him. His sisters had taught him a little honey worked much better on women than making demands. What was it about Tara Reeves that brought out his unreasonable inner caveman? From the moment he'd set eyes on her, he just hadn't been able to help himself.

God knew he didn't have time for a woman in his life. And even if he did, he still wasn't convinced Tara was the kind of woman he'd want in it. Last night's emotional connection had surely just been an illusion, the result of an overly tense situation, and going too long without a lover . . .

Or . . . was all this crazy stuff he was feeling the real deal? Something he should grab onto with both hands and not let pass him by?

Was he genuinely falling for the annoying state trooper?

Bordel de merde. He stuffed the *foutu* T-shirt into his duffel.

This was *not* the time for second-guessing his love life. Or his usual pathetic lack of one. For each minute they delayed, Tawhid and his al Sayika cell slipped further away. Marc needed all his wits about him for the coming chase down.

From nearby came the sound of a chopper landing, and Quinn popped his head into the cabin. "Transpo's here. We're oscar mike."

"Right behind you."

Grabbing his duffel, he ran after Quinn to the clearing between the cabins, joined by Kick and Darcy along the way. He jumped into the helo, the last one on board.

"Rand and Kowalski?" he shouted.

"Driving the Moby," Quinn shouted back.

Marc winced. Ski would be behind the wheel doing at least seventy down the country roads, with Rand in the back at the UAV's control monitors. No doubt he'd be hanging on for dear life, while systematically scanning the last forty-eight hours of aerial footage hoping for a glimpse of the tangos at the research station, so the team could get some visuals on them.

Exchanging a thumbs-up with Quinn, Marc slammed the helo door shut, accepted a mic'd helmet, and strapped himself in.

With any luck, Rand would also be able to nail down their departure time from the station and identify the ground vehicles the terrorists were using. But meanwhile . . .

"Where are we headed?" he asked over the helmet comm.

"Baton Rouge," Quinn came back. "Possible sighting of our targets."

"Already?" Kick said in surprise.

Buckled in next to Quinn, Darcy nodded. "It's a real long shot, but the state police got a report of an incident on the outskirts of town. A nervous gas station attendant called it in. Six men arguing in what sounded like Arabic. One of them appeared to be sick."

She brought up a map grid on her laptop and pointed to a location just south of Baton Rouge. "There."

"Time frame?" Marc asked.

"Just under an hour ago."

Not great, but an intercept may still be doable.

"According to the report, they were driving two cars and a van," Quinn said. "Which could fit. The attendant got a partial plate on one of them."

Darcy worked her laptop like Schroeder at his piano. "I'll have the filling station security footage of the cars up in a jiff," she said, "and I can access live feeds from LDOT traffic cams along the freeways until Rand can retarget the UAV to Baton Rouge."

The sat comm crackled. "STORM Alpha Six, this is STORM Sierra, over."

"This is STORM Six actual, go ahead Sierra, over," Quinn answered Ski, who had apparently taken over incoming comm duty while Rand was busy.

"The Homies report putting response teams in position at the airport, bus, and train terminals, over."

Kick shook his head and spoke into the helmet mic, which Ski could also hear. "Tawhid won't risk public transportation. Not yet."

"Not until he's ready to release the virus," Marc concurred.

Quinn passed him a road map of the U.S. "For which we have to assume multiple targets spread out across the country. Any guesses?"

"With three vehicles, they've probably already split up," Marc said, trying to unfold the map to show Louisiana. In the small confines of the helo, he only succeeded in getting it in everyone's faces. Darcy swatted away the crinkling paper.

The sat comm crackled again. "STORM Command reports they're preparing to run a real-time probability analysis to pinpoint the most likely release areas based on the ground routes the tangos choose, over."

North of Alaska, Kick looked askance. "Based on what? The assumption that these insane zealots are making rational decisions? Tell them good luck with that, over."

Quinn made a face at Kick, then told Ski, "We'll need to be informed of any stolen vehicles along all the possible routes, over."

"Yes, sir. Already requested, over," Ski confirmed.

"Keep me informed, over."

Quinn opened a large steel weapons locker bolted to the floor between the aft seats. It was filled with the usual mission smorgasbord of weaponry. "In case there's any doubt," he said to those on the helo, "our orders are to stop these motherfuckers any way we can."

Wordlessly, Kick scooped up a handful of clips from the locker, then lifted a single weapon from his own duffel—an HK sniper rifle if Marc wasn't mistaken—and started methodically checking it over.

Giving up on the map, Marc thrust it at Darcy, sending her a grin when she rolled her eyes at him. What? Bits of paper and assessments were her job. His job involved a more deadly and decisive arsenal.

From the locker, he grabbed a dozen clips for his Beretta, helped himself to an M4 and a dozen clips for that, an additional combat knife, a few grenades, and several flashbangs. He didn't want to risk messing with explosives INCONUS, so he passed by that stuff. But he grabbed a can of pepper spray. You just never knew.

"STORM Romeo here. Gas station video link is up, over," Rand said over the sat comm.

Darcy clicked a key and turned her laptop so they could all see the screen.

Marc glanced at Kick, who'd suddenly gone absolutely still except for a muscle clenching and unclenching in his jaw.

"That him?" Quinn asked. "You can confirm it's Tawhid?"

Kick gave an abrupt nod. "Yes, sir. That's him. The one getting out of the van."

"Sierra," Quinn said over the comm, "please inform STORM Command we have a positive ID on our target, over."

"Copy that, over."

All eyes turned to the jerky video as the gas station vignette played out. One of the tangos was filling the brown, windowless van's tank while the others gathered by the pump and started arguing. The video had no sound, but the disagreement seemed to be over who would drive one of the two other cars.

"Dr. Cappozi said besides Tawhid and her attacker, there were four others, maybe five," Marc said. "I'm only seeing four, *including* Tawhid."

There was Tawhid, plus a short skinny guy, an older balding man wearing a head cloth, and a bearded man with a potbelly.

"No, five," said Darcy, pointing at a sneakered foot barely visible inside the van through the open sliding door.

"There could also be more inside that we can't see," Quinn said. "Romeo, any chance the UAV can get a body count, over?"

Besides regular optical viewing, the UAV was also equipped with an infrared sensor.

"Sorry, sir. Even if we could see through metal, the UAV won't be in range for another twenty, over," Rand replied.

"Do we have IDs on the other four tangos yet, over?" Quinn asked Rand.

"That's a negative. STORM Command's still working on facial recognition, over."

"Copy that. Okay, until we have names," Quinn said, signaling Darcy to freeze the video, "Tawhid is designated Tango One. Tango Two will be him." He pointed at the bearded guy. "Tango Three's the bald guy, and Tango Four the skinny one. Sneaker guy is Tango Five." As he spoke, Darcy tagged the photos on the screen and sent them to Rand.

Everyone acknowledged, and Darcy pressed play on the video again. They watched the argument wind down and Tawhid stalk back to the van. Tango Three got in behind the wheel of one of the two other cars, a silver midsized sedan.

"Looks like Tango Four won the coin toss," Marc observed as the skinny terrorist climbed into the white compact that Tango Two had been driving when they arrived. Instead, Tango Two joined Tawhid in the van, then all three vehicles pulled out of the filling station and headed back toward the freeway, and shortly thereafter disappeared out of range.

"Sierra, do we have a BOLO out on the bad guys, over?"

"Affirmative," Ski responded. "State police put it out as soon as they got that partial plate from the attendant. But there's not much for them to go on for the other vehicles, over."

Rand interjected, "Alpha Six, I'm working on enhancing the number plates, but the quality on this video is shit, over." Doing it in the back of a fast-moving van probably didn't help, either, Marc thought.

On the laptop, Darcy fast-forwarded through the gas station footage until the state police cruiser arrived on the scene. The troopers were having a casual conversation with the attendant when one of them got a call on his shoulder radio. As he listened, his posture went into alert.

"That call must be the DHS orders to apprehend the suspects," Darcy suggested.

Sure enough, the two troopers ran for their unit, hit lights and sirens, and took off in the direction the tangos had vanished. According to the video time stamp, that had been almost twenty-five minutes ago.

Just then, Ski came back. "Alpha Six, LSP is reporting a white compact matching the BOLO proceeding east of the city on the I-12. No sign of the other vehicles, over."

Everyone in the helo came to attention. This was real time!

Ski gave the coordinates to Darcy and she worked her magic, bringing up the corresponding I-12 traffic cams on the laptop. When the rooftop call number of the reporting police unit appeared, she froze the frame. Yes! The white compact was right in front of it. She reversed the video slowly, focusing in on the traffic. Several silver sedans passed by. But without a plate number, it was useless to try to pinpoint the right one. No brown vans appeared.

"Romeo, can you light a fire under the UAV, over?" Quinn quickly asked.

"Sorry, sir. At top speed already, over," Rand informed them.

"Fucking great," Marc and Kick muttered in unison, eyes glued to the screen.

The UAV was an amazing piece of compact spy technology, but the aircraft was designed to dwell in the air rather than fly quickly through it—its top speed was less than a hundred mph—so moving from one mission location to another took precious time. Which they didn't have at the moment.

The LSP cruiser drove out of range, and Darcy switched to the next traffic cam along the route. A few moments later, the white compact came into view.

Suddenly, it careened to a halt at the shoulder of the freeway.

"Jesus!" they all chorused in surprise. Then, "Shit!" as the state troopers swung their unit nose-first alongside the compact. The doors popped open.

Darcy's hands flew to her cheeks. "God, no."

"*Stay in the fucking car!*" Kick growled at the computer.

But they didn't. The troopers started to get out, weapons drawn.

"*Non, sacre—*" Marc and the others watched helplessly as Tango Four leapt from the white car holding a round canister.

"God*damn* it!"

"Fucking *A*!" Quinn shouted as all hell broke loose on the screen. Tango Four ran right at the cops, holding the canister up and aimed at their faces. "Sierra! Get DHS on the horn *now*, over!"

"On it, boss!"

Too late. As Tango Four shook the can at the officers, he pulled a gun from his waistband. In a split second, the cops dropped, opened fire, and shot down Tango Four where he stood.

"Contacting the authorities to divert traffic," Darcy called out, furiously tapping keys on her cell phone.

"When the fuck did this happen?" Quinn asked her. "Please tell me that time stamp is wrong."

"No, it's really happening now. Real time."

Quinn turned to the helo pilot and shouted directions. "Get us there!" he ordered. Then to the team, "We'll take charge until DHS arrives. Full hazmat gear, people. This is not a drill."

Marc and Kick exchanged a deadly look and nodded in perfect accord. Time to split up the team.

"Boss," Marc said to Quinn. "We can't let Tawhid slip through our fingers. You and Darcy can handle this. Kick and I request permission to go after that brown van."

SHE *must be insane*.

Rebel made a halfhearted attempt to pull her hand from SAC Wade Montana's as he eased his body close to hers in the hallway just outside the four-star hotel room he'd checked them into.

"Last chance to say no."

This was *really* insane. Sure, she'd told herself over and over she needed to find a man to make her get over Alex . . . but this was not exactly what she'd had in mind. Not *this* man.

But then he kissed her. A deep, heavy, body-slamming kiss against the wall that brooked no resistance, and left no doubt as to where it was heading when he opened that door. *Straight into the king-sized bed that took up most of the room.* How long had it been since she'd felt like this? Forever.

She gave up, moaned a low, "Yes," and kissed him back. He pushed her inside and snicked the lock home.

His jacket, then hers, hit the floor as he relentlessly backed her across the room toward the bed, stripping them as he went. His tie and his shoes quickly followed. She stumbled, he caught her, and somehow he maneuvered off her heels and they went sailing. The kiss never let up. His breath was heavy, her moans visceral, and his hands were all over her as he took the kiss deeper still.

Yes. Yes, this could work.

He shoved her skirt down her hips, then his hands were on her there, caressing her backside, gliding over her sex, then up and under her blouse, cupping her breasts.

She gasped as his fingers slipped into her bra and squeezed her bare, sensitive flesh. He thumbed her nipples hard, and she saw stars. The backs of her knees hit the bed and she tumbled backward onto the mattress. He fell on her, devouring her mouth as he swiftly worked her blouse open. Then a jarring rip lifted her feet and her hose vanished; she felt a rush of cool air on her wet folds as he wrenched her legs apart and landed between them. There was a snap of latex.

Before she could catch her breath, his thick, hungry cock rammed into her, thrusting in deep and hard, clear to the hilt.

She bit back a throaty scream. Drowning in a stunning mix of shock and pleasure. How had this happened so fast?

He halted his full-frontal assault with a guttural moan, then scythed even deeper by small degrees, inching up under her thighs with his muscular legs until he could go no further.

"Fuck me, Rebel," he groaned into her ear. "Fuck me till I beg for mercy."

His plea penetrated her mind as abruptly as his sex had penetrated her body. Powerful, carnal, *irresistible*.

"You first," she pleaded and opened herself to him completely. Wanting more. Wanting to feel what it was like to be totally taken, to be possessed by a man who wouldn't stop until he'd gotten what he wanted and had wrung every possible erotic sensation from her body. A man who wanted *her*.

He did a slow grind over her, pushing his hard angles into her soft curves with a crude thoroughness. "Say it," he demanded.

"Please," she begged, with a sharp inhale at the alien feel of his thick cock splitting her apart and stretching her insides to bursting. Her body trembled. *She'd forgotten it felt so good.*

His tongue toyed with the shell of her ear, making her squirm, impaled and helpless under him, drowning in the sensation.

"Tell me, Rebel," he ordered in a gravelly whisper. His hands slid up her thighs, grasping below her knees, and pushed her legs wider still. "What do you want me to do to you?"

He pulled out a few inches and pushed back in, a graphic illustration of the word he wanted from her. And of the compelling power he held over her.

Finally she understood. She shivered, unsure if she could actually form the sounds.

"Is saying it so much worse than doing it?" he asked.

"I don't swear," she said in illogical distress, caught in a web of indecision. And realized at once how absurd that sounded when confronted with her actual position.

He licked his tongue across her cheek. "But you fuck. You fuck your boss. Hell, you fuck a man who might possibly have murdered the last woman he fucked."

And just like that, the uncertainty she'd felt earlier about him returned in a horrible rush.

She had to get up! Get away! She was too exposed. Too vulnerable to his will. Too—

Wait.

Suddenly what he'd said registered fully.

The *last* woman . . . ? She peered up at him. But he and Gina had broken up more than two years ago.

He gazed down at her, a strained smile slowly peeking through the powerful sexual arousal burning in his eyes. "Okay. There may have been one or two others in between."

The admission caused a peculiar reaction to spiral through her belly. Under the circumstances, it *should* have made her jealous. But instead she felt oddly . . . relieved.

Because of Alex? Because she didn't want to be that important to this man . . . because she was in love with another?

No.

Get Alex Zane out of this bed, girl. He had no business being there.

Alex did not want her. He'd made that perfectly clear by his choice of fiancée. And Rebel was not into threesomes. Of either flavor.

She wanted *this* man. The man inside her.

She took a deep breath. Lifted her lips to her boss's mouth. And whispered intently into it, "Fuck me, Wade. Fuck me now."

THE STORM helo made its emergency landing on the east-bound lanes of the I-12 freeway a quarter mile behind where the Louisiana State Police cruiser sat. Traffic had been stopped at the previous exit, and the two troopers who had yet to be clued in to the fact that they might not live to see next week had been radioed with strict orders to keep themselves isolated from everyone, especially the suspect.

As soon as Darcy and Quinn jumped onto the pavement wearing hazmat suits and carrying med kits and their personal duffels in special hazmat gear bags, the helo lifted off again with Kick and Marc still on board. Darcy waved them off with only a brief second of concern. How the frick had *she* gotten stuck teamed up with Quinn? But there was no time to worry about her private purgatory. They had a real, immediate hell to deal with.

The good news was that Tango Four was miraculously still alive. Barely, but there was a chance he'd make it if they got him to a hospital before he bled out.

She and Quinn worked like a well-oiled machine. They'd done enough ops together to know their natural division of labor without exchanging more than a few hand signals and nods. Once they'd hiked to the scene, Quinn swiftly took charge of the suspect, and Darcy took care of the witnesses. In this case, a pair of recalcitrant good ol' boy cops who were convinced whatever shi-yit was in that spray can was nothin' couldn't be cured with two aspirin and a few shots of bourbon. Until she mentioned anthrax. That got their attention real quick. And also prompted the other good news of the day.

"Is that stuff invisible or somethin'?" one of them asked, nervously checking his clothing and hands. "How'r you s'posed to know you got it on you?"

"The residue should look like a fine powder. Where did he spray you?"

"Well, damn, darlin'. Nothin' came out of that ol' perfume can he tried to git us with."

The other man nodded, his eyes darting to where Quinn was zipping the bandaged-up terrorist into a special hazmat containment bag. "We'd thought it was pepper spray and we got lucky."

The two traded the suddenly spooked look of men who'd traveled a lot of miles together and seen death before, but never their own deaths staring them in the face from such close quarters.

"Guess we got *real* lucky."

"Yeah," she agreed. And they weren't the only ones. If what they said was true and the canister had failed to spray the contents, or even released just a tiny amount, it was a huge break.

She told Quinn, who called in the news immediately.

But she wasn't taking any chances. By the time the DHS team descended in their own trio of helos, she'd managed to coax the two troopers into an extra set of hazmat suits and injected them with doses of Cipro from the med kit. She then helped them up into the same helo Tango Four's stretcher was loaded onto, for evac to a secure hospital.

Quinn had been busy, too. He'd chem-bagged the spray canister, and was now giving the white compact car a visual inspection for anything that might lead them to the other terrorists or hint at their ultimate targets.

"Anything usable?" she asked.

He shook his head, holding up evidence bags containing a small Koran, three bottles of water, and a well-worn baseball cap embroidered with the Knicks logo. "Good for DNA. Not terribly useful in terms of destination."

Darcy frowned at the hat. The adjustable band was let out almost all the way. "Does that cap look too big for our guy?"

Quinn studied it critically. "Hmm. Yeah. But wasn't Tango Two originally driving this car? He probably forgot it when he switched to the van."

That made sense. T-2 was a lot bulkier than skinny T-4. "You're right."

"We'll compare DNA, just in case. Good catch," Quinn said.

The DHS hazmat team took over, efficiently testing and clearing the scene. Thank God, no trace of the virus was found. But the whole section of freeway nevertheless had to be sanitized with a special sterilization foam before being released to traffic. Which meant more time ticked by.

Darcy and Quinn were stashed in one of the two remaining helos, awaiting the others so they could all be airlifted at once to a decontamination unit that was being set up in a nearby empty parking lot.

"This is a complete waste of time," Darcy grumbled in angry frustration, trying to get even remotely comfortable sitting in the bulky hazmat suit in the narrow helo jump seat. "We don't need to be *de*contaminated if there was no contamination in the first place."

Quinn was too busy unfolding his stupid map to respond. His jerky movements told her he agreed, but Quinn was never one to complain, even when he was royally pissed off. She could take a lesson.

With a huff, she retrieved her laptop from her duffel and pulled up Google Maps. "You are so freaking old school. What are you looking for?"

"Besides a cold beer and a hot woman?" he muttered.

"Not remotely funny."

Even through the double hazmat visors she could see the sardonic look he shot her. Yeah, yeah, she was a cold bitch. That had been established years ago. She had to be, to keep her sanity in this job.

Or possibly, it was the job that let her hold her much-needed protective shield so firmly in place around her emotions. The shield that kept her from being torn apart by the things she saw . . . and by men like Bobby Lee Quinn. Lately she had begun to wonder. Because somehow Quinn had wormed his way under that shield. And for the life of her, she didn't know how to flush him out again.

"I'm looking for possible targets," he said, expertly unfurling the map and refolding it precisely to the section he wanted.

She wanted to scream and leap over and strangle him for being so damn perfect. She took a cleansing breath and concentrated on her laptop, IMing STORM command for any updates. But there was nothing new.

"We have to go on the assumption that those sports magazines were there at the research station for a reason."

"You think they're looking to target sports venues with the virus?"

"A stadium holds a hell of a lot of people."

"True. What sports are going this time of year?"

"Football. Basketball. Hockey. College ball."

"A lot of stadiums." She suddenly remembered the cap they'd found. "What do the Knicks play?"

After an eye roll of male superiority, he told her, "Basketball." Then his eyes widened and met hers. "At Madison Square Garden."

Madison Square— Holy crap. She tried to dredge up what she knew about the famous New York landmark. Not much, other than . . . "Isn't Penn Station right under it?"

"Yep," Quinn said. "Da-amn. I think we need to report this to Command."

"You don't think we're reaching?"

"Hell, yeah, we're reaching. But right now it's all we've got."

He filched the laptop from her and typed "Knicks" into Google with two hazmat-gloved fingers. It took several tries to get it right, but he smiled in triumph when their current season's schedule appeared on the screen. God, he was cute.

She turned away and crossed her arms against the crazy impulse to touch him.

"We make a good team, you and me," Quinn said into the hovering silence a few minutes later.

"Better than all your other women?"

Damn. She hadn't meant to say that out loud.

"Baby, you know you're the only woman I want."

She stifled the absurd pitter-pat of her heart. Oh, please. The only woman? Yeah, well, at least for the duration of the op.

Not good enough.

Not anymore.

"Let me show you how much."

She had to swallow her retort because several of the DHS guys finally trooped over and started climbing into the helicopter.

Quinn's gaze lingered on her for a moment, but she didn't let herself meet it, smiling instead at the other faceless men and closing up her laptop, anxious to get on with the mission. The sooner they caught Tawhid, the sooner she could get away from Quinn. Regain her equilibrium. And rid herself of the dangerous notion that a man like him, or *any* man, could ever love her for always, instead of just until someone better came along.

It was a quick hop over to where the large decon tent had been set up, complete with a tanker truck hooked up to it. She'd been through the procedure many times before, of course, but never on this scale. There'd been more than a dozen people at the freeway scene, all of whom now had to shower and scrub their suits before getting out of them. After the humans were done, the three helos would go through a similar decon process, which was why the STORM pilot had dropped them so far away from the scene initially.

Well, at least they didn't have to strip naked. Any contamination would be on the *outside* of the hazmat suits, not the inside. Small favors.

As though reading her mind, Quinn winked. Erotic visions of his nude body in the shower last night shot through her head. He couldn't quite hide the lecherous grin that wanted to peek out through his visor.

Cute he may be, but God, was he arrogant.

"Bastard," she silently mouthed.

He just laughed, his ice blue eyes twinkling like the aurora borealis.

And that was pretty much when the realization hit, hard and fast. Her heart sank like a stone. She really didn't stand a fucking chance here.

She was hopelessly in love with the asshole.

And there wasn't a damn thing she could do about it.

TWENTY-ONE

SHE was thinking about him. Well, more precisely, she was thinking about his cock.

Bobby Lee wasn't fooled by Zimmie's seeming indifference as she stalked away from the helo toward the decon tent. No, not one little bit. Even in the waning light of late afternoon, he could see the telltale flush rise to her cheeks at his suggestive wink, and the glint of longing lance through her eyes before she managed to stomp it out again.

He had to admit, he also felt that longing. Acutely.

Screw his decision to honor her wishes. He wanted her, damn it. And she wanted him. She *did*. There was simply no hiding real desire, no denying the true passion they had for each other, no matter how hard they tried.

The real question was why she thought she had to try—and worse, to put an end to their relationship. It didn't make any sense. They'd been sharing bodies since day one. He'd had her under him within hours of their first meeting, and she'd never had any inconvenient qualms about having sex with him in the nearly half dozen years since.

Not until this mission.

What the hell had happened?

He refused to believe her change of heart had anything to

do with stinkin' Fiji. He'd apologized more than once for that idiotic misstep. She'd also denied in fairly certain and insulting terms that she wanted a commitment from him when the crazy notion had struck him like a lightning bolt yesterday in the truck. And it was absolutely *not* because she'd grown tired of him physically. That was just plain not true—as evidenced on the first night he'd arrived at camp and crawled into bed with her.

But that was when the change had come—after they made love that first night, when she'd squeezed out of him that he was taking her command. Could she still be upset about that? She had to know he'd give it up in a hot minute if it meant so much to her. He'd never been on a power trip . . . He was all about getting the job done, not about who was in charge. She must know that about him after all these years together.

But if not that, then what?

Her abrupt withdrawal made no sense on any level. None at all.

And to be brutally honest, the idea of an entire future without Darcy Zimmerman in his bed, ever again . . . Well, that was downright depressing.

Suddenly, his chest hurt.

He strode after her to the decon tent and whipped open the flap. Inside, a dozen hazmat-suited guys were laughing and joking and squirting each other with the flexible red sprayers hanging from the ceiling. Zimmie was in the middle of them, being tagged and bounced from one man to the other. In his head, Bobby Lee knew the good-natured horseplay was a natural reaction, a decompression from the dangerous situation that had ended far better than anyone anticipated. And they were all covered from head to toe in spacesuits for fuck's sake!

He knew that.

But all he saw was a bunch of men flirting and teasing and touching Zimmie.

His Zimmie. Who for no good reason refused to flirt and tease and touch *him*.

Anger flared through him, and he had to physically restrain himself from going in swinging and flattening the whole damn lot of drooling men.

Instead, he forced himself to calmly and meticulously spray off his own suit, then get the hell out of there. As he strode past her, he snapped, "Zimmerman! You have sixty seconds to report for duty. Outside."

The horseplay stopped on a dime. But the moron DHS agents apparently found his order amusing. The startled silence was immediately broken by guffaws and chuckled personal commentary mingled with suggestive speculation on Bobby Lee's motives for taking her away from them.

Before he let fly a completely inappropriate retort, he whipped out through the opposite tent flaps into the adjacent changing area. Furiously, he stripped off his hazmat suit and handed it to the wary attendant, who returned his duffel bag. Then he stalked outside to wait for his recalcitrant lover. The sun was just kissing the horizon; he zipped up his jacket against the chill of the coming night.

It wasn't sixty seconds, but not too much longer before she emerged.

She wagged her head. "Way to improve interagency relations, Quinn," she said dryly.

God forbid she keep from sassing him.

"Oh, is that what you were doing?" he shot back, sick of holding it in. "Sorry to interrupt your fun, but in case you've forgotten, we still have at least four tangos at large."

Her jaw dropped, outrage filling her expression. "I haven't forgotten. How dare you imply—"

He did not want to hear it. "Rand arranged an SUV for us," he cut her off. "It's waiting at the north end of the lot." He took off into the gathering dusk in that direction.

Her clipped footsteps followed behind. "You are being a total butthead, you know that, Quinn?" she called.

He spun around and waited until she caught up, hands planted on his hips, too riled up to even think about what he was doing. She came to a halt mere inches away. Even in his fury, he admired that about her. She was never afraid. Not of him. Not of anything. He knew he was supposed to be the big, tough, black-ops guy, but whenever he was with her, he knew his back was covered. If they were attacked, she would defend him as hard and deadly as he'd defend her. He trusted her with his life in any situation. Any at all. There weren't many people he could say that about. But right now, her bravery only goaded him more.

She jutted her chin. "What?" she demanded, mirroring his aggressive stance. "Just spit it out."

"If you don't want to sleep with me," he growled between clamped teeth, "fine. But do *not* throw it in my face."

She was good, he'd give her that. She looked genuinely surprised. Hell, he was a bit surprised himself. He hadn't really meant to put his irrational jealousy on display.

Her eyes widened. "You mean back there in the—" Her mouth clapped shut. "You can*not* be serious."

But now it was out . . . He leaned down over her, nose to nose. "No? You think I'm not? Hell, yeah, I'm serious. I want to know what the *fuck* is going on. Why the woman I've been sleeping with for five years suddenly cuts me off with no explanation and starts flirting with every other man she meets."

Her lips parted a fraction. Just enough to distract him.

God*damn* it.

His attention zeroed in on her mouth. His blood pounded as it never had before. He was a hairsbreadth away from grasping her obstinate chin and taking those lips with his, dragging her to the SUV and—

Just then a knot of DHS agents tumbled out of the decon tent, laughing and slapping themselves on the back.

Bobby Lee came to his senses with a jolt. He took an unsteady step back from her. *Damn.* He had no business thinking about this stuff now.

Because *his* job still needed doing.

"Quinn—" she said uncertainly.

Jesus God on a freaking brick. This was *exactly* the kind of distraction he'd meant to prevent by accepting her ultimatum. The kind of distraction that could get a man in trouble. And torpedo a mission.

"Forget it," he growled. "Let's go. We're oscar mike."

He didn't wait for her explanation. Or even an argument. He started walking, scanning the darkening parking lot as he went, and saw the silhouette of a man standing by an SUV. That must be their contact.

Zimmie followed, matching his stride but hanging half a step behind. It occurred to him, as his temper slowly ebbed, that on an op he usually let her take the lead. He liked watching her six. Felt better having her in his sights, in case things went south, so he could protect her. But also because he knew she was good at blazing a trail, that she wouldn't hesitate to take the more dangerous route if it meant a better, or more certain, outcome. She was smart as a fox and resourceful as a mama bear. The perfect point man. And usually she relished that position.

All of which made him suddenly uncomfortable that she was deliberately lagging behind him.

He could feel her eyes on his back. And his insides prickled, like they did when he sensed an enemy trap—except it was a totally different kind of inner alarm going off. It was like . . . like he was missing something. Something important. Something about *her*. But for the life of him, he couldn't imagine what it was.

He let out a slow, unsteady breath.

Yeah. He was definitely losing it.

After this op, it was time for a vacation. Time to reassess what was going on with his life. Get himself squared away so this kind of shit didn't happen again.

"Major Quinn?"

He made himself shake it off. "Yep."

The man standing by the SUV handed him a set of keys. "You'll find a lockbox of useful items in the back, along with a stocked cooler." The man smiled at Zimmie. "Miss Zimmerman. There's a monitor and sat link to your team's mobile command center up front, and voice comm sets dialed into the rest of the team."

She smiled back. "Have we located the two other tango vehicles, sir?"

"Rand Jaeger is still working on it. I believe he's narrowed them down to a half dozen possibles each. They're running plates as we speak."

"The silver sedan?"

"Most likely traveling west. You are to proceed on that assumption, make up time and distance, secure the canister, and contain your target. Alive is better, but if confirmed through Command, deadly force may be used. This one does *not* get away. Understood?"

"Loud and clear. Speaking of targets, we have a theory," Bobby Lee said.

"I'm listening."

He quickly went over the meager clues of the magazines and the Knicks cap. "We realize it's a stretch, but thought we should mention it."

The man nodded consideringly. "The Garden would be a huge target. Command will give this one serious attention," the man said. "Excellent work, you two."

"Thank you, sir," Zimmie said.

The man handed Bobby Lee a manila envelope. "Good luck, Major Quinn. Miss Zimmerman." Again he smiled at her. Bobby Lee could feel his dander rising. He told himself it was because she was being so polite to the guy, and his use of Bobby Lee's old military rank. Not many people were privy to that intel, and he didn't like outsiders using it. But the next second the man was gone, melting into the black shadows between parked cars with the casual skill of a seasoned operator.

Jesus, he really needed to get ahold of himself.

Zimmie watched the guy vanish. "Wow. That was Kurt Bridger."

Bobby Lee glanced at her in surprise. "You're joking." She wasn't. "How do you know?"

Kurt Bridger was a legend within STORM, one of the original operatives recruited more than a decade ago from CIA's infamous Zero Unit. A few years older than Bobby Lee, Bridger had risen fast and hard to become a longtime member of Command. Every STORM operator had heard of Bridger, but only a handful could identify him by sight.

"We did an op together once," she said. "Back when I was new to STORM."

For some reason, that bit of information hit Bobby Lee square in the gut. Okay, maybe a little farther south. Jealousy surged through him once again, red hot and completely irrational. "You fuck him, too?"

Instead of denying it, her lips thinned. "You have got a real problem, you know that?"

Oh, yeah, he knew. He just didn't know what to do about it.

She lifted the back hatch and slung her duffel into the SUV, then turned to go around to the passenger side.

Chagrined, hurting, and feeling totally out to sea, he caught her around the waist to stop her. "Sorry," he said contritely, burying his face in her long blond hair despite the resistance he felt in her taut muscles. The scent of her hair and skin saturated his senses, along with the familiar feel of her body pressing into him. He groaned softly. "I just miss you so damn much. Baby, please tell me what I did to make you hate me. I'll make it up to you, I swear I will."

Her stiff posture softened, just a little. "Don't go all dramatic on me, Quinn. You know I don't hate you."

"Then what? Please, sugar, tell me so I can fix it."

She sighed. "Now isn't the time, Bobby Lee. Let's just finish this mission, okay? When it's done, we can talk if you still want to."

"Damn it, Zimmie—"

"Bridger is probably still watching us. You know how Command feels about personal problems. I don't want to lose my job."

Before he could stop her, she slid out of his arms.

Hell, she was right. He was being unprofessional and risking both their careers by dragging their relationship mess into the middle of an operation.

He tossed his duffel into the back of the SUV and slammed the hatch shut. Time to get a serious grip. Command probably *had* caught wind of their affair and sent Bridger to make sure this critical operation's effectiveness wasn't being compromised by it. Because the only other time Command sent out one of their own was to vet a possible promotion. And Bobby Lee sure as hell wasn't in line for one of those.

Jesus. Were they considering kicking him out of STORM? Did Zimmie know, and was distancing herself from him on purpose, to save his career? Or hers . . . ?

A sobering thought.

He climbed behind the wheel, started the engine, and leveled her a look. For a second, he considered asking. But no.

He trusted her. With his life *and* to tell him if he was in trouble.

"All right," he said and gave her a tight smile. "We'll finish this later. For now, get Rand on the comm. Let's go save the world."

But he couldn't help feeling at least a little hopeful. Because for the first time ever, she'd just called him Bobby Lee.

GINA woke up screaming.

"Shhh," a soft, feminine voice soothed. A warm cloth dampened her brow. "You're okay. It was just a dream."

Determinedly, Gina battled back the images still swirling in her sleep-drenched mind. *Blood. Fists. Hate-filled faces.*

She shuddered and opened her eyes. And found herself lying in a narrow bunk in a tiny but cheerful room. It was clean and smelled so good. Like fresh roses. There was a big bouquet of yellow blossoms filling a table at the foot of the bed. Strange. The water in the vase was vibrating. And there was a steady hum in the air. Suddenly, she realized she was strapped to the bed.

"Where am I?" she cried, struggling to sit up but unable to fight the straps holding her down. The terror from her nightmare resurfaced, threatening to morph into reality. She jerked her head frantically back and forth.

A pretty woman with wavy brown hair leaned forward from a seat next to the bunk. "You're on a private jet," she said, touching her shoulder gently. "That's why you're buckled in. We're en route to somewhere safe, Gina. It's okay. You're *safe* now. I promise."

That was when she realized she was clutching the woman's hand. She was squeezing it so hard the other woman's fingers were in danger of breaking.

"Sorry," she whispered, forcing herself to calm down. She tried to unclench her death grip.

The woman smiled sweetly at her and patted their joined fingers. "Don't worry. I'm tougher than I look. Remember me? I'm Tara."

Gina thought back. To her relief, she did remember. *That aw-*

ful place, a terrible fate pressing in on her. And then a miracle.
"You were there, when they . . ." She swallowed hard.

"Rescued you. Yes." Tara's smile widened in equal relief.
"Welcome back, Dr. Cappozi."

Suddenly, Gina remembered the rest. "The virus! Did they
get the canisters?"

"We've recovered one of them so far. Still tracking the others."

Panic lurched through her. "They have to find them. They
must, or—"

"They will." Tara leaned closer. "Gina, is there anything
else you remember? Anything your kidnappers said that
might help to pinpoint their targets?"

She let out an uneven breath and shook her head. "I'm
sorry. Everything's still so fuzzy. I don't even remember getting on this plane."

Again, Tara smiled gently. "They gave you a sedative and
an armful of antibiotics. You slept through the medevac ride
to the airport. Never mind. Think about it later, when you
aren't so groggy."

Gina glanced around and noticed there was no window in
the cabin. "Where are you taking me?"

"To a top-secret, private sanatorium in central New York,"
Tara said. "I'm told you can stay there until you've fully
recovered. For as long as you need to feel one hundred percent safe."

Safe.

It might be a very long time before she felt that way. If ever.

But omigod, she was alive!

She tried to wrap her mind around the fact that she could
be really and truly safe again.

Except, she wasn't.

She hardly dared put her deepest dread into words. The
mere thought made her tremble. "What if he finds me?" she
whispered.

"No one can find you there," Tara said. "Not Abbas Tawhid, not anyone."

She shook her head. "But you don't understand. The CIA—"

"The people who rescued you, they aren't with the government. And they are very aware of the suspicious circumstances of your kidnapping. They took you away from the

terrorists' hideout before Homeland Security showed up. Only a handful of people know you were found alive."

The implications hit Gina with a saturating wave of relief. "Everyone thinks I'm dead."

"For now. STORM Corps thought it would be safer that way."

The knot in her stomach eased a little more. "STORM Corps?"

"It stands for Strategic Technical Operations and Rescue Missions Corporation. That's the organization your friend's husband works for."

She meant Rainie. *Who was now married.* Gina closed her eyes and managed a smile. Her best friend had a lot of 'splaining to do. "Rainie knows I'm alive?"

"Yes. I can't tell you how happy she was to hear you'd been found."

Gina let out a long sigh, that final bit of good news at last allowing the tension to ease from her body. "When can I see her?"

"She'll be there when we arrive. Sleep now," Tara urged. "You need the rest."

The suggestion was all it took. Suddenly, Gina could barely fight the fatigue. "You'll stay with me?"

Her hand was gently squeezed. "I'm not going anywhere."

Safe at last.

Safe from Tawhid. Safe from the beatings and torture, safe from having to betray the country she loved.

She was safe now.

Well . . . almost. Unfortunately, there was one kind of danger she knew her rescuers would never be able to protect her from.

True, with time her body would heal, the terrorists would surely be caught, and everyone would tell Gina she was well and truly safe. There could be no more danger.

But they'd be wrong. So very wrong.

Because until that bastard Gregg van Halen was dead and buried in his grave, she would never be safe from the worst danger of all: the betrayal wrought by her own heart.

IT was the brown van, all right.

Empty.

Merde.

Frustration pelted through Marc's insides like shotgun pellets. A string of curses spilled from his lips as he hammered the roof of the abandoned van with his fist.

Gone.

The terrorists had used the oldest trick in the book. Driven the van into a crowded shopping mall parking lot and left it there. Despite the fact that it would be packed to the brim with shoppers, Marc would bet a year's salary this mall was not one of their chosen targets. They'd stolen a car or two, maybe even had vehicles here waiting for them, but they had no intention of releasing the deadly virus among the throng of shoppers.

Too bad DHS couldn't take any chances. The whole mall had to be evacuated, everyone exiting vetted, and the entire place searched and cleared. There would be angry shoppers, if not mass rebellion to calm down. All of which would take time and precious resources away from the hunt.

Tawhid knew exactly what he was doing.

"*De putain,*" Marc growled, and hit the van with his fist again.

"Yup," Kick agreed, equally furious. But Kick was a sniper and emotion rarely broke through his outward calm. "DHS is going to have a hard time keeping this one quiet."

Orders from Washington were to keep the situation deep under wraps until after the terrorists were caught and the virus threat eliminated. They'd managed to mislead the press into reporting the freeway incident as a lone gunman. But the media had a way of ferreting out the truth if given the slightest foothold. Even if they reported this mall thing as a routine bomb scare, some smart reporter was bound to put the freeway shooting together with this mall closing, reread the carefully worded DHS press briefs, and start asking some tough questions. Despite DHS claiming a national security info freeze, it was all bound to come out sooner than later.

"We need to be long gone before the feeding frenzy starts," Marc said. "Let the locals handle it. Less panic that way."

"Yup," Kick said, but he had his PDA out and was clicking through screens. "Hmm. There's something I want to check out before we split."

"Should I be worried?" Marc asked as Kick picked up the baseball bag that held his HK sniper rifle, ammo, and the rest of his gear and shouldered it.

The other man gave him a sinister grin. "Always." He trotted away down the endless row of cars. "Meet you at the helo in ten," he called over his shoulder.

Behind them, the shopping mall fell under full siege by cops and national guardsmen, lights flashing and bullhorns blaring. An unmarked tow truck pulled up behind the brown van to surreptitiously haul it away for inspection by the DHS forensics team. There was nothing left here for Marc.

"Hey, wait up!" he called after Kick and took off after him. He caught up, and together they loped down a ditch and over a set of railroad tracks, then along a narrow street. As soon as Marc saw the name on the side of one of the buildings, he knew exactly what Kick was thinking.

Evangelical Bible Seminary.

This could not be good.

Still loping, Kick pulled a Windbreaker from his bag and tossed it to Marc. *FBI* was emblazoned in big gold letters across the back. At the same time, Kick tugged on a black baseball cap embroidered with the FBI logo over his headset.

"Job change I'm not aware of?" Marc joked through his own headset mic.

Kick grinned and came back, "Only temporary."

Marc surveyed the main seminary building. It was one of those modern cement-and-glass deals, octagonal with square towers at each of the corners. White lights adorned the angles of the roof, and a flashing marquis advertised special December prayer services every day at seven p.m. It was now six forty-five.

"You getting a bad feeling?" he asked.

Kick nodded. "They would have had to drive right past on the way to the mall. I'm betting this was too enticing to pass up. Maybe create a diversion to help them get away."

Marc agreed.

When they approached the building, Kick pointed to the closest tower. "That's me. You try the front."

Adrenaline spiking, Marc trotted around to the main entrance. Kick's instincts had been right on. Sure enough, someone was inside, causing a stir among those gathered in the foyer. Upset people were shouting down a bearded man wearing a long white tunic over a potbelly, standing in the middle of the huge foyer waving his arms and screaming something unintelligible.

Tango Two.

Marc slipped inside and quickly assessed the interior of the building. The echoing foyer led past a honeycomb of rooms and passages, then emptied into a central, multistoried church area where he could hear a choir singing.

Donning the FBI Windbreaker, he ran for the sweeping marble staircase as he tapped the mic button on his comm. "This is STORM Mike. Come in, STORM Alpha Six; we may have a situation, over."

Below the staircase, the crowd was getting larger by the second; the commotion was attracting people from the offices on either side of the foyer. The yelling grew louder.

A few seconds later Quinn came back, "This is STORM Alpha Six actual. What's going on, over?"

"STORM Mike, this is Kilo," Kick interjected. "In position to cover, at your four o'clock. I am loaded with rubber, over."

Good choice. If Marc couldn't wrestle Tango Two into submission, one shot would take him to the floor without endangering innocents around him. And no blood involved.

Marc scanned the walkway that spanned the highest story of the foyer between the towers and spotted the top of Kick's black baseball cap just behind the gleaming rail. The muzzle and sight of his sniper rifle rested on the white marble like the mouth and eye of a deadly black snake. Marc gave Kick a subtle sign of recognition and sprinted up a few more stairs. There was no doubt in his mind the bearded man causing the scene was Tango Two, but they needed confirmation before acting. He snapped a photo with his PDA and sent it to Rand in the Moby.

"Alpha Six," Marc said in a low voice over the comm, "we have a possible sighting of Tango Two. Sending visual to Romeo to confirm, over."

There was a quiet chorus of swearwords over the comm from the team; then Quinn said, "What's your twenty, STORM Mike, and is Kilo still with you, over?"

"We're at the Bible seminary next to the mall where the van was found. Kilo has nonlethal cover and I am in position to act, over."

"Hold for backup. I'm sending in the Homies, over."

As Marc debated the best strategy in case things went south, Tango Two spotted the large central church area behind him. The choir had already halted in confusion, the seated worshippers rising uncertainly at the hubbub going on in the foyer.

The comm crackled. "STORM Alpha, this is Romeo. We have a positive ID on Tango Two, over."

"Alpha Six, this is STORM Mike. We have confirmed eyes on Tango Two and an escalating situation. Request permission to approach and apprehend the target, over."

In the distance, he heard the wail of sirens.

"Status of the canister, over?"

"Situation urgent," Kick interrupted. "Tango Two is pulling out the canister as we speak, sir."

Quinn swore. "You have the go-ahead, STORM Mike. If you need to, you're clear to take the fucker down, Kick, over."

Before Quinn had finished giving the order, Marc lifted his combat boot and slapped it down with all his might on the marble landing. The sound was like a .350 Magnum going off.

"FBI! Everyone down!" he bellowed.

As one, the hysterical crowd dropped to the floor, screaming and covering their heads in terror, leaving Tango Two standing above them with his hands up and spread like a prophet, oblivious to all but his own chanting.

A millisecond later came the distinctive crack of a rifle.

Tango Two folded like a rag doll in slo-mo. Stunned, but not dead.

Le bon Dieu. Kick was a true artist.

As the enemy went down, Marc leapt off the staircase and landed at his feet. Reaching out, he snatched the canister of lethal virus from the air before it hit the ground, sliding it gingerly into the Windbreaker pocket. Then he grabbed the fast-sinking T-2 and bound his wrists with flex-cuffs.

"STORM Kilo here," he heard over the comm. "Tango Two is down. Repeat: target is contained, over."

"And the canister, over?"

"Item is secured," Marc reported. "What's the ETA on the Homies, over?"

As he spoke, a quartet of navy blue Windbreakers burst through the front entrance, taking charge.

Marc turned over his prisoner and went with the flow of confusion as people jostled to escape the foyer. Once outside, he melted into the darkness, retracing his steps back to the mall parking lot. Five minutes later he was back at the helo.

"What took you so long?" came Kick's teasing voice over his earpiece as Marc trotted up, the FBI Windbreaker flapping on his back. Kick's feet were already dangling from the bird, his back resting against the open doorframe.

Marc had to chuckle. The guy was definitely a phantom. "You sprout wings or something, Jackson?"

Kick sent him a half grin and pulled his PDA from the baseball bag. "Just the wings of love, buddy."

Marc shook his head in amusement, knowing Kick was speed-dialing his wife to report one more bad guy down. And probably to have a little phone sex while he was at it. Listening to their conversations could be downright embarrassing. "You got it bad, *mon ami.*"

"Oh, yeah," Kick cheerfully agreed. "And I ain't never had it so good. You should give it a try, my friend. Put that sexy little state trooper back in handcuffs before she gets away for good."

Marc cleared his throat.

Tara back in handcuffs. *Dieu.*

It wasn't like certain ideas hadn't crossed his mind for those few hours she'd actually been in handcuffs. The thought was appealing. *Bon.* Very appealing. The woman made his mouth water just walking into a room, let alone handcuffed to his bed. It was just . . .

Hell, he didn't know what the problem was.

Or maybe he did.

Mais, yeah, he liked the image of her helpless and in his power. He'd sure liked it last night when she'd broken down and come to him, scared and vulnerable. Needing him, needing his strength and comfort.

To be honest? What he *didn't* like was her being a cop. A

woman who carried a gun could take care of herself. She didn't need a man to watch over her. Didn't need the only things a man like Marc could really offer a woman—his strength, his protection, and his ability to provide for a wife and family. A cop could do all that for herself.

Why would a strong, independent woman like Tara Reeves ever need a man like him?

He sighed.

And yet . . .

She was his. That's what he'd told her last night.

And also the last thing she'd whispered to him before he left her.

He was so damn confused.

Dieu. Love was much too complicated. Maybe he'd be better off just skipping the whole damn thing.

If only he could get the sexy, gorgeous, and all-too-outspoken woman off his damn mind.

TWENTY-TWO

HO-BOY.

What had she done?

Rebel sat in her car, parked in her usual visitor's spot at Haven Oaks, and pressed her forehead against the rim of the steering wheel. She had the heat blowing full blast onto her bare legs, but she was still shivering. She wasn't wearing any panty hose. Because Wade Montana had ripped them off her. Right before he'd—

Ho. Boy.

She blushed to the roots of her hair just *thinking* about what that man had done to her. It had been amazing. Amazingly daring. Amazingly erotic.

Amazingly foolish.

And seriously? The last thing she wanted right now was to see Alex Zane. Or rather, have him see her. Because he would *know*. Instantly. Oh, yes, he'd see it in her eyes—every kiss, every moan, every shuddered climax. Every secret fantasy that it was *him* inside her, *him* making her come, instead of Wade Montana. She was absolutely sure every shameful deed and thought was stamped plain as day across her guilty face.

She groaned again, and bonked her forehead against the

steering wheel for the dozenth time. So much for taking her mind off him.

Just kill her now. *Please*.

But, unfortunately, she had no choice. She had to go in and face him.

Kick Jackson had left her a message that his STORM Corps team had found Gina Cappozi.

Which was incredible news. Flying in from Louisiana, any minute now the rescued hostage would arrive at the sanatorium after a three-hour layover in D.C.—time that had allowed Rebel to come up with a credible excuse for not having dinner with her boss . . . or anything else . . . and making the drive up here instead . . . against every screaming personal instinct. Naturally, Alex was expecting her, having also been alerted by Kick—who'd had to leave *her* a message because her cell phone had been turned off all afternoon. Because she'd been in bed with Wade Montana. Naked.

Had she *men*tioned he was her boss and SAC on the Gina Cappozi case?

Sweet, ever-loving insanity.

Never in her life had Rebel been so tempted to use profanity. "Oh, dear" just didn't quite fit the bill in this situation.

Taking a stalwart breath, she forced herself to pick up her briefcase and get out of the car, lock it, and walk to the front entrance where the familiar pair of guards waved her through with friendly smiles.

Okay. So maybe "Too Stupid to Live" *wasn't* stamped across her forehead in big red letters.

Ho.

Boy.

"Hey, you."

She jumped at Alex's unexpected greeting, and her briefcase flew from her hand. Her frantic grab missed, but he plucked it from midair, tucking it against his broad chest with a superior male smile. "You catch like a girl."

She fanned her face. "Good grief, scare me to death, why don't you?" Her heartbeat was at full gallop. And not from being scared. She avoided his eyes, turning to head for the elevator.

"I've been waiting for you," he said, falling into step beside her.

"Why?" The word shot out of her mouth far too quickly.

His brow hiked. "Uh, because they found Gina Cappozi alive? Remember? The woman you've been relentlessly pestering me about for weeks? The one kidnapped by the same sick fuckers as I was?"

Inwardly, she winced. "Of course. I know. I'm sorry. I'm— That is, today's been sort of—"

He blinked. Then frowned.

She wanted to kick herself. Oh. Rats. "Um, language, Zane," she amended lamely.

Far too late.

His frown deepened. He grabbed her arm, tugging her to a halt in the middle of the reception area. "All right, you. Spill."

It was dinnertime, so several patients and staff members were wandering past on their way to and from the adjacent dining room. This was *so* not the place for this conversation.

"Nothing. Really," she tried to assure him.

He wasn't buying. "Bullshit. Tell me what's happened, angel." He scowled like he was ready to pounce on the first thing that so much as looked sideways at her.

It was all too much. The truth rumbled up inside her, needing to explode like that gross monster from *Alien.*

"Fine!" she blurted out. "I slept with my boss!"

Instantly, *instantly* she regretted it.

Just as instantly, Zane's face went stony, his eyes turning to blank blue slates.

"Montana?" he spat out, his fingers digging painfully into her arm.

She nodded in misery. "Oh, Alex, what am I going to do?"

People were starting to stare. None too gently, he pulled her to the elevator. He didn't say another word, even after they got to his room and he slammed the door shut behind them.

She sat down on his bed, burying her face in her hands while he stalked back and forth.

At length, he stopped and spun to her. "Do you love him?" he demanded.

She dropped her hands. "Are you in*sane*? I'm terrified of him!"

Alex's face contorted. "What are you saying? Did he *make* you—"

"No!" she backpedaled. "Oh, heavens, no. It was all my— I mean, he—" She slapped her hands over her eyes again. "It was definitely consensual. I just . . ."

He halted right in front of her. She could feel the waves of anger coming off his body. His voice was gritty and demanding when he prompted, "Just?"

She dropped her hands to her lap and gazed up at him in a misery. How could she tell him she just wished it had been *him* in bed with her?

"I just don't know what to do," she said.

He snorted derisively. "It appears to me you had no problem at all in that department."

Although she deserved it, his cutting remark stung. "Alex, please don't be ugly. I feel bad enough as it is."

His jaw clenched. "This is not like you, Rebel. How could you do it? How could you have sex with a man you don't love?"

She literally had to bite down on her bottom lip to keep from shouting, "Because the man I love is taken, you dolt!"

She took a deep breath. "I'm only human, Alex," she said. "I get lonely, and Wade wants me. It's nice to be wanted for a change."

She caught his gaze. Held it. Daring him. Daring him to admit that *he* wanted her, too. Last night, he'd come so close to kissing her. Had that meant anything to him? Anything at all? Or had her own lovelorn mind imagined the whole thing . . . ?

He turned away abruptly. "Will you keep seeing him?"

Her heart fell. "I don't know," she answered honestly. "Now that the Cappozi case is closed, I assume he'll be returning to D.C."

"Are you sure it is closed?" Alex said, staring out of the window.

"Why wouldn't it be?"

"Because the government doesn't know Dr. Cappozi has been recovered. The only person outside of STORM who knows is you."

That took her by surprise. "Why the secrecy?" Then she remembered. "Oh. Because of the traitor." The al Sayika mole in the CIA.

"Kick and I are sure the same traitor must have been involved in Dr. Cappozi's kidnapping. After Abbas Tawhid is caught, we intend to find and take down the motherfucker."

"*Language*, Zane."

He turned and gave her a level look. "Did you enjoy fucking him?"

Shock went through her at the sharp shift in topic, back to the previous. Hurt followed close on its heels. She felt her chin raise a notch. "Yes," she responded, though sick with mortification. "Wade is a good lover. How about Helena? Is she any good in bed?"

It was like the same demon that had taken over Rebel's body earlier had invaded her soul, forcing the words onto her unwilling tongue. But it was too late to take them back. The exchange hovered in the air around them like an electric mist, choking with tension, thick with danger, threatening to ignite and burn them both to cinders.

"I wouldn't know," he retorted, a muscle working in his jaw. "We haven't slept together yet."

Her whole body jerked back, as though he'd kicked her. The breath sucked out of her lungs. "But—"

She'd assumed—*Oh, no*. All this time she'd taken it for granted that Alex and Helena were lovers. Helena had certainly implied as much after each and every date they'd had, back before he'd gone missing. It was also the excuse Helena had used to move out of their New York apartment and into her own place. She and Alex needed the privacy, she'd said with a coy giggle. Throwing Rebel into a black hole of envy and jealousy.

"But why not?" she asked him now, stunned.

"That's the way she wanted it," he said dryly. "And I—" He shrugged. "What was I going to say? Please, can I fuck you just once before we get married to see if you're really as perfect as you seem?"

Okay, wow. Did he *really* have to say that?

He took a step toward her. "Or would you prefer, please, can I fuck you just once so maybe before we get married I'll stop having these fantasies about fucking your best friend?"

This time, the shock was like a locomotive slamming into her. "Zane!"

Suddenly, the door swung open. And in breezed the last person on earth Rebel wanted to see, ever again.

"Helena!"

"Hi, you two!" said Rebel's perfect best friend, clapping her hands together like a delighted child. "What fun! I didn't know you'd be joining us for supper tonight, Rebel. So, you'll never guess what I have with me!" She lifted a heavy pearlescent white box from her oversized Gucci bag. "Look, Alex! Darling! Our wedding invitations!"

TWENTY-THREE

"OMIGOD! Gina!"

At the familiar voice, Gina turned her head on the gurney as it was being unloaded from the limo-style ambulance. Seeing a blur of blue scrubs and blond hair sprinting out the doors of the ritzy private medical facility she'd been taken to, tears sprang to Gina's eyes. This was the final proof she needed. Her horrible ordeal truly was over.

"Rainie!" she choked out.

"Gina!"

If she'd been on her feet, they would have crashed into each other, hugging and jumping up and down, clinging and talking a mile a minute, both with tears streaming down their faces.

As it was, they had to settle for the tears. Rainie ran to her side, stalling in dismay for a split second when she saw the extent of Gina's injuries.

With a sob, her friend embraced her fervently but oh-so-gently, then took her hand and tenderly touched her face and hair. "Thank God! Oh, thank God they found you! I can't believe this happened to you because of me. I am *so* sorry, Geen."

Gina couldn't hold back the flood of tears that had wanted to come out since she'd opened her eyes in that awful place to see Rainie's new husband standing over her like a savior. It felt so good to have someone touch her in kindness and love, not with hatred and cruelty.

"This wasn't your fault, Rain," she insisted between the hugs and the tears, wanting to banish the thick haze of guilt clouding her best friend's expression.

Rainie wiped her tears with a sleeve. "No, it *was* my fault. I'll never forgive myself for—"

Gina raised her hands and pressed them to her friend's cheeks. "Stop. There's nothing to forgive. We've both been through hell, but we're both alive. That's all that matters now."

A ragged sob broke through Rainie's attempt at control. "You're right. But—"

"But nothing." Gina smiled through her tears, allowing herself finally to feel a measure of safety. "Just promise me one thing."

Rainie's answering smile was hard-won, but more precious for that. "Anything. Just name it."

Gina met her eyes wryly. "The next time I want to go speed dating, do me a favor and just shoot me."

A choked laugh made it through her friend's distress. That was where it had all started—the speed-dating event she had dragged Rainie to. Where Rain had met Kick, and fate had swiftly closed in on all of them.

"Omigod, will I ever."

They hooked fingers and pinky-promised, and both laughed through their tears as the gurney was rolled past a sign that said Welcome to Haven Oaks.

Safe at last.

Gina had never felt so relieved to be anywhere in her life.

ALL Tara could think about was why Marc hadn't called her.

He'd *promised*.

He'd kissed her, said he knew she was his—in response to her bumbling attempt at telling him how she felt about him— then strode away from the research station, and right out of her life.

Forever?

Oh, God. She should have known.

She'd grown up with a military father who'd been gone overseas more than he'd been home. Waltzing in and out of her life like it didn't matter. She'd seen how lonely her mother was most of her life, and how much she'd needed him when she'd gotten deathly ill with cancer. But short of jettisoning his beloved career, there'd been no remedy.

How had she not seen that Marc had exactly the same kind of job? He would never stay with her, either. Tara didn't want to live that way. No matter how much she loved him.

So okay, it was good he didn't call. Had no intention of calling.

The rat bastard.

"Officer Reeves?"

She snapped to attention. She was standing in the admissions area of the very swanky private hospital where the limo-cum-ambulance had taken her and Dr. Cappozi after picking them up from the small airport out in the middle of nowhere where they'd landed.

"Trooper Reeves," Tara corrected automatically.

The impossibly young male staff member whose name tag said "Bob" gave her a blank look. "Ma'am?"

"I'm a Louisiana state trooper, not a police officer." Though she wasn't dressed as either, having been provided a soft woolen trouser suit and cashmere turtleneck on the plane, to replace her ruined clothes. The knee-length boots were made more for the runway than for running after bad guys. The whole outfit had to have cost more than her monthly salary. Not that she was complaining.

The kid's pierced brows quirked decoratively, and he gave her the obligatory once-over. As if checking out her body could tell him the difference between trooper and officer. Or why a Louisiana cop of any variety would be here in Podunk, New York, or wherever the frigging hell they were, with her heart on her sleeve, crying because some damn rolling stone of a man hadn't called her.

Bitter? Her?

More like crushed.

"Oh. Okay. Whatever," Sponge Bob said. "Anyway, while they're getting Miss Gina settled in her room, we thought maybe you were hungry? Dinner is still being served. If you'd like to follow me, ma'am, I'll seat you."

Food. What a nauseating thought. She wondered idly if they served adult beverages at dinner in a rehab facility. Or whatever Haven Oaks was. Nah, probably not.

But it wouldn't hurt to ask.

Heck, Kid Rock here might have a private stash hidden away he'd be willing to share. Except with her luck, whatever his habit was would probably be illegal.

"Offic—uh, Trooper Reeves, ma'am?"

See? The young could be taught. He didn't even look at her breasts this time. Maybe because she reminded him of his mother. If he called her "ma'am" one more time, she would scream. "Yep?"

"Don't you want dinner, ma'am?"

She forced a smile, all teeth. "No. Think I'll skip it, thanks. But you know what I'd really like?"

"What's that, ma'am?"

She resisted the growing urge to pull out her SIG and shoot the little punk. Too bad she'd never gotten it back. "To speak to someone from STORM."

"Uh, ma'am?"

She sighed. "STORM Corps?"

The kid looked truly at a loss. But before he could send her off to the local weather station, she was rescued by a masculine voice behind her. "Can I help you, Miss Reeves?"

"God, I hope so," she muttered and turned to find a tall, distinguished man with a skier's tan around clear green eyes, a strong, unshaven jaw, and a deceptively friendly smile. Deceptive, because those emerald greens were smart, cool, and assessing. Still, it wasn't the watchful eyes or his short haircut that pegged him as STORM—both Marc and Kick kept their hair well below collar-length. But Tara could have picked this guy out of a lineup in a hot minute. There was just something about him that matched the other team members. *Danger.* Behind the relaxed façade lurked the unmistakable steel of a male primed for mortal combat.

He extended his hand. "Call me Bridger," he said, and they shook. His grip was firm, calculated. "Mind if I call you Tara?"

"If you can help me, you can call me anything you like," she said, unsurprised he knew her name. Everyone around here seemed to.

A corner of Bridger's lips curved. "I'll do my best. Look, Tara, I know you didn't want dinner, but I've been traveling all day and, personally, I'm starving. Any chance you'd join me while we discuss what I can do to help you?"

She let herself be ushered into the dining room, a high-ceilinged, columned affair with glowing antique furniture and white linen tablecloths. Suddenly she felt underdressed, despite the new clothes.

What *was* this STORM Corps, that they ran both covert black-ops missions and posh private hospitals fit for royalty?

Her escort chose a table near the crackling fireplace in one corner. He did manage to surprise her by letting her take the seat against the wall, leaving his own back exposed to the room. So much for *that* myth.

He smiled and said, "Don't worry. I have eyes in the back of my head." And obviously mind-reading abilities as well.

After they ordered, Bridger leaned back in his chair and regarded her thoughtfully. "I want you to know how much STORM Corps appreciates you taking such good care of our special guest," he said. "I know it can't have been easy for you—to have your life essentially ripped out from under you like that. Yet, you didn't hesitate to jump in and help, even a complete stranger."

She shrugged it off, uncomfortable with the praise. "Anyone would have done the same."

"No, not really. But in any case, you needn't worry about your job back home. Your captain has been informed you were commandeered by Department of Homeland Security for an open-ended mission. Feel free to enjoy our hospitality here at the spa for as long as you wish. When you're ready to go home, a private jet will be provided for your use."

Spa.

Private jet.

Wow.

She stared at him. He didn't look like he was kidding.

Well, of *course* a once-in-a-lifetime offer like this *would* materialize the one day in her life there was no way she could accept.

She took a quick sip of ice water. "That's very generous," she said, almost choking on the refusal. "However, that thing I need your help with? Well, actually, I was hoping you could find a way to send me back to the team."

It was his turn to stare at her.

"You know, the team hunting the, um"—she glanced around them and lowered her voice—"kidnappers."

His tanned face remained absolutely neutral. "I'm afraid the team has been split up."

"Oh." Regret fanned through her. Okay. That made sense. Gina'd said she was forced to prepare enough deadly virus for five canisters. Each terrorist must have his own targeted city to get to. And each of them must have a STORM agent tracking him. But . . . if they'd split up, then . . . "That means you've located the suspects?"

Bridger laced his fingers together on the table. "We have a possible lead. But I can't really discuss details."

"Ah. Of course. I understand." So, now what would she do? Now that she'd had a taste of what a real team of equals felt like. People who treated her like she was smart and competent and had something valuable to contribute. And she'd been doing something truly important—like she'd felt when she volunteered after Katrina. Like she'd felt investigating the deadly pollution . . . which turned out to be something even more horrific. How could she go back to being a traffic cop after all that?

Their drinks came, and to her surprise, instead of the diet soda she'd ordered, the waiter placed a draft beer in front of her.

"You prefer draft over bottled, I hear?"

Okay, the man was downright scary. "Who did you hear that from?"

"Pretty much everyone we asked."

Blood sang in her ears. She waited until the server departed, then leaned forward and demanded, "*Asked?* Why were you asking *any*one about my beverage preferences?"

He tilted his head. Waited a beat, then said, "I'm very sorry about your mother."

Her whole body jerked back. She didn't even bother asking what her mother had to do with anything. Her mother was the whole reason she was sitting here now, instead of in her LSP cruiser on some Louisiana back road writing traffic tickets, as she was supposed to be. But nobody knew that. Nobody. Not her captain. Not her father. Not even the man she'd been paddling around the swamps with for two days looking for evidence of industrial waste.

But this man knew.

Which meant he must know everything else about her, too. Obviously from her dysfunctional childhood with an overbearing military father and sweet mother dying of toxic pollution–induced cancer, probably all the way down to the fact that she had spent the last thirty-six hours having virtually nonstop monkey sex with one of his colleagues.

She cleared her throat.

Okay, then.

"Thank you," she said. About her mother.

Bridger's expression remained impenetrable. "So," he said. "I assume the real reason you want to get back to the team is Marc Lafayette."

Thank God for the fireplace next to her. Maybe he'd think the sweat popping out on her forehead was from the heat of the fire and not embarrassment.

"No, actually—"

"I apologize for the handcuffs," he said. "Lafayette went too far with those."

Oh, God. He knew about the flex-cuffs? She grabbed her beer and took a big gulp.

"And forcing you to sleep in the same room with him. That went far beyond his orders."

Oh, dear Lord, just let her sink through the floor now, never to be seen or heard from again.

She waved a hand, trying not to choke. "That's, um . . ."

"If you wish to register a complaint, I'd be happy to—"

"No," she cut him off, swallowing painfully. "Really, that won't be necessary. I'm—" Any second now, her face was going to burst into flames. But as pissed off with Marc as she was, she couldn't let him be punished for doing his job. Hell, she was as much to blame for the resulting inappropriate be-

havior as he was. If not more. "I'm fine with all that. We"—
she swallowed again—"uh, came to an understanding."

At least she'd thought they had. For about the first six
hours after he left her. After that, not so much. She ruthlessly
suppressed the temptation to check her cell phone for
messages.

Bridger nodded. "Good. I thought as much, but I had to
be sure."

Their food came and she eased out an uncomfortable sigh.
It looked delicious, but she didn't think she could eat a single
bite.

"Anyway," he said, digging in. "I may be able to hook you
up with Lafayette again. He and Jackson have arranged to
rendezvous with Kowalski and Jaeger to go over UAV footage tonight, looking for corroboration on that lead I mentioned. Still interested in rejoining the team?"

Suddenly, she wasn't so sure. What would Marc think if
she just turned up? Would the team be as accepting of her if
she and he weren't an item?

She squirmed in her chair. "Believe it or not, I really do
want to help. I saw what those bastards did to Dr. Cappozi,
and she told me their plans for that horrible virus. Wanting to
help STORM isn't about a personal agenda. It's about de-
fending my country against terrorists. I'll gladly assist anyone on the team. Wherever you need me."

He held her gaze for a good long while. Then he gave a
short nod. "Very well. I'll take you at your word. Rand Jaeger could use help in the mobile unit. That would free up
Kowalski to work on countermeasures for the virus."

She squelched the annoying squeeze of disappointment in
her heart about not being assigned to help Marc. But really.
She had to face reality sometime. Better sooner than later.

Somehow she produced a sincere smile. "You're on," she
said to Bridger. "I'd be happy to help with the Moby. When
do I leave?"

He picked up his fork again and pointed it at her meal. "I'll
order up the jet just as soon as you've eaten your dinner."

She'd just taken her first bite when his cell phone vibrated. He apologized and flipped it open. After listening
briefly, he hung up and smiled wryly. "No rest for the

wicked," he said. "I'm sorry, but I need to go up and sit in on the FBI's debrief of Dr. Cappozi."

"FBI?" Tara said, alarm rising. "But I didn't think the government was supposed to know she was found?" The team had worked hard to ensure as few people as possible knew she'd survived, especially anyone working for the government alphabets. "Because of the possible traitor."

Bridger looked mildly curious. "You're aware of that?"

She toyed with her food. "Gina thinks it's someone in CIA by the name of Gregg van Halen."

"So I heard." Bridger gazed at her consideringly. "Look, why don't you join me?"

"Really? I'd like that."

He gestured at her dinner. "Good. I'll have that boxed up for you."

She opened her mouth to tell him not to bother, but he'd already signaled the waiter. She politely said, "Thank you."

"The limo will be waiting for you after the interview, and I'll call to have the jet standing by to fly you back to Louisiana. There'll be instructions on board where to meet up with the team."

"Okay, thanks."

"Don't forget your dinner," he admonished as they rose, winking when the waiter handed her the take-out box.

The man was relentless. Ah, well. Maybe she'd be hungry later.

Later this century, she thought with a sigh.

She took it with a defeated smile at Bridger's back as he walked toward the elevator. "Thanks, Dad," she muttered under her breath.

Without turning, he wagged a finger in the air and called, "I heard that."

TWENTY-FOUR

GINA had been installed in a large, airy room with a big bay window overlooking a moonlit, snow-carpeted flower garden complete with fairy-lighted trees. She was lying on one of those hospital beds that bend up, propped against a mound of pillows. Rainie had helped her take a long, wonderful shower, so she was clean at last. Rainie had also brushed her hair till it shone, and rebandaged her worst cuts. Gina'd managed to eat a whole bowl of hearty soup, and a steaming mug of coffee sat on the nightstand. She felt nearly human again.

At least she was no longer terrified this was all a dream.

Kurt Bridger popped his head into the room. "Hi. This a good time?"

Gina smiled. Bridger was the one who'd overseen her check-in to Haven Oaks. He was with STORM Corps, fairly high up the hierarchy, she judged by the way everyone snapped to his slightest orders. He'd asked her if she was up for an interview right away, so she'd been expecting him. To her delight, Tara Reeves was with him.

"Please, come in," she said. "It's so good to see you again." Tara came over and gave her a hug.

"You, too, Gina. Settling in?"

"Everyone's been so nice." She turned to Mr. Bridger.

"Thank you again. The room is lovely. And having Rainie here to take care of me . . ." To her embarrassment, she felt her eyes filling for the umpteenth time that day. "I can't tell you how much it means to me."

"Glad you're comfortable," he said, stepping up to the foot of the bed. "How are you holding up otherwise?"

Gina nodded. "Still in shock, but in a good way," she confessed, then gave an embarrassed laugh. "Though I can't seem to stop crying."

"You go right ahead," Tara said, squeezing her hand gently. "You've earned every one of those tears of relief. You were so brave."

She shuddered out a sigh. "I only wish I was."

"Of course you were," a woman said from the door. "Incredibly brave." Dressed in a chic, feminine business suit and heels, she was truly striking. One of those willowy redheaded Irish beauties Gina had always envied, with creamy skin and an angelic face. Although . . . her pleasant expression did seem a bit pinched at the moment.

"Special Agent Haywood, I presume?" Bridger asked, stepping over to check the credential wallet she held up.

Wait. She was with the *FBI*? Gina exchanged a look with Tara, who seemed equally surprised.

"Yes, I am. Kick Jackson wanted me to check in on Dr. Cappozi. Make sure she and Rainie found each other."

"Yes, we did. You just missed her," Gina said. "She went to get some dinner."

Tara introduced herself, and said, "You know Rainie Jackson, Special Agent Haywood?"

The agent smiled and nodded. "We met several weeks ago. Here at Haven Oaks. And everyone, please, call me Rebel."

Bridger went to prop himself next to the dark window. "I understand you're also a friend of Alex Zane."

At the name, Special Agent Haywood—Rebel—started. Actually, she blanched.

What was that all about? And why did that name sound so familiar?

"Yes," Rebel said, recovering quickly. "I was liaison to Zero Unit several years ago. Alex was my contact." She turned back to Gina and said, "Alex was best man at Kick and Rainie's wedding. He's engaged to Helena Middleton, my, um, good friend, so I attended, too. Helena was the substitute maid of honor."

That's where she'd heard the name before. Kick's friend Alex, whom they'd rescued in the Sudan.

"I'm so sorry I missed the wedding," Gina said, her voice wavering threadily. Her eyes swam again. Rainie had told her all about the intimate ceremony that had been held right here at Haven Oaks. How she hadn't wanted to marry until Gina was found, but Kick had been worried he'd be sent off on a mission and didn't want to wait. Gina didn't blame him. In fact, she liked him all the more for not letting anything stand in the way of their love. She'd never seen Rainie so happy or confident. Kick was good for her.

Rebel gazed at her with sympathy. "Rainie was so sad and upset that you couldn't be at her side."

Gina dabbed her eyes. "I understand Alex was in such bad shape the doctors wouldn't even let him out of bed for the ceremony."

The agent nodded. "He's doing better now. And anxious to meet you. He's just down the hall." For a second her smile faltered. But just as quickly she composed herself and continued. "Anyway. All of your friends were so determined to find you, Dr. Cappozi. They impressed me so much, the next day I went to my boss and requested a transfer to your case so I could help."

"Call me Gina. Please." She swallowed heavily. "All that time I thought everyone had deserted me." How could she have had so little faith?

"Believe me, they didn't," Tara assured her. "Not for a minute."

"And neither did the FBI," Rebel said.

Gina's heart swelled. "I'm so grateful to everyone."

"We're just glad to have you back safe and sound."

Bridger unpropped himself from wall next to the bow window. "And to make sure you stay that way, I'm afraid you won't be able to contact anyone outside of Haven Oaks. Not for a while. That won't be a problem, will it?"

She blinked. "Um. No, I suppose not. But why? Rainie said they'd already caught two of the terrorists."

Bridger looked grim. "Yes, but we suspect al Sayika has someone working for them on the inside, probably within CIA or the FBI."

"It's Gregg van Halen. I know it is."

"Possibly. But we don't want to take any chances. Not until Tawhid is caught and the traitor is identified for certain."

Her heartbeat kicked up. She glanced from him to Agent Haywood and back. "But . . . the FBI?"

"Don't worry. No one else in the Bureau knows you were found," Rebel assured her. "I'm only here because Kick and I have been exchanging information about your case privately, outside official channels."

Tara frowned. "But . . . if you can't tell the FBI Gina's alive . . ."

Rebel grimaced, and looked at Bridger. "She brings up a good point. I frankly have no idea how I'm supposed to handle this. My SAC—" Her voice did a weird little crack on the "A" and she had to clear her throat. "My SAC is going to know if I lie to him. Which I'll have to, unless somehow the case is closed or he goes away."

"Would you like him to go away?" Bridger asked. The agent's eyes widened slightly and Bridger cracked the shadow of a smile. "Not permanently. Just back to D.C."

"You can arrange that?" Rebel looked doubtful.

"Perhaps a body matching Dr. Cappozi's description could be found somewhere—far from Louisiana, naturally. That would close down the task force until a positive ID could made. Which might drag on for months. Meanwhile you'd be reassigned. He'd go back home. End of problem."

Rebel's smile grew strained again. "That would probably work for anyone else. Unfortunately . . . there's an added complication in this case."

Bridger's lips pursed. "You mean your SAC being Wade Montana."

Gina gasped softly. "Wade? *Wade* is the lead agent on my case? Isn't that a conflict of interest?"

"Indeed." Rebel bit her lower lip and nodded again. "To be honest, at first I thought he'd murdered you, in revenge for—" Her cheeks went all pink. "Well, obviously he didn't. He's genuinely worried about you, Gina. He blames himself for your kidnapping. I really think he needs to be told you're alive."

"Wait," Tara said. "Who is this person?"

"Wade is my ex-fiancé," she explained.

Tara's brows shot into her scalp. "Whoa. Talk about a conflict of interest! How could the FBI have given him this assignment?"

Rebel crossed her arms tightly. "He didn't disclose the relationship to anyone. I only found out by accident. I threatened to expose him, but he managed to convince me of his sincerity."

"You were either very brave or very foolish, Special Agent Haywood," Bridger said.

"No doubt the latter," the agent returned, avoiding everyone's gaze.

Gina frowned slightly. Was something going on *there*, too? Knowing Wade, probably.

Not that Gina could afford to throw stones. Her rat bastard lover sold her out to terrorists, while her lying ex-fiancé tried to find her . . . apparently while banging his subordinate.

But those kinds of complications were over and done with for her. She would never get involved with another lying bastard of a man as long as she lived.

Bile rose up her throat. Not that any man would have her. Not now, after what had happened to her.

"I agree with you, Rebel," Gina choked out, yanking herself back from the precipice of terrible memories. "The rest of the FBI can believe I'm dead, but Wade should at least be told I'm alive. I owe him that much."

"Don't forget you broke up with Montana," Bridger observed, watching her carefully. "Do you really trust him with your life?"

"Of course I do." Gina swallowed. He might have lied to the Bureau, but he'd never lied to her. At least . . . not that she knew of. "You can't possibly think *he's* involved?"

Bridger's shoulder lifted. "Someone on the inside is working with al Sayika. I know you believe the traitor is van Halen, Dr. Cappozi, but until we have proof—"

Not going there. Gina rolled her head back and forth on the pillow. As much to shake out thoughts of her real betrayer as to refute Bridger's theory. "It's not Wade. That much I'm sure of."

Bridger studied her for a moment. "He did check out when we ran his background. Okay. If you're that certain, we can read him in."

"He'll want to see her," Rebel warned. "In person."

Bridger looked at Gina and raised a brow. "Yes? No?"

She pushed out a breath. "Sure. Why not."

"With any luck," Rebel said, "he can get the task force closed down without producing a body."

"We'll work on that, and I'll arrange a visit," Bridger said, then turned back to Gina. "Meanwhile, Dr. Cappozi, are you up to talking about your ordeal now? Anything you might remember is important. The smallest detail could help catch these terrorists. We need to hear everything."

She had to do it. She knew that. Better to get it over with. "I'll do my best," she said. But already fear was rising up through her stomach and lungs to grip her throat like talons.

"Whenever you're ready," Bridger said gently.

Tara seemed to sense her blossoming panic and sat on the edge of the bed, holding her hand soothingly between hers. "I'll be right here."

She closed her eyes and shakily prepared herself for the descent back into hell.

"STORM Alpha Six, this is Romeo." Rand's voice boomed over the headset, satisfaction ringing loud and clear. "Tango Three is on the grid and we have a visual, over."

Bobby Lee straightened like a shot from his catnap in the passenger seat of the SUV. Adrenaline surged through his veins. At last! Finally some real action. This cat-and-mouse game they were playing at was starting to get old.

After seeing what those terrorists had done to the poor woman hostage at the research center, Bobby Lee wanted to catch the bastards and make them pay, almost as bad as Kick and Marc did. What kind of animals would do something like that to a woman? They deserved to be put down.

He exchanged a look of anticipation with Zimmie, who was behind the wheel, then hit the mic of his headset.

"This is STORM Alpha Six actual. What is Tango Three's position, over?"

Kowalski must have been roped into working with Rand in the Moby again, because it was he who answered, "Still on the I-10, nine miles east of Lake Charles, over."

"Thank God," Zimmie muttered about the I-10 part, then said, "Shit," about the tango's actual position.

Intercepting a terrorist in a big city like Lake Charles was not something any of them wanted to chance. Too big of a risk for a goatfuck.

"Streaming the IR video to Zulu's laptop," Rand said. Infrared because it was almost midnight, so visibility would be zilch without it. "Both the sedan and your SUV are tagged. Alpha Six, you are currently four-point-two miles behind the target vehicle, over."

Immediately, Zimmie floored it and flipped the switch for lights and siren. "Damn. We'll never catch up before Lake Charles," she said, ever practical.

On the laptop, Bobby Lee connected a socket to the Moby's feed and examined the UAV video stream when it popped up. They were gaining on the silver sedan, but it was traveling well above the speed limit. Bobby Lee wasn't a math wiz, but even he could calculate that unless they went more than a hundred miles an hour it would take them more than the few minutes they had left before hitting the city to catch the sedan.

"What's the status of the Homies?" he asked. "How far out is the intercept team, over?"

There was a short pause, then Ski came back, "About fifteen minutes, over."

Too long.

"What do you think?" Bobby Lee asked Zimmie. "Catch up and tail him to an unpopulated stretch of freeway, or involve the locals and have him stopped before he hits the city?"

She was gracefully weaving the SUV between the few cars on the road at this hour, going about ninety. She didn't even hesitate. "Tail him. Wait for the DHS team. The locals won't know what they're dealing with. Too dangerous for everyone."

Bobby Lee agreed.

"Romeo, is there an update on Tangos Two and Four?" he asked of the two already captured terrorists. "Are they talking yet, over?" Last he'd checked, T-4 was still in surgery for his gunshot wound, and T-2 had been turned over to the DOJ, but refused to open his mouth other than to spout insurgent bullcrap. Too bad Kick'd had to use rubber bullets on the fucker.

"That's a negative, Alpha Six," Ski answered. "But the doctors say Tango Four should be conscious soon, over."

Bobby Lee hoped the interrogators would have better luck with him. Maybe the anesthesia would loosen his tongue and give them the corroborating evidence the team needed to move on Madison Square Garden. It would be useful to know if that really was where Tawhid was planning his ultimate attack.

The good news was, Lake Charles was not a logical target of any kind, so chances were T-3 was just passing through on his way to somewhere more high profile.

But as Kick was fond of saying, that all assumed these fuckers were rational. And in this biz, assuming anything was a huge mistake.

Speaking of Kick . . . "STORM Mike, STORM Kilo, do you read, over?"

"Yup, loud and clear," came Kick's reply. "We're standing ready at the Moby. You want us to hop on the helo as backup, over?"

Bobby Lee considered briefly. "No. Hold off on that for now. Do you have a location on Tango One yet, over?"

"Negative on that, too," Marc interjected disgustedly. "*De foutre.* Even knowing where he might be heading, the man's a ghost, over."

Which just made Bobby Lee all the more determined to nail T-3 before he slipped off the radar, as well. "All right, people, then let's make sure we catch this one, over."

Together the team swiftly debated the best way to set up the takedown of Tango Three, with Rand coordinating with the DHS team commander. The westbound I-10 passed through a large stretch of unpopulated swampland right around the Texas border, which was ultimately chosen as the best place to close in.

The laptop beeped. "Half mile from target vehicle," Bobby Lee warned Zimmie, who shut off the siren. They were at the outskirts of the city and didn't want to spook the terrorist off the freeway.

A few moments later she shut off the flashing lights and slowed to just over the flow of the traffic.

"There. That's him." Bobby Lee pointed to headlights in the distance. Just beyond, they could see the lighted silhouette of the Calcasieu River Bridge fast approaching.

Zimmie settled into maintaining a steady distance between the two vehicles. Behind the wheel, she stretched her back and flexed her fingers.

Bobby Lee switched off his mic, swept a glance over her drawn face and rounded shoulders, and asked, "You okay?" He'd been up since before six a.m, but Zimmie'd probably pulled an all-nighter while he'd caught those few hours of sleep last night. She'd taken the first catnap in the SUV, but it had been too short and she must be running on fumes.

"No worries," she said. "I'll be fine."

Like she'd say anything else.

"What the—" she suddenly muttered, coming to attention and peering through the windshield.

He turned his focus back to the road and promptly cursed. "Son of a *bitch*!" Up ahead, flashing blue lights were peeling out from an on-ramp, in pursuit of the silver sedan. Bobby Lee hit his mic. "Damn it, Romeo! Didn't anyone warn the locals to keep their distance, over?"

"That's affirmative. What's happening, over?"

Bobby Lee swore again. Zimmie floored it.

Not fucking a*gain*.

"There's a goddamn smokey pulling him over!" Or trying to. But Tango Three was speeding up, obviously not intending to stop. "Somebody get on the horn and warn that— Ah, *hell*."

Suddenly, the silver sedan made a sharp right and veered off the freeway. It cut straight across a grass barrier, then careened onto the road on the other side of it and took off like a bat out of hell. The cop shot right past, missing the off-ramp.

"Shit," Zimmie ground out, hit the lights and siren again, peeled the SUV off the freeway, and gave chase onto the frontage road. "Damn it, this is a one-way street!" Going the wrong way, naturally.

"Where are the goddamn Homies, over?" Bobby Lee called over the comm.

"Four minutes out, over," Ski informed them.

Fuck.

Horn blaring, T-3 scraped past an oncoming car, barely missing it as they sped around a blind curve going south under the freeway. Zimmie just managed to dodge it. Thank God traffic was light at this hour or they'd be metal confetti.

Bobby Lee furiously attacked the laptop keyboard, pulling up the map overlay and zooming in on it, but the wild ride made it hard to read. "Damn it! Anyone, where's he heading, over?"

"Looks like . . . Lake Charles," Kick answered. "The actual lake, not the city. South of the lake a river leads to swamps, then another big ol' lake, and beyond that is the Gulf, over."

Jesus. "Okay. So obviously he's looking for a boat. Is he going to find one, over?"

Zimmie swore as the silver sedan sliced a hard right across the median to the parallel road going in the correct direction. She followed, tipping on two wheels as she made the move. They barreled past a deserted civic center.

"Affirmative," Ski said. "There's a string of private docks coming up in a block or two, over."

"Let him," Zimmie said, gritting her teeth as she fought to keep the SUV apace.

He flashed her a glance. "What?"

"We're coming into a residential area. We can't risk him letting the virus loose here. Let him get on the lake."

Tango Three squealed up to the first dock, leapt from his car, and sprinted for the nearest fast boat.

Bobby Lee made a split-second decision. "You're right. STORM Alpha, we're gonna give him some rope. Romeo, make sure you tag that boat, over."

"Doing it as we speak, boss, over."

"And find me a faster one. Pronto! Also, better inform the Homies the assault is going to be amphibious, over."

No time to call in the Coast Guard. Too bad. They were the experts at this sort of thing.

"Alpha Six, there's a speedboat tied up at the third dock, over," Ski informed them.

"Copy that. There's our ride," Bobby Lee said to Zimmie, pointing. He snapped the laptop closed and swiveled to reach in the back for their jackets and duffels. As soon as the SUV slammed to a halt, he tossed Zimmie her bag and they sprinted for the speedboat.

Jumping aboard, he made quick work of the hotwire as Zimmie cast her off, and the engine sputtered to life. He checked the gauges. A full tank of gas. Thank you, Jesus, he must be living right. "Hang on," he yelled to Zimmie, who dropped into the passenger seat, and they took off into the darkness.

T-3's craft had already disappeared into the black void of the lake, leaving behind only the receding whine of a motor and a rolling wake that reflected the lights of the city behind them.

"What's the plan?" Zimmie yelled, pulling Bobby Lee's NVGs from the duffel and passing them over.

"Plan?" He grinned at her as he slid the headgear on and flipped down the eye scope. "You tell me."

T-3's heat signature popped into view, an orange blur in a sea of solid nothing. He was headed straight out into the lake. Good.

Zimmie slipped on her own NVGs. He grinned wider. He'd always been turned on by the sight of her in night gear. Of both varieties—job-related and bed-related. She was definitely the sexiest—

"Focus, soldier," she snapped.

Oh, he intended to. On both fronts. "Yes, ma'am," he said, and turned back to the job at hand, totally secure in the knowledge that they would get their man.

And suddenly he realized something very important. Breaking up with Darcy Zimmerman would *not* improve his concentration on missions. But what *would* was to make damn sure she was always right there by his side. Together they were unbeatable.

Note to self: request Command that Zimmie be assigned permanently as his partner. Whether she liked it or not.

A cold mist from their rooster tail wafted forward on the

wind. He shook his head like a spaniel, relishing the bracing chill on his face and neck. And the feeling of certainty in his heart.

Rand came on the comm. "DHS reports their strike team is not prepared for a water insertion." A snort burst rudely across the airwaves. "Seems the boys forgot their wetsuits, over."

Bobby Lee rolled his eyes as he turned the speedboat south, following the orange blob on his scope. Tango Three was headed for the river.

"Looks like it's up to us, ladies and gentlemen," he said with lethal determination. "Time to put an end to this wild-goose chase and show this fucker who he's messing with."

EVEN in full darkness and beneath his NVGs, Darcy recognized the look on Quinn's face. Sheer exhilaration. This was what he lived for. The excitement of the chase; the amazing rush of taking down the bad guy and saving the world.

Hell, it was what she lived for, too.

At least . . . it used to be.

So what had happened? Since when had the expression of defeat and surrender on the enemy's face become less stirring than the animation in Bobby Lee Quinn's as he was about to cause that surrender?

Damn.

She was the one who needed to focus.

"What are you thinking?" she asked. "Flashbang or bullet in the head?"

"I'm thinking I wish we could have Rand blow him to smithereens with one strike from the UAV."

She pursed her lips. "A bit like shooting fish in a barrel."

He grimaced. "Save the taxpayers a buttload of money on a trial."

"The Homies'll get all bent out of shape if they can't interrogate him."

He mocked a sigh. "Shi-yit."

"Yeah."

"Okay, then. Flashbang it is."

He throttled up and the speedboat took off like a rocket. She dug in the duffel and pulled out two M84 stun grenades.

He glanced over and hiked an eyebrow. "Two?"

She sent him a challenging smile and shrugged. "Just in case."

He made a wry moue as she pulled out their ear protection and they switched out those for their NVGs. "Oh, ye of little faith."

With a snicker, she drew out a gas mask and offered it to him.

He waved it off.

She continued to hold it up. Stubborn, stubborn man. "Just put it the fuck on, Quinn."

He gave her a lopsided smile. "So you *do* care."

"Hell, no. I just look terrible in black."

He chuckled. "Here. Take the wheel."

They seamlessly changed places, and he told the team, "STORM Alpha, we're moving in. Will be going silent for a few minutes, over."

"Copy that, over," Rand said, and they turned off their headsets.

Quinn took a stun grenade from her and wrapped his fingers around it. He spread his feet on the lurching deck, and readied his throw with a look of sheer concentration, like an athlete determined to win a gold medal.

Standing there all golden and godlike, silhouetted in darkness with the wind whipping through his hair, he was so damn beautiful her throat ached.

With the ear covers on, all Darcy could hear was the pounding of her own pathetic heart as she executed a textbook slingshot and swung the speedboat to just within range of Tango Three's craft.

Quinn let fly the flashbang, its red arming light making a graceful arc through the night sky. She didn't have to watch to know it would land precisely where it should, at the enemy's feet. He wasn't starting pitcher for the STORM interagency baseball team for nothing.

She peeled the speedboat straight away from the target, locked the wheel, and hit the deck with her eyes shut tight. Quinn landed on top of her, pulling on the gas mask. A scant second later, the edges of her vision lit up like daylight and a sharp boom rattled through the speedboat.

Immediately Quinn pulled her up and she grabbed for the wheel again, turning sharply back to the target. Within seconds she'd caught up and came alongside T-3. Quinn leapt across the gap and tackled the stunned and staggering terrorist. Before the man knew what hit him, he was trussed up hand and foot.

Darcy ripped off her ear protection and shouted at him, "The virus?"

Quinn searched the deck, bent down, and triumphantly held up the canister. He tapped his comm.

"This is STORM Alpha Six actual," he told the team. "Tango Three is contained, and the item has been secured."

TWENTY-FIVE

DARCY felt herself being lifted by a pair of strong arms. *Quinn's arms.* Without even opening her eyes, she knew his touch, his way of gathering her up against his chest, his musky, sexy smell.

When had she fallen asleep?

"You should have woken me," she murmured, trying to pry open her heavy eyelids.

"How? With cannon shot? You didn't get any sleep at all last night, did you?"

Uh-oh. He sounded annoyed.

Well, no, as a matter of fact, she hadn't slept last night. That whole jerking-off-in-the-shower thing had interfered with her sleep patterns in a major way. Besides, she'd had work to do. "No time," she murmured, curling her fingers into his soft, warm T-shirt. "Needed to find the bad guys." *And to avoid him.*

Speaking of which . . . Last she knew, she'd been resting her eyes in the SUV at the boat ramp while Quinn turned over their prisoner to DHS. His conversation with the commander had taken forever and a day. She must have fallen asleep waiting.

The SUV door slammed and he started walking, carrying her.

"Hey . . . where are you taking me?" she demanded, which somewhat lost its potency when she slurred all the words together.

"To bed."

She was finally able to prop one eyelid open and peer up at him. His well-traveled face was even more craggy than usual, a thick shadow of dark blond beard on his angular cheeks and jaw. *God*, he was handsome. No way could she end up in bed with this man. She'd be helpless to resist him.

She opened her mouth to protest.

He beat her to it. "Are we going to start this again?" he grumbled, even more irritated than before. "Because if we're going to start this again, I'm just going to drop you right here and you can sleep on the sidewalk."

She clung harder to him because she knew he'd do it, and she didn't relish landing on her ass on the hard pavement. "Where are we, anyway?"

The air smelled . . . warm. And a bit salty. She opened her other eye and glanced around in time to see the dark, silent parking lot of a cute pink motel with a red neon crayfish waving to passersby decorating the vacancy sign. It was so quiet out, she could hear the electricity crackling as the big claw moved back and forth.

He pushed open a numbered door and carried her inside a small, neat room, the main feature of which was a giant bed. Over it were mounted three paintings of crawdads.

"Somewhere in Louisiana, I'm fairly certain," he said. He dropped her onto the bed and started stripping off his clothes as he made his way toward the bathroom.

Oh. My. God. It was déjà vu all over again.

Except this time she didn't follow after him, and she *definitely* didn't watch him shower. She was pretty sure she wouldn't be able to keep her hands off him if she did.

Two minutes later, he came out again. Dry. Totally naked.

God help her.

Her limbs seemed to be paralyzed. She hadn't moved from the spot on the mattress where he'd deposited her. *Couldn't* move as he came and stood in front of her legs, which were still dangling off the side of the bed.

She gave an inward groan.

Damn, his body was magnificent. Tall and broad-shouldered, packed with muscles that had been earned honestly, hauling munitions over mountain passes and rebuilding bombed-out schools and turning winches on stuck jeeps in far-off lands. His short blond hair had been kissed by the suns of five continents, his hands calloused from the arts of war in a hundred different countries, in defense of the one nation he loved above all else.

He was the sexiest man she had ever met, and she had to fight the urge to spread her knees and invite him to take her as he'd taken everything else he'd ever wanted in life. Mercilessly, thoroughly, and without quarter.

What would it be like to be loved, truly loved, by a man like Quinn? Would he be as fiercely loyal to her as he always was to the land he loved?

She shivered as he leaned over her, grasped the hem of her T-shirt, and started to pull it up. There was not a shadow of doubt what he intended to do.

She put her hands over his. Torn. Tortured. "Quinn."

"Are you going to fight me, sugar?" he asked, his eyes burning. "Go ahead and fight me. Because we both know I'll win."

"I thought we were going to talk."

"Tired of talking." He muscled her T-shirt over her head and threw it aside. "Baby, we can do this rough or we can do this gentle. Your choice."

Sweet arousal coiled through her body. It was a game of sexual domination they'd played dozens of times before.

With one difference. This time it wasn't a game.

"Quinn," she said. But the name came out a breathless invitation instead of the warning she'd intended.

He stripped off her bra and dropped it over the side of the bed.

"Yeah, sugar?"

"You need to stop."

He paused. "Why?"

She bit her lip in lieu of blurting out the dreaded words . . . the reason doing this would kill her. She couldn't tell him how she'd come to feel about him. She *couldn't*. At least this way she'd emerge with her dignity intact. Unlike the other times she'd been discarded and replaced.

With a shrug, he started to twitch open the buttons on her BDUs, one by one, pausing to look into her eyes after each new inch of skin was bared. Her whole body tingled with desire for the feel of his touch.

"This isn't fair," she breathed.

He unlaced one of her boots and tugged it off. "You're wrong. What isn't fair"—he did the same for the other—"is you cutting me off with no explanation. You wanted to talk? Talk quick if you want me to stop."

Despair had her shaking her head back and forth. If she told him the truth, he'd be gone like a shot. Oh, he might finish making love to her tonight. But he'd take the first opportunity to get the hell away from her. Bobby Lee Quinn was not a forever kind of guy. Hell, he wasn't even a tomorrow kind of guy. The word commitment was just not in his vocabulary. And she couldn't go through another rejection. Not with her heart so totally involved. Been there, done that.

"You wouldn't like it," she whispered.

"Damn straight I don't."

She cringed. Oh, God, had she said that aloud?

His fingers seized the waistband of her BDUs and started pulling them down. She panicked for real, sucking in a breath at the skin-to-skin contact, and tried to buck off his grip. It was all he needed. Instantly he was sitting on top of her, her wrists held in a viselike grip above her head. He lifted up a bit, and slowly dragged her body up higher on the bed under him, drawing her BDUs down to her ankles with the friction of his legs and the help of his feet.

Still holding her fast, he looked down and caressed her body with his heated gaze. *Oh, God.* She could feel herself getting wet, reacting to the provocation. The man had a way of letting every carnal, lascivious thought shine through in his pale blue eyes. And make her want to experience it all.

The irony was, if she simply ceased fighting and told him to get off, that she was tired and wanted to go to sleep, he'd stop right here.

If she had any kind of brain, that was exactly what she would do.

But his thick erection pulsed against her mound, telling her with every heartbeat how badly he wanted her. Her nipples had long since beaded to tight points, scraping against the hair of his chest, screaming with need. He felt so incredibly good. She wanted to soak it all in, absorb the heady feeling, so she could remember and pull the memory out in the years to come when she cried for want of him.

One more minute, then she'd tell him no.

As though sensing her compliance, her powerlessness against his potent sexuality, he stretched his nude body over her, covering her from head to toe, growling out a feral noise of anticipation.

Bundling her wrists in one strong hand, he ran his other hand slowly over her body, down her hip, her thigh, then cupped it around the back of her knee and pulled her calf up and out of her pants leg. And kept pulling. She realized what he was doing, spreading her knee wide to expose her, and tried to stop him. It was no use. He was too strong.

She bucked in frustration.

"So you want it rough," he crooned.

"No," she denied. But it was too late. She'd already implicitly consented to the game. She yanked hard at her wrists, bubbling over with aggravation. At herself. For wanting him so damn much. For losing sight of the bad ending this was bound to lead to.

"That's right, baby, fight me," he said in a low command.

So she did fight him, in earnest now, testing his strength, his will to have her. Her breath panted with the exertion, her heartbeat pounded out of control. His eyes darkened, cobalt rings forming around the icy blue as he wrestled her down. He was getting more and more aroused. Harder. Thicker. Stronger. He wanted her.

He wanted her.

She thrashed until he had her completely subdued, his body pressed into hers, the strength of his limbs holding hers down so she couldn't move. His cock lay tight against her inner thigh, pulsing with hunger. He slid his hand over it and between them. And touched her.

She moaned, clenching in pleasure at the feel of his fingers on her. In her. Slippery and skilled, gliding through her wet folds, finding the center of her need. Circling in for the kill.

"Quinn," she gasped. "We have to talk."

"So, talk," he said but didn't cease his relentless seduction of her response. He bent down and his lips and tongue performed the same dance of temptation with her mouth. Nibbling, probing, caressing, opening her wider and wider to his pleasure. And hers.

"Bobby Lee, please," she moaned.

A hum of approval rumbled low in his chest. "That's more like it," he murmured. "Keep talking, sugar. I want to hear you beg."

It wouldn't be the first time. One of them often reduced the other to begging during sex. There was no shame between them, no limits. No need for a safe word, because their sexual appetites fit together so seamlessly, so completely.

Another reason she loved the man to distraction. She could always be herself around him. No maidenly pretense.

At his fingertips, she felt the first ripplings of climax. She closed her eyes in anguish. She hadn't wanted to give in. Not this time.

"Damn it, girl, don't look so sad while I make you come."

She gasped as the physical rush took hold and began to suck her into the vortex of mindless, helpless sensation. "I can't help it!"

"Why?" his dark voice demanded, his fingers never ceasing to draw her further into the abyss.

"Because—*oh, God!*" It was no use. Her body seized in pleasure, bowed up in a perfect arch of surrender. She gave herself over to the overwhelming need in her heart. And cried out the words that would seal her fate. "*I love you.*"

A light dusting of snow had begun falling by the time Rebel emerged from the Lincoln Tunnel into Manhattan. The moon was just peeking through the clouds that enshrouded the city in a multicolored, spun-sugar cocoon.

She'd always thought the city glowed under a special spell of magic around Christmastime, with all the festive lights and colorful banners. Especially when the sky was newly awash in the shimmer of a billion tiny snowflakes. It was like living inside an enchanted snow globe, and it never failed to cheer her up. Even the taxi drivers stopped being rude while everyone enjoyed the five minutes of delight.

But tonight she didn't even see it. Her mind was too crammed full of too many things to process at one time, let alone notice the beauty of the night.

Things like the truly horrible experiences Gina had told about her captivity.

And everything that had happened earlier with Wade.

Not to mention the bombshell Alex had subsequently laid on her . . .

Had he really fantasized about being with her the same way she had about being with him?

Fantasies that had been thoroughly crushed by the stinging memory of those white parchment wedding invitations . . .

It was all too much to think about. Especially on no sleep. Her brain was about to explode, her body about to shut down.

What she needed was a hot bubble bath, a chilled glass of wine, and a strong pair of loving arms to hold her close as she slept for about three days. Just hold her.

Yeah, dream on.

Her cell phone rang for the dozenth time. Who was it this time? Wade, or Alex? They'd been playing phone leapfrog, and obviously, neither man was going to quit calling until she answered. She pushed out a resigned breath, picked up the cell from the seat next to her, and pushed the talk button.

"Haywood."

"Was I really that bad?" The deep masculine voice held a note of wistful dryness.

Amazingly, she felt herself smile. His self-deprecation never failed to raise her esteem for him. "Oh, you were terrible. That fourth orgasm you gave me was definitely subpar."

Wade made a noise that might have been a chuckle. But distinctly lacking in humor. "Then why'd you run away?"

She tried to come up with an excuse that wouldn't sound like an excuse even to her. And came up empty.

"Wow," he drawled. "Not even a dead mother or ailing aunt?" The dryness was now Sahara-worthy. With an edge.

She felt awful if he thought she'd just blown him off, but

she really couldn't deal right now. "Sorry. I'm just . . .
exhausted."

"Strange. I can't sleep. Where have you been for the last
twelve hours, Rebel?"

Nothing like beating around the bush.

"Wade—"

"If you won't answer the man you spent yesterday afternoon fucking, maybe you'll answer your boss. Where were
you, Agent Haywood? I've been calling all night."

She winced. "Language, Wade."

"Just answer me, damn it."

She was too tired to fight him. "All right. There have
been . . . developments."

"In . . . ?"

She blew out a breath. "The Cappozi case."

He was silent for a moment. "Impossible. You see, I'm the
SAC on that case, so I would have been notified if there'd
been developments."

"I'm sorry," she said. "I guess we need to talk."

"No shit. Get over here. Right now."

So much for that bubble bath. She checked the dashboard
clock. "Fine. I can be at the office in—"

"No. My hotel room. If I'm being back-ended, I'd rather
get it in private."

His hotel room.

Where the sheets were probably still smoking from yesterday afternoon.

"Wade, I don't think that's—"

"God*damn* it, Rebel! You've got ten minutes to get your
butt over here or you can kiss your career good-bye."

The cell phone screen blinked off. He'd hung up.

She sighed. It was an idle threat, of course. If she went
down, so would he. But she felt his frustration. She did.
However, she was also about to drop from exhaustion. Were
a few hours' sleep too much to ask? Apparently.

She turned the car toward his hotel.

Twelve minutes later he opened the door to her soft
knock.

He was wearing a pair of black sweats that hung low on
his hips, and an unbuttoned flannel shirt. His hair was art-

fully mussed and his feet bare, like she'd gotten him out of bed, which no doubt she had. The crow's-feet at the corners of his eyes were a bit more pronounced and his mouth less welcoming than last afternoon, but other than that he looked as attractive and powerful as ever.

Was she crazy not to jump in and grab this man with both hands? Probably. Wade Montana was a twenty-karat catch and more. She'd wanted a boyfriend. A man didn't get much more made-to-order than this one. So what was her problem?

Like she didn't know.

"Come in," he said stiffly.

Ah, well. No doubt she'd already totally blown her chances. She had pretty much hijacked his case and lied to him . . . if by omission. Not exactly a great relationship foundation.

"Thanks," she said. And noticed the room service table in the middle of the room set for two, complete with burned-down candles and still-cheerful flowers. One meal sat half eaten, the other untouched, along with a bottle of champagne swimming in an ice bucket filled with warm water.

Oh, dear.

She turned to face him. "I'm sorry," she repeated for the umpteenth time.

"So am I. Now tell me what the fuck is going on."

"Language, Wade."

He slashed an angry hand up. "I swear. Get over it. And start talking."

"It's Gina. She's been found."

He froze where he stood. His eyes lasered in on her. "Is she okay?"

Rebel nodded. "A little worse for wear, but okay."

"Where is she?"

She cleared her throat. He was not going to like this. "I can't tell you that."

"*What?*" he exploded. "What the fuck do you mean? I'm the goddamn *SAC* on the goddamn case. You'll tell me or—"

She dug in her suit jacket pocket for Kurt Bridger's card and held it out to him. "Call this man. He'll explain everything."

He snatched the card from her and examined it while she walked over to the small settee and dumped her purse onto it, along with her raincoat. On second thought, she added her suit jacket to the pile. And kicked off her shoes. Then turned to watch him whip out his cell phone and call the number on the card, his face a mask of . . . lord knew. Fury? Worry? Affront? All of the above?

"This is Special Agent in Charge Wade Montana from the Federal Bureau of Investigation," he growled into the phone. "To whom am I speaking?"

This could take a while.

She wandered over to the table and lifted the silver lid on one untouched plate. Lobster. *Ouch.* She lifted another. Salad. She popped a cherry tomato in her mouth. The sweet-tart taste burst onto her tongue as she chewed. Good. But she still wasn't hungry. She eyed the champagne bottle. Maybe he'd hate her less after a glass or two, even if it was warm. Or maybe she'd notice less. She popped the stopper and filled the two flutes, walked over, and handed him one as he talked. He took it but ignored her.

The tepid liquid went down surprisingly easily. Probably would have been really good cold. She was on her second glass when her eye snagged on the bathroom. Which had one of those wonderful giant spa tubs. With jets. A basket of bath items sat on the tiled rim, wrapped in a bow, like a present just for her. She strolled in and pulled an envelope out from the basket. Bubble bath. Lilac.

It was a siren call too great to resist. And it wasn't like she had to worry about Wade wanting to join her. That look on his face had said he'd probably never speak to her again. What could happen? Besides, he'd already seen her naked. She closed the door, turned on the water, and stripped.

Oh, it was heavenly. Hot and bubbly and smelling sweetly of summer flowers. The champagne tickled her throat and relaxed her muscles. She closed her eyes and sighed in pleasure. *Exactly* what she needed. Her mind finally slowed to a crawl and ebbed away.

"Rebel?"

She started awake. Wade was standing over the tub, looking down at her. The hot water had grown tepid. Good grief. She'd fallen asleep.

"You're lucky you didn't drown."

"What? Oh. Yeah." She sat up. Rubbed her eyes. Opened them to Wade's gaze drifting down her naked body. Okay, so maybe she'd miscalculated the part about him not wanting to join her. Her nipples contracted with a zing. And okay, maybe she'd also miscalculated the part where she didn't want him to join her. Memories of yesterday afternoon flowed traitorously through her mind. And her body.

"So. Are we still speaking?" she asked through her tight throat.

He moistened his lips with his tongue and she followed the movement longingly. "Maybe. Are we still fucking?"

Whoa.

She swallowed. She should say no. Absolutely not. Her heart belonged elsewhere, and . . . "Maybe," she said.

His eyes narrowed slightly. "Stand up."

He held out a hand, and against every instinct she took it, letting him pull her up from the water. "Wade, there's som—"

"Shut up."

Okay. He *was* still angry. If the clipped order hadn't told her, the way he wrapped her in a towel and rubbed the streaming droplets of water from her body did. Not rough, exactly. But definitely not gentle. More on the order of if-you-let-me-screw-your-brains-out-maybe-I'll-forgive-you-but-no-guarantees-because-right-now-I'm-hating-myself-for-wanting-you.

Not that she blamed him, exactly.

He tossed the towel aside. Along with his flannel shirt.

Ho-boy.

Even under the thick fabric of his sweatpants his erection looked huge. And hungry.

"Wade—"

"Did I say you could speak?"

He skimmed his fingernails up her body from her hips to her breasts and she shivered in pleasure, her flesh crying out for more. He teased her nipples and she moaned in an agonized mire of guilt and anticipation. The man knew how to turn a woman on.

Reaching up, he pulled out the long pin holding her hair

in its bun and let it drop to the floor with a clatter. He combed the strands with his fingers, arranging the unruly locks in a cloud of red over her shoulders, partially covering her breasts. He stepped right up against her, so the wiry curls on his bare chest barely grazed the beaded tips. The thick staff of his arousal touched her belly. The soft cotton over the head felt moist with his essence. She sucked in an unsteady breath.

"Take them off," he ordered gruffly.

She blinked.

"The sweatpants. Take them off."

She should be more torn. But she wasn't. She wanted this. She wanted him. Even though she knew it was all wrong. Selfish and deceitful.

She lowered to her knees and slowly drew down his pants, revealing his rampant desire. She looked up and their gazes met, clashed hotly. She felt a rush of moisture between her legs. She finished taking off his pants, easing them over his athletic calves and masculine feet. Then put her lips to his inner thigh. Drew her tongue upward. His fingers stabbed through her hair and held her head in their powerful grip. She continued her journey upward. She licked at his balls. Kissed the root of his cock. Brushed her lips slowly, deliberately, up to the head, then took it in her mouth.

Finally he groaned. A deep, seductive noise of want.

Then his fingers tightened in her hair and he jerked her away.

"Oh, no, Special Agent Haywood," he said, low and rough. "You're not getting off that easy."

TWENTY-SIX

IT was one of those immensely frustrating hurry-up-and-wait deals.

After taking down T-2, Marc and Kick had been dropped by the helo in the parking lot of the Baton Rouge motel that DHS had taken over as their base of operations. That's where Ski and Rand had brought the Moby, which was now parked alongside an assortment of DHS mobile units.

There had been a huge spurt of excitement while Quinn and Darcy had captured Tango Three, half an hour ago. Then he and Kick gone with the DHS team to interrogate the prisoner and see what could be learned, if anything. So far no joy, but they'd been ordered to stand down and wait for further instructions.

Since then, operations in the Moby and the DHS ground units had reverted to the prior steady buzz of activity . . . of the strictly intel-gathering and interpreting variety.

The UAV had done several optical pass-overs of the whole region—thankfully both before and after the brown van had been abandoned at the shopping center. A dozen specialists, including Rand and Ski, had been feverishly working on overlaying images to help determine the new vehicle or vehicles Tangos One and Five were using, then to track their possible destinations. In the case of Tango Three's silver sedan, the geek squad had scored a perfect touchdown. But for the van . . . not so much. As a result, everyone was on edge and short-tempered.

Dieu. Marc had had no clue how much monotonous analysis went on behind every successful UAV sortie, nor of the incredible skill a good sensory operator had to possess in order to pinpoint, follow, and tag small targets. As a soldier on the ground, all you saw was the missile coming out of nowhere to blow up an enemy RPG position or insurgent vehicle or whatever. These days, you kinda took that type of support for granted. Never again.

But Marc and Kick were not computer geeks or data squints who could help with any of that. They were both boots-on-ground, guns-in-hands specialists who carried out the orders analysts helped strategize. In other words, they were totally useless at this stage. Once Tawhid's location was nailed down, that would be a different story. But for now, Marc and Kick had been told in no uncertain terms to take a hike.

"Find a bed. Get some sleep," Kurt Bridger had ordered them. "You're making the analysts nervous peering over their shoulders armed to the teeth like that."

Quoi? He and Kick had hiked brows over the comm. Ready to move out at a moment's notice, each of them had a pistol holstered at his hip, another tucked in the back of his waistband, and a really big knife strapped to his thigh. Kick's HK was leaning next to the Moby's exit door, along with Marc's entry kit.

They rolled their eyes at each other and shrugged. "Wimps," Kick mouthed.

Nevertheless, they stepped away from the geeks, grabbed their stuff, and headed back inside the motel to their assigned rooms. Probably a good idea to catch a few z's anyway. They'd been up since the crack of dawn, and God knew Marc hadn't gotten much sleep last night, either. If any.

Because of Tara.

At the unbidden reminder of her, a wave of need and longing washed through him. Which was quickly razored through by a sharp slash of guilt.

He tossed a salute to Kick when they parted at the corridor his room was on and reflexively checked his watch: 12:43 a.m. Too late to phone her?

Alors. He'd said he would call. And at the time he'd had every intention of doing so. Yet all day he'd resisted the almost constant urge to dial her cell phone number just to hear her cute Yankee accent purring in his ear.

Dieu, he was already half in love with the woman, driving himself crazy with thoughts of how it could be between them if given a chance. Despite the short amount of time they'd known each other, he'd never felt so strongly about any woman before. Never thought he would.

Still didn't think he should.

He strode down the hotel hallway, checking room numbers as he went. His must be around the next corner.

What he *should* do was let her go. *Fini.* He was not in a position to give her any kind of relationship. Even if she wanted to be with him, what could he offer?

An arrangement like Quinn and Zimmerman's? Seeing each other a few times a year, screwing their brains out, and then parting, living separate lives until the next time he rolled through town for five minutes?

Or get into a situation like Kick and Rainie? Where he's off on a mission for days, weeks, or even months without her? And she's tucked away in some STORM safe house, unable to hold down a normal job or even go out, because some psycho bad guy had might take it into his head to hurt her in retaliation for something *he'd* done? Married, but forced to be apart, both in danger of being killed . . .

Non, working for STORM Corps, relationship prospects really sucked. Better to stay strong, endure this small heartache, and avoid a much bigger one down the line.

He jammed his hands in his BDU pockets and went around the corner. Just as a woman stopped in front of Rand Jaeger's room and lifted her hand to knock.

Tara!?

Quoi fais foutre?

She glanced his way and her hand faltered. It *was* Tara!

"What the hell are you doing here?" he burst out.

She froze to the spot. "U-um," she stammered. "I'm, um—looking for Rand."

Everything in Marc's body swirled into a vortex of deathly calm. Or was it raging fury? "Rand?" he repeated, not quite believing what was happening. She was here, in Baton Rouge, in the same motel as he was . . . and looking for *Rand Jaeger*?

"Yeah, I've, uh, been assigned to help him."

"Assigned," he repeated, sounding like a goddamn parrot. What the *fuck* was going on? Since when was Trooper Tara Reeves someone who could be *assigned* to a STORM operation? He scowled suspiciously. "Help him with what?"

She dropped her hand to her side. "Anything he needs."

His scowl deepened. Reason flew out the window. "*Any*thing?"

A few long seconds went by before she jetted out a breath and pursed her lips. The only indication of her true reaction was when her jaw muscles clenched once.

"Well," she said conversationally. "I'm sure he won't get too personal in his demands. I mean, you *did* tell him I was coming, and that you and me, well, we have a thing going, right?" She blinked guilelessly. "Except"—she hit her forehead with her palm . . . *He was so screwed*—"oh, wait. You didn't *know* I'd be coming back, because you never bothered to call like you said you would. Therefore, any *thing* we may have had obviously didn't mean *shit* to you." By the end of her little speech, her voice had risen with angry bitterness. "So, never mind," she clipped out, turning to deliberately ignore him.

Merde.

"Tara, *cher*—"

Her hand shot up. "Save it for someone who cares, Lafayette. I'm not interested. Just point me in Rand's direction and I'll be out of your hair."

"*Beb, non*—"

"Seriously?" She wrenched away when he reached for her. "I'm over it. Just here to do a job."

Yeah, sure she was.

"In fact," she declared, "when Kurt Bridger asked who I wanted to work with, I specifically requested Rand." She tried to walk past him.

She was *so* lying. He slapped his hand on the wall to prevent her escaping. *"Arrête!"* He whacked his other hand on the other side of her, bracketing her between his arms. "You think you can just walk away from me?"

"Like you did?" she retorted. "Absolutely. Now, let me go."

"Like *hell.*"

He stared down at her, knowing damn well she still cared, still wanted him—why else would she be so furious?—but not quite daring to kiss her because he had the distinct feeling he'd get a knee in the balls for his trouble.

She closed her eyes, let out a breath. Opened them. Arranged her face in an oh-so-reasonable expression. "Look. I get it, okay? We were thrown together in an intimate situation, and hormones got the better of us both. But when you left this morning, be honest—you never expected to see me again."

A muscle ticked in his face. "Tar—"

"Please, Marc. Just. Don't. Today has been hard enough without you giving me more false hope. Do me a favor, and let's pretend last night—hell, the last three days—never happened. Okay?"

Her tone was both wry and fatalistic, and if he hadn't looked into her eyes, he might have done just that. It would surely be the easy way out. The *smart* thing to do. Take the graceful exit that she was so generously offering. But when he looked into those doleful, soulful green eyes trying so valiantly not to let the hurt and vulnerability shine through that false façade of strength and indifference, he just couldn't do it.

He wanted her too badly. Not just sexually, but in every sense of the word. Maybe even more in other, more important ways than having her under him again. *Mais, Dieu,* he wanted her that way, too.

With a sigh, he dropped his cagelike stance and slid his arms around her. "Sorry; can't do that," he said, holding her firmly against him when she tried to squirm away. "What you say might be true. And I'll be the first to admit I'm a goddamn selfish, sorry-ass bastard of a man. But now that I've got you back in my arms, I can't let you go again. I won't."

"Jesus, Marc. What do you want from me?" she asked, her voice frayed.

"Nothing," he said and drew her closer still. "Everything."

She gave a desperate little laugh. But didn't resist. Much. "Oh, *that*'ll be easy."

"A better question is, what can I give you in return?"

She obviously caught his meaning. Her chin tilted defensively. "All right, fine. What *can* you give me in return?"

He sighed. "Not a hell of a lot."

"There's a shock."

He put his lips to her forehead. Kissed her frown. "You know the business I'm in, *cher*. It doesn't leave a lot of room for a personal life. But it's what I am, all I know. I can't leave it."

"I wouldn't ask you to."

But what was the alternative?

The smell of her skin, the feel of her curves wound through his senses. "I can't ask you to live like that. Never knowing where I am, when I'll be back, *if* I'll be back. It's too hard on a woman."

Despite the certainty of what he was saying, another certainty was making itself known in the slow quickening of his body. *He wanted her more than ever.* And there was no way in hell he'd let her go. Not yet.

"Let me go, Marc," she pleaded softly. "I'll find Rand and that'll be the end of us."

The end of us.

That unacceptable thought sent a vicious pang of need streaking through him. He lifted a hand and pushed a lock of hair back from her face.

"Rand's busy," he said, his groin heavy with the want of her. "He sent me and Kick away so he could work undisturbed. He'll call me when something breaks. He won't need you for anything until then." His cock lengthened and thickened against her belly.

Her green eyes gazed up at him, startled comprehension suddenly dawning in them. "Marc," she choked out. "You have got to be kidding. You just dumped me!"

"Let you go. And not by choice. Let me show you how much I wish I could keep you."

She gave another of those bitter little laughs. "Wow. Does that pathetic line work on all the women you love and leave?"

He cupped her face in his palm. "*Cher*, you are the only woman I've had in two years. Trust me, this is not any kind of bullshit line."

Her eyes searched his. Filmed over. "You are a real bastard, you know that?"

"Yeah. I know." He tightened his grip and kissed her. Hard. And deep. So she couldn't think about just how big a bastard he was being. If he had half a heart, he'd let her go. Let her walk—no, run—away from him and this untenable situation.

But he couldn't. He wanted her. *Dieu*, he wanted to *own* her. He wanted to ram inside her and never, ever come out.

"*Pitié d'amour,*" he whispered in her mouth, touching the tip of her tongue with his. "*Vien. Baise-moi.*"

He could feel her weakening, her body melting into him one stubborn muscle at a time. He pulled her toward his room as he kissed her, digging in his pocket for the key card.

When they reached the door, she put a hand on his chest. "Just so we're clear," she said, her voice rough with desire. "This is the last time. Then it has to stop. You're turning my life upside down and I can't deal with this anymore."

She couldn't deal? What about *him*? Unreasonable anger swirled through him. She just didn't understand. He smacked open the door and pushed her through it, whirled around, and pushed her up against the hollow wood.

"You think this is not killing me, too?" he demanded hotly. "Every time I get within ten feet of you, all I think about is how much I want you. I can't concentrate on the mission, my job, on what I'm supposed to be doing. I'm *completement fou*, totally useless, when I'm around you."

Merde, he didn't understand. Didn't understand how she had gotten under his skin so thoroughly, in such a short time. How she'd made him actually consider giving up the job that had been his whole life, that defined him as a person, just to be with her.

But then her mouth reached for his and he couldn't think at all.

"Thank God," she moaned, licking at him, her fingers gripping his T-shirt in tight fists. "Thank God it's not just me."

Donc. That was the whole problem in a nutshell. It *was* just her. Just her he wanted. Just her screwing up this mission . . . *merde*, just her ruining his whole *foutu* life. Because it was just her he could imagine spending the next fifty years with. Just her who made his blood heat to the point he could think of nothing else but being inside her.

"All right," he swore. "This is the last time. Now, take off your clothes. I'm done talking."

TWENTY-SEVEN

THE last time.

Even as he swept her off her feet and onto the bed, Marc's words echoed in Tara's mind, leaving despair in their wake. Why did he have to feel so damn good? Taste so sexy? Touch her so temptingly?

Now that she'd found him, had learned what real love could be like, how would she ever live without him?

In the blink of an eye they were both naked, their bodies molded into each other, their lips sharing wet, lingering kisses.

"*Ah, cher, si belle.*" He held her close, slipping between her legs. "How could I not want you for always?"

"But you don't have for always to give," she returned, more to remind herself than him. It was so hard to accept reality.

Not when right now his hands and his mouth were kissing and caressing their way down her body, fulfilling every fantasy, every need. Why couldn't *this* be reality, for always? She moaned, arching into him as his tongue laved over her breasts. Determined to enjoy every minute she still had him in her arms. Soon enough he'd be gone, and she'd be back to the all-too-lonely reality of life without him. How would she ever survive?

He found the center of her need and used all his skill to bring her to a slow, powerful climax. And then he surged up and into her. She gasped at the intense sensation of him filling her, claiming her. *Completing her.* "Oh, Marc!" she softly cried.

He gazed heatedly down at her and wrapped his arms around her body. "*Bien?*" he asked.

"More than *bien*," she assured him breathlessly. *At least until he left her.* But she didn't want to think about that now. "Love me, Marc," she whispered. "Please love me."

His eyes softened, and she was sure he was about to say something. But he just pushed in to the hilt, his dark-lashed lids sinking to half-mast and a deep rumble sounding in his chest. And then he loved her.

For the next hours—minutes?—she thought of nothing but him. Felt nothing but him. Dreamt only of him.

Until she awoke to the roll of the bed dipping, and the warmth of his body next to her turning to chilly emptiness.

She forced herself out of the muzzy contentment she'd been surrounded by. "You're leaving?" she asked into the darkness of the room.

"It's past time I checked in," he said. She could hear regret in his voice. Or was that just wishful thinking?

"So, this is it?" she asked, her heart squeezing more painfully than she could possibly imagine.

He pushed out a breath. "Better to be strong. Not to torture ourselves dragging out our good-byes. It'll only hurt worse."

"So this really is the last time . . ." she whispered, sitting up.

He turned on the bathroom light and pulled on his BDUs. "If there were any way to make things work between us, you have to know I'd try . . . But I can't ask you to live that kind of life. Never knowing where I am. Not knowing if I've been hurt or landed in some third-world prison I'll never get out of." He sounded very determined.

"I know," she murmured. "I understand."

And she did. She'd lived that for years with her father. But that didn't mean she had to like it. She watched bleakly as he finished dressing, turned off the light, and picked up his gear.

"Don't I even get a hug good-bye?" she asked, unable to control the wavering in her voice.

The flashing lights around the motel illuminated his face in alternating strobes of red and green through the thin drapes. He swallowed. "I'm afraid if I touch you again, I won't be able to let you go."

Then don't, she wanted to cry out. But she knew men like Marc and her father didn't change. Would never stay. Not for a woman. Duty always came first. Always. Then, if there was any time left over, love and family. But Tara wasn't willing to accept second place in Marc's heart. She'd seen what that compromise had done to her mother.

"Okay," she said, holding down the pain with an iron will.

"Go back to sleep," he told her. "Rand can wait until morning for your help."

"Yeah," she said, though there was fat chance of that happening. She'd probably never be able to fall asleep again.

Suddenly she was shivering cold. So she obediently lay back down and pulled the covers up to her chin. Would she ever be warm again, without him there to heat her blood and her body?

Suddenly, the bedside phone rang, shrilling through the room, startling her right out of bed. She grabbed it, locking eyes with Marc, who'd halted with his hand on the doorknob. "Hello?"

There was a brief pause. "Uh . . . Tara?" It was Rand.

Suddenly she remembered it was Marc's phone. *Oops.*

"Yeah. It's Tara. What's up?"

"Sorry for the, um— We need Marc ASAP. We've finally got a bead on Tawhid."

Instantly she was awake. "Great! Where are you?"

"The Moby, out in the parking lot."

She turned to give Marc the news. But he was already gone. He'd slipped out the door before she even knew he'd moved, leaving a dark, empty void in his place.

Pain razored through her heart. *Oh, God.* Would she ever see him again?

"Tara?"

She forced herself back to the phone conversation, dashing at her welling eyes. "He's on his way. And Rand? Kurt Bridger sent me to assist you. Hope that's okay."

"Are you kidding?" He actually sounded relieved. "I could sure use the help. Ski's been chomping at the bit to get back to his petri dishes."

"Give me a few minutes and I'll be down," she managed.

She hung up the phone, closed her eyes, and exhaled a shuddering breath. Trying desperately to pretend the warm moisture trickling down her cheeks wasn't tears of desolation.

She did *not* need him. She'd survive this breakup. She would endure. Eventually. She always had before when those she loved had abandoned her.

But, oh, how she wished she didn't have to be left behind. How she wished that *this* time things would be different. That this time she'd finally found the happiness that had eluded her for so long. And that, for once in her life, she didn't have to be so damned strong.

TWENTY-EIGHT

ABBAS Tawhid and Tango Five had commandeered a small plane at a private airport about twenty-five miles northeast of Baton Rouge and taken off without filing a flight plan. A costly miscalculation on the part of the terrorists. Warned to be on the lookout for any suspicious activity, the airport had immediately notified Homeland Security.

At that point it had taken Rand all of thirty seconds to locate the plane with the UAV radar, and send Marc, Kick, and Ski running for the bright red Coast Guard Stingray helicopter that swooped down to pick them up in the motel parking lot. The STORM chopper had left to transport Bridger to Command.

Marc stowed his gear, hunkered down in the bay, and clung to a strap as the helo took to the still-dark sky. Adjusting the volume on his headset, he clenched his stomach muscles against the Coast Guard pilot's idea of a giggle—climbing at a steep tilt so his big, tough commando passengers would toss their cookies. As if.

The craft was no-frills, with a big door that had been left wide-open to the frigid blackness of nighttime, and none of the usual amenities. Like seats.

Hell, who needed seats anyway. Marc always felt an incredible adrenaline rush hanging out the door of a moving chopper climbing straight up to two thousand feet, even if he was freezing his butt off. He also had to concentrate not to fall out—which kept him from thinking about pretty much anything else.

Which was a good thing.

Because if he started thinking about Tara and the way she'd looked at him when he was leaving her, he'd—

Non. Merde. Not going there.

Next to him, Kick interrupted his guilt attack by yelling into the comm over the roar of the engine, "This is STORM Kilo. You reading me, Romeo, over?"

"This is STORM Juliet," came the reply, jarring Marc's gut even worse than the pilot's clown maneuvers. "We're reading you loud and clear, Kilo. Your bird is tagged and Romeo is streaming your progress in infrared, over."

Kick frowned and turned to Marc and Ski. "Who the hell is Juliet?" he asked over the headset.

Marc pressed his lips together. *Si foutu amusant.* As a policy, no one on the teams used *tango* even if their first name started with a T, and Rand was already Romeo. So Tara had gotten to choose her call letter.

Romeo and Juliet.

De putain.

"It's Tara," Ski jumped in when Marc was too busy grinding his teeth in jealousy to answer. "She came back to help out Rand."

Kick sliced Marc a surprised glance but didn't say what he must be thinking—what Marc had been thinking since he saw her knocking on Rand's door earlier. She'd claimed she specifically requested Rand. But Marc refused to believe that. It had been the anger talking. So, *why had Bridger assigned her to someone else?* Hell, the STORM commander was legendary for knowing everything about everybody. He must know about their affair. Had he deliberately separated them? Did he have doubts about Marc's ability to do his job while around her? Was it so damned obvious?

Or had she really requested the assignment herself? She *had* been pretty damn pissed off at him earlier, before he was able to turn things around . . . temporarily, at least.

"Good to have you back, STORM Juliet," Kick said over

the comm, ignoring Marc's thunderous scowl. "What's Tango One's heading, over?"

"Feeding coordinates into your PDAs as we speak, over," Rand answered. Probably sitting right next to her in the crowded Moby. Were their shoulders touching? *Dieu.* Marc did not want to think about Tara working so closely with another man.

Not that he had any right to object. He'd made his choice and walked away from any say in her life whatsoever. And that was that.

He just had to get over it. Forget Tara.

He had to think about the job. Catching the bad guys. Recovering those deadly virus canisters. *That's* what was important. Not his pointless jealousy. Or his heavy heart. Or the fact that suddenly the prospect of all those years stretching ahead with only bad guys to share them with made his life seem almost too lonely to bear.

Foutre de foutre.

Giving himself a firm mental boot, he forced his focus back on the mission.

Ski had his PDA in hand, studying the map on the screen. "Looks like our boys are headed northeast."

"On a straight course for Atlanta," Tara said over the comm.

Marc peered over Ski's shoulder. "And beyond that, D.C."

"Or New York City," Ski said, drawing a line with his finger. "Quinn thinks at least one of them is targeting Madison Square Garden."

"They'll never get that far," Marc said.

Kick swore softly. "Plenty of venues in Atlanta. We're still thinking they're targeting sports arenas, right?"

"Romeo, is it possible their plane makes it to Atlanta before us, over?" Marc asked with a curse.

"Barring unforeseen disaster, no chance," Rand assured them. "The tangos only had a fifteen-minute head start, and your pilot's really hauling ass, over."

"All right, people, so how do we take out the terrorists without killing *their* pilot?" Marc asked the team, really wishing they could just blow the damn plane out of the sky with a well-placed missile launched from the UAV. As sortie leader, he'd received orders to bring down the bad guys using any means necessary. But if that meant killing an innocent pilot, no way he'd do it.

Kick patted his trusty HK. "Just get the fuckers in front of a window on that plane, and they're history."

"Yeah, that'll work for the first shot, but the second won't be so easy," Marc pointed out.

"Then I'll have to make sure the first shot takes out both of them."

Against his will, Marc grinned. The guy was a cocky bastard, had to give him that. "I take it you brought your Spidey X-ray vision glasses?" he drawled to a collective team chuckle. Searchlights went only so far. It was pitch-black out, and contrary to what Hollywood would have you believe, real thermal imaging devices couldn't see through the insulated walls of a plane or building—or even glass. So unless the searchlight picked out both men, there was no way of knowing where inside the aircraft the second tango was positioned while Kick took out the first. After the first went down, the second was sure to hit the deck and hide.

"You let me worry about taking the shots," Kick said, stroking the HK like he would a lover. "Just get us within searchlight range."

"The question is how," Marc said, glancing at the glow of his watch. "And we've got six whole minutes to choreograph this operation, people. Then it's showtime."

REBEL lay exhausted and replete under Wade's incredible body. She'd never felt so amazing in her life.

Nor as filled with guilt.

He seemed to have forgiven her. Or maybe had just worn off the edges of his anger through the pure physical force of his lovemaking. If you could call it that.

She'd be more inclined to use the other word he was so fond of. Though not in a bad way. Necessarily. Lust had its place, and apparently that was exactly what they'd both needed.

He rolled off her with a satisfied grunt, breathing heavily as he gathered her in his arms and tucked her against his side. "Damn, woman."

She hummed an unsteady note of agreement. "That was unbelievable."

He tipped her chin up and gave her a long, toe-curling, spine-tingling kiss. "I do like a woman who's not shy of telling a man what she wants," he murmured.

She felt her cheeks go warm. Then glanced at the champagne bottle. It was empty. *Whoops.*

"I only have one question," he added, keeping his hold on her chin.

"Oh?" She nibbled her kiss-swollen lower lip. "What's that?"

His fingers tightened. His eyes went cold. "Just who the hell is Alex?"

RAND was sitting at the control console of the Moby like the wizard of Oz, watching UAV video, mapping overlays, IR streams, and lists of numbers as they flashed by, while tapping keys on a *Star Trek*–like keyboard nearly as fast. Over the comm, the team was furiously debating strategy.

By comparison Tara felt of little use. She'd been tasked with monitoring the team comm, communicating with the helo pilot, and patching through to STORM Command and DHS if necessary. Which felt a bit like sitting in the corner stacking Legos while the big boys played *Resident Evil* on the Xbox. Why did this all feel so very familiar? She'd honestly thought STORM would be different.

"So. You and Lafayette."

At the unexpected remark, Tara shot a glance over at Rand to make sure he'd muted his mic. He had, thank God.

"What about us?" she responded, shaking off her frustration and antsiness.

"Well," Rand said neutrally. "You spent the night together. Twice." His quirky South African accent made the overly personal observation sound more charming than impertinent.

"Yep." Not like she could deny it.

She kept her eyes firmly glued to a small television monitor squawking softly next to her comm center. Rand kept it tuned to Bloomberg, so he could monitor the stock market as he worked. Apparently he was amassing a small fortune despite the recent downturn.

"Yet," he persisted, "you've been avoiding talking about him since you got here. Changed the subject whenever his name came up. Haven't once commented on a thing he's said over the comm."

Which had taken a herculean effort, by the way. She was darn proud she wasn't hanging on his every word as he expertly tightened the attack plan. Good thing, too. He hadn't even seemed to recognize her voice at first. Ski'd had to tell Kick she was Juliet.

"And your point is?" she mumbled.

"No point," Rand said. "Just wondering." A few beats later, he ventured, "So, you're not . . . involved with him?" His mild green eyes met hers in the reflection of the TV monitor. They held a definite shade of interest.

Wow. How to react to that? Rand Jaeger was a computer geek of the first order. An absolute grand master of high tech. Tall, rangy, and sandy-haired, his wire-rimmed glasses framed long-lashed, sensitive eyes that missed nothing. Okay, he had great bone structure, not a bad body once you got past the ill-fitting clothes, and if he'd spend more than five minutes a year outside and put a little color onto that pale skin, he'd actually be a great-looking guy.

But she was *so* not interested. In *any*one. Not just Rand.

"Yeah. Marc and me . . . It's complicated."

Uh-huh. As complicated as one minus one equals zero.

"Uh-huh," he said. Was there an echo in here?

She flipped the TV channel and it landed on CNBC. A well-known female financial guru was expertly explaining to a clueless woman how to fix her disastrous investments. Tara turned up the volume a tad. She'd always liked the outspoken feminist money whiz. Too bad there wasn't a similar show that explained to clueless women how to fix their disastrous love lives.

"Anyway," she added for Rand's benefit, "neither of us is looking for anything serious right now. Especially me."

"Okay, I get the hint," he said good-naturedly.

She smiled at him. "Rand, you're going to make some lucky woman an awesome boyfriend one of these days. But trust me, you don't want it to be me."

"Well, can't blame a *boike* for checking," he said, peering closer at the computer monitor. She got the distinct feeling he'd already forgotten the question.

She toyed with a pencil as commercials played on the TV. Suddenly, she sat up. "I'll be damned," she murmured, reading the announcement on the screen.

"What's that?" Rand asked.

Tara pointed at the screen. "Omigod, look! My all-time favorite celebrity is here in town! She's giving a speech on financial fitness for women this morning at a place called Maravich Center. Boy, would I love to go to that."

"Gawd." Rand made a face. "You can have her. She hates men, you know."

Tara made a face right back at him. Why were men always so threatened by a strong woman? "No, she doesn't. She just advocates for women to take control of their own finances."

"If you say so." He typed a few keystrokes and the thermal image of the helo reappeared, closing in on the tail of a small private plane. He tapped his headset mic to unmute it. "STORM Mike, this is Romeo. You are approaching your tango's six, over."

"Copy that, over."

Tara held her breath as three human heat signatures leaned out of the open helo doors, two with rifles and one holding a portable floodlight. Marc barked out a series of orders, and suddenly, the helo zoomed up to hover piggyback above the plane. If the private plane's pilot noticed, he wasn't reacting with any evasive maneuvers.

Within seconds came Marc's backward countdown. "Ready with the light, Ski. Commence action in three, two—"

On *one*, the helo rose up, dashed ahead of the plane, and did a midair quarter spin. Rand switched the monitor from IR to camera just as a floodlight strobed on, flooding the nose of the plane in light. Kick's long rifle took aim at the windshield, jerked, then over the comm came the loud rapport of a single shot.

"Target one contained," came Kick's calm voice. "Searching for target two."

The helo kept steady pace ahead of the plane as the floodlight panned across its windshield, illuminating a terrified and wildly gesticulating pilot. The air traffic radio band that had previously been deathly silent came alive. "Don't shoot! Please, I'm not with him! He had a gun on me!"

As the frantic pilot rattled off his name and the plane's call number, Marc interrupted. "This is Coast Guard helicopter sierra one. Is the hijacker dead?"

"Yes! My God, right through the forehead! And my windshield is—"

Again Marc interrupted. "We have information that *two* men boarded your plane. Where's the other one?"

"He got off," came the hurried reply.

"Got *off?*"

"Yeah. After they hijacked the plane, they made me taxi down the runway, then turn around and take off in the other direction. He jumped out when I slowed to maneuver the plane around."

A collective "Fuck" sounded over the comm.

Immediately, Rand flew into action on his keyboard. He zoomed in on the dead man, capturing an image of his face. And let out a curse. "Bad news, team. The man Kick took down is not Abbas Tawhid. It must be Tango Five."

With an equally potent oath, Marc ordered the stammering pilot to return to the airport he took off from, where a DHS team would meet him. Then the helo spun away, arcing back and over the plane to follow close escort.

Tara let out the breath she'd been holding all this time and leaned back from the edge of her seat. Good lord, *that* was some amazing teamwork.

Marc issued one last order, startling her. "Juliet, raise STORM Alpha Six and Zulu. Tell them to get their butts back here pronto. Looks like we've got a manhunt on our hands."

"Copy that," she acknowledged. "And request permission to join the search myself, over."

"Permission denied," came the swift reply. "I don't want you anywhere near this guy. And we need you at the comm, over."

Okay, really?

She tamped down another major spike of frustration. "You really do think I'm useless, don't you?" she grumbled, forgetting to mute the comm.

There was a brief pause. "Don't be ridiculous. I'm only trying to protect you," Marc responded.

"How many times do I have to tell you, I don't *need* your protection. I want to help catch these terrorists!"

"You are helping. Right where you are."

She huffed out a breath. "Fine. Whatever." It was like arguing with a brick wall. Maybe she'd have better luck with Quinn when he got here. *He* was team leader, after all.

In the background she heard a subtle clearing of throats. Ah, hell. She'd forgotten they had an audience.

"And in the future, please observe comm protocols," he scolded mildly. "Over."

She counted to ten as her favorite financial whiz enthusiastically plugged her appearance at Maravich Center on the TV monitor. "Yes, sir," Tara answered. "Over and *out*." With that, she ripped off the headset and set it on the console . . . so she wouldn't fling it onto the floor and do a flamenco on the damn thing.

She turned to see Rand regarding her wryly. She ground her teeth. "Is he always this much of a male chauvinist bastard?"

Rand nodded. "Oh, yeah. Growing up with five sisters will do that to a man."

"Yeah, well, I am *not* his freaking sister," she ground out.

"No. It's far worse than that," Rand observed philosophically. "You're the woman he's in love with."

TWENTY-NINE

BOBBY Lee awoke to the loud ringing of his cell phone.

And the certain knowledge that life as he knew it had changed. Irrevocably.

Darcy Zimmerman was in love with him.

If that didn't beat all.

He grabbed the buzzing phone. "Talk to me."

"This is STORM Alpha Juliet. Tango Five's contained and we've got a bead on Tango One," said a female voice that sounded suspiciously like Marc's little state trooper. "What's your twenty?"

He rattled off the name of the motel and its location from a brochure next to the phone.

"Helo's on the way. Be ready in fifteen. I assume I don't have to call Zulu?"

"She's right here."

He hung up the receiver and turned to wake Zimmie— Darcy. *The woman who loved him.* Her eyes were already fluttering open. His heart fluttered right along with them.

"Hey," he said softly and bent to give her a lingering kiss.

"Hey, yourself," she murmured sleepily. "What's up?"

Good question. What *was* up with him?

He wasn't sure exactly how this love thing would play

out, but he knew something big had to give, one way or another. Her heart. His lifestyle. His lifelong insistence on complete freedom from entanglements. The way she'd looked at him last night as they made love . . .

"It's time to get going. They've found Tawhid and are sending the helo."

The hell of it was, the idea of his life taking a radical left turn into such unknown territory didn't even scare him.

"You okay?" she asked, scanning the look on his face with a shade of concern.

"Oh, yeah," he said.

In fact, he felt pretty damn good.

Well. Especially now. After a couple hours of power sex, both of them were replete and numb with pleasure. At least *he* was. And judging by the smile on her face, Darcy was, too.

She tugged on the ropes still looped around her wrists. "Then I guess you'd better untie me."

Last night he'd been too stunned to react to her obviously chagrined declaration of love, other than purely physically. After a moment of frozen shock, he'd simply taken her. Hard and fast. Again. And then his inner machismo had reared up. He'd felt compelled to push it, to see how far he could take her grudging submission . . .

Now he gently pushed a lock of fallen hair off her face. And carefully drew the covers down so he could see her gorgeous naked body.

Fifteen minutes . . . He really did have to undo her bonds. But damn, he liked having her under his complete control. It didn't happen all that often, so he doubly enjoyed taking full advantage when it did.

He stroked a hand over her body. "No hurry. We've got a few minutes."

"Quinn . . ."

"Hmm?"

Not that she couldn't get out of these ropes if she really wanted to. The woman was a Zen master when it came to martial arts . . . and escaping tight places. Hell, he remembered one time they'd been sent down to rescue the wife of a Colombian judge, whom drug dealers were holding for extortion. He and Zimmie had been discovered and captured, and were just waiting for the head honcho to come out any minute to the barn and summarily execute them. Bobby Lee'd been saying his final prayers when she somehow slipped free of the leg irons they were in, crawled through some disgusting sewer trap to escape the stronghold, and had brought in the cavalry in the guise of their backup team to rescue him and the judge's wife, saving the mission as well as his hide.

That night he'd tied Zimmie up and made her show him how she'd done it. Well, naturally one thing had led to another, and pretty soon he'd been too distracted to get out of the restraints she'd put him in, in return.

Filling his senses with her now, he brushed his knuckles over her hips, remembering that heated night. It was the first time they'd made love with one of them tied up. Though truthfully, it tended to be Bobby Lee bound to the headboard. Hell, fine by him. It took a real man, secure in his sexuality, to allow himself to be put in such a position. Bobby Lee had no problems in that department. Aw, let's see . . . lie on his back and let a beautiful woman pleasure him until he was limp from spent passion? Now, there's a tough one. Even for a man who preferred to be in charge, that was a no-brainer.

It was harder for Zimmie to let herself go like that—to put herself so completely in someone else's hands. He'd often wondered what it was in her background that drove her to maintain such impenetrable walls around her vulnerability. But he'd never asked. Wasn't the place of a twice-a-year, no-commitment lover.

But now . . . now that she loved him . . .

Da-amn.

What the hell was he going to do about *that*?

Unable to resist, he canted his body over her and tongued one peaked nipple, tasting her. *So good.*

"Mmm," she moaned, stretching in a graceful bow. He closed his mouth over her and gently sucked; she gasped softly, opening her eyes, and tried to lower her arms but was stopped by the restraints.

He cupped her other breast and thumbed its nipple as he suckled her. "Quinn," she repeated breathlessly, making him smile. "Come on. We've got to go."

"I really think," he said, licking around the puckered areola, "you have to start calling me Bobby Lee, now that you're in love with me."

Her next moan was tangled with a shade of distress. "You are such an ass. Bobby Lee, we need to move. The helo—"

"Yeah, yeah," he said with a half grin and reluctantly reached up to release her wrists.

Immediately, she rolled off the bed and headed for the bathroom. He sighed and went to join her.

"Besides, I never said that," she declared, busying herself.

"Yeah, you did," he refuted, unwilling to let her pretend it didn't happen.

"Then I didn't mean it," she insisted.

Uh-huh. "Don't even try, sugar."

For several minutes she was silent as they got ready, her face a careful mask. Then, suddenly, she pressed her palms flat against the sink and bent her head down, dropping her gaze from the mirror.

"Oh, God. I'm so sorry," she said in a thick whisper, squeezing her eyes shut. "I didn't mean to do this to you."

Bobby Lee moved behind her, put his arms around her. "Why? I'm not sorry. I'm flattered. I'm honored. I'm ... maybe even having similar feelings for you."

Her eyes sprang open and she looked at his mirrored reflection in stunned mistrust. "What?"

Whoa, there. "Did I say that aloud?"

"Very funny." She swallowed, turned stiffly in his arms, trying to escape. "Let me go. The helo will be here any minute."

"It can wait."

"*Quinn*—"

"Call me Bobby Lee, and say it sweet, now."

"Bobby Lee, I swear I'll—"

He sighed dramatically and let her slip away, out of the bathroom, to quickly gather her things into her duffel.

He joined her. "Damn, girl. You could at least *try* to make it easy on a man."

"Oh? Because you've made it so easy on me?" She zipped up her bag and marched to the door, flinging it open. The dawn sun was struggling to break above the horizon, shedding just enough light to illuminate her unhappy features.

Suddenly, he understood. He grabbed her hand before she could stride off. "Aw, baby, is that what this whole breakup thing has been about? Because you were afraid to tell me you love me?"

"No," she ground out. Still avoiding his eyes as he pulled the door shut behind them.

He didn't believe her. "Then what?"

She was mute for several heartbeats. "I don't *want* to be in love. Not with anyone. Especially not with you."

Ouch. "Now, baby, that's just plain hurtful."

She actually snorted.

"Okay, yeah," he allowed, "I'll admit that at one time— all right, maybe up until fairly recently . . . like maybe yesterday—I might not exactly have warmed to the idea. But now . . ."

He turned her face toward him and her big green eyes regarded him uncertainly, warily. *Now or never.* He had to say it. Tell her how he felt. But his words and feelings got all jumbled up in his chest and throat, and he couldn't utter a sound other than a choked cough.

The sound of a chopper welled up in the taut silence.

Those beautiful eyes took on such a forlorn cast, his heart just about broke. "You don't have to say anything," she said, yanking herself away from him and starting toward the back of the parking lot. "Really. It's okay."

"No, you don't understand—" he croaked, chasing after her as she headed for the helo that was landing in an open field behind the motel.

"I do. Under all that uncompromising"—she seared him with a look—"*male*ness, you're a decent man, Quinn. You only said . . . implied . . . what you did so I wouldn't feel so much like a fool."

Double ouch. He tried to stay objective, but did a lousy job. Shouldering past, he vaulted up into the bird and extended a helping hand back down to her. "You feel like a fool for loving me?"

Her eyes went all mushy as she accepted his hand. "No." They took seats next to each other and buckled up. "Not because it's you, but because I should have known better than to let myself fall in love at all."

He pursed his lips and nodded as the helo lifted off. That he got.

She handed him a headset, but he didn't put it on. Laying a hand over her set, he shook his head. He didn't want others listening to their conversation.

He had to come clean. Somehow spit it out. He'd never been one to beat around the bush or prevaricate when it came to decisions before. The watchword of a spec operator was flexibility, adapting to changing conditions, altering strategy to reach the desired endgame. He could see plainly if he wanted to keep Darcy—and he did, badly—he'd have to meet her at least partway.

"You know"—he leaned over and spoke loudly, so she could hear him above the *whop-whop-whop* of the rotors—"a funny thing happened to me yesterday."

She gave an inaudible groan, covering her face with her hands. "Why don't we just skip the humiliation, and—"

"No, hear me out, baby." He leaned in closer. "You know, yesterday I was so damn angry with you I couldn't concentrate on anything. All I could think of was you. Wondering what I'd done to make you change your mind about me. Hell, I was so compromised I knew if I didn't straighten up, I'd be a danger to the mission. So I convinced myself to go along with your ridiculous edict to break up, thinking that would help. Told myself that mixing sex with an op was the real problem." Not that it had ever been before . . . Talk about rationalization.

She rolled her head on the backrest to watch him guardedly. "That's funny?"

"No." He tucked a strand of hair lovingly behind her ear. "What's funny is, it didn't help. When you flirted with those DHS guys, I almost lost it. I was jealous as hell, and I'm not ashamed to admit it." The corner of his lip twisted. "Now, anyway."

A zillion emotions passed through her eyes. "Quinn, what exactly are you saying?"

He eased out a long breath and leaned his forehead against hers. "I'm saying maybe it's time to take our relationship to the next level."

Her mouth dropped open and she pulled back, staring at

him in blunt disbelief. Waiting for the punch line? He cringed inwardly.

"Jesus," he blurted out, suddenly as unsure as he'd ever been in his life. "Are you going to make me spell it out?"

"Uh, yeah?" She still looked like she doubted him. Couldn't trust that this was really happening.

Had *he* done that to her? Treated her so badly in the past as to make her this suspicious?

Time to make amends.

He reached for both of her hands. "It took almost losing you to make me realize how much I want you in my life, sugar. I never thought I'd say this to any woman, but . . . I want you, Darcy Zimmerman. You and only you. Can we come to some kind of arrangement, you and me?"

She blinked. Puffed out a laugh. Pulled her hands away and stuck them under her armpits. "Wow, Quinn. Another eloquent plea. How can I possibly resist?"

He moaned, falling back in his seat and rolling his eyes heavenward. "Damn it, woman! Okay, fine." He turned to her again. Took her face in his hands. "Marry me," he pleaded. "Okay? Please, Darcy, I—"

"*What!?*" She waved him off wildly. "No! Are you in-*sane*? Quinn, that's crazy talk!"

He gave her a warning look. "Darce, I swear to God—"

"Bobby Lee," she cut in. She held him away forcibly, but the warmth that was blossoming in her eyes served to calm his jagged nerves. A little, anyway. "Let's just take this one step at a time, okay?"

But . . . "If you don't want to get married, then what?" he demanded exasperatedly.

She licked her lips. "You're really serious?"

"As hell."

"What if this is a huge mistake?"

"We're both intelligent adults. We'll think of something."

She nibbled on her lower lip. "But what if—"

"Darce. Please. I'm dyin' here. Throw me a bone, at least."

She closed her eyes, then opened them. "Okay. We could . . . Well, we could tell STORM Command we'd like to work as a team?"

He nodded encouragingly. "Good. Yeah. And?"

"And maybe we could even . . . you know, get a place to-gether somewhere. Try living with each other first? Before we do anything drastic."

Relief filtered through him. Not because he didn't want to marry her. But because suddenly he knew with dead certainty he *did* want to.

And okay, *that* scared the crap out of him.

Her way was far less likely to end up in a flat-out panic attack.

"Yeah. I'd like that," he said, smiling at the profound wisdom of the woman he'd chosen to be his for all time. Or had she chosen him . . . ? Either way— "Sounds like an excellent plan."

She finally let him pull her into his arms for a long, sweet kiss . . . the sweetest of his lifetime. "You are one amazing woman, Darcy Zimmerman," he whispered. Utterly stunned that anything like this could ever happen to the boy who'd sworn love would never knock on his door, and if it did, he'd slip out the back way.

"Right back at you," she whispered. "But, Bobby Lee?"

"Yeah, babe?"

"Um. Everyone's watching us."

He glanced up and realized the helo had landed, and the whole team was gathered in front of the open door, grinning like hyenas.

Slowly a smile spread across his face. "What's the matter, people? Never heard a man propose to his woman before?"

TARA'S impatience grew by the minute as she watched the video stream from the UAV and listened to the comm. The rest of the team, along with several dozen DHS agents, were combing through the patchwork of woods, lakes, fields, and river bottom surrounding the single-strip airport where Abbas Tawhid had disappeared. Seemingly into thin air.

Unfortunately, the whole area was crisscrossed by dozens of winding roads trafficked by a light but steady stream of morning commuter vehicles, any of which could be speeding Tawhid away from the searchers. Or worse, already have done so.

It could take hours to find him.

Hours that Tara was more and more convinced they didn't have.

To her chagrin, Quinn had backed up Marc's decision about not letting her into the field. She didn't have the training yet, he'd told her, and Kurt Bridger had assigned her to Rand in the Moby. He wasn't about to countermand a direct order from STORM Command.

But Rand didn't need her. He'd pulled in a handful of experts from the surrounding DHS units, and they were deep into their analysis, including carefully checking license plates one by one with the UAV's extreme zoom. Tara was just in the way, taking up space a real analyst could be occupying.

As she'd sat there essentially twiddling her thumbs, she couldn't help thinking about things. And that was when an alarming theory had started gaining momentum in her mind.

Everyone on the ground was scrambling to catch Tawhid before he slipped out of the search net. They were convinced he was heading for New York City as fast as he could. But the terrorist was not stupid. He had to know law enforcement was combing every inch of Louisiana for him. That today, every federal agency and local PD in the entire country had his face at the top of their Most Wanted posters. Especially in New York. And that it was just a matter of time before he'd be captured.

But for a fanatic like Abbas Tawhid, escape would not be his endgame. Not at this point. When he'd illegally entered the U.S. to perfect his weapon of mass destruction, he must have planned this as his final jihad. Surely, he meant to die here—taking as many people with him as he possibly could and making a bold statement for his twisted cause.

And if he couldn't make it to New York City, it meant that right now he had to be heading for a place where he could do maximum damage with the one remaining canister of Armageddon virus, before he was neutralized for good. Right here in Louisiana.

The team still believed even if Madison Square Garden wasn't attainable, his target was still going to be some kind of sports venue. They were sure they had until tonight to find him because there were no sports events anywhere close scheduled before six p.m.

But Tara wasn't so sure they had that long to find him.

Sitting in the Moby watching and listening to everyone else contribute while she couldn't, she'd thought long and hard about her exasperating situation on the team and with Marc—being undervalued and marginalized in her job because she was a woman. Marc denied it fervently, said it was only because she lacked training, but he belied that by constantly treating her like she needed coddling and protecting, rather than as a professional equal. That had naturally led her to thoughts of similar frustrations she'd experienced as a female state trooper, and even from her own father. Which in turn had led her to thoughts of Gina, and what she'd related of her captivity.

There was no doubt in anyone's mind that Abbas Tawhid hated women with an intense passion; he had repeatedly said as much to Gina. Had consistently degraded her and called her a whore. What had initially triggered his rabid misogyny was a mystery. But he'd tried to rape Gina, the ultimate expression of that hatred, and when he couldn't, he'd beaten her brutally and impersonally, to establish his male dominance and to teach her a lesson about the superiority of men over women being the natural order.

Tara also remembered one of al Sayika's more publicized terrorist attacks: the savage and demonstrative assassination of a Saudi princess who'd tried to bring reforms to the women of her conservative country.

Then, after having all those thoughts, that TV commercial had come on, the one advertising the financial fitness for women speech at the university this morning—a speech that would be filled with an audience of women. Women who sought to become stronger and less dependent on men. Thereby upsetting Tawhid's fanatical "natural order."

And *that* thought had instinctively raised the hair on the back of Tara's neck. Those women would be perfect targets for Tawhid's obsession.

Tango One was headed for the university and that speech. She was sure of it.

But when she'd proposed the idea to the team, the only one who'd taken her seriously was Darcy Zimmerman. Big shock. To their credit, they had all listened politely and even debated the idea for a few minutes over the headsets while they tramped around in the woods.

But in the end Quinn had decided to keep the team searching. "We have hard evidence he's been here, and he's probably still around somewhere, hiding out until the search moves on. Better to get him before he has a chance to let that virus loose. But I will notify the Homies to send someone over to the university to check it out," he promised. Which he did.

That was half an hour ago, and the DHS agent had yet to report back. Had Homeland Security even bothered to send someone?

Tara let out a jet of pent-up frustration and checked the big round clock on the wall of the Moby. 8:05 a.m. The speech was slated to start at nine. She pressed the heels of her hands into her scratchy eyes and counted to ten. Twice.

"Tired?" Rand asked, interrupting her sublime agitation.

She glanced up, startled. They hadn't spoken much after his outlandish suggestion that Marc Lafayette was in love with her. Which . . . omigod, how ridiculous was *that*. Of all the bizarre notions.

She pushed out a breath. "Exhausted." Though, honestly? At the moment fatigue was the least of her worries.

"Go back to your room," Rand suggested. "Take a nap. Sleep off some of that irritation you're feeling. Quinn knows what he's doing, Tara, and Marc . . . well, he's a damn idiot."

One out of two, anyway.

Rand smiled sympathetically and made a shooing motion. "Go. I'll call you if anything breaks."

She debated for all of three seconds. "Thanks," she said. "I guess I could use some sleep."

She grabbed her things off the console and trotted down the steps of the Moby into the chilly morning air. Yeah, a nap really did sound good.

Too bad she wasn't going to get one.

Because, hello? Tara Reeves was a Louisiana state trooper, and she'd be damned if she'd let anyone stop her from doing her job.

She pulled out the keys to Darcy and Quinn's SUV that she'd scooped up along with her purse on the way out. Before getting in, she lifted the back hatch and unlocked the metal weapons case. And smiled in grim satisfaction when she found a SIG-Sauer just like her own. She stuck it in her waistband.

Revving up the engine, she punched the button on the GPS. And told it her destination.

"Louisiana State University."

THIRTY

WADE was not a happy man.

Rebel figured having a woman in the throes of orgasm call out another guy's name would do that to a man.

Talk about mortifying.

Even more mortifying was being forced to admit she was in love with that other guy, implying Wade was just a substitute.

Way to go, Haywood.

All of which was bad enough, but then he'd had to spend the whole morning disbanding the Cappozi task force and trying to explain to Chief Jansson why he couldn't tell him the reason, or even whether the subject of their investigation—meaning Gina—was dead or alive. That must have been a real barrel of laughs.

Rebel was now faced off against Wade in the back of a STORM limo with tinted-out windows, heading for Haven Oaks, where they would meet with Kurt Bridger and Gina. So Wade could assure himself that his ex was fine and this whole weird situation was legit.

"I'm sorry," she said for the umpteen-thousandth time.

He just glared.

"I didn't mean for any of this to happen."

He didn't even blink.

Several miles went by in stony silence.

"For what it's worth, I think you're an amazing lover," she said guiltily, looking down at her hands to avoid his chilly look. It was totally inexplicable to her, because she really *was* completely in love with Alex Zane, but even now, being alone with Wade, so close to his carnally familiar body, she got that tight, sexual feeling in her throat, and her breasts tingled in memory of his touch.

He snorted softly. "You want me to slip off your panties and do you here in the limo? Once more for old times' sake?"

She licked her lips, wishing the thought didn't make her pulse quicken just a shade. "No need to be ugly, Wade."

"Sweetheart, you have no idea from ugly."

Was that a threat? She glanced up at his handsome—if forbidding—face, but saw no real malice there. Anger, yes. Hurt, definitely. Cruelty? No, not that.

"Maybe I don't," she said, deciding a change of subject was overdue. "But Gina does. She's been through . . . a lot."

His eyes shifted, going softer at the mention of his ex-fiancée. It was obvious he really did care about her. To his credit, he dropped the interpersonal conflicts and asked, "What do I need to know before I see her?"

Rebel let out a long breath. How best to prepare him? "She's pretty messed up. Both physically and mentally. She endured a lot. Torture and repeated beatings."

At the word "torture" he flinched visibly, letting out a virulent oath.

"She still blames herself for surviving," Rebel continued. "For doing what the terrorists wanted instead of killing herself."

"Which was?"

"Didn't Bridger tell you?"

"He didn't want to go into specifics on an unsecure line."

"Ah. Well, they made her weaponize a deadly hybrid virus. If it gets loose and innocent people die, I don't think she'll ever forgive herself."

"Jesus," he breathed. "So it's true. Terrorists did kidnap her for her knowledge of viral genetics."

"More like nasal inoculations. They forced her to put the virus into a spray, like she'd been doing with those kid's shots she's been working on, so it can be disseminated easily."

Again, he swore roundly. "And she succeeded?"

"Yes. She also attempted to embed a self-destruct gene into it, so the virus dies instead of spreading to another host. They're testing the recovered canisters to see if she succeeded. But meanwhile, there's still one canister out there at large."

He closed his eyes and was silent for the rest of the trip. She might have thought he'd fallen asleep, except for the pained expression of regret that occasionally flitted across his features.

She just hoped he was thinking of Gina and not her. No, she was not in love with Wade Montana. Not like she loved Alex. But she liked him. Really liked him. And if it weren't for her feelings for Alex, it could easily have developed into much more.

Sometimes life really sucked.

Which was proven in spades when they arrived at Haven Oaks, got off the elevator on the second floor, and met Kurt Bridger. Because standing right there next to him, *naturally*, was Alex Zane.

Seeing him, Rebel stopped on a dime, getting whacked in the shoulder by the closing elevator door.

Help.

She had to physically restrain herself from backing straight back into it and pressing the button that would take her all the way down to China.

"Special Agent Haywood," Bridger greeted her with an outstretched hand. "Good to see you again. Hope you don't mind, I've asked Mr. Zane to sit in on our meeting with Dr. Cappozi. To compare notes."

Mind? Why on earth should she mind having the unobtainable man she loved within striking distance—literally—of her angry lover?

"Of course not," she said, ignoring the glowering men and concentrating on the pleasant one speaking. "May I present my SAC, Special Agent in Charge Wade Montana?" She introduced Bridger and the two shook hands.

Alex's mien went even more thunderous when she introduced him to Wade. He didn't extend his hand. Could he tell they'd spent the night together?

"Heard a lot about you, Zane," Wade said evenly, taking obvious measure of his rival, who was looking particularly healthy today, dressed in jeans and a snug T-shirt that showed off his returning physique far better than his usual loose scrubs.

"Likewise," Alex returned.

"You seem to be recovering from your recent ordeal," Wade offered.

"Let's hope your fiancée recovers as quickly from hers," Alex volleyed back.

Ouch.

"*Ex*-fiancée," Wade corrected coolly.

Bridger, who'd been observing the byplay, raised a brow and cut her a penetrating look.

Oh, swell. Now everyone knew.

"Is Gina in her room?" she asked him pointedly.

He swept an arm toward her door. "Yes. Why don't we go in."

She gave him a strained smile. Sometimes the better part of valor was to run like hell. "Actually, if I'm not needed, I'll sit this out in the dining room. I could use a cup of coffee." Better yet, a stiff drink.

"*No*," both Wade and Alex said in unison.

"You're not going anywhere," Wade said.

Okay, then.

Bridger cleared his throat. "It appears," he said dryly, "that you are needed, Special Agent Haywood."

She pushed out a sigh. "All right. If you insist."

Heaven help her.

She was in such trouble.

SLIDING his headset down around his neck, Marc stamped the worst mud from his boots and pulled the Moby door open. He was dirty, wet, and freezing his ass off. Not to mention about ready to explode in frustration. He only had a few minutes before he had to get back to the team and was just dropping by to get an update from Rand along with a refill on his coffee thermos.

At least, that's what he told himself.

He and the others had been searching now for a steady three hours, through forest and swamps, fallow fields and frigid rivers, and the only thing they had to show for it was the discarded plastic packaging from three space blankets.

Which at least explained how the fucker'd foiled the UAV's powerful infrared sensors. By wrapping himself head to toe in the micro-thin, warmth-conserving blankets, Tawhid's heat signature had disappeared completely from the radar, enabling him to elude sensory detection. The other clever thing he'd done was to spray the discarded plastic wrappers with a generous dose of the deadly avian flu–anthrax virus. When K9 handlers were brought in, two of the search dogs sickened almost immediately, and both died a short time later. The owners had been quickly rushed to the hospital and dosed with Cipro and antibiotics. After that, the searchers were ordered to wear protective gear, and all dogs were pulled off the detail.

Needless to say, the morning had not gone well.

And it hadn't helped that the only thing on Marc's mind the entire time had been Tara.

Tara, Tara, and more Tara.

This couldn't go on. Something had to be done about this unacceptable situation before he screwed up completely. Or lost his mind.

He ducked halfway through the Moby door, scanning the interior for her. And frowned. The place was packed with geeks, all concentrating on their monitors. No Tara.

"Hey, Rand," he called, propping himself on the doorframe. "How you guys doing in here? Any leads yet?"

"Getting close," came the answer. Rand spun in his chair. "You'll be the first to know when we've got a bull's-eye on Tango One." Something in Marc's face must have given him away, because Rand added, "Tara's not here. She went to take a nap."

Marc shrugged, pretended to be indifferent. "None of my business."

"That's right," Rand said with a perfectly straight face.

"You go on and keep your distance. That way she'll know you're a complete asshole instead of just suspecting it, and I'll have a much better chance with her." His lips curved up tauntingly.

Jealousy slammed through Marc from the tips of his toes to the ends of his hair, and all parts in between. *Especially* the parts in between. *Le foutu tayau!* He had to ball his fingers into tight fists to keep from stalking over there and wrapping them around Rand's nerdy little neck.

Le bon Dieu mait le main.

He took a few seconds to compose himself, then answered neutrally, "Good luck with that." He turned on a toe and closed the Moby door behind him with a loud snick.

As if Tara would ever in a million years fall for someone like Rand. After being with *him*.

Would she?

Hell, no. *Not if he had anything to say about it.*

Marching back to his room, he jammed the key card in and whipped open the door. He looked like a swamp rat and probably smelled worse, but too damn bad if he offended her delicate sensibilities.

"Tara?" he barked. He wanted her awake. *Now*. To hear what he had to say. Which was . . .

Merde. God only knew, because *he* sure as hell didn't.

But no soft Yankee yawns or even angry retorts returned his brusque greeting. The only sound in the room was the echo of his own harsh breath.

He flicked on the light. The bed was empty. Hadn't been slept in since the maid made it up right after they left, hours ago.

Dieu. She must have gotten her own room. He should have known. After the way he'd left her this morning, she wouldn't want to be within a mile of him while she slept. He got that.

So why did it feel like such a slap in the face?

Tamping down his visceral reaction, he went to the front desk, flipped up his credentials, and asked what room she was in.

With excruciating slowness, the brain-trust desk clerk checked through the motel's antediluvian computer. Then shook his head. "Sorry. There's no one registered by that name. Tara Reeves doesn't have a room here."

Marc narrowed his eyes, possibilities hurtling through his mind. The one that surfaced and stuck made him see red.

It took him thirty seconds flat to double-time it back to his corridor and find Rand's door. He didn't bother with niceties. Just raised one booted foot and bashed it in. The door whacked against the wall, vibrating with the impact. Almost as much as he was vibrating with anger.

The room was dark.

But the bed was empty.

Merci Dieu.

Slashing a hand through his hair, he pushed out a long, calming breath. Steadied himself with a shaking hand against the corridor wall.

Bon. Where the hell was she?

An emotion that felt a lot like despair curled through his gut like a copperhead. Had she finally had enough of him and chucked it in, mission and all?

It didn't seem possible. Just a couple of hours ago she'd been so determined to be up-to-her-pretty-green-eyes involved, so adamant about her new female financial speech theory, so—

Mon Dieu. Her *theory.* Of course!

He glanced at his watch. Nine thirty. What time was that speech supposed to start? Ten? And where? Had she ever said?

He pulled out his PDA and realized he had no idea what her number was. *Merde.*

He trotted back to the Moby and stuck his head in. "Rand. Where is that speech Tara was talking about?"

The other man blinked at him. "The university. I think. Why?"

"She's not in the motel. Could she have gone there?"

"Well, she did mention she'd like to. But it seems weird she'd just take off without saying anything, though."

"Would you have let her go if she'd asked permission?"

"I told her to take a nap." Rand shrugged. "But she was feeling a bit shoved aside and useless. So yeah, I probably would have."

Marc let out an oath and pressed his fingertips to his temples. *Shoved aside and useless*. This was all his fault. He was the one who'd asked Quinn not to let her onto the search team. The thought of her being in the same universe as a monster like Tawhid—

Dieu. He really had to stop thinking of her as his woman, and start treating her like a competent member of the team. Which she was.

And she *wasn't* his woman.

Not yet, anyway. But he decided that had to change. And soon. Before he went completely off the deep end.

"Is there a problem?" Rand asked.

Good fucking question.

He shook himself mentally. *Back in the game, Lafayette*.

Was she in danger? Probably not. They'd all decided there was a low probability the university speech was a target.

Low, but not impossible, his nagging unease insisted. The idea did have enough merit that Quinn had notified DHS, and they'd sent a man. Who hadn't reported anything amiss.

He got her cell phone number from Rand and exited the Moby, dialing as he walked back to his room. It went straight to voice mail.

"Damn it, Tara! Where the hell are you?" he demanded after the beep. *Bon*. Not the best way to get her to call him back. He stomped down on his blossoming apprehension. "*Cher*, you can't just disappear like this," he said reasonably. "You need to check in and let us know where you are. We're worried about you." He swiped a hand over his mouth. "*I'm* worried about you. Call me. Please, Tara."

When he got to his room he changed out of his wet clothes and debated whether or not to notify Quinn.

Was he being a worrywart? Was this buzz of unease humming through him just his out-of-control protectiveness for a woman he loved, born of growing up watching over his five wild-and-crazy sisters?

Probably.

And yet . . . Something flip-flopped in his stomach when he considered the possibility—the *slight* possibility—that Tara could be right and they should have listened to her. That Tawhid was there at the university, about to spray his virus of

destruction over a crowd of helpless women. *Including Tara.*
Mon Dieu.

Should he go to her rescue? Sacrifice precious search time
on the off chance that Tara's feminine instincts were correct?
That she needed his help?

But if she needed help, why hadn't she called him?

Because she was fine, that's why. He was just being
paranoid.

Time to get back to the team.

He slid his headset back on and was about to tap the on
switch and call Quinn when his cell phone rang. He snatched
it up. "Tara?"

He could barely hear the answering whisper, "Marc, omigod, come quickly. It's Tawhid. He's here!"

TARA pressed her back against the solid wall behind her,
swallowing several times to keep her stomach inside her ab-
domen where it belonged.

She'd finally found the DHS agent, in a backstage dressing room.

Dead.

In a pool of blood.

His throat had been viciously slit and gaped open like a
grotesque mask that had slipped down too far, still oozing
blood onto the floor. He had not been dead long.

"*Tara!*" Marc's voice on the cell phone cut through her
daze. "Talk to me, *cher*!"

How long had she been standing there after dialing on
pure instinct, frozen with horror and revulsion?

"Are you hurt?" he demanded in alarm. "What's going
on? Tara, I swear if you don't say something, I'll—"

"I'm here. Sorry," she croaked out. She had to pull herself
together. Seriously. *Tawhid was close by*. This vicious attack
couldn't be the work of anyone else. "I found the DHS guy
Quinn sent. He's dead." She shakily described the scene,
gathering her wits about her as she did.

"Where exactly are you?" Marc asked. She could hear a
door slam in the background.

"I'm backstage at the Maravich Center. LSU."

"*Bordel du merde*," he ground out, and she could tell he'd started running. "The Maravich Center's a fucking *sports* arena! Why didn't you *tell* us?"

Okay, so they had both been right. Small comfort now. "I said LSU. But I don't follow sports. Sorry, I had no idea."

"All right. Get the hell out of there," he commanded. "*Now*. I'll be—"

"No way," she cut him off. *She was a cop. She could handle this.* "I won't let that bastard hurt these—"

"Tara, don't you *dare* approach Tango One without backup!"

"There may not be *time* for backup. What if he starts spraying the audience, or has already—"

"We can get them to the hospital immediately. Ski and the CDC have developed measures to fight this thing."

"Then I'll be fine, too. I promise I won't get within knife range of him."

Marc let loose with a flurry of Cajun French—she assumed more swearwords. "*Cher*, you have to wait for backup. Wait for *me*."

"Just hurry," she urged, making up her mind, and snapped the phone closed. For good measure, she switched it off.

Pulling out the SIG from her waistband, she clipped her LSP shield to her jacket pocket. At the last minute she swiped up the DHS agent's baseball cap from the floor where it had fallen and tugged it onto her head. Didn't want there to be any doubt who was the good guy here. With a final deep breath, she cautiously opened the door to the backstage corridor and slipped out into the dark, silent hall.

THIRTY-ONE

FILS *du putain.*

It had taken nearly six minutes to collect the team from the field, rush back to the STORM helo, and take off. ETA to the Maravich Center: two more minutes. Total: eight minutes since he'd lost contact with Tara.

A lot could happen in eight minutes.

Marc hung up after reaching Tara's voice mail for the dozenth time and clamped his jaw tight as a vice against the urge to roar out his anger. Anger at himself. *Why hadn't he listened to her?*

"Calm down, buddy," Quinn told him, peeling off his muddy jacket. "She'll be fine. She's a smart and resourceful lady. She's a good cop."

Darcy was furiously typing on her laptop, capturing schematics and other data about the center that Rand was sending, forwarding it to their PDAs as she searched for weak spots. "The arena looks pretty standard," she said. "Not many places he can hide out."

"He doesn't want to hide out," Kick said, passing out the Kevlar. "He's after max casualties. He'll be spraying that virus everywhere. On people, seats, handrails, door handles, you name it."

Darcy jetted out an agitated breath, pulling a vest over her head. "Which means when those who've been exposed leave the center they, in turn, will infect anyone they come in contact with."

"Unless Gina's self-destruct gene works," Ski's voice reminded them. He and Rand were hooked in and standing ready with logistics and medical help over the comm.

"Let's pray it does," Darcy said, retrieving her Glock from Quinn. "Otherwise, we're all screwed."

"The good news is, Tawhid will also be infected," Quinn said with somber satisfaction, strapping his own weapons to his body. "Maybe we can lock him in a closet somewhere until it kills him."

"He won't live that long," Marc gritted between his teeth, snapping a new clip into his Beretta and stashing three more in his vest. Orders were to bring down Tango One, dead or alive. And there was no doubt in his mind which option *he* was going for.

His small, tight-knit STORM family all paused in their preparations for battle and glanced at him, sympathy in their determined gazes. They knew what Tara meant to him and would do everything in their power to see she came out of this alive. He knew that.

But he also knew shit happened. Things you couldn't control. Unless she left the premises, there were no guarantees he'd ever see her alive again. Never see her sweet face, or hear her sassy backtalk, or touch her incredible body, ever again.

And she refused to leave.

He battled back the cold, debilitating fear flooding his gut. She was too brave for her own damn good.

Kick watched his agony with understanding eyes. "You have to learn to trust her," he said. "I've seen Tara in action. She knows what she's doing, Marc. Let her do her job. Trust her instincts. It's the only way you'll survive working with her in this business."

Quinn and Darcy exchanged a tender look of agreement. "Listen to the man," Quinn told him. "He's right."

Easy for him to say. Darcy was born for this work. Tara was different. She was . . .

Non. Kick *wasn't* right.

"Who said anything about working with her?" Marc
ground out irritatedly. Why were they all ganging up on him?

"She came back to us, didn't she?" Darcy said. "Requested to be on the team."

"That was just to be close to me," he responded without
thinking.

Darcy rolled her eyes. "Wow."

Quinn grinned. "Keep tellin' yourself that, buddy."

Marc opened his mouth but didn't have a chance to retort
because the helo finally swooped down in front of the
Maravich Center's main entrance. But it just hovered. Why
weren't they landing?

He looked down. His heart leapt to his throat. Streams of
screaming women were running out of the center doors onto
the sidewalk under them.

Foutre de merde!

"That's not a good sign," Kick said.

"No shit," Quinn muttered.

Marc slammed open the helo's sliding door and leaned
out, gesturing wildly and shouting, "Get out of the way! Let
us land!" For all the good it did. The panicked women ignored his orders. Or maybe they just couldn't hear him over
the deafening roar of the rotors.

Darcy was already on the horn to center security, asking
for someone to come out and clear the area. She shook her
head. "They've only got ten men on duty, all inside, trying to
control the crowd."

"Fuck it," Marc said, leaned back in, and grabbed the rap-
pelling rope secured next to the door. "I'm outta here."

He launched himself out of the bird and three seconds
later he was on his feet, running for the building. In the distance he heard the wail of many sirens. *Merci Dieu.*

"Where?" he demanded of no one in particular as he
sprinted through the double glass doors, weapon in hand.
Several women pointed inside toward the arena. His gut
clenched. That's what he was afraid of.

He stormed through the opening and muscled his way up
to the railing of a mezzanine walkway that overlooked the
big coliseum. What he saw nearly made his knees give out.

Down below in the middle of the arena, Tawhid and Tara

stood at center stage in front of the podium facing each other, each with arms outstretched, aiming their weapon at the other. Tara had her gun; Tawhid held his canister of death. A classic Mexican standoff.

With one exception.

Even from halfway up the stands, Marc could see the fine mist of spray that floated down over Tara's head and body. And she was just standing there *talking* to the fucker.

Non!

Panic surged through Marc's watery limbs.

Why wasn't she shooting?

"Shoot him!" he shouted at the top of his lungs. "Shoot the bastard!" But no way could she hear him. And even if she could, she couldn't shoot. The speaker and her entourage were behind Tawhid in her direct line of fire.

He whipped up his Beretta and took aim above the jostling crowd. But not his. Then reason and training kicked in and he lowered it again. He was well out of range and more likely to hit an innocent bystander than his target.

That's when he realized what Tara was doing. By talking to Tawhid, attempting to negotiate, she was diverting the terrorist's attention away from the speaker while she and the others were being slowly backed offstage. Tara was sacrificing herself for the safety of the others. Until someone else could take the shot.

Hot tears pressed the backs of Marc's eyelids as he watched the woman he loved being infected over and over again with the deadly hybrid virus. With that kind of exposure, it would be a miracle if she lived.

Non! She *couldn't* be taken from him! Not now that he'd finally seen the light. Finally realized what a fool he'd been to walk away from her.

At last he'd found the woman he'd been searching for his whole, lonely life. He wasn't about to let her go. Not like this.

He wouldn't let it happen. He. Would. *Not.*

Raising the Beretta again, he turned to charge down the stairs, determined to kill Abbas Tawhid any way he could. Regardless of the consequences.

But a strong hand gripped his shoulder and wrenched him back.

"Wait," Kick said, taking up position next to him on the landing. He calmly spread his feet and raised the sight of his HK to his eye. "I'll take him down."

Marc put a restraining hand on his friend's arm. "No. Let me." This was *his* responsibility.

Their eyes met in an exchange of intense clarity. Wordlessly, Kick handed him the sniper rifle.

By now the speaker was several paces away from Tawhid. There was no chance of hitting her by accident. Or Tara.

Marc snapped his body into a solid shooter stance and lifted the rifle to his shoulder. Aiming for a spot above the enemy's ear, he took a cool, steadying breath . . .

And pulled the trigger.

TAWHID'S head jerked violently to the side. Blood sprayed from his skull in a liquid funnel of crimson.

Tara's heart stopped in her chest, then restarted with a lurch. *Thank God. At last someone had come!*

As the terrorist's body twisted and fell to the stage, her arms and legs started to shake like a carnival ride. But for some reason she couldn't move them. Couldn't get her elbow unlocked to lower her weapon. Couldn't move her feet to get out of the way of the disgusting puddle of red spreading quickly toward her shoes. She watched it as though in a trance, suddenly fighting to get her breath.

She wanted to look around, to see who had finally come to her rescue. Was it some brave security guard? *Was it Marc?* But it was as though her body had turned to a stone pillar in the midst of an 8.0 earthquake. A *collapsing* pillar.

Tawhid's lethal spray crawled on her skin like ants. She could almost feel the horrible disease boring its way into her flesh and organs. Her whole body itched, her lungs burned. Her stomach rebelled.

God, she was *dying*.

An unbidden sob burst from her throat.

Around the stage, people were going crazy. Running, screaming. Shoving one another to get away. *Stop panicking!* she wanted to shout at them. No need! Tawhid was dead!

But, then, so was she.

A sudden vision of the dead family in the swamp swept through her mind. The virus worked quickly. She could be gone in a matter of hours. Or minutes. In horrible agony.

Before she'd had a chance to tell Marc how she really felt about him. How much she loved him. How she had died a little inside when he left her. How she'd have done anything, anything in the world, to keep him, to have him love her back.

"Tara!"

She heard the faraway call. *His voice.* Another bitter sob escaped. *Please let me see him just one more time.* If only she could stop shaking and turn her head.

Hot tears trickled down her cheeks. Maybe it was better this way. This way he'd be free, as he wished. And she'd be spared the unbearable pain of living without him.

"*Tara!*"

She sucked in a shuddering, half-sobbing breath. Except she didn't want to die. Not like this. She could deal with pain. She had before, and—

A large body hurtled up onto the stage with a crash. *Marc!* He rolled to his feet. "Tara, look at me, *cher.*"

He had to stay away! Her head started to shake back and forth as her eyes sought him. He was lunging toward her. "N-no!" she gasped out, then coughed. "D-d-don't come any closer!"

Too late!

He put himself between her and Tawhid's lifeless body sprawled on the blood-covered floor, blocking her view. He reached out for her gun arm, grabbing her wrist with one hand and grasping the SIG in the other.

"D-don't touch me!" she cried, coughing on the words. Trying desperately to pull away. "I'm infected!"

"Like I give a fuck about that," he said, his voice steady, but more intense than she'd ever heard it. "Tara, give me the gun."

She looked down at her own hand holding the SIG in a death grip, and struggled to relax her fingers. She also struggled to breathe. "Please, Marc," she wheezed, "I don't want you to die, too."

He succeeded in prying the gun from her hand. "Nobody's dying here except the bad guy. Now, look at me, *cher.*" He guided her trembling arm down to her side.

Black spots danced before her eyes. She swallowed thickly, feeling her body start to shut down. She looked at the man she loved with all her heart. Coughed again. *She had to tell him.* "Marc, I need to—"

"Save your strength, *beb.* I'm getting you to the hospital." With that, he swept her off her feet and into his arms.

"Marc," she croaked, desperate to get his attention, but it came out in a racking cough.

It was no use. He was sprinting with her at full tilt up the stairs, shouldering his way through the parting crowd. She lifted her hand to grasp his shirt and hang on and saw that her skin was already breaking out in angry blisters. *Oh, God.*

Unable to hold her head up any longer, she let it loll against his chest. She closed her eyes. His unique, comforting smell surrounded her, calming the terror in her heart. At least she would die in exactly the place she most wanted to be—in his arms.

"Hang on, *mon amour,*" he told her, his voice thick with emotion. "You've got to hang on. Do it for me, *ma douce.*"

They burst out into the chilly winter air. She was jostled and she heard Kick say from far above, "Hand her up," and she felt Marc let her go.

"No," she whispered in panic, trying to hang on to him.

"I'm right here." Then once again she was in his arms.

Her body gave a shiver, and she felt her mind slipping away. With her last ounce of strength, she lifted her lips to his ear.

And just as everything faded to nothingness, she whispered, "I love you."

THIRTY-TWO

A black shadow moved across the pristine blanket of newly fallen snow directly below the bay window in Gina's room.

She bolted up, disoriented. Frozen with fear.

Where was she?

Her pulse beat out of control, the horrors of her captivity avalanching over her—Tawhid, the torture, the unspeakable terror . . .

Then she remembered. STORM. The rescue. Haven Oaks. The phone call last night.

He was dead.

And she'd survived. She was safe now.

But what had awakened her?

She gasped as the black shape glided swiftly over the icy whiteness under her window, drawing her attention. It was the shadow of a man, as distinct as a black woodcut against the virginal white of the snow.

She couldn't see the man, just his shadow. He hugged the edge of the building as he prowled along, hidden from view unless she were to lean out the window. But she couldn't do that, all attached to various tubes and wires as she was. Not that she would ever dare to. She may have been fearless once. But no more.

She clutched her blanket tight to her body as the shadow disappeared around the corner and told herself it was probably just a security guard. Or a staff member out for a late-night smoke. But knowing that didn't help. Her heart thundered in dread, anyway.

Because . . . *Oh, God*. There'd been something terrifyingly familiar about the way the shadow had moved, the broad set of its shoulders, the distinctive way its close-cropped head cocked to one side to listen. The cruelly handsome aquiline profile . . .

Gina grabbed the panic button by her bed and pressed it blindly, over and over.

Two nurses rushed into her room, along with one of the two STORM guards posted to this wing. One of the nurses was Rainie, thank God.

She ran to her side in alarm. "Gina! What's wrong?"

The other nurse hurried over to check the monitors above her bed, which were beeping out of control. The guard drew his weapon as he did a thorough visual sweep of the room. "Are you all right, ma'am?"

Her pulse was thundering. "Someone was trying to get in!" she cried, grabbing Rainie's hands and hanging on for dear life. "Oh, Rain, he's after me!"

Rainie looked around worriedly. "Who?"

"Where?" the frowning guard asked at the same time.

Gina trembled so hard her teeth started to chatter. "Th-there," she said, indicating the bay window. "He was c-c-creeping under my w-window."

The guard strode over to the bay and checked below. "No one's there now, ma'am. You're sure it was a person, not a deer?"

"Yes!" She started to say the bastard's name, but stopped herself. She had seen only his *shadow*. How could she be so sure it was him? They'd think she was imagining things, that she was crazy. Hell, even *she* thought she could be hallucinating. But she still couldn't stop shaking.

"It was h-him," she said between teeth chatters. "I know it w-was."

Rainie sat down on the edge of the bed and put her arms

around her, holding her close in a comforting embrace. "It's okay, Geen. Whoever it was is gone now. Try to relax."

The guard pulled his walkie-talkie from his belt and headed for the door. "I'll send a guy to check it out. But don't worry. Even if someone managed to breach the grounds, there's no way they can get up here to you. There are guards at every entry, two on this corridor alone, and it would take a monkey to get up to your window from the ground. Not to mention our state-of-the-art alarm system." He smiled reassuringly before he went out. "Trust me, Dr. Cappozi, you are perfectly safe here."

She nodded as though she were reassured and allowed the other nurse to fuss with her monitor and the IV until the beeping began to slow, and fluff her pillow and wrap another blanket around her because the clueless woman thought she was shaking from the cold.

"Would you like something to help you sleep?" the nurse asked sympathetically. Gina hated the way everyone looked at her with pity in their eyes. Everyone but Rainie. Rainie was the only one who seemed to understand.

She shook her head. "No, thanks."

Rainie motioned the other nurse out, then reached up to smooth a lock of hair from Gina's face. "Honey, I know Wade's visit yesterday upset you. That's all this is, residual stress from that."

The visit *had* been disturbing. Ever since Gina broke up with her ex-fiancé last year, things between them had been strained. But when he'd helped her try to find Rainie when she disappeared, Gina thought perhaps he'd forgiven her for dumping him. At one point, he'd even asked her for another chance—not that she would ever go back to him. But now he was blaming himself for her kidnapping, believing he had inadvertently put her on the terrorists' radar.

To make matters worse, he seemed to have become involved in some kind of bizarre love triangle with his subordinate, that pretty redheaded FBI agent, and Alex Zane. The tension during the meeting had been thick enough to slice.

But the real kicker had been Rebel Kurt Bridger asking question after question about Gina's last "boyfriend," the CIA Zero Unit operator suspected of being a traitor in league with al Sayika.

Her pulse skyrocketed just thinking about the rat bastard, let alone speaking his name.

No doubt Rainie would think she was just projecting her fears and conjuring phantoms that didn't exist.

But she wasn't. He *was* out there. Somewhere just beyond her window. Waiting for her.

"Why is he still after me?" she murmured in despair. *So soon.*

One day she would let him find her. But not yet. *Please, not yet.* She wasn't strong enough to face him. She couldn't even get out of bed, let alone have time to learn the skills she'd need to confront him fearlessly. To ask him why he'd done this to her. Then look him in the eye . . .

And plunge a dagger straight into his black heart.

"You do know you're safe now, right?" Rainie asked her worriedly.

"No," she whispered. "I won't be safe anywhere. Not until he's dead."

"He *is* dead," Rainie said, obviously thinking she meant Tawhid. "And the others are all behind bars."

"I know," she said, swallowing hard. "It wasn't any of them I saw."

"Then who? Who did you see out there, Gina?"

She gazed up at her friend, terror clawing at her throat. "It was Gregg van Halen," she whispered. "He's come to kill me."

"MARC is a complete wreck," Darcy declared as she joined the rest of the team in the dining room of the Haven Oaks Sanatorium. "*Somebody's* got to make him get some sleep."

Around the table, six skeptical pairs of eyes met hers.

"Good luck with that," Kick said wryly, pulling his

wife closer to him on the bench and giving her a mock frown. Rainie looked utterly exhausted, too, having been up nearly as long as Marc, helping to monitor Tara Reeves upstairs as she fought for her life. They'd all been taking turns sitting with her and Marc. But Rainie was also Dr. Cappozi's nurse, and Gina's PTSD seemed to have kicked in with a vengeance over the past two days—hallucinations and all. Rainie had been stretched thin to say the least.

"Trust me," she said now, pushing away the remains of her dinner, "Marc won't let himself sleep until Tara is past the worst."

Darcy took a seat next to Bobby Lee. "How much longer until the worst is over?" she asked with real concern. Of all the people exposed at the Maravich Center, Tara had taken the worst dose of the terrorist's bioweapon. Before invading the stage, Tawhid had sprayed all the hand railings in the center, which had managed to infect nearly five hundred people. Luckily, they were all rushed to a containment center and treated soon enough to stave off most of the symptoms. And to everyone's amazement—mostly Dr. Cappozi's—her embedded self-destruct gene had actually worked. Not a single secondary infection had occurred. The Armageddon virus had been stopped cold in its tracks, thanks to her bravery, skill, and foresight.

But poor Tara Reeves had breathed in enough of the lethal concoction to take her down almost instantly. She'd been at death's door ever since . . . more than three days now. The doctors said it was a pure miracle she'd lasted this long. Which gave everyone hope that she might actually pull through in the end.

"She's a fighter," Rainie said. "If she gets through the night, she should make it."

"Let's all hope she does," a man's voice said behind Darcy. She turned in surprise to see Kurt Bridger. The man had been more visible on this op than in all the five years she'd worked for STORM Corps. Actually, it was nice to know the top brass were taking an active interest, not just in the completion of a mission but in the fallout, too.

"Hello, Commander Bridger," she greeted him. She introduced him to the others, most of whom had never met the legendary STORM commander in person. "Won't you join us?"

All business as usual, Bridger waved off her invitation. "Thanks, but no. Just came to check in on Miss Reeves, and to let you know that your team has been given a week's R and R. But stay on grid, everyone, so we can find you all if necessary."

Somber "Thank you, sirs" sounded all around the table, but Darcy was pretty sure not one of them had any intention of leaving Haven Oaks until Tara's fate was decided . . . one way or the other.

Bridger turned to go, then halted and turned back. "Oh. I almost forgot." He dug in his inside jacket pocket and produced a bronze-colored envelope. He handed it to Bobby Lee. "Major Quinn, new orders. You report for reassignment in two days. Sorry your leave can't be longer, but we need you active as soon as possible."

With that, he strode off.

Darcy's heart stood still as her gaze collided with Bobby Lee's. *Reassignment?*

"Fuck," Bobby Lee murmured, his jaw clenching. "Goddamn fucking hell."

With everything else going on, they hadn't had a chance to talk to STORM Command about their altered relationship, nor put forth a request to work together.

"Oh, Darce," Rainie said and reached over to squeeze her hand. "I'm so sorry."

"His timing really stinks," Ski said, but Darcy wasn't quite sure if he meant Bridger or Quinn.

The rest of the team nodded sympathetically. They'd all been incredibly supportive about the engagement. Apparently she and Quinn were the only ones who *hadn't* known they were meant to be together forever.

"Come here, baby," Bobby Lee said and drew her down onto his lap. He gave her a reassuring kiss. "This isn't going to change anything. Just a little inconvenience. We'll straighten it out in no time."

She swallowed her selfish disappointment and kissed him back with a pout. "I was really looking forward to having you all to myself for a while."

He winked. "Yeah. Me, too."

Rand pointed at the envelope in Quinn's hand. "So, where've they got you going this time? Tierra del Fuego? Mogadishu? Detroit?"

With a weary curse, Quinn ripped open the envelope and unfolded the paper inside. Darcy tried to read what it said, but he deliberately held it behind her back.

He frowned as he started to read. Seconds ticked by and he didn't say anything. In fact, his face grew more and more incredulous.

"What?" she said.

"Jesus," he murmured.

Okay, now he was scaring her. "Quinn. What does it say?"

"Enough of this mysterious bullshit." Kick leaned across the table, snatched it from his hand, and started reading aloud. "To Major Bobby Lee Quinn from Headquarters, Strategic Technical Operations and Rescue Missions Corporation . . ." His brows flicked up and he stole a wide-eyed glance at Bobby Lee. "Fuck, man."

This couldn't be good.

"What?" she demanded.

Ski grabbed it away and started to read. "Blah, blah, Quinn, blah, blah. The STORM Board of Command hereby informs you of your—Holy shit!" His astounded gaze cut up to Quinn's.

Okay, now she was officially terrified.

Darcy let out a growl. "Damn it! If someone doesn't tell me what it says, I swear I'll—"

Wordlessly Bobby Lee swiped it back from Ski and handed it to her. She tried to read what was in his eyes but couldn't even begin to decipher the look he gave her.

Heart pounding painfully in her throat, she began to read the letter:

To Major Bobby Lee Quinn from Headquarters, Strategic Technical Operations and Rescue Missions

Corporation. The STORM Board of Command hereby informs you of your promotion to the position of full commander. Please report to headquarters to assume your duties on the STORM Board of Command within two days of receipt of these orders.

Congratulations, Commander Quinn. You've earned it.

THIRTY-THREE

IT was time. Time to say good-bye.

Rebel took a deep breath and knocked on Alex's door, dreading the next few minutes more than she'd ever dreaded anything in her life.

It jerked open, and there he stood. Half naked as usual. Looking so sexy and tempting she had to stick her hands under her armpits so she wouldn't reach out and touch his broad, golden chest.

Why did he always *do* this to her?

"Hi," she said.

"Come in," he said stiffly and moved to let her enter.

For a split second she debated the wisdom of being in a room alone with him. Unfortunately, what she had to tell him was not something she wanted to blurt out in the hall where anyone could hear. Besides, nothing would happen in there. He didn't exactly look delighted to see her.

Surprise, surprise. The last time they'd seen each other was a few days ago at that disastrous meeting between Wade and Gina. Disastrous in the sense that the tension arcing between the two men had been impossible to miss, and even poor, traumatized Gina had realized something explosive was going on between Rebel, Alex, and her ex-fiancé.

Which was when Rebel had decided that she had to take the bull by the horns and end this crazy thing with Alex. It couldn't continue. The lying and pretending was killing her. He was her best friend, but the situation was classic *Othello*. Their precarious relationship was not doing either of them any good. It had to end. She had to move on. So she could find someone who would love her back and be with her. Someone like Wade.

"Thanks," she said and brushed past him into the room.

She faltered. An open suitcase lay on his bed.

He was packing.

"You're leaving Haven Oaks?" she asked, striving for a calm, modulated tone that didn't betray her alarm.

"The terrorists have been caught, Rebel. Abbas Tawhid is dead. I think I'm safe to go outside now," he said with the slightest shade of sarcasm.

She chose to ignore it. "But what about the al Sayika mole? The government traitor who betrayed your unit in Afghanistan, and Kick in the Sudan? He's still out there."

"I'm very aware of that. It's why I'm leaving. STORM is putting together a team to flush him out. I asked to be part of it."

She stared at him in dismay. "You've joined STORM Corps? Alex, are you *nuts*? You're in no shape to—"

"Thanks," he cut her off irritatedly. "I really appreciate the vote of confidence." He turned to the dresser and started pulling clothes from a drawer.

"You were a prisoner! Tortured, beaten, and starved for over a year! Alex, you've got to give yourself a chance to heal. It would be insanity to—"

"Rebel, what do you want?" he interrupted. "I'm a little busy now."

Hurt cascaded through her at his cold dismissal of her concern for him, and obviously of her, too. Not that she didn't deserve it.

Okay, no. She *didn't* deserve it.

So she'd slept with another man. That made *her* the bad guy here? Alex was engaged to be married—to one of her oldest friends! What did he expect her to do? Become a nun and wait for him to change his mind? It was crystal clear he had no intention of doing so. Not after that searing near-kiss and dropping the bomb about wanting to sleep with her . . . and then ten minutes later when Helena came in with those dratted wedding invitations, pretending nothing whatsoever had happened and everything was perfectly fine and normal and he couldn't wait to get married?

Please. She might be a fool, but she wasn't stupid.

Fine.

She drew herself up and stared at his back as he bent down to the bottom drawer. "I came to say good-bye," she said. And pretended her heart wasn't breaking into a million pieces.

For a microsecond, she thought he froze in mid-motion. Wishful thinking. He continued pulling out clothes. "Yeah? Going somewhere?"

Her heart squeezed painfully at his indifference. "I've been transferred."

He turned and stared back at her, his lips pressed into a thin line. "Really? When did you put in?"

"Three days ago." The day after the disaster . . .

"That was quick."

"Helps to know people in high places."

His eyes narrowed almost imperceptibly. "Montana?"

She nodded.

"Ah. So you're transferring to D.C. Should have seen that coming."

"Norfolk, actually. Agents aren't allowed to fraternize in the same office."

A muscle ticked in his cheek. "Just two hours away, if I'm not mistaken."

"More like three."

He spun back to his suitcase and dumped the clothes into it. His broad back went ramrod straight. "Close enough. I take it you two are an item now."

She wasn't exactly sure how to answer that. Not that she wanted to leave any doubt in his mind that she was moving on. But she had already decided to put on the brakes with Wade . . . It would be unfair to him if she couldn't commit totally. "Not an item, exactly. We're taking things slow. Seeing where they lead."

He snorted. "Not much doubt about that."

Again, hurt seeped through her. "Alex—"

"No." He turned back to her. "Sorry. You have every right to be happy. It's not like I—" He stopped abruptly. "No, it's great. Congratulations, Rebel. I wish you all the luck."

"There's nothing to congratulate," she said, fighting an unbidden wobble in her voice as she flooded with desperate, irrational disappointment. "It's a lateral move. And Wade and I . . . We're just . . ."

Alex's look chilled her to the bone. "Keep in touch. Helena's going to miss you."

Rebel's stinging tears struggled to break free. What about *him*? "Yeah," she said and swallowed. She gazed at him for an endless moment, but he remained stubbornly mute, his face a cool blank. "Well. I should be going. Still have to pack up my apartment." She made a pitiful attempt at a laugh. "Don't suppose you need a place to live? You could sublet."

His expression remained impassive. "I'll be moving in with Helena."

She thought she'd been hurting before, but at this last bit of news, hideous pain surged through her entire being. Quickly she turned, blindly reaching for the door handle, praying her tears wouldn't fall before she got out of there.

"That's great," she echoed. "I'm sure you'll be very happy together." How could he not? Helena was the ideal woman.

Before she could jerk the door open, he said harshly, "*Rebel*," and suddenly he was right behind her.

Her limbs started to shake.

He didn't touch her. But stood so close she could feel the warmth of his body on her back. The electricity from his skin leapt onto hers, raising the fine hairs on her trembling arms and the back of her pulsing neck. She didn't open her mouth to answer. She didn't dare. Didn't dare move. For fear of what she might say . . . or do.

She just waited.

And felt the heat of his breath sough lightly through her hair. "Rebel," he murmured, quietly this time.

Every cell in her body yearned to whirl and throw her arms around his neck, lean in, and kiss him hard and long, until there was no doubt in his mind how she felt about him.

Make him see, make him change his mind. Make him . . .

But she couldn't.

He belonged to another woman. Her friend.

She bit her lip to silence herself; her heart pounded out of control.

And still she waited.

Until at last she heard him sigh softly. "My angel," he whispered. "Good-bye."

THIRTY-FOUR

"**I'M** going to make an espresso run. Can I get you anything, man?"

Marc raised his head from where he'd been resting it on his folded arms on the edge of Tara's bed and glanced bleary-eyed at the speaker. Rand. Which meant it was the midnight-to-three-a.m. shift.

"*Non, merci,*" he said, his voice gravelly with weariness. "I'm good."

"No, you're not," Rand told him. "You're about to fall apart. You need to get some sleep."

"Can't," he answered automatically. He'd heard it all before, about a million times now, and always gave the same answer to friend and doctor alike. "I want to be here for her when she wakes up." Which always produced the same awkward silence in response.

They all thought she was going to die.

But they were wrong.

She couldn't die.

He wouldn't let her.

Through sheer force of will he'd stayed awake, talking to her, telling her the plans he'd made for their life together, telling her how much he loved her, how it would kill him if she gave up and let go of her precious life.

Dieu, once he'd even gone down to the hospital chapel to pray. When was the last time he'd been in a church? Or even whispered a silent prayer to God?

"Okay," Rand said resignedly. "I'll be back in a flash."

"Take your time," Marc murmured. "I'll be fine."

But that was a big, fat lie. He wouldn't be fine. Not until she opened her beautiful green eyes and smiled at him once more.

For the past three days and nights she'd just lain there, her disease-compromised lungs assisted by a noisy breathing apparatus, her beautiful mouth marred by a hideous plastic tube, the pale flesh below her collarbone tinged with blue and punctuated by med lines and catheters. Her small, slender hands were covered by vicious sores . . . and a generous layer of ointment and gauze, preventing him from touching, let alone holding them—on doctor's orders. Thank God the rest of her skin had been covered by protective clothing when Tawhid had sprayed that devil's concoction over her and that she'd been wearing that DHS cap. The rash on her face was starting to fade.

But so were her vital signs.

He didn't miss the increased worry on Rainie and the doctor's faces when they came in to check the diminishing numbers on the various monitors.

Tara had been fighting so hard. But after enduring the ravages of the toxic symptoms for three days, her body was starting to give up.

And there was nothing Marc could do to stop the downward spiral. Nothing but talk.

But he wasn't about to give up, too. So for the past six hours he'd been talking to her nonstop. Until his voice had gotten so hoarse Rainie had made him stop to drink a cup of honeyed tea and rest for a bit.

But now that Rand was gone and he had a few precious moments alone with her, he had to tell her again. Make one last, desperate attempt to bring her back to him. Back from the dead.

He looked at her, so small and helpless on the stark white bed, surrounded by all the cold, impersonal medical instruments, and desolation swept over him. His eyes filled with tears.

"Ah, *cher*. Don' leave me, *fille*. God can wait. I need you here on Earth with me."

He reached out and stroked her arm, brushed his knuckles gently over her cheek. He couldn't stand not being able to hold her.

Swallowing heavily, he knew this could be the last chance he got.

Fuck doctor's orders.

He lurched up from the chair, knocking it over backward, and carefully climbed in next to her on the bed, sliding under the sheet. He nestled his body up against hers, so cold and frail. Slipping one arm gingerly under her shoulders, he placed the other lightly over her chest, burying his face in her hair as he gathered her close to him.

"Please, *cher*," he choked out in an anguished whisper, bleak tears running down his face. "Forgive me. All those days before, I was such an idiot. I love you so much. Please, Tara. Don' leave me all alone. My life is worth nothing without you. Come back to me, *fille*. Come back."

THIRTY-FIVE

GOD, she hurt.

All over.

Inside and out.

Her lungs burned like the fires of hell.

Her brain pounded like Thor's hammer.

And her heart . . . her heart ached with a pain so intense it took her breath away.

Tara had dreamt of her mother. Her dear, sweet mother, who'd been taken from her much too soon. Mama had been crying, pleading with Tara to come to her. Except . . . no, that wasn't right. She'd been smiling, holding her loving arms open, surrounded by a beautiful, bright white light. Tara had run to her and been gathered up in Mama's warm, comforting embrace, sweet words of love and reassurance whispered in her ear. Tara had been so happy, it had felt so good, she'd wept with joy. Oh, how she had missed Mama all these years!

But then Mama had set her away and told her softly that she must go, return to the world of pain and the suffering. They couldn't be together. Not yet.

Tara shuddered out a silent sob. She didn't want to go! She was so tired. Tired of fighting against the inevitable.

God, how she hurt! Her body was a chaos of agony.

She couldn't even swallow without feeling she was being ripped apart from the inside.

How could Mama ask this of her?

Then, slowly, bit by bit, Tara felt something else. Not pain . . . but something warm and soothing against her fevered skin. A body. A large, gentle male body that held her carefully, protectively, in his arms, like she was a precious, delicate doll. A body that promised to watch over her for as long as it took for her to come back to him.

She fluttered her eyes open, tried to look at him. But she couldn't move. She tried to speak. Terrible pain flashed through her throat, streaking clear to her toes and back. She closed her eyes again, and eased an exhale through her nose, clinging to the feel of his skin against hers, to the warmth of his breath stirring the hair against her temple. Wondering at the moisture . . . Were those her tears she felt on his cheek? Or were they his on her . . . ?

Very slowly, the ache in her heart loosened, eventually giving way to a quiet joy.

Surely, this man loved her as much as Mama!

But something was wrong. Somehow she sensed his silent grief, the profound sadness in the shallowness of his breath and the fragile way he held her.

Was *he* the reason Mama had sent her back to the suffering? To be with him?

Perhaps.

Yes, that must be why she had to endure.

For him.

Because what would happen to this gentle, vulnerable man if she chose to slip away and leave him forever . . . ?

Perhaps she should dig deep and find one last, hidden ounce of strength to fight this terrible thing that had nearly robbed her of her will to live.

For him.

The man lying so still next to her.

The man she loved to her very soul.

Because she was afraid if she gave up . . . he just might, too.

"MARC?"

Tara's mind floated in that twilight zone between conscious and unconscious. Just awake enough to know that she had spoken. And that she'd been here in this bed for a long, long time.

Her throat was beyond sore, his name more of a whispered rasp. But he must have heard it—his large frame dislodged itself from her with a jerk.

"Tara? Are you awake? *Cher?*"

With excruciating slowness, she licked her parched lips. "I think so," she whispered.

"*Mon Dieu!*"

She felt him bound up from the bed and start to call out to someone.

With all her strength, she lifted her hand and reached for him, squeezing his arm when she found it. "No. Wait."

He froze. "But, honey, you need a doctor right awa—"

"Not yet," she croaked, swallowing. "Water."

"Jesus," he swore and suddenly a straw touched her lips. She sucked on it greedily. "Whoa, slow down, *cher.*" He gently withdrew it.

"How long?" she rasped.

"Five interminable days and nights," he said, his voice strangely twisted. "We thought . . ."

Then she felt his hands on her cheeks, touching her, stroking the hair from her face. The bed moved and she felt his lips brush gently over hers as his arms surrounded her and he folded her against his chest. Just as he had before, while she lay dying. "*Merci Dieu.* Ah, *merci Dieu.*"

"More water," she whispered, coming a bit more awake. Reached for the straw again. Found his hand. "My throat hurts."

He let her take another sip. "They had you on a ventilator until yesterday. You gave us quite a scare, *fille.*"

"Sorry," she whispered. "For not waiting."

His eyes grew shiny as he gazed at her. "I swear to God, I don' know what I would have done if I'd lost you, Tara."

"You saved me." She knew in her heart it had been him who pulled the trigger. She held him closer. Savored the feel of his solid, sheltering arms around her. "I knew you'd come for me."

"I'll always be there for you, *cher.* From now on. I swear I will."

Her heart swelled as he laid his cheek against hers. It was scratchy, like he hadn't shaved in days. It felt so good. So real.

"Tara, I've been such a fool," he said, brushing his lips over hers. "When you told me you loved me, I ran scared. I didn't think I could handle a woman as strong and independent as you. I thought it would make me less of a man. But the truth is, you make me a far better man."

"Oh, Marc," she murmured, closing her eyes at the tearful emotion welling inside her. Afraid like crazy to hope too much.

Was she really conscious? Or was this just another wonderful, wishful dream?

"*Je t'aime, mon cœur*," he whispered. "I love you with all my heart, Tara."

Her tears brimmed over. Was it true? Could this really be happening? She looked up to see his warm brown eyes gazing down at her, filled with love and promises.

"Please tell me I'm not too late," he said.

"God, no," she rasped, joy bursting through her like rays of the sun through a storm cloud. She swallowed painfully. "I'll always love you, Marc. No matter how dense you are."

"*Merci Dieu*," he said with a soft smile. "'Cause sometimes I can be incredibly dense."

She melted into him. Held him in her trembling arms. "No more than me, for letting you go."

"That's never going to happen again. I swear on my life. Marry me, Tara. Be mine forever."

She blinked up at him. Surely *this* was a dream. "Really?" she asked, her voice a thready whisper. "Do you mean it?"

"With all my heart."

"But your job . . . What about—"

"There are plenty of domestic assignments I can put in for. I'm getting too old for the rough stuff overseas anyway."

"You'd do that for me?"

He smiled. "*Mais non*. Purely selfish, I assure you."

She wasn't so sure about that. But she wasn't about to argue. "Yes," she said happily. "Oh, yes, I'll marry you!"

No more pain.

Well. Maybe a little in her body . . . that would heal. But

the big pain in her heart was gone. Banished by the true love of an amazing man. A man who loved her for who she was, just as she was. Who'd have thought it possible? Except she knew. Thank you, Mama.

"I love you, Marc," she whispered.

"I love you, too, *cher*," he whispered back.

"You'll stay with me?"

"I'll be right here. As long as it takes."

And this time when she slowly faded into a peaceful sleep, it was with a big smile on her face and endless joy in her heart.

Turn the page for a preview of the next romance
from Nina Bruhns

A KISS TO KILL

Coming soon from Berkley Sensation!

ONE

THEY *were using her as bait.*

Dr. Gina Cappozi could feel them following her. All day she'd had that peculiar sensation of eyes on her back, the spill of goosebumps on her flesh for no reason, a tingle in the hairs on her neck . . . It was obvious the STORM Corps special ops guys were doing what they did best—lurking in the shadows, watching her from doorways and alleys, scanning the busy Manhattan streets for danger. Always there for her. Always watching her back. Waiting patiently for their mutual enemy to appear. Or so it seemed, at least.

She wished they would just go away and leave her the hell alone.

Their constant presence was meant to be reassuring. It should be a comfort knowing they were there watching out for her. But it wasn't. Because even though they'd once heroically saved her life, and were now supposedly protecting her, she also knew those spec ops guys had an agenda— to get their hands on *him*, their hidden enemy, any way they could.

And she was their Judas goat.

Well, too bad. They'd have to wait their turn at the bastard. Because *she* wanted him even more than they did.

Him—her nemesis. Captain Gregg van Halen.

Gina glanced around as she quickly took the steps down into the black maw of the Lexington Avenue subway tunnel. No familiar faces lingered in the crowd as the crush of mindless, workbound humanity carried her along in its wake. Would she be able to give her babysitters the slip this time?

Or maybe they'd tired of her game of hide-and-seek, and had already gone away and left her on her own.

Maybe it was van Halen she could feel stalking her.

Good. Let the bastard come.

Just let him try and hurt her. She was ready. Her body was healed. And her mind . . . well, her mind was as healed as it was going to get. For now.

She was armed, of course. She never left her Upper East Side brownstone without her weapon of choice. Hell, even inside her home she was never without her knife. Nowhere was safe for her, indoors or out. Not as long as van Halen still drew breath.

She wrapped her fingers firmly around the handle of the razor sharp Ka-Bar knife tucked in her coat pocket. Oh, yes. She'd been practicing, all right. Lunging and plunging her knife into the heart of a straw target, over and over, until little piles of cut straw lay scattered on the ground all around and its cloth covering was sliced to ribbons. Day after day, week after week. She'd decimated a hundred targets or more, much to the chagrin of her self-defense instructor.

She was confident now, no longer terrified of the mere thought of coming face-to-face with the man who'd haunted her nightmares for the past six months. The man who had sold her to terrorists and walked away without a backward glance.

Really, what could he do to her that she hadn't already endured? Nothing, that's what. He couldn't hurt her. Not this time. Not her body. Not her heart. He wouldn't take her by surprise again. He wouldn't get the chance.

No one would. Not ever again.

Because Gina Cappozi was taking her life back.

And Gregg van Halen was going to die.

That was for damn sure. The very hand that had lovingly

stroked his skin and caressed his body to fevered arousal was going to be the same hand that ended his miserable life for good.

And if she was very, very lucky, it would happen today.

STORM operator Alex Zane had never been claustrophobic before.

But then again, he'd never been a lot of things before . . . until the events of the past two years had taken their heavy toll. So he shouldn't have been particularly surprised when the insidious panic swept over him, stealing the air from his lungs and thrusting him into a living nightmare of hallucination. But he was.

Fucking hell, not again.

Alex struggled to take a breath. Frantically, he fought against the menacing desert mirage as it eclipsed the brick and asphalt of the city outside the SUV windows. Afghanistan closed in all around him, binding him in a breathless straightjacket of horror. He tried desperately to block the piercing phantom screams, in reality long since silenced.

No! This was all wrong!

He was in New York City. On his first op for STORM, he'd spent the day sitting in a vehicle on stakeout—not on some Godforsaken mountaintop fighting insurgents. He should be seeing tall buildings, hearing the blare of horns and the chatter of businessmen on their BlackBerries.

Just another damn flashback . . .

In his mind he knew that. But it didn't help. The screams grew louder as he battled to drag himself from the twilight of an illusion so real it made him doubt his own sanity.

When the fuck had he fallen asleep? He had to pull himself out of it, bring himself back to the present!

But it was no use. The panic had sunk its sharp talons firmly into the chaos that was his scarred mind. The scents of spring flowers and a nearby restaurant were rudely swamped over by the fetid smells of dirt and human misery, drowning him in memories he'd give anything to forget. He squeezed his eyes tighter. Slammed his hands over his ears so he wouldn't fucking hear the cries of his lost Zero Unit teammates. Wouldn't react. Wouldn't be forced to relive the searing agony that inevitably followed.

"No!" he cried.

Too late. No way out of the nightmare now.

He hugged his rifle to his body and burrowed his back into the rocky hillside above the Afghan village where he'd been sitting for hours, waiting for the signal to attack. Screams of pain echoed through the heat-shimmering air like sirens of death.

His COM crackled and his team leader's urgent voice broke over the headset. "Zero Alpha Zulu, this is Zero Alpha Six, do you read me?" Kick Jackson sounded steady. Competent. In control. *Unlike Alex.*

He grasped at Kick's voice, clinging to it like a shipwrecked sailor. "What's going on out there Alpha Six?" Alex asked, fighting the panic. *Fucking breathe, soldier!*

Kick's voice barked out, "Do not move in! It's a trap. Repeat, do not—God *damn* it! Drew! Get back here!" Kick swore again, and Alex could hear his sharp breaths, like he'd taken off at a dead run. In the background, the terrible screams grew louder. "Abort and withdraw!" Kick yelled, cursed, then the COM went dead.

Suddenly, an explosion ricocheted off the mud walls of the village below. Alex flung his rifle onto his back and scrabbled up the rocky hillside to take a look. No way was he retreating, leaving Kick and the others to—

A dozen village men surged over the ridge just above him, pointing their weapons at his head and shouting. His pulse rocketed out of control. *Fucking hell!* He spun in the dirt and launched himself down the slope. He hit the COM. "Zulu going down!"

His attackers swarmed after him. He had to lead them away from the rest of the team!

No! Don't do it! his mind cried out. *Don't—*

Gunfire erupted all around. More screams. His own?

Fire scorched across his temple and pain burst through his shoulder. He jerked and stumbled. The world tilted, then went black. But miraculously, he was still conscious. Terror crushed his chest. He scrambled up again and ran. Blind.

A flashback! Just a flashback!

Oh, God. Please let him snap out of it!

He ran straight into a human hornet's nest. Vicious hands grabbed his arms, fingers yanked painfully at his hair, gun butts slammed into the soft organs of his body. He cried out in agony, striking back, kicking with all his blind fury.

His captors just laughed. And beat him until his flesh turned to red oatmeal.

Then they bound a rope around his ankles and threw him to the ground.

A raw sob escaped his throat. Fuck, no! No. No. *Fuck no!*

"Alex?" Kick's reassuring voice floated in on a cool breeze.

Alex tried to yell an answer. But his throat had strangled closed on a mute cry. He knew all too well what came next. And there was nothing to do but endure it. *Again.*

Or go completely insane.

Which he might do anyway. *Again.*

"Alex?" Kick called from far away. *Too far.* He'd never reach him in time.

The motor of a Jeep roared and gears ground. He thrashed against his bonds. *Fucking damn it to hell!*

The rope around his ankles yanked taut. *Oh, God, this was really happening.* He tensed his body. Prepared himself for the hideous pain.

"Alex!"

The Jeep jerked forward. So did he. A bloody layer of skin stayed behind on the ground.

He couldn't help it. He screamed.

"Alex! Wake up!" The order was firm and clear, like the voice of God. It would not be disobeyed.

Alex surged out of his trauma nightmare, wrenched upright with a lurch, and hit his head on the SUV's solid roof liner.

Back in Manhattan.

"Shit!" he cried, gulping down a painful gasp of much-needed air. *"Shit."* He grabbed the steering wheel and gripped it to steady his throbbing, reeling head. Harsh breaths stung his lungs as he forced himself to calm his raging insides.

Too slowly the debilitating panic and adrenaline subsided. Until, finally, he was able to haltingly unclench his fingers and stomach.

"You okay?" Kick asked at length.

Alex exhaled heavily. Looked up into the worried face of his best friend, who was white-knuckling the edge of the open SUV window, leaning in. Not touching or reaching for him. Just observing, at the ready. He'd been through this before. They both had.

"Fuck," Alex said shaking like a goddamn leaf. "Fucking hell."

"Yup," Kick said. Perfect understanding weighted his intense gaze. That day in Afghanistan when Alex was captured, Kick had been half blown up by a land mine and left for dead. It had been a long, long road back for both of them.

And it wasn't over yet. Not by a long shot.

But *hell.* Alex had really thought he was ready to go back to work. After all, the injury-induced blindness was gone, his body weight was back up to where it had been before the tender loving care of his al Sayika terrorist captors had starved it in half, his muscles were again firm and rippling . . . under the web of angry red scars. He no longer flinched at sudden sounds or movements.

Much.

It was just the fucking claustrophobia that still got to him. Who'd have thought simply sitting in a closed vehicle would trigger it? He sighed. More damn fodder for his damn shrink.

He steadied his fingers and slashed them through his hair. "I don't know how long I've been out. Did I screw up? Did I miss her?"

Her being Dr. Gina Cappozi, the object of the surveillance he may have just goatfucked all to hell. Gina Cappozi had also been a captive of al Sayika for three months, but here in the States, and for entirely different reasons than Alex. And after her rescue, as they had after his, the decimated terrorist organization in their inimitable logic had blamed her for their failure, and put a price on her head. A big one. Double the price they'd put on his and Kick's. Everyone, including Alex—hell, especially Alex—was expecting some fanatic jihadi to show up and collect on it any minute.

Thus Gina's protective detail, of which he and Kick were part. The operation was being run by STORM Corps—Strategic Technical Operations and Rescue Missions Corporation—Alex and Kick's current employer.

Initially, Alex had been on Gina's tag team, but he'd kept jumping at shadows, absolutely certain she was being followed by someone other than STORM. But no one else on the team had spotted any kind of tail, or danger, or anything suspicious at all. It was just him being paranoid.

Big fucking shock.

So he'd been reassigned to watch her brownstone—a throwaway job no one had thought he could possibly fuck up . . . though no one had actually said it aloud.

How wrong they all had been.

"No worries," Kick told him now. "Dr. Cappozi's fine. She just got on the subway."

It suddenly dawned on Alex that Kick was supposed to be on tag duty today with Kowalski. "Then what are you doing here?" he asked. "Are you sure nothing's happened?"

"Gina's safe," Kick reassured him. "But there has been a development. NSA picked up some interesting chatter overnight."

Alex was instantly alert. "What kind of chatter? About al Sayika?"

Kick nodded.

Alex narrowed his eyes. For many years both he and Kick had worked as operators for an outfit called Zero Unit, which was an ultra-covert black-ops unit run from the deepest bowels of the US Central Intelligence Agency. But after the deadly disaster in Afghanistan, and another near-debacle six months ago in the Sudan, Kick was convinced al Sayika must have a mole working for them—either within Zero Unit itself, or for someone higher up in CIA, or in another agency with close ties to the ZU. How else could the terrorists have obtained such accurate details of both ill-fated operations? Details solid enough to sabotage the missions and leave most of the team dead.

Alex agreed with Kick. They were dealing with an inside traitor of the worst ilk.

So they'd both quit Zero Unit and joined STORM Corps, a similar but non-governmental spec ops outfit. They were fairly certain that STORM had not been infiltrated by the terrorists. Last year the organization had staged Dr. Cappozi's rescue in Louisiana, as well as Kick's retrieval of Alex over in the Sudan—all without leaks from their side.

Dr. Cappozi's current protection detail was just part of a bigger mission: to find and eliminate the scumfuck traitor working as a mole in the US government for the al Sayika terrorists. In other words, the person directly responsible for Alex's torture and imprisonment, Kick's terrible injuries, and the hideous deaths of their teammates.

For Alex and Kick, this mission was one of pure revenge.

Kick finally opened the SUV's door and got in. "Quinn called a meeting," he said. "He wants us back at HQ, ASAP."

"What about the Cappozi place?" Alex asked, glancing uneasily at the three-story brownstone before hesitantly reaching for the vehicle's ignition. "What if I'm *not* being paranoid and—"

"Johnson and Kowalski have her six on the subway. And they're bringing in Miles to finish your shift here," Kick told him. "She'll be in good hands until Marc and Tara take over their regular watch at nine tonight."

Alex pushed out a breath. "All right," he conceded, checking the dashboard clock. It was just after five. "I guess that works."

Kick raised a brow as Alex put the SUV in gear. "You good to drive, bro?"

Alex gave a humorless chuckle. "Worried about my mental health?"

"Hell, yeah. I need to stay alive. Newlywed and all, remember?"

"Like I could forget," he muttered with a wry curl of his lip. Despite the dead-serious mission, Kick had been relentlessly happy since tying the knot. Not that Alex begrudged his friend. He was glad *one* of them was happy, at least.

He gunned the engine to life. "And damn, Kick. In case you hadn't noticed, *every*one behind the wheel in this town is fucking crazy. Trust me, I'll blend right in."

GREGG van Halen followed Gina Cappozi onto the subway car at the last possible second. Making sure she didn't dart out again just before the doors closed.

She didn't. Didn't even try.

Not that it surprised him. For the past week, since returning home to Manhattan after her lengthy convalescence upstate, his former lover had done nothing to avoid being found. Nothing to escape the malice that lurked in the corners of the darkness, seeking to hunt her down.

Almost like she was taunting him. Or fate. Except for the occasional furtive, hollow-eyed gazes she gave her surroundings, you'd never know she was in a constant state of terror.

Avoiding the vigilant observation of the STORM agent tailing her, Gregg casually grabbed the center pole in the subway car along with the horde of commuters anxious to get home for the night. The sliding doors slammed shut and the wheels lurched forward with the distinctive rattle and squeal of the New York subway.

He turned his back on Gina. He didn't need to face her. In fact, he preferred watching her in the flickering reflection of the grimy window. Better to keep the rage from showing in his face and giving him away.

Her dark green eyes went to and fro as she clung to an overhead bar, her gaze alighting for a quick perusal of each passenger before shifting to the next. Always moving. Always searching.

For him.

He allowed himself a grim inward smile. So nice to be wanted.

She'd never see him, though. Yeah, she'd see a man, a tall man. But not *him*, not Gregg van Halen. Not until he chose to show himself. Which he wouldn't. Not with those STORM clowns following her every move. But he could be patient when he had to be.

Gregg had been invisible for so much of his life, it took no effort at all to remain so. Even in plain sight, in broad daylight, he was a true shadow-dweller. A ghost.

A spook.

His lips flicked up. An apt double entendre. Because the description went far deeper than his job.

The shadows themselves drew him. Dark obscurity spoke to him. Even now, it whispered in his ear, beckoned to him from the pitch black void just beyond the strobing flash of subway window where he watched his own reflection, and that of his woman.

Alas, he could not answer the call and slip back into the void. There was something he must do before returning to the sheltering comfort of anonymity. He must deal with the overwhelming fury in his heart. And take care of this woman. His lover.

Dr. Gina Cappozi.

Because she had seen him.

In the mirrored film noir frames of the moving window, he searched her face for any sign of recognition. Or of alarm. And found none.

But within himself, crouching right next to the anger that simmered and roiled in his chest, he felt a bone-deep physical recognition of her. And had a sudden, overwhelming need to put his hands on her. A need so potent and visceral it nearly sucked the breath from him.

He *knew* this woman. Knew her intimately. Knew her flesh and her fears. He had plunged deep inside her and felt her quake with the pleasure his presence there had brought her. And felt her tremble with the fear of his absolute power over her.

He wanted to feel her quake and tremble again.

But she would never allow it. Never accept him again as she once had.

Because he had betrayed her.

He had betrayed everything.

He battled back a surge of sick fury. Steeled his insides and beat back the clot of unwanted emotion. Anger would not help. Only action would.

As the train screeched around a curve he released the

pole, letting his body wedge into the clutch of commuters surrounding her. No need to hold on. His balance was perfect, honed through years of hard physicality on his job as a mercenary for Uncle. Bit by bit, inch by inch, he eased closer to her—the backward bump always accidental, the sideways step seemingly unintentional. Until his back was at her front. Not quite touching.

But, oh, so close.

Close enough to catch the familiar, tempting scent of the woman he'd once tied to his bed and taken in ways that had both thrilled her . . . and frightened her to the marrow.

He'd always frightened her. From their first wary, agenda-filled meeting, he'd scared the pants off her. Literally and figuratively. It was part of his attraction. And hers. She had once loved the thrill of it. But now . . . now she hated him. Hated him with a passion that nearly matched his own.

At the sanatorium up north, from his hidden vantage points on the grounds he had watched her body slowly heal from the terrible trauma she'd gone through. But in her mind the terror still loomed as large as when she'd been a captive. She'd learned to defend herself, studying deadly moves, plunging her knife into the center of a man-shaped target over and over. Imagining it to be his own black heart, no doubt.

Over the months he'd observed her, one thing had become abundantly clear. Gina Cappozi wanted him dead.

And *she* wanted to be the one to kill him.

Too bad he couldn't let that happen.

The train sliced through the black tunnel, lights flashing to the cacophony of the steel rails. He cocked his head to the side and inhaled, picking out his lover's unique fragrance from the potent olfactory brew of refuse, burning brakes, and the perfumed sweat of a thousand bodies that permeated the subway car.

She glanced around uneasily. Nervous. Instinctively sensing a predator close by.

Impassively, he read an ad sign hanging on the wall, keeping his face hidden. She anxiously caught the eye of the STORM agent across the car from her, who shook his head reassuringly. She shuddered out a breath, and tightened her grip on the bar above her as once again wheels screamed and the train pulled to a herky-jerky stop at the next station.

Passengers all around disgorged, jostling them so her body was wrenched away from his. New people crowded around. He steered closer. The doors slammed shut again.

Heedless to the danger, he turned, and deliberately stepped up right behind her, this time his front to her back. She was tall, especially in her work heels, but he was taller. Much taller. Heartbeat accelerating, he spread his feet and grabbed the bar next to her.

He hovered over her. *Close. So close.* Silky strands of her long black hair tickled his nose . . . smelling of the woman he had stripped naked and taught to pleasure him as no other woman ever had.

His body remembered those nights. Achingly well. He could still hear the echoes of her groaned sighs and throaty moans as he took her. Could still feel the touch of her fingers and the tip of her tongue as she explored his body with mutual shivering delight.

His cock grew thick and hard, remembering.

Again the brakes squealed, the car slowed, people shifted in readiness to exit.

He nearly vibrated with the urge to touch her. To step into her. To press his body right up against hers and feel her succulent curves fitted against his unyielding muscle. Just for a fleeting moment.

But he didn't dare.

She must have felt the air around them quicken. Must have sensed the taut, electric thrum of lust that pulsed through his whole body for want of her. Must have inhaled his eager male pheromones as they sought a way to lure her to his bed again. For suddenly, she went rigid. Her knuckles turned white on the bar she clung to. Her head whipped around and she raked his features with a fear-sharpened glare.

But he had already looked away. Averted his face so she couldn't see the hunger prowling in it like a trapped tiger. Wouldn't read the intent lying there, in wait. Waiting for the right moment.

To take her.

The train jerked to a halt and she stumbled backward into him. She gasped. He didn't move. But she felt it—the long, thick ridge that the memories had raised between his thighs. Her breath sucked in. Her hand dropped. To touch him?

He knew better. She was reaching for her knife.

But too late.

He was already out the door.

It wasn't time. Not quite yet.

But soon he would have her.

Very soon.